PRAISE FOR ELISSE HAY

Rory is officially one of my new favorite urban fantasy and supernatural suspense characters. She's smart, powerful, insightful, and tough—and full of care for those who need defending. I'd want her on my team for sure. Elisse had me at the Shakespearean title and locked down ownership of my heart and soul on page one with this fantastic story and lively prose. Her books are insta-buys for me from now on!

— LISA EDMONDS, BESTSELLING AUTHOR OF THE
ALICE WORTH SERIES

VILLAINS BY NECESSITY

SOMETHING WICKED
BOOK TWO

ELISSE HAY

Dedicated to Wayne. You know why. Don't make me write it out. (But also, I love you.)

AUTHOR NOTE

This story was written on the Wadawurrung lands of the Kulin Nation and is set in the lands of the Bunurong Boon Wurrung and Wurundjeri Woi Wurrung peoples of the Eastern Kulin Nation.

I pay respect to First Nation Elders past and present. Sovereignty was never ceded.

CONTENT NOTES

This book contains content that may be distressing for some, including sexism, sexual harassment, family violence, violence, alcohol and other drugs, transphobia, and xenophobia. Extensive trigger warnings are available via the author's website.

If at any point you become distressed or numb, please take a break and reach out to your supports. Your wellbeing is important.

ALSO BY ELISSE HAY

The Something Wicked Series

Foul is Fair

Villains by Necessity

Met by Moonlight

Thunder, Lightning, Rain

CHAPTER 1

ARTHUR WALKED ABOUT HALF A STRIDE AHEAD OF ME, HIS HANDSOME face totally blank as we headed back to the East Melbourne Coven. We'd survived what should, hopefully, be the last official interview with the police after all the shitfuckery with his uncle Edward Van der Holst. Drugs. Murder. Riftrunning. Faeries. Lycanthropes. Egos. All that good stuff.

I kind of felt for Arthur. Edward had done a pretty solid job of setting him up to take the fall if the cops ever got close. So much for familial loyalty.

If I hadn't stuck my neck out to back him up, he'd have copped an accessory to murder charge and a bunch of others, too.

Of course I *had* stuck out my neck, because that's the kind of witch I was. And my thanks? Not even him acting as my thrice-cursed windbreak on the way back. I huddled lower in my jacket and scowled at his back.

Maybe I could call up Detective Taig O'Malley, bat my eyelashes, fan myself. "I'm so sorry, Detective," I could sigh. "I don't know what came over me. I think Arthur must've scared me right out of my senses. Why, he must've been in on it all along."

Except I wouldn't. Because I wasn't *that* shit. Even if he was.

1

But thinking about it didn't cost me my high moral ground.

The amusing part was, despite all his petty posturing and puffing, my legs were still longer than his. He was working *hard* to stay ahead.

As if hearing my thoughts he paused at the slightly wonky post box beside the walkway to our coven, his hand on the recently graffitied gate. His gaze swept me, lip curled in derision. I stopped and planted my hands on my hips.

I could think of comfier places to confront the jerk. But I could think of worse ones, too. At least out here there weren't any nosy witches listening. Aside from me.

"If you'd just done your job—the job you were actually *hired* to do! —this wouldn't be happening."

"Thanks," I said, brightly, and smiled with lots of teeth. "Did it occur to you I *did* do my job, and now *I'm* being punished for it?"

"The way you fawn over Taig," he said, disgusted. "No, it hadn't. You obviously like the attention. Is that why you did it?"

Rage pulsed in my veins. There had been zero fawning. Taig and I were friends. I was very happy snuggling up to Beo Velvela, even if he *was* technically my client and theoretically off-limits due to my alleged power over him.

I mean, I *hoped* I had some power over him, since I was halfway in love with the big lump.

"Oh yeah, King," I shot back, mockingly. "Spending hours with cops just makes me *so* happy. It's not like I'm now about four days behind in my observations. It's not like now I need to put in extra hours to make sure the leprechaun family who's just transferred can get uniforms and devices for their kids so they can start school on—"

"As if you even care!" he half-shouted, throwing his hands up. "You're in it for the fame! And now *me* and *my coven* have had our names dragged through the mud!"

The fury at my temples drummed. I could so clearly see the way my fist would cut through the air. The force would reverberate down my arm, nestle in my shoulder, burn in my knuckles. "*Your* coven," I repeated, mockingly.

"Yes!" And he raised his hand, one finger drawn in threat. "*My coven!*" And the finger jabbed forward in accusation and attack.

My wrath was red-hot. In that moment I gave exactly zero shits that he was a bad-arse wizard.

My body knew the moves. I shifted, felt my shoes on the wet cement with the slick leaves and grit as the soles gripped faithfully. And as I rotated, I felt the damp, icy wind pick up my hair and toss curls into my face.

Fuck you, wind.

Fuck you, wizard.

I knocked his finger aside but crushed the urge to grab that wrist. I knew exactly how it'd feel when it broke and oh hells it was *right there*. "Don't you *dare—*"

An arrow bloomed in his chest.

My heart stopped for an instant. His face was frozen and if it wasn't for the way his pupils dilated as he stared, I would've sworn time stood still.

My cold fingers coiled around my wand. Traffic rumbling along the street, ignorant. Proof that the world still turned as I reached for my magick. His hand swept up like it was pulled by a string, past the lapel of his charcoal woolen designer jacket to the shaft protruding from low in his shoulder.

Through this dome none shall leave or come unless it is with me. The spell rippled and flowed from me. Blood bloomed in the fabric of Arthur's shirt and the song of a bell ringing met my ears.

With the breath still frozen in my throat I cut through our surroundings with my gaze. There weren't any obvious culprits but every detail jumped out at me. The light was almost gone, partially due to the hour but also because of the thick clouds gathered overhead. Parked cars sat in the gloom, unmoving. An older woman toddled down the road towing a cart of groceries, her big coat wrapped tightly around her bent frame. A young guy with headphones over top of his blue and white striped beanie walked a dog and scrolled on his phone.

Fuck.

"All right, Arthur," I said, grimly, turning back to my jerkoff line manager and digging out my phone. "Don't pull out that arrow. I'm calling the ambulance." And whoever had shot him—with a medieval fucking *arrow*, no less—was probably long gone since their second attempt had just hit my ward.

It'd be less paperwork in the long run if they'd had better aim. I could hear my Oma's voice in my head. *Measure twice, cut once.*

He collapsed, right there. Plonked down on his arse on the wet cement like some sort of cartoon character. With his mouth hanging open he stared up at me like he'd never seen me before.

Something about that made unease crawl up my spine.

The wound was too high on his chest to have hit anything *incredibly* critical and there sure wasn't a geyser of blood, but maybe my judgement was clouded by the liberal amount of adrenaline I was currently enjoying. Still, while his color was a bit high, it sure wasn't the white of shock. "You okay there, King?" I asked, resisting the urge to shove him at some paramedics and get home to a bucket of ice cream and forget this whole shitstorm.

He blinked owlishly. "You're beautiful when you're in action."

I froze. I was *what?*

And then the arrow just fucking *vanished*. Right there. From his chest. A hole remained in his shirt, welled and overflowed with blood. And he just sat there staring at me with wonder.

Okay, I'm going to need more than ice cream.

Gracelessly I yanked the scarf from around my throat and felt it catch on my keys, then the edge of my wand. The concrete was wet under my knees and I focused on that, not the pounding frustration. *I just can't get a fucking break.*

"Who's on this afternoon?" I asked, trying to distract him, keep him calm, and also avoid saying anything that'd cost my high moral ground. I liked the view.

Someone had just attacked him *on the street*. Would the second shot have killed him if I hadn't been there to throw up my ward? Maybe he'd back off, now, if I'd just saved his measly life.

And maybe he wouldn't.

Well, my own reflexes just made shit harder. I tossed the nub of my wand to my other hand so I could grab him in a vice. The silk scarf I pressed hard against the wound. I'd *absolutely* get done for murder if I didn't get this oxygen waster some help. Because that's how my luck went.

"On?" he repeated, the word strangely light. "Your hands. So warm. So strong. Oh, hells, Rory. Oh, please." He let out a long, shaky breath, tears welling in his eyes as he stared at me like a lost puppy. "Please," he said, the word shaking as his hand locked over mine but did nothing to increase the pressure on his wound. "Oh, please. Never let me go."

Well, shit. This arsehole wasn't bleeding out and he didn't seem to have a punctured lung. "Not letting you go, Arthur," I told him, though I really, *really* wanted to. "But I need you to keep the pressure on while I call for help." And then scrubbed away his touch.

"Yes," he breathed, his expression tender.

I had no idea what he was agreeing to. Or maybe he had no idea what he was agreeing to. My head was spinning. There had been no more bell-like noises, so whoever had hit us wasn't trying again. And Arthur was just sitting there, staring at me like I was the answer to his every hope and dream.

Not me. I was a fucking nightmare.

"Left hand, King," I demanded of him.

He lifted it and I took it with my wand hand, juggled until I had him holding on the pressure. Where were my thrice-cursed helpful bystanders? How was a Melbourne street so *quiet*? The one fucking time I needed a nosy neighbor and instead I got...*this*. Arthur. Gazing at me with utter adoration.

I pulled out my phone but hesitated once I got there. He wasn't in any immediate danger of dropping dead. Unless he told me I was beautiful again. Then all bets were off.

Opening my call log, I brought up the number for my most useful connection and hit call. "Detective Taig O'Malley," the sexy, up-all-night voice declared from the other end.

"Hey, Taig. Rory. I got a problem."

A chair squeaked in the background. "Where and what?"

"The coven. Arthur's been shot. By an arrow, not a gun."

"An—okay. Hey, Clint, got us a situation at the coven. Grab a car, meet me out front." Arthur leaned closer, his expression one of bliss. I leaned back and his face fell. Tears welled.

The *fuck?*

"What're we looking at?" Taig asked me. Background noise rose and fell on the end of the phone. "Doesn't sound like magick."

"It was absolutely magick," I said, irritated. "The arrow vanished after, I don't know, some seconds. Or minutes. And Arthur is really weird."

"Weird?"

"Yeah. Weird. You'll see."

"I'm not weird," Arthur breathed. "I love you, Rory."

Oh.

Oh, *no.*

CHAPTER 2

"Love potion," I told Taig, feeling sick. "I'm going to get him inside, see how bad the wound is. It isn't going to knock him out anytime soon."

There was some amusement in Taig's voice when he said, "make sure *you* don't, either. We're seeing enough of each other professionally without me having to follow up an assault charge."

I rolled my eyes at the phone and hung up. As if he'd get me on assault. As if Arthur would even press charges. Not until the spell lifted. And, shit, self-defense.

It took some juggling, but I got Arthur into the unusually empty coven.

The tiny kitchenette, done in government issue greys and full of the fussiest decor your grandmother could stand, was where I guided him. The multitude of embroidered tea towels were awesome bandages.

Who the fuck shot anyone with an arrow dipped in *love potion*?

Pressure. I needed pressure. And fucking yarrow. "Hold this," I told him, impatiently. "I have to go out to the garden."

Instead of holding it he dropped those poor ruined tea towels and grabbed me. "No—no! It's too dangerous! You wait. Here. Yeah." He seemed to come out of his daze, pushing off the bench as blood bloomed against the white of his shirt. "I'll go. I'll do it."

I folded my arms as he swelled with pride and purpose. "Oh, yeah?" I asked, mildly. "What're you doing, then, King?"

He blinked at me. "Protecting you."

For fuck's sake. "By going out to the garden."

He blinked again. Bloke looked like a bloodstained, upper-class goldfish. "Yes."

I grabbed the fallen tea towels, tossed them into the sink. The next fistful I grabbed and shoved hard at him. "Sit your arse down, King. You wouldn't know the herbs I need if they were sorted and labelled on the bench, so just..." he went to grab me again and I evaded, another wave of fury rolling through me. "Don't touch me without permission."

He deflated, suddenly, like a hot air balloon. "I'm... sorry. Rory. But... it's too dangerous. What if you get hurt?"

"Then we'll have herbs to slap on me, too." The heat of my anger wasn't dampened at all by the pathetic expression he wore. "Mate, I am not paid to clean your blood off the floor. Get pressure on your wound so I can go and help you." *Again. Because of course.* Did I get some sort of long service leave for providing excellent support to arrogant arsehats?

Like a sack of potatoes, he tumbled into a chair and did what I'd ordered. I didn't hang around to give him more time to argue. Where the fuck was my coven when I needed their old school assistance? I strode out into the cold, hyper-aware of the way the winter wind tugged at my hair, smelling like rain and exhaust, the hum of traffic, the steady footfalls of a jogger intent on their run. My focus split between my surroundings and my search for the plant..

The yarrow was half-hidden behind a rose bush that was probably older than me, and certainly better maintained. I snapped the fine, feathery yarrow leaves with a vicious snap of my wrist. *Elders give me patience. Or good legal advice.*

The door slammed behind me when I stomped back in and I didn't even *mean* for it to. I could almost *hear* Cici's exclamation of horror at how I'd trashed their garden.

Well, my garden was barren of fucks right now.

"Where's the coven?" I demanded of Arthur, striding into the tiny kitchenette and turning the tap on blast to rinse the yarrow. I ignored the way liquid splashed up around the sink, the way it soaked into the tea towels thrown there earlier. The way the water ran red with his blood.

Who in the ever-loving fuck shot *arrows*? With *love potion?* I could totally see shooting Arthur. But with a *love potion?* Hells, no. Bullets, thank you.

Arthur was staring at the benchtop listlessly. Probably still sulking because I'd forced him to sit himself down. Typical. "It's six," he said, the words cracking and crumbling.

Well, no wonder. I tossed the leaves down. *Fine. No other witches.* But where was Taig? The cop shop was, what, ten minutes' walk away? Was he stopping for *coffee?*

That thought actually brightened my mood. He'd get me one if he did. He was a good sort.

"At least you don't want me dead," Arthur said, despondently, as I reached for the buttons of his shirt.

"I don't want you dead," I said, yanking aside the thick, luxurious fabric of the guy's shirt. Probably cost more than my whole outfit, this shirt. And he had a singlet. Of course he did. "I just want you to be less of an arsehole."

"I—I'm not an arsehole." But the response lacked all of the customary Arthur arrogance. In fact, the way he raised his voice at the end, the hesitancy of the words, almost made it... a question?

I didn't stop to think on that. "We're all arseholes. You happen to be a specific flavor of arsehole that I object to." I reached over and grabbed the scissors. "Elders, Arthur," I heard myself say impatiently, "keep the pressure *on.*"

He did, looking like a puppy I'd just kicked. *Tears* welled in his eyes and he hadn't tried to weaponize his dimples in more than ten minutes. Guilt seeped through the anger as I cut the singlet above where he held two peach-and-blood colored tea towels against his wound.

He looked so deflated. So lost.

This wasn't my fucking *problem*.

Snatching up a fistful of yarrow, I crushed it in my palm and still had plenty of anger after that tiny act of temper. The smell of it filled my head and I was transported back to Oma's garden as she hosed off my scraped knees and put the bruised leaves onto the wounds.

"Lift."

He did. Blood flowed. As I pressed the half-mashed leaves to his wound, I couldn't help but notice the bare branches of the tree outside the window moving in the wind. Adrenaline flooded my system again as my brain saw threats in every shadow. I pushed it away, grabbed the tea towels, flipped them with my other hand and put them on top of the yarrow.

It'd hold him. He wouldn't drop dead in the next five minutes.

"You're so gentle. So competent. You look perfect in a kitchen, Aurora."

"Rory," I corrected, out of long habit. As for the rest…Elders, there was a lot to unpack there, but I was definitely in the mood to just burn the whole suitcase instead.

Love potions were *so hard* to undo.

The door opened and I glanced up as Taig strode in, his expression carved into its customary painfully neutral lines. The vice around my chest eased and his face softened, just fractionally. Guy didn't have a coffee, but I'd forgive him.

"Didn't bother with sirens," he said, as a how-do-you-do and sorry-I'm-late all in one. Arthur tensed as he looked between Taig and I. I remembered his earlier accusation and pressed harder on the jerk's wound. "Clint's doing a quick sweep."

Clint. Another jerk I wouldn't mind getting shot. Taig's new offsider was going to be a major thorn in my side, I just *knew* it. Where he found leftover red flags, considering how hard Arthur hoarded them, I had no idea, but he managed.

"You're remarkably cavalier about Rory being in danger." I was sort of relieved to see the way Arthur put his shoulders back and shot the words at Taig like some sort of accusation. Familiar was good, right?

"Not many witches in this town I'd worry less about," Taig said casually, flipping open a notebook and clicking a pen as he pulled up a chair beside us. "You're lucky she was with you, Arthur."

The trust made a tendril of shame worm through me. I shifted, ignoring it, and took Arthur's hand.

His eyes snapped to my face and I could feel his focus in my veins. A wave of pity for him swept over me. I lifted his hand to the makeshift bandage. "Hold it," I said, and it came out far more kindly than I would've wanted. Which is to say with any kindness at all. I stepped back, my jaw tight. I'd have to get the fuck-knuckle to a healer, too.

"I better call in the paramedics," Taig said, frowning a little at Arthur.

"No." The refusal was fast and hard. "Rory will look after me."

My stomach turned at the idea. Before I could respond, though, Taig made a quick note and said, "From the top, then?" His manner was as bland as unseasoned potatoes.

"We were about in the gate," I said, briefly, knowing he'd need just the basics. "Taking some swings at each other, and—"

"I'd never hit you," Arthur objected, horror dripping from every word.

I took a deep breath and his eyes dropped down to my chest. I took another and reached for my patience. It wasn't his fault he was off his face on hormones. "We were arguing," I amended, to keep Arthur from bickering over minutia. *Easier to stop fish from swimming.* "Arthur was shot with an arrow. I cast a ward. A second arrow bounced off it, I assume. I didn't see, but I heard it hit." Come to think of it, I probably should've tried to grab it. Unless they were auto-disappearing? What the fuck kind of spell was that? And could I use it on my dirty dishes?

Taig didn't look up from his notebook. "Clint'll find it."

"Doubt it. The first disappeared within about twenty seconds."

His pen scratched away quietly on paper. "Clint's good at what he does." The words were said with painful neutrality that made me suspect Taig liked him as much as I did. "Disappeared? Sparkles, smoke? Levitation spell, recall spell?"

"None of that." I shook my head, trying to remember the details. "Nothing. Just gone."

Arthur turned to Taig deliberately, his expression in familiar disdainful lines. "It would've hit Rory if she hadn't dodged. Show a bit of compassion, *Detective*, or you'll be hearing from your superiors."

I managed, through sheer force of will, not to roll my eyes. "What makes you say that?" Taig asked, pausing in his notetaking.

I opened my mouth to clarify but Arthur, apparently back to his old self, said over top of me, "She moved. We were—disagreeing. She's fast on her feet, you know."

Taig made a non-committal noise. His pen didn't move. "You're confident Rory was the target?"

"I am," Arthur said, flatly. "And you need a police guard on her, *now*."

"Hold the fuck on," I cut in, and ignored the amused twitch of Taig's mouth. "I do *not* need a police guard and you do *not* know squat, Mr. Hormone Junkie."

He straightened and did his level best to stand over me, glaring and puffing his chest out. It was very hard not to laugh.

"I'm going to look after you whether you want me to or not."

The *conviction* in his words. The guy was funny in the same way a puppy was when it fell over its own feet. I gave him a nudge toward his seat and felt the anger ebbing away, leaving tiredness in its wake.

Clint blew in with a flurry of wet leaves.

"Females appreciate being looked after," he said as if he was talking about adorable kittens and not humans.

I saw red.

"Want it or not," Arthur said, melodramatically, "it's what she's going to get."

Air whistled through my teeth and filled my chest as I went on the offensive.

And then ice speared from a ring on my right hand straight into my bones and agony roared.

An image overlaid my reality like it was branded on the inside of my eyeballs.

A blonde woman, quiver on her hip and wand in her hand, lifting her booted foot and driving it into Dierdre's door. Wood shattered beneath the force and her expression didn't change from the neutral lines of a focused predator.

Deirdre.

Clint's voice rose and fell in the background. Arthur. Their words tangled up in a stream of unintelligible nothing, even compared to their usual trash fire.

I fell back, groping for the kitchen bench. Another step. The pain was deep and huge, the shock of it, of the reality, sending frost straight to my heart.

The door exploded inwards in my vision and the sound of their conversation was overlaid with what I could see and feel. The all-consuming agony of it.

My charm.

The bitch shattered my charm.

And she was going after my witch.

My hand was so cold it burned, stole my breath, made the world go grey. I shook my head and tried to clear the vision, tried to push back, to get control. I was gripping my wrist. My fingers clamped down on the freezing flesh, felt the icy bite of my own skin. Someone had tried to kill us. Now they were going after my client.

Not on my fucking watch.

"*Stop*," I managed to get out, through the rolling images in my head, the splinters of broken spell, the visceral pain of my own protective charm doing its work, and their general shitfuckery.

A hand settled on my waist, then was roughly removed. There was some sort of movement, snarls. Fighting? I shook my head again. She was walking down Dierdre's hallway. The noise didn't match. It wasn't her. It was around me. But I watched as she checked the bathroom, closed the door behind her. The woman's mouth opened, closed, as she prowled down Dierdre's little hall.

Shit, I wished I could hear her words, not the arseholes around me. But I knew the look of a hunter.

"Just breathe, now," I could hear from close to me. "Breathe, Rory."

I sucked in air. The pain in my hand was *huge*. That bitch had done a number on my spell, all right, and now—

"We're in your coven," Taig was saying, his voice low and calm. "You're safe."

He didn't get it. I set my teeth and squeezed my eyes shut. "Taig. Broken charm." And I held my hand out in front of me, unable to see past the gorgeous bitch who had chewed my protections up so effectively.

"Arthur," Taig said, suddenly impatient. "Can you—"

Fuck being rescued by that paper-pusher again. I shook my head. There was nothing he could do, anyway, and the charm would take the brunt of it. "Dierdre." And she was the one witch who could fix Arthur's hormones up, too. Coincidence? The thought dragged across my brain like shattered glass. I tried to think through the pulsing, ripping pain. "Fuck." I sucked in more air. "Dierdre, Taig." Did he know who she was? The world was moving around me and I could see it going down, still, that familiar prowl, the doors opening, closing. *Hide, Dierdre.* "My witch. Dierdre Summers. Witness protection."

"What about Dierdre?" he asked, in that calming way he had.

My head *hurt*. I dug through my mind for counter-spells but they didn't come. Once a spell was smashed—

The sound of something cracking filled my head and the agony stole my breath. My vision went dark.

Fury pulsed, hot and dark.

Deirdre had been through enough and there was no way.

No.

Way.

I was letting that bitch hurt her.

CHAPTER 3

The first thing I saw was the kitchen bin with its lavender-scented liner under my face. There was a smattering of blood droplets on the bottom. I couldn't quite count them.

And there was Taig's hand. I was pretty sure it was his. I recognized the ring on it. It was probably charmed. And someone had a good grip on my hair and were holding it back. Seemed like a Taig thing to do.

"Elders," I breathed, as the pain rolled over me again and my vision blurred. The blood droplets became clouds. I blinked and they snapped back into focus.

"At least let me get her a tissue for her nose." Arthur's words were like icepicks into my brain.

"Yeah, no." The low, sexy rumble was close to me. "You look comfortable there, Arthur, and Clint's doing a good job on that shoulder. She'll come 'round."

I lifted a hand, felt it flutter helplessly. "Round."

"Going to vomit?" Taig asked, bluntly.

Straightening, I ignored the trickle of blood down the back of my throat as I peered at Taig. I hadn't had a charm broken like this since… since… *ever.* "If I do, I'll aim for those two."

Amusement tugged at his lips and the hand holding my hair was removed. I lifted my head a little more. The room whirled gracefully, slowly, around me. A quick grab for the bench kept me upright. There was no paper towel, of course. The wash cloth was embroidered though. I grabbed a clean one to hold to my nose and breathed around the pain.

Holy. Fucking. Shitballs.

"You need water, healing. An Unbreaking Tonic." Arthur again with the words.

Joke was on him. The only tonic I was drinking was with gin.

"So. One of your spells was broken," Taig said, putting the bin down and going to wash his hands in the sink beside me.

The words. The noise. Hells. "Yes." The visual popped back into my mind.

Witch. Big, combat boots. Lupetec armor or what looked like it, and the rest of the Retrievals kit, too, plus a quiver.

Shit. Deirdre.

I pushed off the bench. "I have to go get—"

"I'll drive you," Taig said, like we were debating whether to get pizza. "We'll check it out together. You can tell me what happened that made your ring flash like a blown light globe."

I glanced down at my ring. Urgency drummed in my heart, but I was in a bubble of calm. Swimming, almost.

The rose quartz that had sat there for years on my hand, charmed by my Oma was now blackened and cracked.

Oh, wow. Oma was going to be *impressed.* "She put a *lot* of power into breaking the charm I put on Dierdre's place," I explained, shaking my head.

"Who?" Taig asked, grabbing his notepad and wandering closer to the door, keeping a watch on me.

"The witch that broke into Dierdre's and shot Arthur." I shook my head. *Come on, brain, don't fail me now.*

Taig's eyes sharpened. "Recognize her?"

"No. But how many people with a bow and arrows do you see every day?"

"The law doesn't believe in coincidences, Caretaker," Clint told me, looking at me dispassionately.

"The law follows up on leads, though," Taig said, the words impeccably neutral and underscored by the loaded look he shot at Clint. My feet worked. Shit, I had good feet. Best knees ever, too. Barely even wobbled. I zoned out their bickering and let Taig ride shotgun over arsehole Clint from the front. Pig-headed Arthur insisted on coming, too, cluttering up the back seat. Thank the Elders it wasn't raining. They'd parked behind the coven. They'd need to do a twenty-point turn to get out, but that wasn't a me problem. I collapsed into the back and shut my eyes.

The strange fuzziness receded, and I was left with a dull fucker of a headache and a hand that felt how I imagined freezer burned meat would, if it had a feeling.

Taig was on the radio, or whatever it was. The conversation was a mess of cop-speak. From far away I heard him say, "Is there a Retrievals team available? I've got a violent witch possibly on location." Whatever the response was mustn't have pleased him, because his follow up was, "I don't care about the budget, Sunny. We need to mobilize *now*."

Arthur's hand crept over the back seat toward me. I shot him a look designed to eviscerate and was again taken aback by the concern on his face. Yep, not something I was accustomed to from him.

"... I'm aware that's not protocol, but legally she's the victim's Caretaker, *and* she's the only Retrievals trained witch in the goddamn city, apparently."

Me. That was me. I swung my eyes back to Taig's profile as Clint eased us into traffic. I saw his beady eyes on me in the rear-view mirror and hoped his arrogance didn't get us killed in a car accident. That would just be a far too mundane way to end my day.

"Sure," Taig said, going from impatient to perfectly calm in a heartbeat. "Let's bring her in. You can meet us at the scene and transport her." And then he hung up.

I blinked. "What'm I doing?"

He half-turned to look at me, his gaze assessing. "Your color's better. They want us to take you in. Both of you."

"And we should." Clint accelerated harder than I felt was necessary, weaving in traffic. And then I remembered Deirdre. Urgency drummed in my breast. Where was my head at?

"Sure we should," Taig agreed, straightening. "But we've got a time-sensitive lead and some excellent backup if things get hairy. So, we won't."

Clint snorted in derision and shot me another look. I didn't flip him the bird, but, shit, it was tempting.

"It's dangerous," Arthur jumped in, and I just let my head fall back. I couldn't deal with this guy. "She's hurt. This is negligence. Your duty of care—"

"*She* is right here," Taig said, his voice milder than the message he was delivering. "Rory, you in a state to consent to this?"

The question dispersed some of the mist in my head. I'd been hit for six and there was no point denying it, but damned if I was going to hop out of this car and go and present to the police station just to twiddle my thumbs.

Deirdre had escaped her abusive ex and come into my care. I wasn't letting her down.

"Yeah," I said, and my voice sounded strangely normal. Calm, even. "I'm on board."

"Rory," Arthur said, gently, as we sped past parked cars and rain-soaked streets, "you're hurt. Broken spells aren't a small thing and if she went through your charm, she's powerful. She's already tried to hurt you once. Whoever she is, she could use lethal force. You could be hurt. There's no reason you need to be present. It isn't part of your job—you're supposed to refer everything like this to the relevant authorities. I can manage this. I know what we're up against is probably very dangerous."

And he was so adorably sweet about it. Like this was a whole new concept to him he was sharing. He was a toddler figuring out something and being so excited he just had to tell someone.

"... could be carrying other potions, some of which can be lethal.

Even if she isn't, the chances of her knowing how to weaponize magick means this is a very dangerous situation."

Taig cleared his throat. "Arthur, you do know Rory's more qualified in this field than you, right? And debatably, in better shape than you."

He bristled. "I know she's making a mistake because her kindness is clouding her judgement. She's emotional—"

"Arthur." I put my hand on his arm. Poor little man. He'd be ripping my head off, usually, for going off half-cocked without a Risk Management Plan. Instead, he was mansplaining my job to me. What a way to show his magickally induced love. "Trust me, okay? And back me up. That's what I need from you."

He melted right there in front of me. Elders, I was a bitch. "I…I want to. But you need to be looked after."

Why the hells not play this game? I knew we were close. He could very well seal me in the car, so I'd play the cards I had. "Yes, I do. And the way you can do that is by sticking with me. Just like with the lycans we fought."

Something flickered over his face. "I saved your life."

And wasn't that galling. "Pretty sure we worked as a team, King."

I doubted if Arthur even heard. "We're a good team."

"Yeah," I agreed, unclicking my belt. The noise echoed. "Go, team." And, ignoring the pain spearing through my head and the way my belly lurched, I opened the door and followed Taig around the back of the building. My eyes skipped ahead, seeking the entry to Dierdre's apartment.

Arthur was so close behind me I was worried about having my heels trod on.

I tried to remember what I'd seen of the enemy's movements. Where she'd been. What she'd touched. Whether she'd set traps. But it was all blurry in my head, now.

Someone stared out from their window in a neighboring apartment, talking into the phone, their eyes wide as they watched us. I saw Clint flash them his badge.

Bracing myself, I caught up to Taig as he topped the stairs and rounded the corner to Dierdre's place.

The broken door didn't shock me. I'd seen it happen. "Was this a spell?" he asked, drawing his weapon.

"Yeah. Boot meets wood; magick of squats and glute bridges," I said impatiently, shoving past. "Dierdre!"

Silence.

The place smelled like hearty vegetable soup and homemade bread. My heart broke, just a little.

"She closed the doors after checking rooms," I told them, unsurprised at how calm I sounded. The energy simmering under my skin, the heat of impatience and the throbbing urgency was all familiar. This was my bread and butter. *You can do this. This is fine. Everything is fine.*

Deirdre was gone. I could feel it.

The greatest risk right then was from the untended food, so I managed that and I breathed. It took them less than two minutes to secure the place. I had the soup in the fridge before they'd returned, because she *was* coming back.

"She's gone," Clint told me, totally unnecessarily. "Who is this witch?"

"Protective custody," Taig said, briefly. "Fill you in later. I'm calling in Retrievals. Screw the budget."

"No sign of struggle," Clint disagreed.

Taig, already lifting the phone to his ear, just pointed at the shattered door.

Arthur hovered near my elbow, his eyes everywhere, his expression grim, but I was already sifting through what I knew. Retrievals would take anywhere from ninety minutes to three hours to rock up. I'd done that dance. You could cover a lot of ground in three hours. And if there was no sign of a struggle inside the apartment, no corpses, no blood… she'd taken Dierdre alive.

I dug out my work phone. I was a passable tracker in the bush, but here? Not a chance. Not without any of the obvious signs like footprints, blood trails or broken trees. All I had was urban jungle. And that witch had already disappeared on me once.

"Hello, Caretaker," Beo said from the other end of the line, and the words were perfectly polite.

Hope and guilt warred. I had no idea what impact this would have on us. Things were rocky enough already without me asking for a favor. Especially a public favor. "Hello, Beo. I've got a situation at work."

He was quiet for a moment, then asked, "Are you okay?"

I hated this charade. I could feel Arthur's focus on me and I knew I couldn't misstep, no matter how much I just wanted to vomit it all out and have Beo hold me. "I'm in need of someone who's able to track a client through the city—fast. Do you know anyone who could help?" *Will you please help?*

"Give me the address," he said—no questions and absolutely no hesitation.

This man was too good for me. My heart ached. I held my love close, kept it buried, and passed on Dierdre's address.

"I'll be there," he said. "You look after you, Rory."

And, from him, it wasn't overbearing. I ached.

One way or the other, I needed to be in his arms tonight.

"You called Velvela?" Arthur demanded of me the moment I tucked the phone back into my pocket. I didn't know or care if it was jealousy or hurt in his tone. At least he wasn't having a go at me about it. Ah, the merits of having a love-punched boss.

Taig, whose call was also over, narrowed his eyes at me. "He coming on in an official capacity?"

"Wasn't discussed," I said, honestly. My head was too fuzzy to play games well. "He's helping, though."

"Who is Velvela and why is he helping?" Clint asked, with a long-suffering sigh.

"He's a lycanthrope Alpha on Rory's caseload," Arthur said, pacing across the room, his movements jerky, his eyes skimming the surfaces. I doubted he was taking note of much of anything. "He owes us."

I didn't correct him, even though it wasn't true. If anything, I owed him a few. And that had nothing to do with the orgasm tally, because who even counted them?

"You want him to *sniff* this witch out?" Clint demanded.

"Breach of protocol, involving civilians," Taig said, the words almost amused. "Good solution, though. Retrievals estimated at six hours; teams must've been busy. They're having to split an active group."

The thought made me feel queasy. I'd been there, done that. You went in with a certain amount of people because that was what was needed. Splitting teams increased the risk exponentially. Choppers weren't stealthy.

Split teams were dead teams.

"Cancel the call, Taig."

There wasn't the slightest change in his expression. "Protocol, Caretaker."

Fuck protocol. And since when did he care? I gritted my teeth, tried to think. "Fine." The next best option was to stall it, let them get a whole team. Safely. "You put a rush on it, didn't you?"

He looked at me like he was reconsidering whether I should even be there. "Of course."

I pressed my aching hand to my aching head to hold in my thoughts and watched as Arthur's gaze followed the movement like a dog waiting for a bone. I couldn't help but feel for him. "We'll either have her in hand or be tracking her the hard way in a few hours, Taig."

Arthur strode into Dierdre's cupboard. He flicked a light on, chased away the early winter gloom.

"Call them back," I told him, tiredly. "Tell them we've found a way around." I couldn't help but ask, as he began to rummage, "Arthur, what are you doing? This is a crime scene."

Taig tucked his hands into his pockets and wandered over to me; Arthur shot him a wary look that I doubted had anything to do with the laws he was breaking.

"Making you a tonic," Arthur answered, sulkily.

I somehow managed not to roll my eyes. Shit, if it kept him busy.

The dude was wounded and making *me* a tonic? Dierdre's pot plants would love it.

"You know something I don't?" Taig asked me, quietly, coming to a stop at my shoulder.

He smelled like sandalwood, rain and coffee. It made my head spin, a little, and not in a bad way. I cleared my throat. "Pulling half a team off an active mission, Taig…"

"It's their job."

"It was mine." This close I could see the grey flecks in the pale, piercing blue of his eyes as I met them head on. "It's not worth it, Taig. I know the score. Trust me."

His gaze went to my blackened, cracked ring. "You want to do this alone?" And the words were no nonsense, rough, but not quite a warning.

I thought of Beo's unquestioning support and managed to hide my smile, if not some of the tension that ebbed out of me at what was very obviously one last check in before he capitulated.

"I never said that, Detective."

CHAPTER 4

"I DIDN'T REALIZE WIZARDS COULD MAKE POTIONS," CLINT SAID, managing to somehow sound curious rather than blatantly misogynistic.

Taig shot him a loaded look but took his call outside. Well, I could deal with jerks. Plonking my butt down on one of Dierdre's chairs, I said, mildly, "You're remarkably well preserved for a Neanderthal, Clint."

I didn't miss the way Arthur's brow furrowed as he quickly glanced between us. "It's a tonic, not a potion." He dropped a crystal into the heat proof jug with finality. "We need them when we practice combat spells."

Which made them manly, of course. I was surprised it didn't have steak and jizz in it. I mean, I hadn't been watching closely, but I was pretty sure I'd have noticed those additions.

"You got a photo of her, Arthur?" Clint asked, personably.

Seconds dragged by and I struggled with impatience as Arthur fumbled his phone out and passed it over after a few quick taps. "That's her," he said, going back to his potion. "I'm glad I can help. I know Rory's worried."

Clint made a noncommittal noise. I rubbed at my aching temples, wishing I could just throat-punch this witch and get to bed.

"She single?" Clint asked.

It was a normal question, and Taig had said he was good at his job. Clint would know, surely, the greatest risk to women and children were the ones close to home. But when I glanced up, he didn't have his notepad out, but was just standing, looking thoughtfully at Arthur's phone. And his expression made my skin crawl.

"Yes," Arthur said, absently. "Divorced, I think? Or... no, I don't think she was ever married."

"She's got time yet," Clint mused, angling the phone screen to get a better look.

Where was Taig to pass me something to puke into when I needed him? There were so many responses all jammed up in my head that all I could do was sit and stare. We weren't really going there, were we?

As if summoned, Taig returned and immediately Clint put Arthur's phone aside with a casual nonchalance I didn't buy for one second...

"Arthur, how long will that take? If there's time before backup arrives, I'd like to interview neighbors, but I need you two out first," Taig said.

The moment had passed and I was as disgusted with myself as I was with Clint. By the time I managed to find the words to tell Arthur, "Leave it," he'd redoubled his efforts and was rummaging through Dierdre's jars frantically enough that the sound of them crashing into one another made me wince.

He actually stopped, though, and looked at me.

Since when did Arthur listen to me?

"You... don't want my help?"

Elders, those puppy eyes made me feel like a bitch. "Will it get me up and running in the next half an hour?" I asked, forcing myself to be pragmatic.

He looked down at the jar in his hand. "No. But it'll make you just feel hung over tomorrow, instead of all week."

Tomorrow? Deirdre needed me *now*. "By tomorrow we'll have

Retrievals on board," I said, shaking my head. "Better to let these two canvas the area, see if we can get a head start on the legal bullshit at least." I hesitated, though. If it gave me an edge…"What's in it?" I asked, suspiciously. As soon as he opened his mouth, I waved a hand. I didn't actually care. "It's fine. I'll trust you." Words I never thought I'd say and hoped to shit I never said again. "Just do it. Meanwhile, have you two got some sort of database of witches who practice illegally I could look through?"

"Back at the precinct," Clint told me, with a nod. "I can take you."

Yeah, no thank you. "I've already started debriefing Rory," Taig said, as if he could read my thoughts. "I'll take her when we get back, Clint, if you get Arthur. We'll send some beats to clean up the neighborhood. Gerri's on the way to manage the coven."

Distracted, Clint frowned over at Taig. "Gerri? Isn't Johnno free?"

I zoned them out and went over to where Arthur was whipping ingredients together with a fork, apparently not even feeling his wound. "Hey. Go easy."

He jerked like I'd hit him. "What? I won't break it. The jug, I mean."

"No. On yourself." I eyed him warily, wondering again exactly what concoction he'd been hit with. Surely a skin full of love juice wouldn't be enough to let him move so freely?

"Oh." He shrugged and went back to whisking. "Sure. Yeah." He cleared his throat, his eyes flickering up to Taig and Clint. "What… what *do* you want in a man, Rory?"

My heart felt warm, suddenly, and too big to fit in my chest. I rested my elbows on the bench, held that feeling close. *Beo.* That's what I wanted. But I couldn't say that, could I? "I want a good one."

He didn't respond for a moment, murmuring a spell over the jug and making it go a cool green, then take on a cloudy, yellowish glow, until it looked a bit like the sort of snot that sent you to the doctor. "Done." He grabbed a strainer, sat it over a glass and, as he lifted the jug, asked, tentatively, "Am I not good, Rory? I thought … I thought I was okay. I tried to be."

My heart twisted as I watched the liquid run through the strainer. The crystal, sprigs of herbs and some seeds I hadn't seen go in all were caught. "I know you did. Do. We all do. I guess we all value different things." And even if I knew he'd be a sanctimonious jerk the minute this potion was negated, I felt for him. But I wasn't going to lie. The dude was a douche canoe. No amount of puppy eyes would make me offer him any false reassurances.

"Detectives." My head jerked up fast enough to make the blood pound painfully at my temples. "Caretaker." Beo stepped over the broken door carefully, bag over his shoulder and brilliant green eyes on me. My heart warmed at the sight of him but I kept my face impassive. "Zane's outside. He can keep up on the bike," he told me, tone impersonal. But I knew he was wondering.

Things suddenly felt a lot more in control and the relief of that was huge. I drank up the sight of him as his gaze raked the surroundings. It was so long since I'd kissed him good-bye this morning. He skirted a sliver of wood, the jeans on his legs molded to the strength of him. The way his shirt stretched taut over his chest as he twisted to avoid an indoor plant. The man filled the space.

The man filled my heart.

I breathed and, once again, held that warmth, that softness, close. And then I noticed the faint bulge of a bandage on his shoulder.

Confusion swept through me. He hadn't been hurt this morning. He'd have told me if something was going down. *Jiu-jitsu injury?* I couldn't ask now.

To hide the feelings smashing around inside my ribs I took the tonic Arthur passed me without a second glance. *Dierdre. Focus.* "We've got a rogue witch who smashed my charm," I told Beo, and waved my aching hand at the broken door. *Get your head in the game.* "And kidnapped a client. Retrievals are hours away. Reckon you can find her?"

His eyes had gone to my hand and his expression turned flinty. He hadn't looked at the door, but I saw him studying me for injury. What could he see, sense? I felt completely naked in the most welcoming, comfortable way.

Then I realized how silent the room was.

He must have, too, because he took another step closer to me and held out his hand expectantly. "Your ring."

I lifted my hand toward him hesitantly. "It was a protective charm. It was broken when—"

"Whoever broke it left their magick upon it." He took my hand and the ache suddenly seemed a lot less. Heat radiated into me and I drank it up, wishing I could wrap my arms around him. "I caught the scent on the wind earlier." His eyes flickered to the drink in my other hand. "That looks like it'd do you good, Caretaker."

I winced and lifted the cup as he raised my aching hand gently to his face. The intimacy of the action made discomfort and delight creep up my spine. I focused on the vile taste of Arthur's tonic rather than the strength and warmth of his fingers. There was no way I couldn't remember the way he buried his face in my neck and moaned as he inhaled me.

Shit. Tracking a dangerous witch. My client kidnapped. And I was halfway to finding an excuse to grab Beo and fold myself into his arms in a back room. Stairwell. Elevator.

The tonic was utterly vile and that probably saved me from being overtaken by my own fragility. My belly rolled as the potion hit it. I should've known better than to trust Arthur, even in Pathetic Puppy Form.

Beo lowered my hand, his eyes narrowed. "Witch, you said? That's all?"

Some of the fog blew out of my head. My attention honed in again. "Why? What do you smell?"

He shook his head a little, a faint frown on his face. "That. And something... different."

"Vampire?" Taig asked, briskly. "Fae? She could be coerced or charmed."

"No." The word was final. "Not from my world."

Unease danced under my skin. I met his eyes. "And it changed the smell of her magick?"

Even though it wasn't really a question, he said, "Yes."

My mind spun.

An amplification potion might explain why she'd burned through my charm like a bushfire in February, but I didn't like it. Amping had serious long-term side effects. No one who actually valued magick would touch it except in a life-or-death situation—and she held all the cards, right now.

"Potions," Arthur said, firmly. "They change magick. Makes sense they'd change its scent."

"And we already know she's used them," Taig agreed, his pen scratching as he noted this. "Could be why she's targeted Ms. Summers."

Things magickal of this world was a pretty short list. There was human magick, some First Nations connections... and angels or demons.

Fuck. If it wasn't potions...

Beo gently released me. "I want to walk through. Make sure it's the right scent."

"Sure. I'll accompany," Taig said, snapping the notebook closed.

"I'll go catch Zane," I offered, since there was nothing else to do. Beo nodded to me and turned down the corridor. Arthur, predictably, stuck to me like a burr. "Can I get you to put through the paperwork to get Beo clearance?" I asked him, because, Elders curse it, having a love-drunk boss had to have *some* perks.

"Of course." He was frowning, though. "It won't be finalized in time for him to be... here."

"Time stamp it from when we realized Dierdre's place was broken into," I suggested, then remembered who I was talking to and winced at his expression. "Look. It's two minutes. *Technically* we made the call then. We couldn't make it earlier. The man—"

"Lycanthrope."

I didn't like his tone. "Beo has been investigated inside out and upside down. He's not a bad guy or we'd know it. He's doing us a solid. It's the least we can do." And I'd caused the guy enough drama, what with clueing his murderous brother into the whereabouts of the child Beo had taken in to protect.

I could see from Arthur's thoughtful expression that this made sense, somehow, to him. "It wouldn't be fair of us to ask him to help and then not do the paperwork, would it?" I asked, to seal the deal.

Arthur gave a curt nod. "And you're in no state to do it," he agreed, pulling out his phone. "I'll get you to put your signature on it, though, so I can okay it."

Ah, the power of administrators in love. No mountain of paperwork too tall, no ocean of red tape too wide. "Thanks, King," I said, and there was gratitude and warmth in there I didn't even have to work for. I was a total bitch and he was being played—but, shit, Beo came first.

At the bottom of the stairs, he held the door for me, his expression one of pleasure. "You're welcome."

Guilt gnawed at me as I went into the underground excuse for a car park where I knew Dierdre didn't have a vehicle. Like me, she rode the trams. Like me, she loved the old rattlers. *Where are you, Dierdre?*

Zane waited beside his motorcycle. The first thing I noticed was a bandage on his head and my mind skipped back to Beo.

Had they *fought?* They were like brothers. He lifted a hand in greeting. "Hey, Rory. Arthur." He cleared his throat, shrugged his arms a bit in his jacket, then pulled it closed. "Good night for it." I shot him a disbelieving look and he ducked his head to hide a smile. "What happened to you two, anyway?" he asked his feet.

"Later." I was so done with explanations that went nowhere, and I had to wait to interrogate him. "What's the plan?"

"Plan?" he peered up at me. "You needed a tracker. We're here."

Butter wouldn't melt in his mouth. "Okay. Two of you?"

He shrugged and relaxed a little. There was a second helmet on the bike behind him. I'd never seen any of the lycans ride double before. "Sure. Cars'll have a hard time following. Figured this way, I can call in the location once he gets there."

My heart squeezed. Beo was going to shift. Break a few laws. Put himself at risk. And he'd do it without even asking me why.

Shit, maybe the man was *too* good. And maybe I wasn't. "I didn't realize he'd need to shift, Zane."

"Well, maybe he won't. But if you want this done before the rain hits and muddies the tracks, then." He shrugged again. "You know Beo."

I did.

Maybe Arthur's tonic was helping, because I was able to think a little clearer, now, to realize I should've known.

He'd be so much faster, so much better at following a scent, in his lycan form. "Shit."

Zane flashed me a fast grin. "You never seemed to think so before." Then his eyes flickered to Arthur as if realizing his mistake. But Arthur's attention was on his phone as he rapidly input data into online forms.

I just swung a fist at Zane's shoulder in a lazy punch and he didn't flinch. So, he hadn't taken too much of a beating, whatever had gone down. "Shut up, you brute. When did you have a haircut, Zane?"

He ran a hand through his blond mop. "About two days ago. Like it?"

"Did they take off a millimeter?"

He looked injured. "It isn't that long."

"Do you like men with short hair?" Arthur asked me, lifting a hand self-consciously to his own impeccably maintained short back and sides, phone forgotten in his hand.

I saw Zane freeze, his eyes flicker to me in question. If even *I* could hear the hope in the guy's voice, I hated to think what it would sound like to someone with Zane's hearing. "I just like to tease him," I told Arthur, rather than try to figure out an answer.

He studied my expression, confusion on his face. "So… you don't like short hair?"

"Hair isn't really a factor," I said, because he seemed to need an answer. "I was just joking with Zane." Whose hair needed cutting, despite his protests. "Just being friendly, making small talk."

"Oh." Arthur nodded, as if this made sense and angled his phone again to keep working. "Banter. Right. Not flirting." But he paused before re-commencing typing, looked at me for confirmation.

"Right."

He let out a breath. "Okay." And off he went.

Yep. Queen Bitch. That was me.

Zane raised an eyebrow at me. I just shook my head a little and drew my jacket closer against the chill of the night, trying to figure out what I knew about Dierdre. But the facts and information just swam in my mind. At least my hand didn't hurt so badly now that Beo had held it. And maybe that was purely psychological, but short of curling myself into his arms it was about the best I could get.

Arthur came over and offered me his phone. I skimmed the information on the screen—it wasn't much, our forms weren't phone-friendly—before giving him a dodgy electronic signature. Arthur smiled at me. Two dimples. "Almost done."

I just didn't have the headspace to deal with him. "Thanks, Arthur. I really appreciate this."

He went back to it. "You're right. He's an asset in this situation, and we need to keep it above board."

As he sent through his approval for the request with my name and signature on it, I had to wonder if it'd stand up in court should the fact that he was lovestruck ever be mentioned. Probably not. I didn't really know, though. Still, I had every faith in Arthur's tenacity and adherence to the rules. Technically, this *was* a rule. Even if there was some creative interpretation happening.

When Beo came down the stairs he was flanked by Taig and Clint. Zane straightened from his slouched position against the bike and threw one leg over. "Give your bag to Rory," Zane said, when Beo dropped it on the cement and unzipped his jacket. "Don't need it with us."

Beo's eyes met mine briefly, but it wasn't in a search for acquiescence. "Be safe," he told me, quietly.

The hairs on the back of my neck rose.

Potions.

Or Angels.

Or Demons.

I watched as Clint split off from Taig and took Arthur up the narrow exit from the carpark to the road above. "What did you find?"

I asked Beo, coming to a stop beside him and holding out a hand for his shirt. The shift wasn't kind to lycan's clothes.

"More of the same." He dropped it into my hand and the fabric was warm and soft. I'd held him, smoothed my hands over his back, when he'd put this on this morning.

And I didn't miss the way he twisted to hide the bandage on his shoulder from my sight.

"Does your paperwork cover shifting?" Taig asked me, dragging me back to reality.

He knew it didn't. "No."

Beo didn't pause, just reached into the bag and pulled out a black vest in a very familiar fabric.

Lupetec.

He had lupetec gear.

Unease rippled through me. We didn't know where the fabric came from. Just what it did. And what it cost.

I didn't stand and watch. I knew what the man looked like getting dressed and I damned well knew he was wounded. Did lupetec survive their shift? Should I be stopping him?

"I can look the other way," Taig was saying, quietly, grimly, "within reason."

"Rory needs help," Beo said, flatly. "So does her witch. We'll figure the rest out as it happens."

Taig's brows rose, just fractionally. "I'll get Clint to meet you out front, Rory."

"He's one of the decent ones," Beo said of Taig as I made myself busy folding his shirt and tried not to worry about what might've just been given away. "You don't have to do that."

I shrugged and tucked it into the bag. The lupetec vest he had on was the fabric we used as armor in Retrievals. Flexible, cool when it was hot and warm when it was cold, tough enough to stop almost anything except a full-force lycan bite or vamp strike. Outfitting us in that fabric cost the government a bomb. It was a tightly controlled resource. And not machine washable.

Beo tossed his belt into the bag, his shoes. "What's up with Arthur?"

"Love potion. Also, shot."

"Poor guy." He unzipped his pants and I looked away. Right here in the parking lot? I supposed it was quiet. "I wondered why you weren't ripping his head off."

I shrugged, feeling awkward. "Well, you know. I'll kick a guy when he's down…if I put him there."

There was some amusement in his voice when he said, "Always liked that about you." A few rustles. "You know what it could be that we're tracking?"

"Got some ideas." And they all stopped me from imagining him naked. "None of it's good."

"Figured that myself. You'd better go."

I glanced back to find him in lupetec shorts. I didn't ask where they came from. I knew it wasn't legal. "Does that survive the shift?"

"Yeah." He crouched to zip the bag. "Go on, Caretaker," he said, the words gentle as he passed the bag to me. "Zane's got your number."

I hesitated. "Are you sure—"

"I'm sure I want to kiss you and get out of here," he said, the words a low promise. "We'll get her back. So, you go play nice with Arthur and don't pull punches with that new guy."

I let out a long breath. "You don't want me watching you shift."

His eyes stared straight into my soul. I didn't shy away. "Things are complicated enough, aren't they?"

My heart ached. "I guess." And, trusting his superior senses to know if it was safe, I tilted my head up in invitation. "Kiss me. For luck."

His hand went around the base of my neck, his fingers coiling in my hair. I adjusted the bag so it didn't get between us. The heat of him eased some of the aches I couldn't quite shake. His mouth was firm. Warmth unfurled in my veins. I drew on his strength and felt his hand tighten fractionally. "You're in my bones," he murmured, against my lips.

My heart swelled. It wasn't the first time I'd got the lycan-equivalent of *I love you*, but it was still new enough that it made me pause. "Be safe, Beo."

"What about me?" Zane asked, from behind us. "Do I get to be safe?"

"After you get a haircut," I told him, easing back.

Beo looked puzzled. "He had one a few days ago."

With a shake of my head, I said, "Cool. Great. Bye. Not looking." I hefted his bag over my shoulder and turned to the darkness-clad streets. The aches in my body were there again, now, but they weren't so bad, really.

In his bones.

His strength. His foundation. That's what it meant.

No pressure, though. Not like he was the biggest, baddest bloke around. I heard Zane's bike rumble to life behind me and a chill went up my spine.

The biggest, baddest bloke we knew about.

CHAPTER 5

"Where to?" Taig asked from behind the wheel as I hauled myself into the car and shut the door on the arse-bitingly cold wind.

Where to?

Shit, I probably should have asked for vague directions, shouldn't I?

"Give them a few minutes," I said, as Zane's bike sped past us. Arthur was staring at me openly. In the rear-view mirror I saw Taig watching us closely. Only Clint's eyes were narrowed on the dark outside the car.

Hoping Beo could stay out of sight, I cleared my throat and wished I still had my scarf. "Maybe just follow that general direction." It was the best I had.

"I don't think they're both on that bike," Clint said, suspiciously.

"Who could tell," Taig said, blandly. "It's so dark. Pretty sure I saw two people, but, hey, they accelerated fast."

Good old Taig.

"You really care about Dierdre," Arthur said quietly. "I mean, I knew you did. You talk mean but you'd do anything for your clients."

I really felt for the guy. There was no way he'd be saying this if he weren't TKO'd. "It's my job."

"It's more," he disagreed. "You're a… an egg, Rory. Hard outside, soft inside."

Taig, in the front, cleared his throat. I struggled not to react too. An egg. I was an egg.

Lilith would get a kick out of that. "That's the sweetest thing you've said to me." I couldn't think of another response.

He looked offended. "I called you a strong, independent woman within five minutes of meeting you. I recognized it immediately."

And he'd done it unironically, too. "Guess you did."

"You, ah. You haven't commented. On me."

I had, actually. Just nothing good. "You've been hit by a love potion, Arthur," I said, trying to be as gentle as I could. "You've probably forgotten we don't like each other."

"But you're kind and sweet and hot as hells," Arthur said, confused. "Why wouldn't I like you?"

I sighed. I doubted his bubble was poppable, but I couldn't *lie.* "Because I'm a loose cannon." Pretty sure he'd accused me of that at some point. At least mentally. "I consider rules to be guidelines and I won't sleep with you."

"You follow rules," he objected. "Tonight, you did."

Sort of. "Mm."

"As for the rest, well…I guess, unpredictability is not something I usually like, but—but maybe I just need to see things from your perspective. Maybe that'll help. And maybe you'll benefit from a routine focused day, too."

Routine focused day. That's what he was offering me. Come for the admin, stay for the routine.

"As for sleeping with you…I wouldn't hold it against you if you didn't see me like that." The hurt in his voice said, very clearly, that he would. "I, ah. I don't remember asking you out."

No, I'd nipped that in the bud. "Look, Arthur…" *come on, brain.*

"You're wasting your time," Clint said, from the front. "I'm telling you, Arthur, women nowadays don't understand their market value. Just take it easy, bro, you know what I'm saying?"

"Whoa," Arthur said, shocked. "Are you saying Rory isn't good enough for me?"

"Okay," I said, my head ringing. "Okay, at no point did I or any other woman ask for an evaluation of my market value from a bloke whose entire personality is 'arsehole'—I'm not up for sale, mate, and if I was you couldn't make the payments, so just sit down."

"Yeah," Arthur added, emphatically. "Sit down, Clint." He frowned a little, though, and studied Clint's position as if checking to see if he'd stood up. I wanted to hit my head against something very solid.

Taig cleared his throat again. "Rory, can you give us a description of this witch?"

I knew what he was trying to do, and I didn't like it. "Sure. After you put your sidekick in his place."

Taig did a quick head check before he merged. I had no idea why he bothered changing lanes. It wasn't like we knew where we were going. "There are some conversations I'd prefer to have in private. But she's right, Clint. And I'm absolutely fine with having you out on administrative leave while you do sensitivity training. I report this sort of thing, and I follow up if that training doesn't stick. We'll speak more later."

Clint snorted. "That's rich. Don't think people don't talk, O'Malley. I know what you did a few years back. You and me, we're no different."

Arthur murmured something and, suddenly, I couldn't hear them. Not their conversation, not the background road noise. *What had Taig done a few years ago?* That was…interesting. I arched a brow at Arthur.

"Just a Silence Ward," he said, shrugging. "Clint was upsetting you."

"Arthur," I said, reaching for patience. "You should check in before you make decisions for people. I can cast my own Silence Wards."

He looked like I'd kicked him in the balls. "Oh. I can lower it—"

"Look." But what the fuck did you say to your irritating, self-important, but doped up boss?

He waited while I sifted through options frantically. "At… what?" he asked, awkwardly.

Shit. "Clint's an arsehole. But he's an arsehole I can deal with."

"But… I thought you said we're all arseholes."

I don't think I'd ever had so much actual attention from Arthur. I turned a little in my seat to face him as best I could. His eyes skittered away from mine. I'd hurt his feelings and it was no wonder. He was basically a walking feeling right now. I couldn't imagine how horrible that would be. I put aside my curiosity about Taig for now.

"I was being flippant. No one is perfect. But there are different flaws that are less of a problem. You know what I mean?"

He shrugged. The movement should've hurt him, but if it did, he gave no sign. "Not really. I thought…I thought I was okay. I thought I'd been okay to you. I know…I know I said some stuff, when I was upset. About you sleeping with other people, and whatever. I'm sorry. I was just, I don't know…"

Being yourself.

"I guess I was just insecure," he said, weakly. "I never knew if you liked me or not. Sometimes I thought you did, and then sometimes I couldn't tell, and sometimes you were just…mean." His gaze flickered up again but he didn't meet my eyes.

Poor Arthur. I wanted to put a bow on him, squeeze his cheeks, give him a hug, and tell him to have another go. But not at me. Still, if he was going to listen, then I had to try, didn't I? And where the fuck was Beo? We'd been on this merry-go-round for, what, ten minutes?

"I don't know what you want," Arthur was saying, words thick with misery. "I know what you need, but not what you want."

I drew in a deep breath and didn't let my anger reach boiling point. "Okay, well, maybe that's the problem, Arthur. You *don't* know what I need, except basic stuff—safety, shelter, food, connections." And, *finally*, my brain kicked in. "You want to know what a good man is?" His eyes raised, zeroed in on mine. He hung off my every word and I felt the pressure like cement shoes. "A good man is someone who listens to what other people say, who makes space for them to speak and—and live, and exist. He's someone who knows his own power and protects the people who have less power, makes sure they can get what they need. He creates a space for that. He lifts them up." Yeah. Nothing about steak. Definitely no jizz involved.

"I...don't know how to do that?" he admitted, tentatively, almost questioningly. "I think...I try?"

He was trying all right. "If you aren't sure if you've done that, ask your exes," I said, with a shrug. Shit, that'd be a horrible conversation. "Let them know you want to learn and grow."

"I don't want to talk to them," he said, flatly. "I want to talk to you."

"And I'm telling you, you can learn from your mistakes." He was so damn vulnerable. "We *all* make mistakes. A good man tries to learn from them. Ask people's opinions. Don't try to explain them away. Wonder *why* they have those opinions. What situations led to them feeling the way they do? Because everyone's feelings are valid."

"What about mine?" he asked me, the words small and sad.

"Yours, too," I agreed, aching for him. "Yours, mine, the homeless, a snotty nosed two-year-old. We all are important. We need to ensure we can all have the ability to get the basics, though."

He looked at me like I had just jumped through a rift. "You want me to give my apartment to the homeless?"

"No, Arthur." I couldn't help it. I offered him my hand. I squeezed his cool fingers comfortingly. "I want you to recognize that you're lucky. You're someone with a lot of privilege. Use that to help people without. Don't let jerks like Clint talk down about women. Don't invite Lilith to wizards' only events. If someone dismisses someone else's struggles, stop them."

"What about my struggles?" he asked, and this time it wasn't quite as pathetic. "I worked to get where I was. Family helped, but lots of people have family. I'm good at what I do, but it isn't easy."

I was not equipped to have this conversation. My head ached. My heart ached. "Everyone has struggles. But you *do* have family, who *did* support you." Also tried to get him thrown in prison, but I wasn't going there. "No one is saying you don't work, but remember you're running a race where you got a head start. You're still running, sure, but there are others who are on the track whose lane is quicksand. That's what I'm trying to say, Arthur. Good men see that. Good men will try to help people run their own race."

A bit of a smile touched his lips. "Because we aren't really competing, right?"

Relief rushed through me. "Nah, not really. Not unless we're jerks."

"That's a complicated metaphor, Rory," he said, on a sigh. "But I think I'm sort of following. If I have questions, can I ask you?"

I didn't try to hide my smile. "You can." And didn't that take all?

"Could you love me, if I was that sort of man?" he asked me, deadly serious. "If I helped pull other people out of quicksand?"

"You…" I tried to unravel that. "You don't pull other people out of quicksand. You might try to get their lane re-paved. Um. Like, now." I blew out air. If I mixed metaphors, I'd lose him. "Okay. So. I'm in quicksand with Clint. You can't just kill Clint."

His eyes narrowed. "No, that's illegal."

"And immoral," I added, because the two didn't always align. I'd probably make an exception for Clint, but, hey, he'd taken some shots at Dierdre. Fuck him. "But what you can do is…like when Taig came in and deflected."

Arthur's brow furrowed. "He said something about being wanted being better."

"Right. So he wasn't, like, going head-to-head with Clint. That would've made me feel like shit. I would've had to sit there and watch them argue about women's rights. Instead, he sort of steered it into neutral territory, got us back on track." Arthur was nodding thoughtfully. "He made it clear that he doesn't agree, but he did it in a gentle, general way. Because he had the power in that situation. He could've just kicked Clint out, reported him." *Maybe he should've.* "This way I didn't have to feel any guilt about someone maybe losing their job."

"Why would you?" he asked, shocked. "It's his fault."

I drew in a deep breath. "King, I am *not* qualified for this conversation, I have to say. If you want to discuss the impact of privilege, you really need another tutor. And I encourage you to go there. I'm not an expert. I screw up all the time. I just do the best I can."

"Okay." He dug out his phone and I could see him typing into notes. The guy actually was making a to-do list. I peered at it. *Ask exes how I can do better. Research impact of privilege. Find examples of helping make space.*

My heart just about broke. I kind of hoped that potion didn't get lifted before he'd ticked at least some of them off. And, hells, I really hoped this didn't backfire.

"I don't know if I'll ever love you, Arthur," I told him, as he resolutely saved it. "But I know someone can. And I know you're worthy of it. This stuff… it'll help you be a better person."

The breath he let out shook. "Thank you. For being honest."

"Hey. King." He looked up, tears in his eyes. *Here I am, kicking puppies.* "You're in my coven. I've got your back, okay?"

"It's my coven," he disagreed, but it was said with a bit of a smile.

"Fight you for it," I said, with a wink, to lighten the mood.

Horror flickered over his face, then concern, and finally, resignation. "You like running risks."

My belly rolled and, as if on cue, my phone rang. "Occasionally. Usually, I like making sure shit gets done. Rory here. Drop the ward, King, it's Zane."

CHAPTER 6

THE RAIN WAS HEAVY AND COLD AS I CROSSED THE DESERTED PARKING lot to the abandoned industrial building with its smashed windows and layers of graffiti. I looked around for Zane but couldn't see him.

The headlights from the car lit up the side of the building and the slumping wire fence beyond. The clamor of the rain made hearing hard.

Not a good setup for us. But at least Clint was still in the car, talking to dispatch.

I had my wand in my hand, Arthur at one side and Taig at the other. Neither of them bitched about the weather. I wasn't about to, either, even though my socks were already soaked.

Taig had called in the address, but they weren't sending in beat cops. They weren't trained for this type of clusterfuck.

"Rory!"

I tried to look in the direction of the shout without getting a face full of icy rain.

Beo, Zane a half-step behind him, jogged over to us. "Situation?" Taig asked, lifting an arm in a half-hearted attempt to protect his face.

"One person inside," Beo said, the words directed at me. "Place reeks of magick. And something else."

I nodded grimly. "Hear that, King? Get the counter-curses ready."

"Do we know who's inside?" Taig asked, stepping in front of Arthur to slow him. "Victim? Perp?"

Beo glanced at Zane, who shrugged. "Either it's Rory's witch, or the attacker rolled in her scent. No smell of death. One heartbeat."

"Shit, I could've used you a few times," Taig muttered. "Wait—or come wait in the car. I'll update Clint, get him on our six. How much warning can you give us if the perp returns, Velvela?"

Beo stood, relaxed, in the rain. "Plenty."

"Willing to wait with Clint?" Taig pressed.

Beo's eyes flickered to me, then back to Taig. "Of course. You go ahead, I'll catch him up."

I didn't watch as Zane and Beo moved toward where Clint lurked in the cop car. Dierdre was in that building. I trusted Beo to be okay.

The entrance of the warehouse was perfectly framed by graffitied double doors hanging half off their hinges. Complete darkness lay beyond.

"You feeling okay?" Arthur asked me, hovering at my elbow.

I was feeling focused. The rest had fallen away in the rush of adrenaline that had spiked when we'd pulled up. I didn't waste words, just kept pace with Taig.

Magick, and something else. Something of this world.

Determination filled my bones with steel. Maybe I was biased, but it seemed like shit from this world was always the worst.

Taig stopped beside the door, peering into the darkness. "Dierdre?" he called. "It's the police!"

From deep inside I thought I heard a muffled shout.

With his hand going into his jacket, Taig moved forward, only for Arthur to step in his way.

"Traps," Arthur said, brandishing his wand with a flourish before stepping into the dark.

Or, he tried to.

The sound of a ringing bell made my head ache and I wanted to laugh. That was *my* gig.

"Impenetrable Ward," Arthur said, frowning. "I can try to break it. But I'm not very familiar with them."

No, he wouldn't be. I was the only living magi I knew about in the Southern Hemisphere who could pull that spell off. And it amused me, a bit, that this bitch was trying to weaponize my own specialty against me. I didn't worry much about how she'd learned it. If *I* could figure it out, it couldn't be as hard as everyone made out.

The blow back from breaking that ward would knock that witch on her arse. If we could do it. But it was a solid 'if'. "Breaking Wards is a Class C offense," Taig said, grimly. "We know she's here. We can post a watch and wait for Retrievals."

Arthur looked at me and raised his brows in question.

Wards were my thing. You didn't know how to make one without knowing how to break it.

Arthur's hand went to my arm and then stopped right before touching me, his eyes on the wand attached to my keyring. "It's broken. Your wand. It's snapped."

I brushed him off, irritated at the reminder. "It's fine." I'd gone from 'if it's not broken, don't fix it' to 'if it works, don't knock it' in one horrible afternoon. And we didn't have time for me to explain that even if I'd wanted to. "Hey, Taig," I said, gathering my magick, the words that would channel it. "What's over there?" *From without or from within, this dome will not impact where I go.* The words came, hard, clear and strong. The magick behind them didn't feel quite right, but I pushed through.

Another sound like a hammer striking a bell filled my head, but it went on, a clamor of discordant chimes. Like a bell falling, maybe. Satisfaction darted through me.

I lifted my face to the rain to feel its icy stroke and smiled at the thought of her seeing us as she reeled in pain.

Knock knock, bitch.

"Santa's watching, Caretaker," Taig said, dryly, stepping inside.

I snorted, following after him. He hadn't looked away, but he wouldn't rat me out. "If Santa is so all-seeing, all-knowing, then that jerk knew the reindeers were all harassing Rudolph and just let it go until it suited him to exploit Rudolph's red nose. So Santa can go fuck himself."

Taig's grin was fast and hard as he swept his flashlight around. "I do enjoy your—"

Fire.

Searing, choking, dazzling.

My heart leaped into my throat. I went down as it swept up around us like a cyclone, driven to the ground by a solid weight on top of me. I had no idea whose arms were around me. Out of sheer reflex I reached for my magick, my one tried and trusted tool. *Through this dome none shall leave or come unless it is with me.* But it felt wrong— fragmented, tattered.

Heat. I couldn't breathe. Couldn't hear.

My magick—

The broken charm—

As I will, so shall it be. I pulled it back in and kept my face on the floor. Dirt, rat shit, some sort of wrapper—all unimportant. I needed something smaller. A smaller spell. Something targeted. A shield, buffer—

Through this shield you can't touch me.

The shield spell coalesced, formed, and held. "Arthur!" I shouted, over the roar, desperately fighting to breathe. The barrier in front of us redirected flames, but they weren't the deadliest thing here. Smoke billowed threateningly. "I can't hold the shield! Rain! Rain!"

Words. The rise and fall of a spell. I couldn't make out individual sounds but I knew the rhythm, the flow, in my bones. Arthur, casting a rain spell. He'd heard me. Taig was trying to pull me outside, but there was no way we'd get through that.

Natural or magick, that fire meant business.

Fury pounded at my temples. Deirdre was in there, alive. She had to be. She'd be inside some sort of ward. And I'd put money on the fact that I'd be able to break it...if I could get to her.

My head spun. I tried to breathe shallowly. And when I heard the roar of a downpour, felt the cold, wet drops not as individual drizzle but like a firehose full blast, I had a flicker of relief.

Hissing, sizzling, steam and smoke. *Double double,* I thought, grimly amused. The weight on top of me eased and I lifted my head just a little, spat out whatever the fuck had ended up in my mouth. *Toil and trouble.*

"The building!" Taig shouted from beside me. Some of the pressure on me eased as he moved away, but Arthur was mostly on top of me still.

I glanced up. Smoke shrouded the concrete floor, piles of steaming litter and building refuse. There was a half-melted or half collapsed drum near the wall to the far side of us. Rain, steam and smoke made visibility shit. I had no idea what Taig was bellowing about.

"What?" I asked, half-turning my head. Even moving that much, with the pressure of the water, was a tall ask. And, right then, I didn't mind. It beat the shit out of being burned alive. I'd never considered myself a classic witch.

An ominous crack seemed to go on forever. *The beams. The roof.* I got my hands under me, my heart in my throat. Whatever ward Dierdre had to be in, I hoped it was tough enough, because this whole shitshow was going down.

Then the rain vanished. Or, rather, I couldn't feel it, but I could hear it, see it all around, rivers of whitewater. And a massive paw with neatly trimmed nails and long, wet hair appeared in my vision, too close for me to assess how gigantic it truly was. A huge leg was attached. And an undercarriage with dark, glossy fur.

My heart stopped in my chest.

Lycan.

Creaking came from all around us. *Beams, walls, roof?* I couldn't breathe, much less think.

"Elders—" I heard Arthur choke.

That was a lycan paw. That was *my* lycan's paw.

And then the sound of timber splintering. Falling roof tiles shattered around us. Something sharp and hot hit my face and I shielded myself with my arm as the whole world came apart.

Movies made it look quick, or at least dramatic in slow motion. But in reality, shit collapsed slowly or in waves. Even knowing that, even having seen it, my heart was in my mouth and it was all I could do to breathe through the smoke and humidity and terror.

And Beo was our shield. If he was so much as *scratched*—

Fuck. That. Witch.

Who the fuck used fire wards and love potions? Where was this woman's sense of class?

I felt Arthur try and move at one point and a low growl came from our lycan protector. I yanked Arthur back. "Wait!" I shouted over the roar. "And kill the rain!"

He said something, but it wasn't discernible to my ears over the pop of bricks exploding nearby. I felt the ripple of shock go through Beo above us and horror arced through me.

He'd known we couldn't get out. So here he was.

I reached out and put my hand over a part of the paw I could see, my heart aching. Carefully he put my hand beneath his paw. The rough pad scraped, but he was infinitely gentle, just like he always was with me.

My heart swelled. I drew air in, then let it out slowly. I was soaked to the skin, couldn't smell anything except smoke, and felt like I'd just run a marathon. But we were okay.

The sound of immediate aftermath came from nearby; shoes scraping against concrete, wet clothing, half-muffled coughs. I glanced over to see Taig had his collar flipped up over the lower part of his face. It had been white earlier. It sure wasn't, now, but it looked like a good idea to me.

I added collars to a list of things I wanted on clothing, right under pockets.

"Clear?" I heard Taig say, and realized the roar of the rain had eased to the natural flow that had, earlier, felt like a downpour.

There was a deep rumble from above us. Taig glanced at me as if I could speak growl. I just shook my head. "He'll move when he's confident," I said, because that made sense to me.

"You okay, Velvela?" Taig asked, glancing upwards. I didn't follow his gaze. I could see all the dark hair, the seemingly endless bow of his chest. A ripple of unease went through me.

I'd known what he was.

A part of me sort of wanted to see if that fur was as soft as it looked. Another part of me wondered if it was really rain that made hair clump together wetly on his legs.

From behind us in the darkness, Zane shouted, "He's fine, but stay still! The west wall hasn't gone yet!"

I had no idea which way west was or where we were in relation to said wall, but if Zane—and Beo—said to sit, I'd sit. I dropped my aching head back down onto my arm and tried to gather some strength for the next push.

We had to get Dierdre and get the fuck away from here before this witch returned because she wasn't pulling her punches and this building was less than no protection now.

"Fire Ward," I said, and the words were scratchy. "That's, what, Class B?"

"Usually, yes, but this scale? A," Taig said, and, curse him, there was a bit of amusement in his voice. "I definitely noticed this breach."

I snorted. "Yeah. Me, too."

"Must've mistaken that ward earlier though. Couldn't have been one. Right?"

"Right," I agreed, feeling strangely disconnected.

"Pretty sure the rain was all natural too," he went on, thoughtfully. "Lucky us."

Oh, fuck, I'd forgotten messing with weather was, like, off-the-charts illegal. Well, not off the charts. Taig could chart that, if he was an arsehat. "Love me a good winter storm."

Arthur chose that moment to say, "No, that was my spell."

Taig cleared his throat.

"I'll explain later, King," I said, on a sigh. "Just trust me, okay?"

He was quiet for a moment and then said, suspiciously, "Are you flirting with Taig, Rory?"

"Oh, for fuck's sake." I sighed and climbed to my knees. "No, you big lump, we're pretending none of us broke the law because illegal and immoral are two separate things, and Taig here is smart enough to know when to focus on the *immoral* part of the equation." I took my hand back from Beo and stood, carefully. Shit, I could almost straighten under him.

I refused to think of another lycan, another time.

A quick glance around showed warped, fallen roof, smoldering beams and walls that were blown out to show the gravel and weed parking lot beyond, lit by the glow of a few stubborn coals and the wash of Clint's headlights.

A sickening crash from nearby had me ducking and lifting my arm to shield my face as bricks spewed over the dark ground before us. But the noise was far more dramatic than the reality, and I felt Beo moving carefully from his position on top of us. A twisted metal beam slid off him. It hit the ground and my stomach lurched to see the size of it.

He'd stood in a collapsing building to save us.

Get Dierdre. Get out.

"Light, Arthur?"

Obediently, Arthur murmured a light spell. I straightened, my head spinning.

The destruction was enormous. Shattered bricks, melted iron, smoldering beams, cracked cement. To complete the post-apocalyptic picture, a chocolate bar wrapper floated drunkenly down the makeshift river beside us.

A shout came from the direction of the patrol car. When I turned to look, I saw the door that had been off its hinges was now much closer to the patrol car. The brick wall it had been attached to had exploded outward into the darkened driveway. A thistle lay, half-flattened, its purple flower resolutely poking up between some brick and mortar. *Hey, that's me. I'm a thistle.*

Taig raised an arm. "We need to get clear," he said to me, the rain washing soot and smoke off his skin. "No one's survived that, Rory."

I saw a blurring in my peripheral and averted my gaze as Beo shifted. Arthur, the ignorant jerk, turned to look. I heard his reflexive puke a moment later. *Rookie mistake.*

"She'll be warded," I said, ignoring the fact I was shaking.

The bitch had pumped more power into the death trap than she did into the protective ward she'd put around the building. Well, label me unimpressed and ship me to Tasmania.

"Everyone okay?"

The words were rough. Beo was back in his human form standing beside a half-melted drum of some sort. Like us, he was smoke streaked. There was a big red mark on one of his arms and deep gouges on another. I took a step forward to check him over before I caught myself.

"Yeah. Yeah. Thank you."

He jerked his head to one side of what used to be the building. "She's over there. I don't have shoes. I'll have to shift to get back to Zane, or be picking glass out of my feet for a week or two."

My heart twisted and I breathed through the ache. "Shifting sounds wise. I'll get her." I couldn't touch him, hold him, press a kiss to his head. I wasn't allowed. And it hurt.

He could have been killed. We would have been. And I couldn't even acknowledge that. *Not yet.*

Arthur, whose guts were apparently empty now, staggered over to me. "I'll protect—I mean. I'll go with you. In case you need me." And then he coughed hard enough that I almost patted him on the back.

I drew a deep breath and swiped my sleeve over my forehead so I didn't end up with too much grit in my eyes. We set out across the rubble that had fallen off Beo, picking our way carefully through the carcass of the building.

The area Beo had pointed out was a perfectly round, untouched segment that had probably once been a back room. As Arthur followed behind us, his light spell made the shadows from our movements dance and jerk in a way that kept my adrenaline running. I could see Dierdre wearing a comfy, oversized hoodie and slippers, her red hair plastered to her skull in the rain, her eyes trained on us. "It's warded," she said, as I approached, her face twisted in grief. "I'm so sorry, Rory..."

Arthur rapped on the very obvious ward, his expression one of deep consideration. "It's another Impenetrable."

"No. Really?"

"Yes," he said, quite seriously. "Can you penetrate it?"

All of the childish jokes that swam in my head made me feel mildly spaced out. "Hold my beer," I muttered to Arthur, whose gaze flickered down to my hands. For Taig's benefit, I added, "Look away, Santa."

"Can I request a new nickname?" Despite the wry complaint, Taig turned. "Fire department's on the way."

I drew in a breath and let everything fall away. I was done. I needed a shower, sleep, TLC, sex, and fried potatoes. The order that happened in was totally negotiable.

The words for the spell came slowly, the magick slower again. "You okay, Rory?" Arthur asked, and grimly I fought to keep my focus. Shit, a shattered charm wasn't a joke.

Well, this bitch'd be feeling worse than me tonight.

From without or from within, this dome will not impact where I go. I sent the magick out, hard, into the seams, into the cracks of the spell. My head rang from the resounding sound that followed but, *shit*, that was satisfying.

Taig crossed the threshold of the ward, lifting his badge. "Ms. Summers, I'm Detective Taig O'Malley—"

She hit me like a missile, her arms going around me, sobs shaking her deceptively willowy frame.

"Told you," I murmured, folding her into my arms. "I look after mine."

CHAPTER 7

As I watched, Taig took a set of mugs out of the drawer. None of them had cute sayings on them. I didn't care if it was a hotel or not, I expected something funny or adorable on my mug.

"Can you stay?" Taig asked me, under his breath. "I need to interview her. She's doing it tough already."

I read between the lines. She'd gone with him under sufferance but hadn't been questioned yet, because she couldn't be. "Sure." He wanted me to hold the space for her. Well, that made two of us.

"You down for asking the questions?" he asked me, passing me a pitiful little single-serve cup of milk. I pulled a face at it. "Hey, not all of us drink coffee the color of their soul."

I paused in the process of taking my coffee. "Are you telling me your soul *is* black… or mine is milk-coffee-colored?"

He shrugged. "Take it how you like it."

And there was something about those words that made my blood heat. Oh, he hadn't added any innuendo, no side-eye, no tone change. *Shit. That voice.* He could've sold matches to bushfire victims with that low, promising rumble. "I can ask her the questions," I said, shrugging it off as I made up Dierdre's tea. "If you throw them my way."

"We'll see how we go."

I nodded my agreement and with a hot drink in each hand I went over and took a seat beside Dierdre. I was probably going to wreck their couch with my sodden, smoky clothes and I didn't even care.

With the beat cops making their own cuppas and lingering by the door, I watched Taig flip open his notepad opposite us. "I know today has been intense," he said, clicking a pen, the study of a compassionate businesslike detective. *Weird combo. Works for him.* "I need to ask you some questions to try to avoid another day like this one."

She took a deep breath and nodded, bracing as she lifted her eyes to mine. "I'm sitting in," I told her, casually. "If that's okay."

"I...but you must have plans, or..." she drew in another deep breath. "This isn't something you have to do, Rory."

I sent her a wink, settling deeper into the chair. "Arthur's bringing junk food." And going home to change his socks. Apparently being wet made their seams uncomfortable? Anyway, *my* concern was the food. And the witch. "If I leave now, I have to get my own. I never say no to free food."

"Especially potato-based," Taig said, wisely. "She basically works for it."

"It's true," I agreed shamelessly. "I can leave, if you want. But I'm happy to hang out."

It took us awhile to settle her in, work her around. She consented to being recorded. I felt mildly sick and totally ignored that.

Eventually Taig sat back, crossed his feet at the ankles, and picked up his mug.

I figured that was my cue. I hadn't been trained in any of this shit. I knew I wasn't supposed to ask a leading question, but what *was* a leading question, anyway? "So, you kind of mentioned earlier you saw the woman who grabbed you."

Deirdre's eyes stayed glued to the tabletop. "Yeah."

I turned my now-empty mug around between my palms. Hells, if I got subtle now, she wouldn't recognize me. "What's her name?"

"I don't know," she said, quietly. "But"—her gaze flickered to Taig and she paused for a moment—"she worked with Tobias. He called her Amor."

A chill ran up my arms. *Tobias and Amor. Well, there you have it.* I knew the name of Dierdre's abusive ex who they hadn't managed to track down. Last I'd heard, he was wanted in a few states for some hefty crimes. "What's Amor's story?" At Dierdre's confused look, I waved a hand. "What does she do? You said they worked together."

Her eyes danced away. The tip of her tongue darted out of her mouth and touched a cut in her lip.

I shot Taig a quick glance. She knew more. I knew she knew more. I just needed a bit of space to—

My phone rang.

I gritted my teeth, glanced down at it, saw Arthur's name. The possibility that it was critically important was slim, but not none. "I'm sorry," I said, standing. "I'll be right back."

They both said polite words while I grabbed it and let myself into the tiny bathroom, shut the door after myself. "What?" I hissed. "I can't talk, I'm trying to help interview Dierdre." I wasn't very good at it but that was irrelevant.

"Okay," he said, sounding mildly miserable. "Do I buy her underwear?"

Elders. "Yes." Was it weirder to be given underwear, or go without? Fuck it, I didn't know. "But not a bra." There was *no way* he was going to be able to get that right. I couldn't even get it right for myself half the time, and they were my tits. "A crop top—like a sports bra?—in her size. It'll be better than nothing and give her some power to choose."

On the other end of the phone, he blew out a long breath. "Is choice…empowering?"

"It is when you don't have any." I was pretty sure? "I gotta go, King. Basics. Comfy. Neutral colors."

"Okay." He sounded pathetic. "Okay."

Pity reared its ugly head and I sighed. "Hey, Arthur. No one expects you to get it perfect. Just remember, anything is going to be better than what she's got."

"Yeah. Thanks, Rory. I'll, ah. Let you get to it."

I wanted to tell him to hurry up with the food, because after coffee my system was unhappy about the delay in snacks. But I didn't. "Call if it's an emergency."

Since I was locked in the bathroom and had already derailed shit, I quickly checked my phone. I hadn't had time to debrief Beo; as soon as I saw a message from him, I opened it. *If you're up for it I want to see you tonight. Yours or mine. Any time. Just let me know. XO*

I tapped out a fast reply. *I'm keen. Will come to you. Could be very late.*

Dierdre was staring into her empty cup when I got back to my soggy, dirty spot on the couch. I settled beside her, picked up my mug and thrust it tiredly at Taig. "Coffee me. Deirdre takes her tea white, mid-strength, one sugar."

He nodded and, without hesitation, took our cups. I put my elbows on the table and let myself relax. "Look. Would it be easier to just talk? I don't care if it's out of order or whatever. They can figure that stuff out."

She shut her eyes and curled forward the way I was, her elbows on her knees. "Hells, Rory. I thought…I thought I'd got away. I thought it'd be okay."

The grief in her voice cut me to the core. "We're not done yet," I promised her, quietly. "I eat witches like Amor for breakfast. Used to. New job, new menu." A tiny smile quirked up one corner of her mouth, and she shot me a look that had just the tiniest spark of humor. "Hit me. Then I can field questions for," I jerked my head toward Taig.

She leaned a little closer, her eyes round with sorrow. "I'm sick of it. They don't…they don't want to hear. They just want the answers. I don't have any."

Tears welled. The sleeve she used to dash them away was probably about as absorbent as latex, it was so wet. My heart ached. "Yeah." I shrugged, wishing I had more to offer, but I couldn't deny her reality. "I believe survivors, Dierdre. And I'll back you 'til the very end. You know that."

Her barriers crumbled. I could see it in her shoulders, in the softening around her eyes, in the set of her mouth. "What if it sounds crazy?" she asked, softly.

Could I be worthy of that trust? *Elders, probably not.* "Never use that word myself. It's been weaponized against too many folks. But I can promise you this; I've seen stuff, done stuff, that in a movie would leave critics scoffing about how unrealistic it is."

The breath she let out was long and shaky. She nodded and I took it as agreement. It was a start. "Hit me, before he gets back." I jerked a thumb in Taig's direction.

She laughed, but it was a sad, hollow sound. "I made love potions and he used them on me. I didn't even know."

The cold from my wet clothes seeped through my flesh into my bones. "That isn't crazy," I said, very deliberately. "That's *smart.* One whiff of that stuff and you'd be gone."

She looked down at her hands, her mouth twisted. "I was. I didn't tell them that. I didn't think they'd believe me."

Her hair slipped, curtaining her face. I looked down at my hands, clasped loosely between my knees, and wondered what the fuck I was supposed to say. "I can't vouch for them," I admitted, because I had no real idea if they *would.* "But I do."

She'd been cooking love potions for her ex and Amor. Arthur had been hit with a love-tipped arrow shot by Amor. Who'd cooked the potions? How much had she left behind?

"The police cared about the rifts," she said, softly. "I knew they would. If I tell them the rest...if they knew I lied about..."

I didn't look at the recording device on the table. *Shit.* "I don't know what will happen. All I know is that you're in danger and I want to help. The more you give me, the better equipped I will be when I catch up with them."

"Don't," she whispered. "Don't go after them, Rory."

I moved forward a bit more, a bit closer into her field of vision. She glanced up, meeting my eyes. My heart broke for her. "When I was thirteen, I killed a vampire who was about to drain a kid over the road." I'd done it with my coven, but, still. "I made a living as Retrievals for years. I still contract. I'm not easy to kill, Dierdre."

She laughed again and it wasn't quite so sad, now. "I saw that, tonight. I thought for sure…"

Taig arrived and she didn't speak further as he set our drinks in front of us. "I'll be a few moments," he said, apologetically.

Damned manipulator. He just wandered off to speak quietly to the cops while Dierdre sat and watched, warily.

"What should I be on the lookout for?" I asked her, wanting more.

Her expression was frozen for a moment before she picked up her tea. "I don't want you hurt."

Well, fuck, I was getting tired of this ride. "I'm going to do this, with or without info. You know that, right?"

She didn't smile, just stared at her tea while the conversation on the other side of the room petered out and silence spread. The hum of the city in the background was comforting. I picked up the coffee. He'd added a splash of cold water to it, or hadn't boiled the kettle all the way. Whatever the reason, it didn't burn my tongue and I was grateful.

"I think…I think he's working with something."

I wondered if the words would even reach the recorder. How sensitive was it? Not as sensitive as Clint, I was sure of that. "I figured that," I said, idly. "Got it narrowed down to angel or demon."

Her eyes flickered up to me, shock in her face. Shock, and guilt.

Yeah, she knew.

And I needed to pry it out.

I breathed through the shame that squirmed through my chest. "You didn't think I'd be able to tell?" I asked her, aiming for a light tone, some easy banter.

"Not even *I* knew until recently when I started to put it together. How could you…you don't even know my file. It's closed."

"Never read any of it." And on the other side of the room Taig was doing something on his phone that looked important from the frown on his face. I would've put money on the fact he was stalling.

Here was me, being a turncoat.

"I told you, Dierdre. I'm good at my job. I get *paid* to hunt these things." Maybe not those *specific* things, because that was a whole level of nuclear fuckery right there. But I wasn't going to do anything to stop the flow of information.

She glanced in the direction of Taig. "Look, they believe he forced me to make rift juice to sell. But that wasn't his whole business."

Shit, that's bad enough. Where the fuck had he got the recipe, who had he sold it to? My head spun with the possibilities. That wasn't today's issue. Probably. "They believe that?"

"That part," she amended. "I...I tried to tell the first officer. About the rest. He laughed, Rory." The tears in her voice would've been enough to make rage rumble through me even if I didn't know her from a bar of soap.

"I am very much not laughing," I promised her, flatly. "I am about as far from laughing as you can get."

Her eyes danced warily once more to Taig. "Tobias...he had a side business. He told me he was a marriage counsellor."

I felt sick while my brain leapt ahead. I opened my mouth to guess what came next and save her the pain. Then I closed it. This wasn't my story. "Oh, yeah?"

Her cold smile didn't sit well on her face. "Yeah. He actually did some relationship counselling for a while. Turns out there's good money in doping people with love or anti-love potions."

How the fuck did that make money? "Okay. Sorry. Not a criminal mastermind. He did...what?"

She let out a shaky breath. "He was paid to arrange for a specific person to fall in love with someone else, or out of love with them. That was his bread and butter. The rift juice...it was mostly to stay sweet with the people he got the ingredients from."

People actually *paid* to force love on someone?

"I brewed the potions," she whispered, brokenly. "I thought...I thought he was helping people love themselves. He organized every-thing. Amor made it happen."

It all clicked, then. Not why people were so fucked up; the triad that had worked so well. Dierdre was a phenomenal potion maker. Amor seemed like an excellent hunter. If this guy had the brains to put the two together...

I hoped every arsehole on his books got nailed for coercion. "I'm assuming you didn't know."

She turned the tea in her hands and shuffled her feet. "I was scared of him. I'd reported him to the police." Her mouth twisted in a bitter smile. "He was stalking me. I was terrified. I remember being terrified. And then." She looked down at the milky brown water in the mug. I watched it, too, as it shook. And I ached. "And then I wasn't scared." She was quiet, for a moment. "I heard things. But it didn't…stick. Not until…it did." She spun the cup slowly between her palms. "When I accidentally exposed myself to the violets…" she shook her head, her voice thick. I struggled to hold back my questions. "If I thought I knew enough to help…but they're already after him for the rift potions." She looked up at me, her eyes full of tears. "I don't want to go through it all again. Please, Rory. I can't."

I drew in a deep breath. "You mean dealing with him and Amor?"

The tears trickling down her cheeks made my heart just about rupture for her. "No. The investigation. The questions. The *looks*. The judgement. The statistics on false reporting. I just…I just want it to be simple."

Didn't I know how that felt? I set down my coffee resolutely. "I'll talk to Taig," I said, quietly, hoping like hells the recorder wasn't too sensitive. "I'll do what I can. But whatever happens…" I met her eyes squarely. "Sisters stick together."

CHAPTER 8

"You two don't mind if we just step outside a moment, do you?" Taig asked, hearty as beef stew as he went past the watchdogs, opening the door for me already.

Arthur was standing there, juggling bags. Food. My body sang. "Are there hot chips?"

"There are chips," he said, apologetically. "Can't vouch for the temperature." I waved him in, my head spinning as I got Dierdre's clothes to her. I grabbed a hamburger and a container of chips. "That one's got beetroot," Arthur warned me. "Didn't know if it was your thing or not."

"Beetroot is absolutely my thing," I assured him fervently before shoving some chips in my mouth. "You're on watch for five."

He nodded and took out his wand, setting it neatly beside his meal. Once again, I followed Taig out as the uniforms took their burgers happily. He was obviously a fast-food aficionado. He opened the burger wrapper one-handed and made a 'give it to me' gesture with the other.

"How much did you follow?" I asked him, wondering whether I should just have an accident with my coffee all over the recording device on the table.

"Some. Enough to know not to come back over." He inspected the burger. "I like love drunk Arthur. How're you holding up?"

"Great." I didn't even stop to consider the question. "Just between you and me." I paused. He'd been decent so far. More than decent, really. But should I trust him?

He raised his brows and took another bite.

I sighed, looking at the wan chips in their little cardboard box. Arthur was right to be concerned about their temperature. I'd received dick pics hotter than those chips. "Summary; she tried to spill the whole story to the first responders, got laughed at, edited, is now terrified of coming forward."

He finished his mouthful and wrapped up the rest of the burger, a look of distaste on his face. "Okay. You got the rest?"

"Enough to outline it. She cooked love potions, he made deals, the bitch witch shot the target full of said potion, money exchanged hands." I considered the chips again, but my stomach was no longer on speaking terms with me. "Not just love, but that seemed to be the focus."

"Well." He rubbed his face. "Shit."

"Yeah. Shit."

"And she doesn't want this to be made official." He held up a hand. "Of course she doesn't. So. What've we got?"

I threw a chip at him. "Stodgy takeaway and cold socks."

He arched his brows, but there was laughter in his eyes as he looked between me and the chip now at his feet with all the dignity in the world. "You missed your calling, Rory. You could've been a crackerjack detective."

I sighed with as much drama as I could manage and fluttered my lashes. "Why, thank you."

"Who knows. Maybe you'll get recruited yet. I hear VicPol want witches."

I pulled a face. "Sure, to burn at the stake. Thanks, but I like my steak medium-rare." He took out a notepad, juggled his burger, and wrote something down. I peered at it.

The guy had taken a note of my *steak* preference?

He snapped it closed, raised his brows. "Yes?"

The humor of the situation tugged at me. I couldn't unpack that right now. I didn't know if it was smooth or just weird. It was a later problem. "Amor shot Arthur full of love potion to take us out. She knew I was Dierdre's Caretaker, which means she's done prelim research. Non-lethal hit, just enough to give her time to get to Dierdre's, get clear, get Dierdre back to shitstain ex and get her cooking potions again."

He nodded slowly, studying me like I was a living clue. "If she'd hit *you*, she would've had a lot more breathing space. And Arthur was sure she was aiming for you."

The thought made the contents of my belly sit like wet cement. "I really don't want to think about what he might've done if the shoe was on the other foot."

"Neither do I," Taig agreed, neutrally. "But you're right. Non-lethal. You're out of the picture, probably forgetting all about work. When she breaks through your charm, would you even care?"

The cement in my belly rolled. "Okay. Solid strategy."

"Brilliant. Simple and brilliant." He took one of the chips from my box, inspected it. He sighed, bit the chip in half, fell back against the wall, and stared at the ceiling. "They've got her down as a family violence victim. There's a warrant out for him for the rift juice. Really, this wouldn't add to the case. If they ever get him, he's going away for life as it is."

My heart swelled. "You'd look the other way?"

"It doesn't change much, does it?" he asked, clinically. "We already *know* Arthur was hit by a love potion. We *know* Amor is a crack shot with a bow, we *know* she's willing to use magick with lethal force, we *know* she's after Dierdre. What potions Dierdre has brewed is already part of her initial statement." As he talked, he straightened and ticked points off on his fingers. "I don't remember if love was on there because the guy had her brewing *rapid decay*."

Horror spread through my chest. "Fuck."

"Yeah, fuck. So, really, everything pales beside that. We've got what we need to make an arrest. We've got information to clue us into this woman's MO. Should it be evidence? Yes. Am I going to drag a traumatized woman through the process that just reinforces her trauma for no real benefit?"

I let out a long breath, feeling the tension ebbing. "You're a good bloke, Taig."

"And you sound so sad," he said, a bit of a smile tugging up one corner of his mouth.

I *was* sad, I realized. Sad to the core. "It's a sad situation." I passed him my chips, feeling sick. "Thanks, Taig. For not being an arsehole."

"I'd say any time," he mused, mock-thoughtfully, a glimmer of humor in his eye, "but I don't know I could keep that promise."

I snorted and flopped back against the wall beside him. "I am done. So very, very done."

"Ten bucks says if Amor rocked up now, you'd take her down in a heartbeat," he said, lifting another chip and watching it wilt between his fingers. "Guess I've got a recording to delete."

I turned my head, feeling my hair scrunch and pull. It was going to be a mass of knots. I didn't even care. "I can spill coffee on it?"

"Ah. Tough, smart, able to break wards that are defined by being unbreakable, *and* thoughtful." There was laughter in his pale blue eyes. "I'm glad we're on the same side, Caretaker."

Something about those low, heartfelt words made my blood heat. My brain zipped back in time and I remembered the way his hand had held my hair—*all* of my hair—gently at the base of my head. The intimacy of that struck me. And the fact the man knew how to make someone comfortable. I could think of *so* many applications for that. My body hummed at the thought and I could just about feel the steam rising off me as his eyes dipped, for a moment, down to my lips.

It was right there.

I could've taken it.

I could almost feel the kiss. The heat of it. The hunger. There was no humor in his face when his gaze met mine again and my heart twisted.

I was going back to meet *Beo*. The guy who'd literally protected me from a falling building tonight. Who'd broken laws for me.

The man who was in my bones.

"I should tell Dierdre," I said, my legs somehow keeping me upright as I pushed away, leaving the heat and wanting behind. "She'll be relieved."

"Sure. I'll, ah, I'll be right there," he said, his voice a little lower than usual.

Another ripple of wanting went through me and I breathed around it. *Fuck. Yeah. Not just me on this ride.* "Yeah, okay." Elders take these hormones and his sexy fucking voice and his goddamn *mouth*—

I shrugged it off, refocusing on what mattered here. Because the faster I got it done, the faster I got to curl up beside the man I *wanted* to be with.

Get in. Do the job. Get out.

Angel or demon, witch and wizard.

Deirdre.

She was why I was here.

And it was Beo I couldn't wait to get home to.

CHAPTER 9

HE OPENED THE DOOR FOR ME BEFORE I COULD KNOCK. HE'D showered, and his apartment smelled like ambrosia.

"Cooking?" I asked, as he let me in.

"Couldn't sleep." The way his eyes raked over me made it clear why he couldn't sleep. That I'd caused him so much worry made me feel about two centimeters tall. "I'd love a kiss if you want one."

Elders, this man. The skin of his arm was warm under my hand and my heart ached with that tiny contact as I lifted my face in invitation. The brief meeting of lips reminded me that I stank like smoke. So I toed off my shoes and headed for the laundry.

He followed along behind. "What happened?"

The answer was huge and I couldn't find all the words. I was tired and fragile. "Plenty of 'see you next Tuesday' action. Thank you so much for today."

"See you next Tuesday?" He asked, frowning.

I shoved the mostly-dry pants off my hips, emotions broiling. I was channeling my dad when I was tired. I didn't know how I felt about that.

Before I could explain the bad joke, I saw him mouthing the words, poised with the laundry powder in his hands and a line between his brows. *C. U. N...* I knew the moment the penny dropped because his expression cleared and he arched a brow. "Why are we insulting genitals?" Before I could agree that some of today's major players were way less useful than the anatomy I'd specified, he went on. "You know I'll always be there for you. I would've been there, tonight, if you'd let me know you were leaving. I would've come to bring you home."

I met those big, beautiful green eyes of his and felt the truth of his words in my bones. My heart ached with the sweetness of him. "It's almost three in the morning. I wouldn't do that to you."

"Would you let *me* cross the city at three in the morning, alone and injured?" he asked me.

It was a rhetorical question, but still I said, "I'm not injured." And, tiredly, I tossed the last of my clothes into the wash.

"She made you *bleed,* Rory, and broke your wand." He closed the lid of the machine with finality. It sang cheerfully as those words bounced around in my exhausted brain. "I'd like to know what happened. I'm worried. But you don't have to explain."

Apparently I did. But I was freezing, so I headed to the bathroom, knowing he'd hear me wherever I went in his apartment. There were so many perks when it came to hanging out with lycans.

"I'd set a charm on Dierdre's place to protect her. The witch broke it, which hurt me, but not, like, a real injury."

He reached around me to open the door to the shower, brows furrowed and lips forming an objection.

I pressed a kiss to them. "Okay, a real injury. But a magickal one. The nose bleed was just a symptom. Brain overload."

"You're telling me your brain could be injured if your spells are broken?" he growled.

Elders, I didn't want to do this. I turned on the shower, freezing cold. "I mean, maybe? But magickal injuries are separate. I don't know, Beo. I'm not a Healer."

"Yes, you are."

Fuck. I shied away from the icy water and scowled at him. "Look, I can't give you the academic answers, okay? It's different. It *feels* different to a regular headache." *Kind of.*

He reached out slowly to cup my face, broadcasting the move so I could refuse it. Instead, I turned my face into his big, welcoming palm and pressed a kiss to the pad of his hand.

His thumb sweeping over my cheek was the comfort I hadn't known I needed. I drank it up and breathed in the familiar smell of him. When steam rose, I stepped into the warm water gratefully and he stayed there, at the edge of the shower, ignoring the spray as it dampened his clothes. And he just watched me, his eyes full of concern.

When he was still there after I'd rinsed away the shampoo, I sighed. "I'm not dropping dead today, you know."

He withdrew a little, hunching his shoulders in a move I'd never seen from him, like he was self-conscious. But Beo was as secure as a rock. I paused with a hand full of conditioner, startled by this. *Isn't he?*

"Sorry to make you uncomfortable. I'll go see what I can do to help you recover from a magickal injury, I guess."

"No, it's fine." He was *genuinely* worried. More worried than he should've been. And that was…weird. "What's going on?"

He shot me a veiled look. "The witch in my bones had her wand snapped and magick hurt tonight. You would've been killed in that building, Rory."

Probably. "I wasn't. And I could've managed it, maybe. Or Arthur would've." I did what I could to hasten my time in the water, even though the heat was bliss. "And my wand wasn't snapped tonight. It's been like that for—" I had to look away from those green eyes, suddenly. *The heat of the afternoon sun.* "—ages." I dipped my head under the water to buy myself time, focusing on the feel of it hitting my skin, the sting of the heat against still-cold flesh. The gut-twisting memory eased, somewhat. "Anyway," I said, swiping away the water on my face and reaching for the soap he kept for me, "I like it. It's a convenient size to fit on a keyring. If I want to do fine work, I've got a full-sized backup." But my specialty was bulldozer style.

He was quiet as I lathered up, then said, gently, "I'll let you wash in peace."

The sound of the door closing behind him made shame rise like bile, burning my throat and coating my tongue. He'd known I didn't want to talk. He did, desperately. And he still hadn't pressed.

I leaned my head against the cold tiles of the shower. What was I supposed to say? *Your brother broke it when he tried to rip me apart? Jokes on him, it still works!* Cue high fives.

Today just wouldn't fucking end, would it?

I swallowed away the lump in my throat. He was out there worrying needlessly. I had to find some way to alleviate that. And to figure out what was *actually* going on, because this couldn't be just me. He and Zane had both been hurt, and they hadn't said shit about it.

With that in the fore of my mind I killed the shower and dried off quickly. He'd laid out one of his shirts for me and I pulled it on, heading into the kitchen.

He was sliding a tray of slice—what would be slice—into the fridge and reading something on his phone when I came in. "This says we can get you some sort of potions to help you heal your magick system. Apparently, most humans' magick will heal eventually, but quite slowly, especially if they have autoimmune conditions, which can sometimes mess with it, or—"

I took the slice before he dumped it on the floor. "I've had Arthur's Unbreaking Tonic."

He shot me a droll look. "Yes, I know."

Well, we had reason to not be entirely trusting when it came to Arthur. "Honestly, Beo, I'll be fine."

"You would've died tonight, Rory."

I was getting tired of hearing that. "I didn't," I said, again, clinging to patience with my fingertips. Anyone else and I'd have just up and left. "Thanks to you. And tomorrow is another day."

"And if I'm not there tomorrow?"

If he'd said that without the layers of grief and self-doubt, I'd have bitten his head off. But he just stood there, holding the fridge open, looking at me like I was about to vanish.

And, shit, if I'd seen him almost killed, I'd probably feel the same. So I drew in a deep breath, gathered up my compassion, and eased the fridge door from his hand. "Would it make you feel better if I made myself a potion?"

"Yes." And the word was full of relief.

Way too much relief.

I kept my suspicions to myself, regretting the offer instantly. I'd probably made that potion twice in my whole life. "Okay." I needed sleep. I was exhausted, but not sleepy. I knew the hum of determination-fueled energy would come at a cost. But I wasn't leaving Beo so worried, even if I had to make an unnecessary potion from memories almost two decades old.

"What can I get you?" he asked, looking around his kitchen with concern. "If you need something from elsewhere, I'll go."

And the inference; *you stay where you're safe.*

Beo would never *say* that, but he may as well have. I set my teeth over the snarled response and reminded myself how I'd feel were the shoe on the other foot. "Just quiet. I need to—" I waved a hand, taking out a mug. "Be present."

He stepped out of the way, folding himself down behind the bench on one of the tiny stools there. I tried not to think about how uncomfortable he must be as he watched me from worried, unblinking eyes.

I drew a deep breath and focused inwards, feeling the cold tiles beneath my bare feet, the weight of the hurt at the base of my skull, the beat of my heart. Around my neck, my charmed pendants were warm. My fingers coiled around them and I breathed out slowly.

What did I need, right now, to heal?

Who was I?

A lump formed in my throat and I stood there as the grief welled inside me. I needed vinegar. A lot of vinegar. And a shake of cinnamon.

The ingredients swam into my mind and felt right. Trusting myself, I turned to his pantry. The vinegar was there, ground cinnamon, potato chips, coffee grounds. This was who I was. This was what fed my magick. Whatever that said about me wasn't important.

I didn't measure anything, adding what I needed, going back for more ingredients. Chili, salt, the tiniest drop of vanilla. He didn't have any oranges but he had lemons and that seemed like a fair substitute.

Regrets rolled through me, the shame making them stick in my mind, tarry and black. I should've been able to catch that witch. I should've been kinder to Arthur. I should've knocked Clint's teeth out. I should've been able to make Dierdre feel safe. I shouldn't have worried Beo.

Tears burned my eyes and that felt right, too. I let them come. Maybe it felt like my whole life was a series of fuck ups, but I was still here, still trying, and that wasn't going to change.

I needed fire. Not a lot. So I put my hand over the mug. *Burn, witch,* I thought, letting power trickle into the spell, feeling the tattered edges of it. *Burn.*

It flashed, fast but contained, on the surface of the mess in the mug. *As I will, so shall it be.* The smoke coiled through my fingers, smelling like overcooked potatoes.

My whole body hurt. I didn't know why, but it did. I closed my eyes again and reached for the spell to infuse the essences of the symbols within the mug into a potion and struggled to remember the words. They just weren't there.

Not surprising, really. I was a different witch than I'd been when I'd dabbled in potion making. And if I regretted who I'd become, well, that was a later problem.

New words swam into my head slowly. I breathed them out as they came. *"For better or worse,"* I murmured, searching my heart, feeling all that hurt, *"I need to do this."* Yes, I did. *"I can do this."* No, that wasn't quite right. It didn't fit. Doubt swelled and I acknowledged it, then put it aside, and ran back over the words I had so far. The next part floated into my head clearly, then. *"And I can."* It felt right. It felt *true. "So I will."*

I pulled it all together, letting my breath out slowly around the sob that was stuck in my throat. *For better or worse, I need to do this. And I can, so I will.*

The mug heated suddenly and I snatched back my hand.

Cinnamon and vanilla combined with vinegar didn't smell the greatest. It'd taste even worse. I had no doubt. I looked down at it and watched the surface glow with purple light.

That was me. I was a puddle of coffee grounds and soggy chips, floating in vinegar with a slice of lemon.

My hands shook as I rummaged for Beo's strainer and I tried to ignore it, wiping tears onto the shoulder of my shirt.

"Did it hurt you?" Beo asked, the words perfectly neutral. "Can I help?"

"No." I found the strainer quicker than I wanted, but I didn't keep rummaging. He probably would've known. I just stood awkwardly in his kitchen, feeling more vulnerable than if I'd been naked, and waited for the potion to cool.

"Do you want me to heal your—" I waved my hand at his bandaged shoulder.

He shook his head. "Forget it." My tired brain thought that idea was funny, but the laughter was dust in my lungs. "You cast two spells without a wand."

"Small ones," I agreed, because it was easier than trying to question him now. He didn't want to talk about himself. Well, that made two of us. "On things I was physically touching."

He nodded, studying me like he could the find the information he craved stamped on my face. And who knew, perhaps he could. "You spoke that last spell. You don't usually."

"I had to make it up," I admitted, glancing down at the mug and giving it an unnecessary swirl.

"You make up your spells?"

"Sure. You make up your recipes. Or modify what you find, to suit you." I shrugged. "Magick is just like cooking. Some people treat it like a science, others like an art, but most are somewhere in the middle." He kept watching me, kept listening, so, in lieu of anything else that either of us wanted to discuss, I went on. "Just like cooking, anyone who wants to learn, can, but different styles work for different people. I was raised by a woman who never owned a set of measuring cups in her life. She taught me to approach it like an art.

You find what speaks to you, and you explore it—with a small number of exceptions."

This must've made sense to him, because his expression softened. "Rigidity wouldn't have suited you."

He wasn't wrong. I took one of the bowls he'd washed after his cooking spree this evening and set the strainer atop it. "No. Pretty sure I'd flunk the university magick studies' courses they offer." The liquid was still warm, but it was close enough and I was done talking, so I tipped it through the strainer and watched the deep purple liquid slide through. It was going to have coffee grounds in it still. *Fiber.*

Beo stood and discarded the soggy, stinking mess as I poured it back into the now-empty mug to drink. "There's a lot of vampire activity, at the moment," he said to my back. "Please be on guard."

I lifted one bejeweled hand. "Charisma-proof."

"Their Charisma is only one of their weapons."

I paused as my tired brain kicked in. "Is that how you and Zane got torn up? Was it on your turf?"

He put a hand gently on my waist before I could turn and face him, pressing a kiss to the back of my head. "I'm looking after it," he murmured into my hair. "You look after you. There's enough going on that I can't help with." And at the end he added a word, something growled, something gentle. While my mind deciphered the words my body was already relaxing back into his arms. The weight of them around me was a physical relief and my heart sat lighter in my chest. "Please, just look after you."

"I'm fine, Beo."

His chest swelled against my back and the warmth of his breath tickled my ear. "I was so scared you'd hate me if you saw me." The words were so soft I could barely even make them out. "But I just couldn't leave you. I couldn't let you be crushed, even if it meant losing you." The raw emotion in those words ripped me apart. I tried to turn and face him but his arms tightened, keeping me pinned. "You hadn't mentioned it. But I know it's there." His lips were pressed to my temple and that fucking sob was back in my throat. I pushed away the memory of his big paw on my hand. "It's here. Forever. I know what that's like." And his lips came again, firmly, by the corner of my eye. "I hate that for you, Rory. I hate that I can't fight your battles."

Who in the ever-loving fuck *was* this man?

Feet rooted to the ground, I stared at the mug in front of me as his breath hitched, as he buried his face in my hair. If I'd made him cry by going off half-cocked tonight, I'd probably never forgive myself.

"I'd hate it if you did," I offered, gently. "I'll be more careful, and today was a whole comedy of weird shit. You know it isn't usually like this, Beo."

One of his arms dropped from my waist and his hand burned my thigh like a brand, those big fingers splayed over my cold skin. "I know who did this to you," he said, and now there was fury as well as that sadness in the words. "I know who scarred your body and your mind. And I *hate* that, when I held his life in my jaws, I didn't take it." He pushed away and every single tired, emotion-sodden sense rocked in the wake of his fury. "Drink your potion. I need to cool off."

A moment later the door closed behind him. I didn't reach for the potion, though, but down to where I could still feel the bite of his fingers on my thigh. The scars there were so faint I didn't think anyone could see them. I hadn't noticed them in months. Blood roaring in my ears, I felt my heart break for him.

If he'd killed his brother, I probably wouldn't be here. And I had no doubt Beo knew that, too.

Tears burned my throat. I washed them away with the vinegary potion.

. , ' ' 0 0 ● ◦ ● ◦ - ● ◦ 0 ◦ ● ◦ ' ◦ ●

He tried to apologize when he returned.

I put his mouth to better use.

After the last pangs of hunger had been abated, before the sweat had even cooled on our skin, we slept tangled up in each other. And I didn't dream.

Movement, sharp, hard, urgent, woke me. The darkness was total.

My body was moving. Falling. Landing, hard. My heart was in my throat, energy flooding my limbs. I barely felt the jolt of the floor, the warmth of the covers.

Beo's hands gripped me, hard, held me down and I writhed, bridged, almost won free before he said, "Stay down!"

The note of violence in those words ended my struggles. I stayed, silent, unmoving, and strained to see anything.

In the dim glow of his clock, I could just make out the faintest silhouette of him above me. He was sitting up, his face turned toward the window. The drumming of my own heartbeat in my ears was background noise I zoned out as I strained to hear what he could.

Nothing.

No movement, no sound. Just the usual background hum of traffic on the freeway, the sound of a car engine as it approached somewhere nearby. I let some of the air out of my lungs and felt his grips on me ease as he untangled his legs then climbed off of me. Questions crowded my mouth. Before any of them could be aired he was snarling something.

His anger made the hair on my arms rise. My heart was jumping like a rabbit and there wasn't enough air. "Beo?"

"Wait," he ordered.

My mouth went dry. And then something changed.

I couldn't have said what exactly it was. I recognized all too well the sudden rise of nausea, the way he drew in a breath, the vibrations in his chest that indicated speech. But there was no noise. Not a lack. A total, utter absence. And his hand went over my eyes.

He's shifting?

Panic burned, icy cold, through my veins. I held myself still and frantically tried to remember where I'd left my wand.

But then his hand was lifted and he climbed fully off me, leaving me lying in a tangle of covers and sheets, the carpet still cold beneath me. A word fell from his lips, spoken with fury and disgust. Not in our tongue. Not in any human tongue.

The nausea hadn't abated far, but he hadn't shifted. I lay, still, listening to him moving. My wand was beside my phone, on the bedside charger. I tried to figure out which way I was facing, moving one hand tentatively as I sought the base of the bed to orient myself. I couldn't have gone far, could I?

Light flooded the room and I blinked, turning away from the brightness. My hand bumped the base of the bed.

We *hadn't* gone far. He'd sent us over the side of the bed furthest from the window. "Stay there," Beo ordered.

Fury pulsed. "The fuck?" I scrambled to get up and get my wand. Spells swam in my head, hard and powerful. They were right there, ready to use. Ready to weaponize.

"Fae," he said, briefly. "I need to check it."

Faeries.

I got to my feet and searched for a shirt. He was gone.

Fucking *gone.*

I yanked open his cupboard, ripping out a shirt, and had it over my head before I remembered I had a few items of clothing here.

It took me approximately fifteen of my hummingbird heartbeats to have leggings and socks on and get out of the bedroom. I grabbed my shoes, perched where I'd left them under a heating vent. The laces of my boots were swollen and stiff. I'd go out without underwear or a bra. I wouldn't go out without tying my damn boots up. *That* got you killed.

Furiously I did the laces up. *Loop, loop, pull.* There was a cold breeze and I knew, I *knew,* the arsehole had just up and left. Naked. Fucking *naked.* And left me to—what, sit, make tea? Perhaps a hot breakfast?

What in the ever-loving *fuck?*

The front door was open. I was in full stride, all senses on alert, all feelings roaring, when I barreled straight into him returning.

He caught me around the waist. I was pulled back in as he closed the door behind himself. For once the sight of him naked didn't do a thing for me. "What the fuck?" I demanded, furiously, not too angry to see the wounds on him. What had *happened?*

"Had a visitor while we slept," he told me, holding me there for a moment, his face in neutral lines. "Why were you following?"

"Why was I—" I pulled back just so I could shove him in the chest.

He fell back half a step, but I had a nasty feeling that was just so I didn't hurt myself. "Looking after you is *literally my job*."

"I know." He let out a breath, ran a hand through his hair. "Sorry, Rory. Coffee?"

Coffee. Sorry? That was *it?* "What did you find?" I demanded, following him into the kitchen. "What did you see? What *happened* to you?"

"Didn't see anything. They were too fast." He went over to the kettle, flicking the switch. "Smelled them. They hadn't been there long." He took out two mugs, still naked. I knew I was cold. It was far away information, but it was there. If he felt it, he gave no sign.

Had he checked the perimeter? In the buff? "Next time," I said, reaching for patience and coming up empty, but faking it anyway, "*tell me.*"

He glanced at me, his face carved in painfully neutral lines. "You aren't the best at assessing situations, Rory."

Everything inside of me went cold. "Excuse me?"

He dumped coffee into mugs. "How many times in the last month have you almost got yourself killed? I'm not planning on dragging you into anything that'll…" he trailed off and this time I could see from the light in the pantry the way his mouth moved, his chest rose, just like he was speaking.

But there was, again, that utter void of all sound. And his eyes were an abyss.

I turned and managed to grab the sink in time to direct the vomit that burned out of my body.

Elders.

I shoved my hair out of the way, let my body rebel while my mind tried.

Tried.

Tried to make sense.

He was there, then, running the tap, holding my hair. "I'm sorry," he said, and he sounded tired and sad. "I didn't mean to make you sick."

I spat out the last of the bile in my mouth, rinsing it away with a shaking hand, scooped some water out of the faucet and washed my face. That wasn't his lycan shift. But it was the same magick.

I'd never seen or heard *anything* about that.

Lycans had shifting magick and were tough as nails. End of story.

"What was it?" My words were supposed to be a demand. They sounded more like a pathetic mewl.

"I told the pack to do perimeter checks earlier," he murmured, his hands gentle on me. "Zane was just letting me know they were all okay."

I clutched the stainless-steel sink edge and let that soak in as the water ran beside me, icy cold.

They could communicate, magickally.

Zane was a couple of kilometers away. Three? Four? Shit, for all I knew, he was ten. "Why did I not know this was a thing?" I asked, straightening.

He shrugged, returning to the coffee. "I didn't know you didn't know. Now you do."

How neat. How civilized. "Wow, Beo, you're really making me want to see what noise you'll make if I crush your balls, you know?"

He passed me a coffee. "There was a risk. I let my pack know. I checked it out. I need to do that, Rory."

Because his brother knew where he was. Beo. Beo's pack. Beo's niece. Because I'd told his brother.

Because I'd put them all in danger.

And he blamed his brother, still. Not me.

Guilt ripped at me. I took the coffee and he left; his steps quiet. The view from Beo's kitchen window was of the apartment building over the road in all its end-stage-capitalism glory. The coffee burned my tongue. *Well, doesn't that fucking fit.*

Okay, so, I'd brought this on him, this hypervigilance. And, fuck, noticing a faerie watching me sleep wouldn't make me my most level headed self either. And only a few hours ago he'd all but come undone with fear for me.

Swallowing my pride burned a whole lot more than the coffee.

I took a deep breath, listened to his soft footfalls approaching. "I'm sorry," I said, stiffly. And took another mouthful to wash away the taste of it.

"It's fine." He stood beside me and lifted his coffee. Together we stared at the ugly building over the road, silence stretching between us for an eon. "I can communicate with my pack. They can communicate with me. Alpha thing." I saw him shrug in my peripheral vision. He was wearing a shirt now and I didn't even care. Could the faeries be working with his brother? I felt sick.

I brought this on his pack.

"I should go."

He was quiet for a moment, staring into the darkness. "I won't stop you. I want you here, though."

The reality of the day stretched out before me. Work. Coven meeting today at ten. Deirdre. Associated paperwork. Retrievals would be on deck soon. Arthur, still love drunk.

That was going to make for an awkward conversation or three when I got in. I checked the clock; it wasn't even six. I didn't even bother trying to calculate how much sleep I'd had. "I'm sorry, Beo," I said again, because it was all I had.

"I know." He set down his coffee, turning to me. "We're okay, Rory. We'll manage it."

There was weight in those words I couldn't quite make sense of. The accusations he'd flung at me—no, no they hadn't been *flung*, but, shit, they hurt all the same—surfaced in my mind. So maybe I'd gone in guns blazing a few times in the past when I shouldn't have. But I was still here, and that wasn't just because everyone else kept me alive.

"I don't want to be looked after."

He studied my face and there was the shadow of grief in his eyes. "I know," he said again, and I tried to ignore the niggle of annoyance. "And I respect that. You've got a strong," he tapped his chest. "Spirit. But there's always someone stronger."

I ached. Thought back to those flickers of grief last night. "Who'd you lose?"

He picked up his coffee again, eyes sliding away. "Too many to name. I trust you. I don't trust the world, though."

I struggled to figure out how I felt about that. "I don't, either."

A bit of a smile tugged at his mouth. The grief was replaced by appreciation. I felt the cold of my damp boots seeping into my socks and realized I was coming down from the adrenaline rush. "I'll make you breakfast. You're going to need good fuel to get through the day."

Food was the furthest thing from my mind. I let him do it anyway, knowing what he was like. "So." Neutral topic until I figured out which way my arse was pointing. *Yeah. Smart.* "Vamps, hey?" Subtly, I tried to assess the bandage on his shoulder, comparing it to what I'd seen. That damage hadn't been caused by a falling building. Was he tangling with vamps without letting me know?

"Mm. Not too many on our turf, but I'm hearing about some pretty serious conflict in other areas." He took some berries from the freezer.

Curse it, I was in for one of his patented healthy smoothies. I hoped he was out of spinach. Unless he had kale instead. Fuck kale. "Oh yeah?" I asked, trying to make it sound idle. "Lycans and vamps? Vamps and magi?"

"Lycans," he said, shaking nowhere near enough berries into the jug for the little blender thing before replacing them. I looked at the sad pile with resignation. As my Oma always told me, anything that tastes that bad has to be good. I hid my expression with my coffee cup as he went to the pantry, returning with an assortment of nuts and seeds in recycled jars. "Not surprising. Without Van Der Holst, there's room for maneuvering, and vampires are the best maneuverers around."

The thought didn't make me any happier than the seeds he was shaking into the jug. "Great. Cut off one head, two more spring up."

He didn't glance up at me as he asked, mildly, "Had much to do with vampires?"

I wasn't fooled by the casual tone. "Yes. And look, still alive."

He shot me a quick glance. "Mm. Nice shirt."

I glanced down. My nipples had beaded with the cold. I wasn't used to that being *visible*. "Thanks. It looks great on the floor."

The green of his eyes warmed and his hand slipped a little further than I would've wanted, sending seeds spilling into the jug. I winced and the smile spread from where it had been tucked into one side of his mouth. "It's good for you."

"Yeah," I said, trying to be gracious and failing. "So I hear."

Before he could respond, my phone rang. My work one.

I pushed off the bench and dashed to the bedroom, half-falling over the tangled bedclothes on the floor and scrambling to answer before I could really process what was happening.

"Aurora Gold," I said, double checking the time on my personal phone.

"Hey." Arthur. I didn't relax. "Sorry if I woke you. I know you had a late night."

"Didn't wake me," I said, grabbing my personal phone and stuffing it into the pocket of my leggings. "Everything okay?"

"Yeah. Um. I thought you'd want to know. Retrievals arrived. They're keen to interview you. I told them I wasn't sure what your hours would be today. But." He cleared his throat. "I thought you could make the choice."

A pang of sympathy went through me. Arsehole Arthur would've set up the meeting for me either before or after the staff meeting and just sent me an invite. Lovestruck Arthur probably had been tempted to chase them off. "Thank you. I appreciate it." And I did. He was having a go. "Got a number for me?"

"Uh—the wizard I spoke to—his name was Nicholas Rubikeyv? Or something like that. He said you had his number." And there was just a little hurt in his voice.

Warmth spread through my chest and the old, familiar sense of failure. "Nic? Yeah. That's my old team." And if they were on Dierdre, then I didn't have to lose any sleep over her. "I'll set it up. You made my morning. Now I won't have to worry. Thanks, King." In the background, the whir of the blender sounded and my mood deflated. But

Nic would know somewhere to get hot cinnamon donuts. As consolation prizes went, it wasn't a bad one. "See you at the staff meeting."

"Yeah. Sure. Uh, Rory." I paused and he said, "Never mind. I'll see you later."

Weird. Poor guy. "No worries. Bye." I hung up, trying not to borrow trouble, and walked out to find there was zero green in the smoothie. Thank fuck. I could deal with the gruel looking concoction, but kale probably would've pushed me over the edge.

As Beo gave the jug a shake to get the last of the berries off the bottom my personal phone rang. I recognized the name and smiled. "Hey, spell-slinger," I said playfully. "I hear you're trying to muscle in on my turf."

"This city's big enough for the two of us, Sunshine," Nic drawled from the other end. "Hear you got yourself into some fun without us last night. Why're you so bright this early?"

Beo lifted his eyes questioningly and I shrugged a little. "Oh, you know me."

"I do. Hence the suspicion." The blender whizzed again for a moment and Nic said, immediately, "What was that?"

"That was my breakfast being prepared for me," I said, leaning against the bench.

He snorted. "You don't do breakfast, unless it's the R-rated variety."

"Maybe I just didn't stick around long enough for you to find out," I sent back, enjoying the banter. "So, you've got my witch."

"You stuck around plenty," he disagreed, but there was laughter in his voice. "I remember you bitching about how sticky you were, in fact. Yeah, I got your witch." I saw a smile tugging at Beo's mouth and knew damned well he was following the conversation. "We're not going to keep her long, though. Got an archer to catch, I hear. Love potions. Life gets weirder every day."

I watched Beo split the smoothie into two cups. "You aren't going to stake her out, wait for her to be hit again?"

"Got somewhere else to be." He sounded a little regretful. "But we won't leave you high and dry."

This wasn't what I'd assumed would happen. "Can you track her?"

He snorted. "Come on, Rory. Who're you talking to?"

"Yeah, okay." Nic *was* a half decent oracle. And he did the paperwork to keep that legal, too. Mostly. "I'll give you what I can. It isn't much."

"Well, it can't be much *less* than I got from your boss." He sounded amused still despite the complaint. "Wanna get a coffee?"

I looked down at myself. I might have a bra somewhere here that wasn't wet and didn't stink of smoke. Or—no, no I didn't. "Um. I'm going to need a bit of time."

"I can deliver," he said, easily. "Tax deductible. Don't care if your hair is everywhere. I've seen it before. And the rest."

He had, too. I took the smoothie Beo passed me and swallowed the request for Nic to deliver donuts. "Look, as charming as you are, Nic, I need to get home and change before work. I assume you've got some other strings to pull while you wait."

"You're the last one, Sunshine." I took a mouthful of the concoction and didn't puke. *Winning.* "I can meet you at yours. I won't even ask where you've been."

I considered the time. With travel, trams, showers… "will Vix be there?" She'd keep him in line and on time.

He was quiet.

My heart sank.

"Sorry, Rory," he said, quietly. "I thought Bethany told you."

I took a big swallow of smoothie, turning to the window. "You can. Later." I felt sick and didn't want his donuts anymore. "Look, I can meet you at—"

"No, don't bullshit me," he cut in, brutally. "Fuck, this is why we don't trust powers that be, isn't it? I'll come get you. I got a company ride. We need to catch up. Team comes first."

Beo's face was set in lines of compassion. He offered an arm and, taking a breath, I stepped into the hug. Briefly. "I'm not on your team anymore, Nic," I said, and there was no regret there anymore. Just emptiness.

"Yeah, well, that's our loss," he said flatly, no more teasing, no more bullshit. "I get you're at a guy's place. Don't care. Won't say a damned thing to anyone. I don't care if you told Bethany to eat a bag of dicks, Roars. She earned it. She still should've passed shit on. It's her job."

I hesitated, let out a breath. "Yeah. Okay." It would be easier to hear it from him in person. "Thanks."

He snorted again, but I could see his face in my mind, twisted in disgust, now, not mirth. "Don't thank me. I should've just called you. Come on, witch, give me your coords."

Mouth dry, I gave him the apartment building, got his ETA, hung up and downed the smoothie. It rolled in my belly and I ignored that and the coating of grit and goodness it left in my mouth.

"Tonight?" Beo asked me, the words quiet.

"Yeah." My day swirled through my head. "Maybe."

He reached toward me and waited. I didn't close the distance. I didn't want his comfort. *Just another day, just get through it.* I'd done more on less sleep. I'd bounce. "Rory."

"I'm fine." I was. More than, to be honest. I was good at my job.

Maybe, if I'd been there, if I could've stayed in the team…

"Okay." The hand fell. "I'm going to go chat with Zane. See what we can find out about faeries in the area. I've got class tonight."

That was an eon away. "Sure." I didn't need to go. "I think I'll crash tonight at mine."

He shrugged. It didn't matter to him, but I did. I knew I did. I couldn't feel it, right then, but I knew I did. "Seems sensible. I'll wait to hear from you. I'm happy to come to yours, later, if you want." He rinsed my empty glass. "See how you feel. No pressure."

Elders. I touched his arm, registering the heat of his skin. "Thanks."

"Any time." He set the glass aside. "I mean that literally."

"I know you do." My heart ached. "I've got to go."

He glanced at the time but didn't correct me, even though we both knew I'd be standing out the front for at least five minutes waiting for Nic. "Be safe."

"Yeah." I leant over, brushing a kiss over his lips. "Always."

He didn't correct that, either.

CHAPTER 10

The morning was a blur. I was caught up on the latest shitstorm by Nic between caffeinating and changing, gave him what I had, the official, the unofficial that I knew he'd keep to himself. By the time I got into the staff meeting, I was solidly in survival mode, and I stayed there while I took minutes assessing the flow of information.

No one else mentioned vampires, but I couldn't keep what Beo had told me to myself. So, without looking up from my laptop, typing as I spoke, I said, "Got a client who tells me we've got increased vampire activity in other districts, some here."

"Haven't heard anything," Arthur said, frowning. "What makes him say that?"

Him. Not 'them'. He knew which client I'd spoken to. *Fuck.* "I didn't ask a lot of questions, but they're clashing with lycans elsewhere. We need to keep our eyes open."

He glanced around the table. Most of the witches there were more interested in sampling the latest jams Janet had brought in for morning tea. I didn't blame them. It was pretty good jam, honestly. "Anyone else heard anything?" he asked.

Beside me, Lilith shifted in her chair. A long skein of black skirt slipped down off her knee to drape down to the floor. "One of my clients said something," she agreed, glancing at me. "Yesterday afternoon. Said she'd heard rumors about a big play."

"Vampires always make 'big plays'," Janet said, pushing the jar of what looked like it might be plum jam of some persuasion to Cici, who'd been making eyes at it for about seven minutes. "Then we make big stakes, and the problem is over. We'll keep our ears open, but it'll blow over. It always does."

I didn't add that to the minutes, but I did note Lilith's observation. The thing was, it might blow over *our* heads, but someone, somewhere, wore that storm.

Or it raged, unchecked.

"Any idea what this big play is?" I asked Lilith, glancing over at her.

"No specifics," she said, with an elegant shrug. "But the rumor had enough strength behind it to worry my witch. She isn't the panicky type."

I didn't ask exactly which of Lilith's clients it was. Yet. I'd have coffee with her later, get the full scoop. "So. Eyes and ears open," Arthur said, firmly, glancing around. "You all know vampires' skillset, yes?"

No one said anything out loud. No one needed to. The pitying looks shared around the table spoke volumes.

My heart went out to him, just a little. He wasn't *trying* to be patronizing. He was just naturally good at it. "We haven't had vamps flagged while I've been here," I said, to the table at general. "What's the safety plan?"

"Don't invite them in," Bernie told me. Then, "If they're cute, get them to pay for a hotel."

The very typical Bernie advice was met with some amused smiles, a few laughs, some sighs.

"Do we have charms?" I asked her, raising my brows. "That 'can't get inside without an invite' clause holds less water than the saucer under the daylily. They know *all* the loopholes."

She waved it away with a queenly swish of her jam-coated teaspoon. "Wood is everywhere."

Right. So, that's where we were at. I looked at Arthur, feeling rather grim. He shrugged a little. "We aren't legally able to do much. We're Caretakers, not police, and certainly not Retrievals."

And there I was, being put in my place. Never mind that what I'd learned in Retrievals had made me a better Caretaker. "We're Caretakers," I agreed, noting the total lack of management plan in the minutes because fuck them. "Not sacrificial lambs. We won't know how serious this is until we're in the middle of a burning building that's about to collapse on us."

The table went quiet. And then someone murmured, quietly, "Can I have the—thank you, Janet."

"That's what the police are for, sweetheart," Cici told me, smiling at me like I was three and using the wrong utensil at a family dinner.

Frustration simmered. "We've got a power vacuum," Lilith said from beside me, leaning forwards. "Rory's right. Without Van Der Holst, there *is* room for machinations, and they *love* power play. We need to take this seriously."

No wonder she was my best witch. Under the table, I offered her my open palm. She gave me a quiet low five.

"We will," Arthur said, firmly. "I don't want any of you hurt. I'll investigate risk management strategies employed elsewhere," he told me. "And decide—" he stopped. Swallowed. "And bring some proposals to the next meeting."

That was in a weeks' time, but it was also super sweet of him.

I noted it in the actions and decided not to mention that, in times of crisis, dictators did it better. We weren't at that point. That we knew of.

I shuffled my day so I could check in on Dierdre. She had been moved to an apartment with approximately enough room to swing a small stunned cat, but had her own clothes on and looked a bit brighter when I got there. Her police guard was no longer in the room; a patrol car sat over the road.

I wasn't stoked about the security, but I checked the charms on the place and took the cup of tea she gave me while she prepared ingredients for a potion. "It's for Arthur," she said, as she worked. "Detective O'Malley explained what happened."

Relief rushed through me. I recognized most of what she used, and a lot of the techniques, even if I wouldn't have been able to replicate it. The smell of crushed herbs, the grind of mortar and pestle, took me back to my Oma's kitchen. "He'll be glad of it. Once he's done it."

She shook her head a little, her mouth a hard line.

I sat in the silence that followed my comment, watching her white-knuckled hands as she ground ingredients to a coarse powder, then shook them into a jar. *So. Maybe not so glad.* And who would know better than Dierdre the cost of all that false conviction, those engineered emotions?

"Want to tell me about it?" I asked, because I had no idea what else to say.

"No." She took out a pair of heavy gloves and her eyes flickered up to me. "Sorry. I, um. I don't want it in my head."

"Fair." I watched as she took a jar set aside. The label on it read *Midnight Violets*. "I know the team going after Amor. They're good at what they do."

"They'll need to be," she murmured. "Stay back. This one is nasty."

I took her warning seriously and straightened from my position slouched on the bench. She took a metal implement I might've seen during science class back when I was fifteen and more interested in making things burn. Into the jar it went and a tiny part of withered black petal was broken off and lifted. She held her face well away from it, positioning the jar near the open window. As she withdrew the piece of flower she broke a little bit more off against the glass, then a little more, until I didn't even know if there was any left.

"What is that?" I asked, slightly concerned by the way she was tilting her face away, as if it was a steaming dog turd. "Wait. Don't answer. Don't want you breathing in extra right now."

A nod was my answer. The metal tong things carried the tiniest fleck of the Midnight Violet and put it in the bottom of a glass jar, then were placed carefully in a separate jar and the lid of the violets tightly sealed. Still not removing her gloves, she went to the stove, took some boiling water, and measured some over top of the violet.

The process probably only took two minutes. By the time she was done, the water had gone a deep, vibrant purple and she was sterilizing the metal tool she'd used, still in her gloves. "It's a fae flower," she told me, eventually. "Tobias—my ex. He got them for me."

I looked twice at the innocuous little jar. That was a Class A felony, right there. "Um. Legally?" Shit, I was turning into Taig.

"There are other ingredients," she said, a bit hesitantly. "That you can use. Midnight Violet is the best. The low—from the sudden withdrawal of all the oxytocin—is bad. It hits you harder and faster. But it's also short lived compared to the Earth substitutes, and the other risk factors aren't as high. Some anti-love potions have horrendous risks attached." She swirled the purple mix sitting on the windowsill, eyeing it critically. It was eerily beautiful. "Clotting. Hemorrhaging. Mass organ failure."

"All the fun stuff." So, her ex didn't just trade for cash. He traded for faerie flowers. Probably other illicit substances.

And Dierdre had turned those substances into products.

My heart ached for her. I hadn't missed the complete lack of information about why she still had it.

It was her insurance policy.

"It'll take a little while to cool," she told me, dropping a few shavings of something I hadn't seen her prepare into the bottle. They dissolved, and the liquid went a cheerful pink. "This isn't nice, but it's the safest, when properly prepared."

"What side effects do you need to watch for?"

"Self-harm and suicide," she told me, and I got a glimpse of her professional healer persona. "Make sure someone is with him for the first twenty-four hours. He might not want it, but he needs it. That's the highest risk time. Any trouble breathing, full body rashes, dips in blood pressure, call triple-oh. Avoid asthma inhalers for a week; if that's a problem, preventers are safe."

I kind of wanted to smile at her calm, reassuring air. "I'm glad you're here, Deirdre," I told her, honestly.

She looked up at me and there was surprise on her face. Surprise, and gratitude. "I am, too," she said softly.

I contacted Arthur on my way out, bottle of potion—now a dark red—in one hand, Deirdre's warnings in my head. I was happy to take it in to work for him after grabbing a bite to eat with Lilith, but he just about fell over himself to come and "catch up" with me.

There were some conversations better had in private, but I steeled myself for this particular one as I went into the cafe up the road from our coven. Lilith was, mercifully, late. Arthur must've almost run the whole way because he was waiting for me, and he'd ordered me a coffee already that was steaming opposite him.

"So, I've been thinking about what you said about the vampires," he told me as soon as I sat down. "I've done some research, and in other countries, where they're more of a problem, they have a standard tool kit. A charisma-proof charm is pretty common. Most countries—"

I opened my mouth to comment, shut it again. But, to my surprise, Arthur *didn't* talk over me, but halted awkwardly and peered at me with a sort of semi-apologetic air that made me wish he hadn't. "I was going to mention that the charisma-proof charm doesn't go well with a lot of other charms. We have to choose."

"Well, actually, there's some research into that field that's quite interesting." He settled back in the chair, taking his fancy pants coffee with him, and looked just like the old Arthur. "You see, often we use common gems for our charms. But in fact, rare gems are known for—"

"Arthur." I put down my coffee, held up my bejeweled hand. "I buy my own diamonds, mate." He blinked at my rings as if he'd never noticed them. He probably hadn't. I was pretty confident he'd noticed my tits, though. "You can't ask a bunch of women approaching retirement age to redo all their charms, fork out for diamond or Otherworldly magickally enhanced charms—"

"Wait, you know about that?" He stared at me in awe like I was an astrophysicist or something.

It was not the response I was used to and it jarred me back into the moment. I set the potion bottle before him. "Take this." And the gentleness of the words surprised me. "I hear it's a rough twenty-four hours, but you'll be you again."

He didn't move. The background noise of the cafe crested and flowed into the silence. I became acutely aware that I'd never second guessed whether Arthur should take it. And, okay, the puppy thing was annoying but it had eased.

I didn't hate this version of Arthur.

But I didn't want him to be better to me if he didn't have control over his own emotions.

Considering I'd imagined murdering the bloke once or twice, that realization struck me as...profound.

I took a pull from my coffee and got out my phone. Some work emails; one from Janet with the recipe for one of her jams. I scrolled on, surprised Lilith hadn't mentioned she'd be late.

"What if I like this?" The words were hesitant. "What if I go back to being the arsehole you hate?"

My heart twisted. "Arthur," I said, searching for kindness. "Even if you don't, I can't love you like this. It would be like slipping you some easy yes potion and then having sex with you."

Tears beaded in his eyes. "I know. That you won't—feel the same." His throat worked.

Shit, I was a bitch.

"I can live with that. If...if you don't hate me. And... you don't act like you do." The words were thick with emotion. "Friendzoned for life doesn't seem as bad as being hated."

I reached out over the table, offering him my palm. His hand was warm and soft when it settled into mine. I left the 'friendship isn't second place' talk for now. "I think we've learned a lot about each other." And I was *not* prepared for that. "You won't forget that. Neither will I."

He reached out tentatively with his other hand, glanced up at me, waited for me to withdraw, then, when I just met his gaze, enveloped my hand completely, leaning over that connection of skin and bones like it was a babe on a battlefield. Fuck, my poor feelings. I was done.

So done. The potion just sat there and I just wanted to grab it and pour it into him.

"I've never felt this good. About anyone." He lifted my hand to his mouth in supplication. "Please, Rory. I don't want it to end."

My heart broke. For him, for Dierdre, who knew what this felt like. "Arthur. That isn't real love. Real love lets you see flaws and get annoyed, and… and be *you*."

"I don't care," he said, and the words were too loud, too forceful, too desperate.

I saw Lilith enter in a flurry of winter wind, her brilliant purple hair a chaotic swirl around her. I shot her a quick warning look and her eyes went huge as she looked between Arthur and I.

I had to wrap this up. I couldn't do it any longer. "Do you trust me?" I asked Arthur, levelly.

"Yes," he said, hopelessly. "Yes."

The question had been rhetorical, really. "Go home. Take the potion. Call someone to be with you. Someone you trust. A friend, or family member. Call *me*, if you need someone. But take it. For me."

His tears beaded. "I'm a burden." The hurt in his words made the statement sound almost childish. He let me go, standing on unsteady legs. "I've always worked hard to do the right thing. I just…I just didn't know who to trust. I guess I didn't think. Not deeply." He let out a shaky break and my heart twisted for him. "It's okay. I'll do it. Thank you, Rory."

"And go to the hospital," I said, spotting a lumpy mess under his shirt where he'd been shot less than a day ago.

With tears running down his face, he nodded, smiling unconvincingly. "Thank you," he said again, taking the potion with him.

Fuck.

Fuck.

"Okay," Lilith said, sliding into the chair he just vacated. "What— and I cannot stress this enough—in the actual fuck?"

I dropped my head onto the table. "I am a horrible, horrible person."

"No, *he's* a horrible, horrible person. You're an impulsive, hormone-driven hot mess. Difference. So." She cleared her throat. "Do I need to repeat myself, Roars?"

I peered up at her through the mess of black curls now all over the place, desperately needing her solidarity. "He got hit by a love potion. I just manipulated him into taking the cure."

She set down her phone firmly. "Tell me *everything*. Right now. I don't care if I have to buy you six bowls of wedges to hear the whole story."

It didn't take six bowls of wedges to get her up to date, only one and a muffin that I dissected while we spoke. And it felt so good to offload onto someone who was as blown away as me that I kept going. I told her about that morning, what had happened with Beo.

"Sounds like Mr. Thorough's got a deep, dark past," she said, using the nickname she'd made up for Beo while amusement sparkled in her eyes. "Pretty sure this is the bit where you swoop in and rescue him with your feminine wiles and comforting bosom."

"Bitch," I said, amused despite myself, feeling better, now. "My feminine wiles are not of the swooping variety. Stalking, exploding, annihilating—sure. I don't," I lifted my hands, left some muffin crumbs on the table, and made quotation marks with my fingers, "swoop."

She was smiling at me like she knew something I didn't. "Uh huh."

That earned her a piece of muffin thrown with high precision but low speed at her face. She laughed, knocking it aside. "Some sister you are. I'm sitting here pouring out my heart—"

"More like your hot sex stories," she said, rolling her eyes. "Come on. I've got a two o'clock back at the coven. New intake."

Grumbling out of principle, I stood, paid, huddling down into my woolen coat that was more practical than sexy, and braved the winter air. A storm was rolling in. "Those clouds look like fuckers."

"Bad omen," she said, absently, as some crows cawed their way past us.

I rolled my eyes. "You know what's bad luck? Being superstitious. There's nothing wrong with a winter storm."

"Not if you have a good book, hot chocolate, a blanket, and a hot guy to grab your arse."

I nodded agreement, feeling lighter. We cut down an alleyway, in no hurry despite the threat on the horizon. I didn't give a shit about weather and crows were just your cleverer than average birds of prey. "I need to get chocolate."

"I need to get a hot guy," she sighed.

I bumped my shoulder into hers, playfully. "Or two."

She pretended to consider it. "Look, I don't want to be greedy, but…"

I laughed. We crossed an intersection and I pulled out my phone, my heart sitting lighter in my chest, and opened up the last message from Beo. I *did* want to see him tonight. Even if it was just to fall asleep in his arms.

He had a dark past. We all did. I wasn't going to swoop in, but I'd definitely stand with him.

The thought was grounding, but the pleasure zipping through my veins, the warmth in my heart, froze.

I glanced up, my skin crawling, alarm ringing in my head. And I caught a glimpse of a woman, maybe late forties, in biker gear at the mouth of the alley ahead of us leading back to the main road.

With brilliant, unforgettable green eyes.

Lycanthropes.

Probably from my lover's deep, dark fucking past.

Were they coming after him, too? The thought made all the air freeze in my lungs but I didn't let anything show. I needed a few seconds. Just a few. To warn him. My thumbs moved on the phone. *Ambush.* I didn't alter my course. Glancing back down, I slowed my pace.

I hit send, barely seeing it. "Hold on," I told Lilith, forcing my voice to be even. "Just want to quickly…" in a text to her, I typed. *Get out silver and wand.* There were typos. I barely noticed as I held it out for her.

They'd hear speech. This method of communication wasn't fast. It'd have to do, though.

While she glanced at the message, I took a look around that I hoped appeared nonchalant. Four people behind us. Two more appeared from the alley ours had intersected.

"Got it," she said, and reached for her wrist.

My phone rang. *Beo.*

Running steps and blurring forms. The phone rang. Rang. My wand, in my hand, the bite of my keys.

That was my cue and I didn't need any extra stage directions. *"Take this shape and shift it. Silver spear, I need you near,"* Lilith was saying, turning, spinning. Her hips bumped mine. I moved, too, feeling the heat of her at my back.

Eight, at least.

Fucking *eight* lycans.

They really wanted me dead, didn't they?

My blood was electrified, and I watched for what felt like eons as they charged toward us in their lycan forms, now, a sea of giant beasts shouldering each other in the narrow alley. My heart roared in my ears and I held the spell in my head, felt the breath in my lungs threatening to explode. I needed to time it right. I had to.

The woman in front of me had shifted too. I recognized her by her green eyes and longer hair. And the giant fucking teeth.

The air was icy. The city hummed. My phone wailed. And I felt the words sharpen, harden, infuse in my mind. *Through this dome none shall leave or come unless it is with me.*

The ward caught the green-eyed leader perfectly, her head on one side, her body on the other.

Behind me I felt Lilith move. Around me, the noise of ringing bells from lycans being turned back. The head of the leader rolled to a halt as I took it all in. The rain-drenched surroundings, the smell of blood, the lycans throwing themselves fruitlessly at the barrier.

And Lilith's giant silver spear driving forwards.

Two had got through.

My.

Fucking.

Timing.

Was.

Off.

I couldn't double-cast. I couldn't hold two spells.

My phone stopped ringing and I didn't have time for fear.

Lilith's spear went high, then low. She spun, her skirts swirling low and her purple hair swirling high. Like a beautiful, deadly dancer she moved with grace I didn't have time to envy. With my heart in my throat, I watched, helpless. And above us, I saw—thought I saw—a small, crouched figure that my brain instantly categorized.

Faerie.

Lilith tagged a lycan and the other was there, looming over her, going for her throat. Her whole fucking head. I leapt on the tagged beast, sending a vague prayer to the Elders that the blow from the silver had weakened it. I couldn't check on Lilith, I had to just trust and hope.

Oh, fuck, I had to hope.

My boot found the graze her spear had left on its side and it snarled in fury, swung its head toward me.

The ward gave us a couple spare meters. They'd cross it in split seconds if I lowered it. I wouldn't have time to recast.

I couldn't hold it and cast again, too.

"Rory!" I heard her shouting, but couldn't turn or look. I danced with this oversized, magickally enhanced bag of teeth and steel. It lunged. I did, too. It attacked. I spun. It leapt and I rolled under it. The blow I delivered to its underbelly didn't even draw a snarl.

"Silver me!" I shouted. A foot came down, clawed and huge. I felt the weight of it, the crushing power. Burning pain arced from my foot and leg. Not really full-on pain. Not yet, anyway. It was spinning, snapping. Its hindquarters hit the ward and it was thrown off balance.

I heard bones splinter. A noise of pain. Something wet. Something final.

My heart.

Dropped.

Through the wet cement.

Lilith. Not Lilith.

As I will, so shall it be. The ward collapsed around me.

They would all—

BURN—

The spell was hard and hot. The edges of it were molten in my mind. Tears seared my cheeks.

Burn, witch, burn.

Screaming. Human, lycan—I didn't care.

Lilith.

The fire was dazzling. The reek absolute.

I felt the weight, the piercing, crushing force of a bite, then flames. Ripping myself free of its jaws, I kicked away and struggled to keep my feet.

Sirens, screaming.

Screaming.

Screaming.

CHAPTER 11

"A Burn spell of this magnitude is a Class B offence," Clint was saying as he clicked the pen in his hand, his expression one of painful calm. "The damage to surrounding buildings is extensive."

My head was ringing. I leaned against Lilith's good side. I hadn't had time to splint her fucking *arm*. The paramedics weren't even here.

The lycans that had tried to eat us were still on fucking *fire* and this arsehole was just—

"Self-defense," Lilith said, the words rough. "Permissible."

Clint looked around us, taking in the rubble around us. "We'll see." And I suspected he was looking forward to that process.

I barely even cared, though, I just looked at Lilith. I didn't know if Beo was safe, but she was. Her purple hair was still impeccable, her skirt still billowing dramatically around her booted feet. Only the pale lines of her face and the angle of her arm under the velvet jacket she wore gave any sign that she'd gone toe to toe with a lycan and won.

"Where'd you learn the spear?" I tried to ask, but the words got jumbled.

She blinked at me. "You look like shit."

"Function over fashion, witch."

"Yeah. That jacket of yours sure isn't fashionable." I scowled at her comment. "But it didn't burn." She narrowed her eyes at my arm. "Are you *bleeding?*"

"No," I breathed, in mock-horror. "A lycan took a chunk out of me, why would I be *bleeding?*"

A bite would've taken the limb. I'd got lucky with a graze. But I was pissy enough to claim the whole shebang and not even acknowledge that it still didn't hurt.

The ambos arrived and managed us onto stretchers. The scene was crawling with fire fighters and cops, and bystanders with their phones out. I laid back and let it all happen as I was wheeled out of the alley toward medical care. All I could think of was Beo.

* * *

Magickal healing is amazing—pain relief second to none. But by fuck it knocks a woman out.

In the hours days minutes after I'd been patched up, I might've felt the heat of him. Surely, I'd recognize the strength and gentleness of his hands smoothing my hair or his lips pressing a kiss to my head. I knew the strange, not-of-this-world speech as he murmured sweet nothings in my ear.

But when I woke, he wasn't there. Cici was, stabbing her needle into a long stitch with rhythmic, practiced movements that I watched in my magick and drug induced haze for seconds, hours, minutes while hospital noises washed over me. I slept.

The semi-familiar routine of healing began. The meals, the vitals checks, the "how are you feeling?" doctors. I couldn't contact Beo. I had no idea where my phone was, or whether it'd be safe to call. I dozed. Worried. Dozed again.

The lights had dimmed, signaling night, when I woke to Taig pulling back the curtain around the bed.

Relief rushed through me and I struggled to sit up. If Taig was around, things would be okay. Could I ask him about Beo? Shit, what would I even say?

"Lost quite a bit of blood," he said, stopping by the whiteboard beside me where my name had been written. "Two unprepared witches taking out six lycans lying in wait. Pretty intense odds, Caretaker."

I arched my brows. "Does this mean I don't have to work with Incelius Prime?"

His mouth quirked. "Detective Smith is required on another case."

I shoved a bit of hair out of my eyes. He was blurry. But the cotton wool in my head was no worse than…other times? Yeah. I was fine. "Lilith okay?"

"She's good. Been in to check on you. Home now, sleeping, if she's lucky." He propped a hip against the bed and folded his arms. "Gotta say, I'm glad she was with you."

Unease skittered up my spine. "Oh?"

"Oh," he agreed, and his eyes were travelling over me critically. "Thought you'd want to know Mr. Velvela and his pack were also targeted by a group of unlicensed, shifted lycans this afternoon. We suspect it's another attack by Duke."

My mouth went dry. Zane's face. Beo's shoulder. "Another?"

His expression was impassive. "You didn't get the summary I sent through? Clint discussed it with Arthur a few days ago."

My head spun. How many attacks had he warded off? Why hadn't he *told* me? And—was he okay? "And?" I asked, unable to voice the rest.

"Looks like they'd got warning this time," he said, meeting my gaze. He was leading up to something and I couldn't breathe properly. "They're all okay. A few scrapes. Velvela was in here, earlier." He cleared his throat. None of my anxiety had eased. It sat in my breast, a hot, hard knot. "Couple stitches."

I didn't let myself wilt. "What're you dancing around, Taig?" I asked, feeling sick.

"Nothing."

I didn't believe him. "It isn't cop business, is it?"

He hesitated, shrugged. "No. Which means it's yours. So. On a separate note, I have to interview you, Caretaker. Doc says you should be up for it by now."

Doc could go fuck themselves. "Yeah. Sure. Totally lucid."

A bit of a smile tugged at his mouth. "Hit me, Rory." And he drew out his recorder, held it beside me.

My bed was mine overnight. I got awesome drugs and slept like a brick. My phone, when I eventually got energetic enough to find it, was silent. I sent Beo a message but got no response.

Trying not to worry, I was discharged into Janet's paint-splattered hands the next day, escorted home in a blur, tucked into bed and didn't crawl out of it until after midday. Still nothing from Beo.

Taig wouldn't have lied to me. But Beo might've modified the truth. He'd already hidden how serious the situation was from me. Something had to be wrong.

I opened my messages. Double checked. Nothing since that night he'd helped recover Dierdre. *Call me or I'm going to drag my very battered arse over and kick in your door.* The text was sent. I sat on the edge of the bed, feeling overtired but generally fine, looked at the smoke-and-blood mess that were the clothes I'd worn back from the hospital. That was a later problem.

The shower eventually got hot just as my phone rang. I killed the water, grabbed it. "Hey."

"So tell me," Lilith drawled from the other end. "Why didn't you put the ward up earlier?"

"Oh." Her voice was a relief, even if it wasn't Beo's growl. "Figured the less that got away, the less to jump me later. Sorry." I eyed myself in the mirror. Barely whiter than my usual pasty self. But my hair was definitely a natural disaster. I held up a singed end. "I need a haircut."

"You need a lot of things, Rory," she said, affectionately. "I'm glad you're okay. Was a bit worried until that arsehole burst into flame."

"Yeah, well." I dropped the hunk of hair. I wasn't going to tell her I thought she was dead for a minute. "Did you see how many got away?"

She snorted. "No. Or when they left. I had slightly bigger problems."

"Yeah. They're pretty big, all right," I agreed, grimly. "I'm going to go scrub some of the stink off."

"Solid plan. Want an ice cream dinner with me later?"

My mind went to Beo. "I'm going to pick a bone with someone."

"Oh? Want backup?"

My heart swelled. That's the kind of friend Lilith was. "I'll let you know. Pretty sure I can take him, though."

"Ah. *That* kind of bone." And the sound of her amusement, and the kettle boiling in the background, was so wonderfully normal. "Well, may it be hard and long lived. Blessed be, Roars."

I didn't have any laughter in me. Something was wrong. I was going to figure out what that something was.

And, yeah, maybe *then* there might be some memories made.

With that thought I hurried through the shower, trying to sift through information.

Faeries. Lycans. Beo. No sign of vampires—but why were there *faeries* watching?

I didn't bother trying to do anything except get a bit of water out of my hair and tie it back. It was a later problem.

My phone was silent.

Worry and anger warred in my chest. I slowed down long enough to grab coffee and a few handfuls of chips.

A smart woman didn't go to war uncaffeinated.

She could, however, opt to go in her favorite hoodie, especially if it was almost old enough to buy its own beer.

I was reaching for my phone as it rang, but it wasn't Beo. "Hey, Nic." I couldn't ignore his call, even if he was about the furthest thing from my ravaged field of fucks. "Make it quick."

"She's circled back," he said, and then there was a sudden blast of wind. "Bang's on the phone to the cops. Shit, Rory, this witch knows her stuff."

My blood was ice. I grabbed keys, flying out the door. "Talk."

"Traps galore," he said, frustration in his voice. "We've got another call. Vamp in Springvale. Kids involved. We're going to get pulled, Rory."

The cement under my feet vanished. I felt sick. I didn't stop or hesitate. Tram stop. Fastest way. The sun was a memory warming my skin. The wind was bitter. "When?"

"Officially? Probably once the chopper lands. I'm just waiting on Bethany's call."

Fuck. *Fuck.* I couldn't say, *no stopping a vamp from draining kids isn't as important as Dierdre.*

I could absolutely say, "I fucking hate this, Nic."

"I'm with you," he said, grimly. "Elders, am I with you. But not today."

The call ended. I jumped onto the tram and was about to dial Lilith when it lit up with an incoming call.

Beo.

My heart leapt into my throat. "Hey." I grabbed a seat and wished these hunks moved faster.

"Hey." He didn't *sound* hurt. "I'm calling to let you know we're relocating. Permits went through."

My head spun. "You're…" of course he was.

He couldn't risk his pack.

His niece.

The city blurred around me as the pieces all fell into place. Beo's grief. The injuries he'd sustained. He knew it would come to this. He'd held them back, and for how long, all alone?

My options spun through my head like disco lights. And none of them involved walking away.

Deep, dark past, meet swooping bosom. Lilith was going to get a kick out of this. Because he wasn't alone, and he didn't need to protect me.

Hurt and shame was a hot ball in my chest. He had some reasons to distrust me, and we both knew it. Even if he didn't, he'd never ask me to give up my career and go on the run with him. The man was so damned wonderful. I wasn't letting him down again. It didn't matter if I couldn't work in the field, if I became a pariah. We could figure out anything. But right now—

"Look, I've got a situation I need to sort out, but then I can see what I can do." I had to look after Dierdre, though. He'd understand. I'd just need a few days to get an exit plan.

Thoughts of the lease I'd have to break, the boxes I'd have to pack, the utilities I'd have to cancel spun through my head as the tram rocked around me.

"You aren't second place," I told him, firmly. I loved him. Shit, I loved the whole pack. "But this is life or death for someone, Beo. I promise, I'll call you the minute I'm free. We'll make a plan."

"No." The word was calm and measured. "Your home is Melbourne."

Fury splashed through me hot and fast. "You don't get to tell me where my home is."

"I do get to tell you that you aren't coming with us." And the words were gentler, now.

I didn't want gentle. I wanted to knee him in his weasley fucking *balls.* "Oh, yeah?"

"If you hadn't been with another witch today, Rory..."

"I'd have had a higher fucking kill count." I saw a commuter glance at me, then away, didn't give a single shit. "Are you seriously saying you're trying to protect me right now? And what's with the lying, the sneaking? You've been attacked *how many times,* Beo? That's some heavy-handed shit that I thought you wouldn't pull."

"Maybe it is," he agreed, quietly. "And I'm sorry. But it's better this way, Rory."

The blood pounded in my head as landmarks around me blurred. "You spineless fucking coward, Beo," I snarled, feeling the way the phone bit into my head, pressing my earring into my skull. "You really fucking played me, didn't you? All those times you pretended to respect me, you stood back and let me defend myself. Where you just waiting for me to *fail?* You said you'd stand beside me, and now *this?* I thought you were a better person, Beo. I really fucking did. You had me eating out of your thrice-cursed *hand,* you lying fucking *jerk.*" I stood. The tram was solid under my boots. Somehow.

The fire burned in my veins. "I will be waiting for a fucking apology, you jellyfish of a lycan," I hissed through my teeth, punching the button to get off and hoping, from somewhere far away, that the stop was right.

Deirdre.

"Don't keep me waiting for too fucking long because you are *not* irreplaceable."

My phone rang. I held it away from my head.

He'd hung up.

The arsehole had hung up.

I saw red. And I saw the name of the incoming caller.

"What?" I snarled at Taig. "How did you get this number? This is my personal phone."

He cleared his throat. "Hi, Rory. Got a warning about Dierdre. Amor is potentially making contact in the next thirty minutes. Retrievals has been—"

"I know." And the words burned my lips. I jumped out of the tram as soon as the doors let me, strode to the connection. "I'm fucking on it, okay? Unless you want to wrap me in cotton wool and tell me the big boys will deal with it?"

"Same team here, Caretaker," he said, the words neutral. "I need you on site. We've got a police team, but they're going to take a bit of time, and they sure as hell aren't Retrievals. Unless you don't want to play with the big boys today?"

Blood drummed in my temples. I could've ripped the fucking tram stop apart right then. "Fuck, Taig, I'll do better than you big boys in *heels*," I spat, watching the slowarse fucking tram rumble to a halt in front of me, the doors slowly open. "Get the notepad ready. I'll show you how witches get shit done."

CHAPTER 12

THE FIRST THING I DID WAS DROP THE CHARMS I'D SET. I DIDN'T NEED another headache and I didn't have a charm to soak some backlash this time.

Something else for the to-do list. Haircut, new charm, washing, rip Beo's throat out. I was going to have a busy week.

Deirdre's door was whole when I got there. Fury drummed in my head, heart, and lungs.

In my *bones.*

Maybe it showed, too, because her eyes went huge when she opened the door. "Get in," I said, flatly. "And hide."

Amor wasn't the only hunter in these woods.

She wouldn't follow the same pattern. But she was thorough and smart.

Deirdre went for the classic option of the shower. "Can—can you see me?" she whispered.

I looked at her from my position by the bathroom door. Her silhouette was clearly visible through the shower curtain. The window above was too small, too cloudy, for it to be a potential point of entry, but it was most definitely enough to illuminate a silhouette.

"No," I lied. "Stay there. I'm going to get into position in this room.

When you hear us clash, call Taig. Put it on silent, then on speaker. He'll hear what's going on."

Her indrawn breath was loud in the quiet. "I…I don't have his number."

I walked across the small bathroom, flipped my phone to silent, brought him up, and passed it over. "Here."

She looked up at me, eyes huge in her pale face. "Where are…the police, or…"

"Coming." There were no hiding spots, but enough makeshift weapons. "Repeat what you need to do."

"Call Taig. Make sure it's silent. Turn it onto speaker."

I nodded. "And if I fail?"

Her eyes filled and overflowed. "I—I can't—I don't do curses, or…"

I waited until the maybes and the what-ifs had run their course and she was focused on me. "You survive," I told her, quietly. "You do *anything* to survive. If that means going quietly, you go quietly. If it means doing what she wants, you do what she wants."

Her tears rolled. My stomach didn't.

"Okay," she whispered. "Please, Rory, she's dangerous. We could run—"

"You don't run from predators." And that was all there was to it.

You could avoid, sidestep, or retreat, but as soon as you bolted, you were gone.

I put my wand between my teeth, turning to the bathroom wall and checking out the ceiling. Shit was going to be expensive to fix.

Then I kicked some footholds into the drywall and started climbing.

If I had my battle charms, if I'd known what I was up against so I could choose the right collection *before* it got to this point, I wouldn't have had to anchor myself with a ward. I'd have had more options.

But I had nothing except my wand, the spells in my head, my standard charms, and an entire *ocean* of rage.

Dierdre's sobs were half-muffled. On the ceiling like a spider with my wand in my teeth I was very, very grateful I'd tied back my hair. It was annoying like this. It could've been deadly if it was out.

My hoodie was probably going to buy it. Alas, poor hoodie, I knew you well.

I should've called Lilith.

The thought occurred to me as I listened to my heartbeat, to Dierdre's sobs, to the rise and fall of the city around us. And hadn't I been about to, except fucking arrogant, spineless arsehole Beo?

Really, if I ended up dead, they should send *him* the bill for the extensive plastering they were going to need after this.

From my position, I inspected the gaping holes in the off-white plaster. It'd be hidden by the angle of the door opening, at least until she did a room check. If she even bothered, with Dierdre so clearly outlined.

Not many people looked up, though.

Glass shattered and my heartbeat tripled. Through the curtain I watched Deirdre fumbling with the phone. There was a blast of noise before the quick beeps that signaled she was turning down the volume.

Wrong order. But that wouldn't matter.

The door exploded open. Booted foot, lupetec leggings, bare hands, jacketed arms. I had to assume she had the full sleeve armored shirt, though.

Fuck. Weak points were face and hands, maybe throat, maybe toes. Ears, eyes, seams.

Blonde head. Bow in her quiver. Knife at her hip. Wand in hand. "Come on, Clara," she said, impatiently. "Tobias has been waiting *months* and you know he can't—"

I drew in a breath and ended my ward. Gravity was a fucking *bitch.*

Just like me.

I hit her shoulders and drove her to the ground, struggling for grips. Her jacket slipped. I was thrown into the mirror. The shattering of glass came from far away as my head whirled. I went low. *Take out her knees. No—no, armored.* She crashed into the toilet but the angle was wrong to do damage to her. Roaring filled my head. Her fist met my face and I barely felt it except as a change in balance, a dull, background annoyance. I went for her eyes but she ducked, and I drove my fist through the cursed plaster.

The flash of steel caught my attention. *Knife.*

I drove my knee up in reflex. *Protect the midsection.* The bite of the blade, the burn in my leg, didn't slow me.

Spells clamored in my head. *Not yet. Not yet.* I could only have one active. *And she—I need to time it so—*

We ended up on the ground. I caught her in a triangle choke between my thighs. *Pressure.* Her pretty blonde hair was chaos. Her eyes were a beautiful cornflower blue.

Then they flickered—brown eyes, brown hair—before she went back to being an Aryan poster girl

Illusion.

Her knife was lifted in a panicked move. *Rookie mistake.*

I squeezed harder and it came down on me, biting deep. *My. Fucking. Thigh.*

The soundtrack of Dierdre's sobs warped like some sort of DJ trick. Whacka-whacka-whaaaow.

The muscles in my legs wouldn't hold. I grabbed her hand on the knife, driving my fingers into the sensitive webbing between hers. She hissed like a cat but didn't let go. Bitch tried to yank out the knife.

Fuck, no. I need that blood inside me.

Her thumb in my hand bent and broke. The sound of splintering bone. *Sunlight, warm, on my face.*

A grunt of pain reached my ears after I'd registered her letting go. I fell away. Tiles. Bathmat. And shards of mirror.

Gotcha.

The spell ignited in my head. *Yeah, bitch, let's dance.* A harmless spell, but a great distraction. *Homefires, answer my call. Homefires, don't let me fall.*

Fire sprang up around us, crawling up her body, clawing at her face. Homefires were harmless. And yet—there was *smoke?*

I grabbed a shard while she counter-spelled but didn't hear her speak the words.

Fucking. Retrievals. Trained. Bitch.

Her laughter was low and hard. "Parlor tricks?" she asked me, waving away the last of the smoke as she approached.

Fury pounded in my temples. I had to get close. Slashing her wrists wouldn't take her out quickly enough. I had to go for the throat or the eyes. "Look, I've had a bad day," I said, my voice sounding like it came from a lousy speaker phone. "Cut me some slack, okay?"

"Yeah, you look like shit." She lifted her wand.

Anger rolled through me. She wasn't going to get into arm's reach again.

I couldn't ward. I'd kill Dierdre. Hatred flashed through me at the limitations of my very *circular* ward.

I aimed at her feet, encased in steel capped boots.

Burn, witch, burn.

She stopped to defend. The reek of burning leather, plastic—rubber? —Whatthefuckever—clogged my throat but I couldn't breathe anyway. I hip-escaped and took out her knee. She wouldn't be hurt, but I didn't need it to hurt. Just to knock her—

Into the hallway. She hit the wall. A generic picture of generic flowers in a generic vase smashed beside us. I was on her, heart roaring in my head, every cell focused on her. The glass cut into my hand. I lunged and she fucking *dodged.* I drove my knee into her face. *No armor on* that, *bitch.*

The door exploded. "Police!"

About fucking time. I drove my knee into her face again just for luck, then staggered off her.

She raised her hands. "I surrender!" she said as they flooded the room like blood into water. Her boots were still smoldering. "I surrender!"

"Put your wand on the ground," Taig was demanding down the muzzle of his gun.

As if he'd fire in these quarters.

She spat blood and sent me a disgusted look. She was moving onto her knees and tossing her wand in front of her.

If my leg hadn't suddenly reminded me it had a giant fuck-off knife in it, I would've kicked her wand away. Instead, I just climbed to my feet. On a scale of one to dead, that hadn't gone so bad, now, had it? I didn't need to be looked after. Taig was talking—cautioning, arresting. And her gaze cut to me. She was smirking. Her eyes were milky.

My heart.

Froze.

Angel.

"Angel!" I screamed, levelling my wand, casting. *Breathe not through this ward.* It bounced. The air around her shimmered.

No magick would work on her, now.

They don't know. They don't know—

I had to.

She was smiling on her knees. Her face was tipped up and her lids dipped to half-mast over eyes that were going white. Her lips moved.

I pulled the knife from my thigh. Launching across the tiny distance, I hit her hard. She fought but I fought smarter and took her back. The reek of roses filled my nose. *Fuck. Fuck. Fuck.* From this angle, all I could access was her throat.

The knife cut through her like butter in a heatwave. Blood pumped, *sprayed over the leaflitter and rock*, and she kept struggling.

"Rory!" The shouts were just reverberations in my skull. Blood spurted against the wall in time with her heartbeat was the beat holding the rhythm. *The fine mist that settled over the rocks, drying quickly in the afternoon sun.* "Drop the weapon!"

I tossed the knife at some faceless cop but kept my hand in the woman's hair as it went from blonde to brown, waiting for her to bleed out. It seemed right...and safer.

"Hands behind your head!" someone was bellowing at me.

They weren't going to fucking shoot me. I glared daggers but dropped Amor's hair. There was a dull thunk on the cheap linoleum floor. Good thing lino was easy to clean. *The roar of helicopter blades sending leaves swirling.* "Put your hands behind your head," Clint said, his gun pointed right at my face.

My face?

I did, feeling the adrenaline start to ebb. Considering I'd got a slow start, today had been a pisser already. I struggled to breathe evenly. Clint approached me with handcuffs at the ready. I let him settle the fucking things on without complaint. If it was serious, they'd gag me. "Don't come out yet, Deirdre," I shouted. "Taig will come get you."

I could feel her sobs, even though I couldn't hear them over the rights I was being read. I was being taken for questioning. *Unlawful killing.*

Clint sounded pretty smug about it. There was your gratitude.

Taig came over but was pushed aside. "Conflict of interest, Detective," Clint said, the words flat. "You understand."

Conflict of interest?

My heart sank. I'd given Dierdre his personal number.

Well, shit. With my hands behind my back and my wand in Clint's hand, I limped out of the tiny apartment past the swarm of cops. Where the fuck had they been twenty minutes ago? And now I was going to have the book thrown at me.

At least there were no angels. I ordered witch, not wings.

The interview room was not comfortable, but the hospital had been worse.

Wheels turned slowly. I rested my head on my handcuffed arms and tried to nap, or at least gather some energy. I'd only done what I'd needed to do. They would've been singing a different tune if they'd had a witch possessed by an angel to deal with. Assuming they ever sang again.

While my body lay heavily on the chair, pain drugs pumping through my system and my leg still managing, somehow, to hurt, I turned it over in my mind.

The angel involved explained a lot of the questions—how they'd got the recipe for rift juice, the extra power behind the witch, their brazen disregard for morality. Which angel was it, though?

All I knew was it smelled like roses.

I had to get hold of my Oma. Nic. I had to ask questions, find answers.

Would Dierdre's shitstain ex back off, now Amor was toast? Who the hells *was* she? Ex Retrievals? A dropout from the course? Or just accessed some of the training, somehow, got the gear from someone else? From an ally Overworld they did favors for? Curiosity killed the cat, but satisfaction brought it back.

Beo.

I hoped Dierdre had got out without seeing too much of the gore. I hoped she was being looked after. The one good thing about Taig being barred from me was that it meant he'd have her in hand, and I trusted him to do a half decent job of that.

Maybe I dozed. The door opened and Clint came in with a uniform beside him. Groggily, I watched as he sat opposite me at the table. "Hello, Caretaker. This is Sergeant Greene."

"Hello, Detective, Sergeant." I kept it civil and patted myself on the back for it.

"We have multiple officers who witnessed you killing an as yet unidentified witch who had given herself into our custody. I will remind you that your job does not permit lethal force. Again. For the second time this week." He flipped through some notes, found a page, and pretended to read the information as if he didn't know what had happened.

"Ask your witnesses if they smelled roses," I said, tiredly. I didn't want to do this dance.

"Roses."

"Roses," I repeated, flatly.

His brows rose. "Anything else, Caretaker?"

"Yeah," I agreed, feeling the first bubbles of rage and trying to pop them. "Her eyes were going white."

He took a few notes. "And the significance?"

"She was calling an angel."

He paused, looked up at me. "An…angel."

"Yeah. You know. Opposite of demon." Honestly, did they hand out supernatural detective badges as a gimmick in breakfast cereal?

"Angels are positive beings," he said, calmly. "And mythical ones. They're protective."

Maybe drive through kids meals? Tiny burger, fries, juice box, detective license. "Angels are as real as demons. They're two sides of the same coin. They want different things from us, use different methods, but at the end of the day we're the juicy steak for both."

He took some more notes. "Juicy steak."

Elders, my kingdom for Taig. "I'm not an expert in the academic stuff," I said, with a shrug that reminded me I'd blocked her fist with my face. It wouldn't be my first black eye. "I know their strategies, warning signs, and how to deal with them." Not that we really could. But we could hold the line, force them back. That was about the best you could hope for. "You want a dissertation, call a professor. There's plenty around." *Maybe, like, three. In the world.*

"So." He looked up at me. "You killed the victim—"

"Hold up. Victim is Dierdre."

His eyes narrowed fractionally. "You killed the witch in question because she smelled of roses and you thought you saw her eyes go white."

She'd also negated a spell, but I didn't think I could prove that. And anyway, fuck this specific man. "Yes. Mid-summoning ritual."

More notetaking. "Talk me through a summoning ritual."

"Can't," I said, with a shrug. "Never done it. I just know it's generally done on the knees. You need a bit of time for it. I assume it's a long spell."

"Spell?" he asked, barely making any notes. "She didn't have her wand. Nor did she speak."

Who said *nor?* Really? "No wand, but casting spells?" I barely resisted making an exaggeratedly shocked face. "Sounds like possession to me. You don't need a wand for that, just to have sold your soul. Or whatever it is angels ask for, I don't honestly know. Again, not my thing." I saw Greene beside Clint glance down and carefully arrange his face to ensure he didn't smile. *Cool, a fan.* "As for her speaking—she was Retrievals trained. She was also in lupetec. You wouldn't hear her casting."

"Anything else?" Clint asked, loftily, clicking his pen in finality.

"Yeah." I sat back, my arm aching from where I was forced to hold it with the cuffs. "Can I get a cup of coffee? Black, no sugar."

They came in a few more times with questions. Each time they'd obviously gone and looked into things I'd said. The possibility of being charged with murder grew further away, but my coffee didn't get any closer. I had no idea what time it was when the door opened and Arthur walked in, steaming cup in his hand.

The man looked like he'd crawled out of a six-month bender arse first.

"Are you okay?" I asked him, as he set the coffee in front of me. And then, hard on the heels of my concern came the memory. *The potion*. Fuck, I hadn't even checked in on him. Hadn't even *thought* about him.

There was a flicker of surprise on his face. "Yeah, I'm fine." He sat beside me. "They're finalizing the paperwork now."

"For?"

"Your release." He nudged the coffee a bit closer. "You almost got done for murder."

"Some thanks," I muttered, taking the coffee. It was the perfect temperature. I had to wonder if Taig was behind it, or Arthur. "They called you in, hey?"

"I'm your supervisor."

Right then, he looked like he needed to supervise eight straight, a shower and a shave. "Weird, without a District High Wizard, isn't it?" I asked, realizing the ramifications of the lack of hand on the wheel. So many little things would be falling between the cracks. "Who contacted you?"

He sent me an unreadable glance, then shrugged. *Ah. Secrets.* Which meant Taig had—off the books.

He stretched out his legs and lifted a hand gingerly to his shoulder. So, now he felt it. I eyeballed his wound. If there was a bandage there it was far neater. "Can I do anything to help?"

That flicker of surprise again. "No." Then, "But…thank you."

I shrugged. "It's what covens do. Watch out, you'll have a freezer full of casseroles in no time." The coffee was wonderful. I poured it into my body, glad of the warmth.

It didn't fill the hollow, though.

"So."

He lifted his eyes to mine, waiting for me to continue.

"What time is it and what's the plan?"

He opened his mouth to answer and then went silent as the door opened. A very neutral looking Clint walked in, keys in hand. "Caretaker Aurora, you're being released from custody while we investigate the murder of Lucinda McFarlane."

I zoned out the rest. *Lucinda McFarlane.* It rang zero bells for me, but it was nice to know she had been a real person.

"I'm going to see what I can do to get you back to work," Arthur told me, tiredly, as I was escorted out with two uniforms who were taking me back to my place. They needed my clothes for evidence. I sure had plenty of that on me.

"What do you mean?" I asked, pausing outside the door. It was dark. My body clock said it was midday. *Fucking body clocks, what do they know.*

"During an investigation, Caretakers are placed on administrative leave," he said, his voice a monotone. "But we need you on board. Had sightings of vampires last night where they aren't permitted."

Of course. Without Beo—

"Sure. Well. You have my number." I paused, glancing at him. "You do have my number. Right? My personal one."

"Why would you give me your personal number, Rory?" He looked shrunken with defeat.

I held my hand out. At his blank, apathetic look I said, "Give me your phone, King, so I can save my number."

I added myself to his contacts and sent myself a message, then enjoyed the trip back with the uniforms in a thick, awkward silence.

Bernie arrived about ten minutes after I'd seen the back of them. "Well, look at you." She clicked her tongue, walked past me into my home, peering around. "Enjoying the bachelor life?" She set down a massive bag on my table and pointed at the couch.

"Yeah," I said, through numb lips as I took the seat she'd indicated.

"'Atta girl," she said, with a big wink. "Get some boys to keep your wine cupboard and downstairs entertaining area full." Another wink.

Downstairs entertaining area? I looked at her blankly as she started healing magicks. *Was that a euphemism?* It had to be. This was Bernie.

The familiar fog of magickal healing rolled over me. I sank into it, grateful for the reprieve from the rage. She let herself out. I stayed right where I was on the couch and slept.

When I woke, I was cold and alone.

No notifications. No messages.

Empty.

I rolled over, curled up, and slept again.

CHAPTER 14

Lilith stood in my doorway with a bottle of gin, a bucket of salted caramel ice-cream and a giant serving of chips.

"Hello?" I said, confused. "Did I miss your call?"

"I come bearing bad news."

I looked pointedly at the food again. "And the antidotes."

"That's the goal," she said, grimly.

I stepped back and snagged the chips from her, dumping the wrapped bundle on the coffee table and flipping it with the ease of long practice. "Okay," I said, spreading the paper. They were hot enough and I was hungry. "Hit me."

She fell onto the couch opposite me, regarding me over the pile of salt encrusted carbs. Her face was set in lines of worry. "So, I've picked up a few of your clients while you're on administrative leave."

I paused, feeling sick. "And?"

She exhaled slowly. "And Beo's pack, including him, have transferred. New South Wales."

My belly twisted. I grabbed a chip at random. "Oh. Is that all? Shit, you had me worried." I threw the chip into my mouth. A sharp edge, fried to perfection, stabbed my tongue. I just grabbed another. Salt that wound. Burn out any chance of infection.

Lilith sat there, still. "Rory...Beo's gone."

"Yeah, I heard you." It was real. "Fuck him. Any other updates? Did you pick up Celia?" My siren was a constant pain in my arse.

She sat there for a moment and watched me eating. "You told me a week ago you were more than halfway in love with him."

The knife went home. I barely felt it, but I knew it was there. That familiar burn. Not pulling that out until...later. Future me problem.

"Is this like an emotional version of 'it's just a flesh wound'?" And she was still watching me like I was going to collapse any minute.

I shrugged again. "There's plenty of fish." Maybe he'd end up swimming with them.

The thought sent pain searing through my chest. I glanced down at the golden fried deliciousness.

They tasted like dust.

She reached out warily and took a chip. She nursed hers as I ate mechanically. "Any news on Dierdre?" I asked.

"She's home. Shaken, not stirred, thanks to you." I ignored the accusation in there. Yeah, I'd been going to call her. Before the rage kicked in. He was wrong. I wasn't a liability.

"Vamps?" I asked her, considering whether drinking gin on ice was a good option. Shit, it wasn't like I had to work tomorrow. I didn't even know what fucking day it was.

"Yeah." She nibbled on the chip that was probably cold by now. "They took out one of Janet's families, looks like."

I sat up, energy humming. "What? When? How? What family—not the ones from Germany?"

"No. A group from up north. Queensland, I think." I wracked my brains trying to remember Janet's caseload. "They aren't mentioned much in meetings. They don't cause trouble, keep a low profile." She took a bigger bite of the chip. "They're relatives of the Victorian Minister of Magi."

My stomach sank. "Oh. Fuck."

"Yeah." She let out a long sigh. "Great time for you to be out. Tell you what, I don't like it. Too many whispers, Roars."

"We got protection on some key folks?" I asked her, my mind spin-

ning. If this was really happening, if they were *actually* going for it…
"Anti-charisma potions, at least?"

"Like who?" she asked me, her mouth twisted in disgust. "They get a family member. Family member calls in important person. Trusted location, easy company, and bam. We'll get a system as cooked as—as our legal government."

When she put it like that, it was a lot less alarming. "I guess vamps suck our life forces, not our souls," I mused, and stuffed another chip in my mouth. "That's something."

"Honestly, six of one, half a dozen the other." She shrugged, but she looked jaded. "I want ice-cream. This is depressing as shit."

I opened my mouth to respond and my phone squalled, jarring me. I glanced over.

Arthur.

What the fuck was Arthur calling for?

I reached over, seeing Lilith's eyes go wide with shock. With a quick eye roll that I hoped said *long story*, I answered with, "Hey."

"Aurora. It's Arthur."

Something about his tone, about the way he said my name, had my total attention. "What's happened?"

"Nothing. I think." He cleared his throat. "I may have…I may have just spoken with a vampire. I'm not… sure."

I looked around for shoes. "Are you okay?"

"Yes. Yes, I'm totally fine, but I don't, uh." He cleared his throat again. "There aren't any procedures to follow for instances when a suspicious person who may or may not be a supernatural knocks on your door and tries to get an invite. I thought…well, *you* know a lot about this stuff, and…"

And he was lost.

My heart ached a tiny bit. "Stay inside. Do not open any windows or doors. Get a wooden spoon."

"Rory, it…I don't think I…"

"Humor me, King," I said, grimly, going into my bedroom and hunting for a bra. "Once you've got a wooden spoon in hand, text me your address, then get a coffee brewing for me. I'll be right there. We'll go over it together and figure out next steps."

He blew out a breath. "Yeah. Sure. Black, right?"

"First, wooden spoon."

"Yeah. Got it already. See you soon."

Lilith stood in the doorway while I pulled my hair back, threw on a bra and jumper. "No wonder you get into trouble all the fucking time," she sighed, as I stomped into my runners. My boots were evidence, curse it.

"I do *not* get into trouble." And the bite in my words took me aback. I shook my head. "Sorry. This is weird. Why *Arthur?*"

"He's one of five wizards who currently run the only organized Magi defense this city has," she said, grimly. "Until there's a new District High Douche Canoe, they all vote."

I snorted. We were about as organized as a herd of cats. "Defense?" I asked, disbelieving. "What, Cici going to stitch them up?"

Lilith didn't smile. "She stitched up Edward Van Der Holst pretty well."

Shit. I deserved that. "You're right," I admitted, even though it didn't feel great. I grabbed my third favorite hoodie and remembered the other was at Beo's. *Gone.*

"So, cut it with the lone witch act," she said, grabbing up the chips and thrusting them at me. "It's bullshit. I'm driving, so get Maps going. I do not want that loser's address in my recents."

I took the chips and followed her out onto the street, trying to be gracious about it. There was no 'lone witch' act happening. Was there? And, fuck, I *was* a lone witch.

It started raining as we climbed in. I continued to eat, because the food was there, while my maps told Lilith where to go. It was politer than I could've been.

Arthur's address was a fancy apartment in a fancy apartment building. Sleek glass done in modern lines, lots of chrome. The elevator stank like ego and uppers. He opened the door as soon as I knocked, wooden spoon in one hand, coffee in another. Aside from a lack of tie, he was the same defeated bloke I'd seen earlier. Or yesterday. Or whenever.

He looked awkwardly between Lilith and I. "Hope I'm not a third wheel," she said, in a tone that said she wasn't actually sorry, and shut the door after us with finality. "Three's a good number. Right, Arthur?"

"Uh. Sure. I can—how do you take your coffee, Lilith?"

I skimmed my eyes around the place. Fastidiously organized, modern and soulless. Pretty much what I expected. "Vampire," I said, cutting through the bullshit. "White with one while you talk."

He paused, passed me my coffee with another quick glance at Lilith, waved us through to the kitchen. An ocean of gleaming counters, top-end appliances, and empty space. His spice rack, if he had one, would be alphabetized, I was sure of it. "It's probably nothing," he said, in a strangely un-Arthur, apologetic way that I'd never seen pre-shooting.

"Cool." I slid onto stainless steel, minimalist, and uncomfortable stool. I wasn't planning on getting comfy. "Tell us anyway."

"I, uh." He went to a coffee machine. "Didn't mean to… interrupt."

"Vampires," I reminded him, my head starting to ache. I probably needed water. I drank coffee instead.

"Yeah. Well." He shrugged. The machine whirred. "I just got home. Had a late video conference. She just," he shrugged again, went to the fridge. "Knocked on the door. Full fat okay, Lilith?"

"Do you have skim?" she asked, lazily.

"I…have full fat."

"Then that's fine." And she shot me a look to share in the irony of the conversation. I don't know how convincing my return smile was, but, fuck. "So. Woman knocks on your door."

"She kept…staring at me. Leaning forward. Touching my chest." He didn't look at us as he poured the milk into a frother. He was shifting a restlessly, almost rocking on his feet. I wasn't used to wanting to grab the guy and hug him, and I didn't like the feeling. "Her eyes were strange."

"How?" Lilith asked.

But I knew.

I knew how they became deep, dark, and promising. I knew the effervescent euphoria that almost oozed out of them, and the way their victims moaned for more. I knew the husks they left behind.

"Were you followed from the meeting?" I asked him, cutting in over Arthur's faltering description of an awkward attempt to charm him. "Are you wearing a charisma-proof charm?"

"I don't think so." He looked worn as he carried the coffee over to Lilith. "And no."

"Anti-charisma potion?" I dug out my phone. "Wood?"

"No."

I had no idea why the fuck he wasn't vamp food, but why wasn't important right now. What mattered was that he hadn't let her in, and she hadn't been able to weasel her way around. "You are the luckiest wizard alive," I muttered, standing and pacing away as I lifted my phone to my ear. I listened to it ring.

"This is Taig," the recorded message said in that voice that should've been bottled and sold as an aphrodisiac. "Leave a message."

I hung up. *Fuck messages.* Instead, I called the station. "East Melbourne Metro police," the voice on the other end said. "You're speaking with Sergeant Greene. Can I help?"

"Hi, Sergeant," I said, instantly forgetting his name. "My name is Aurora Gold. I'm a Caretaker in—"

"Hi. Rory, right?" he sounded far more friendly. "Taig isn't in right now."

I had no idea what the fuck they all thought I had going on with Taig and I didn't really care. "Yeah, okay, fine, but I need a Supernatural Detective, or at least someone in the know."

"If this is an emergency—"

"If it was an emergency, I'd've called the emergency line," I cut in, feeling my patience fraying. "Look, mate, I've got vampire problems, okay? It isn't urgent in the next five minutes, but I need to talk to someone tonight."

"Vampire?" he said, briskly. "Give me your address. I'll see if I can get hold of Taig or Clint, but someone will be around this evening."

I opened my mouth to request anyone *except* Clint, including the more qualified cockroaches they had in their staffroom, but closed it. *Fuck it. What do I care?*

Of course then I had to explain what I knew to Arthur and Lilith, and then sit with them in the awkward silence once we'd all run out of things to say. "Hey, Lilith." She looked at me like I was a teenager one step away from having my phone confiscated. I had no idea why. "You got your work phone on you?" I knew she did. She'd come from work. "If you do, might be worth giving Dierdre a buzz. See if the potion she made Arthur might have any crossover with the charisma protection one."

"Charisma protection is a small window," Lilith said, but she dug out her phone. "An hour, tops. Any stronger and the side effects are wicked."

Yeah. Like serious mood changes.

She stood and wandered off. Arthur rested against the bench nearby looking like shit reheated—too briefly. "You eaten?" I asked him.

"Not yet." He went over to the coffee machine. "Another? I'm having one."

"Yeah." I assessed him impersonally. He'd lost weight. Or condition. I had no idea what sort of maintenance that body needed. Seemed like a whole lot to me. Unless you were a lycan, that is, and then it was just a few more acai berries and kale in your smoothie.

I stood and pushed that away. Down. Out. Instead I went to his fridge and peered inside. Ignoring his awkward side-step as I rummaged, I took quick catalogue of the contents. Broccoli, cauliflower, spinach here, too, for fucks' sake. Cottage cheese, feta cheese, a million more types of cheese, meat. Lettuce, two—no, *three* kinds. "Do you not have carbs?"

"I'm keto."

All I knew about keto was that it didn't work if you liked potato. "Is there anything here that isn't okay?" I asked, eyeballing it.

"For what?"

I shot him a look from under my lashes as I peered through his fridge. "I'm going to cook, because you look like shit and I'm bored. Can I use anything?"

"Oh, I have meals planned."

I could tell. It was eight-thirty and he hadn't moved on it. "Sure. What's tonight?"

"Steak and steamed vegetables," he said, after a brief pause.

That actually didn't sound so bad. But I didn't feel like making steak or steaming veg, and he looked like he needed some help. "I'm thinking broccoli soup."

He looked at me like I'd just declared the sun was coming up in the north.

"Look, if you don't hate broccoli, you won't hate broccoli soup," I promised, taking out the bacon and going to his pantry. The garlic was under 'g'. *Of course.* "I thought I would," I went on, to fill the silence as I went to work. "Hate it, I mean. When I was, I don't know, early primary school, my dad had a go at a veggie garden." The sizzle of bacon was soothing. I poked it with a spare wooden spoon and enjoyed the rhythm. "We had so much broccoli that we couldn't give it away. I know a lot of broccoli recipes. And this one is actually not half bad."

"I can't see your dad miscalculating so badly," Lilith mused, sliding back onto a stool. "He's a planner, isn't he?"

I snorted. "My dad's less organized than *me*. He just knows how to talk shit better so no one knows." I started massacring an onion. "It's a skill I hope to continue to develop."

"Your shit talk is pretty good." And Lilith was grinning at me. "I can't believe you're seriously making broccoli soup. Or that you know how to make something not involving potato."

"You can put potato in it," I offered, brightly. "Thickens it. King here doesn't believe in spuds."

Arthur just sat tiredly at the bench, staring into the dregs of his coffee.

Lilith shifted, shooting me a quick searching glance. "So, Dierdre has a theory." I glanced up from the broccoli I was rinsing. "Vamp's charisma works on sending hormones haywire. That's why it's easier to protect against than faerie's direct coercion. She, ah." She glanced down at her hands. "Mentioned that the anti-love potion Arthur took probably has sent him into a chemically induced depression deep enough to give him a level of protection."

"Well." I chopped the end off the broccoli. "That's the best news for depressed folks that I've heard in a while."

Arthur glanced up at me, a bit of a smile tugging at his mouth. "How long do I have this superpower?"

"Dierdre wasn't sure," Lilith said, with a shrug. "Safest to assume you don't, rather than rely on it and end up dazzled."

Silence descended again and I couldn't help but wonder whether I should be waving farewell to Lilith. She didn't need to babysit Arthur. I probably didn't, either, but I had nothing better to do.

No one waiting.

While the bacon, onions and garlic browned I dug out my phone, sent my childhood best friend, Aspen, a quick message to see when she was free this week. I wasn't sitting around feeling sorry for myself. Fuck that. I had nothing to be sorry for.

His loss. His cowardice. Not mine.

Time crawled. Arthur eyed the soup I'd prepared for him warily. "Shut up and try it," I said, plonking a spoon in it. "If you don't like it, I'll take it home and you can have dessert steak."

Lilith took her token bowl, just to say she'd had broccoli soup, and sampled it delicately. "Huh," she said, brows raised. "Okay. I'll give it to you, Roars, that's actually edible."

"You're welcome. And you may as well go after you're done, because I've got no idea how long Melbourne's finest will take to rock up."

She arched a brow at me while Arthur wasn't looking, arching her brow in his direction. I pulled a face. No, I wasn't trying to make a move. But really, two of us was overkill considering the danger was probably past. "Know anyone in the other covens?" I asked her, as she spooned up the soup. "Might be interesting to see if any other Arthurs got a late-night caller."

"Already on my to-do list tomorrow morning," she told me, with a nod. "Also, we need to figure out how his address was leaked." She scooped up the last of the soup. "Did we ever figure out who sent those faeries after you?"

The memory of the faerie on the roof of the building when the lycans attacked went through me like lightning. "No," I said, glancing over at Arthur. "But remind me to talk to you about that. Later."

She shot me a quick, unreadable glance. "Sure. Well, I guess I'll bounce, then. Tomorrow, Roars?"

"Yeah. Maybe. I owe you ice cream." Arthur stood, walked her to the door while I started on the dishes. "I'll call you," I shouted after her. "Arthur, where are your containers?"

He got the leftovers organized while I cleaned up after myself. The clock said nine fifteen.

It was about to get super awkward.

Before that happened, though, there was a knock at the door. The relief that I felt was probably disproportionate to the situation, but I didn't let that stop me.

Arthur went to the door, wooden spoon in hand. And when I heard the low, sexy tones of my most trusted detective, another wave of relief went through me. Whatever the fuck was going on, he'd help manage it.

I lingered in the background while Arthur talked them through what he'd told us. He sounded more confident now. I suppose valida-tion was a thing.

Taig was giving the standard 'we'll do what we can' spiel at the end when Clint glanced at me and murmured something in Arthur's ear.

"She's here because she knows supernaturals, especially violent ones," Arthur said, in his haughtiest private school boy tones. "And because I called her. She buys her own diamonds, Detective. She doesn't need or want my money."

Taig glanced up from his notepad, his eyes narrowed. I swirled my coffee in the cup, rage rolling delightfully through my belly. "Says a lot about you, though, Clint," I offered sweetly. "Covens stick together."

He shot me a look of disbelief. "You're a nice guy, Arthur," he said. "And women don't like nice guys."

Taig's mouth opened and I was content to just sit back and take shots at each other, but Arthur got in first. "I've recently learned they do, actually, and if they don't like you, it's because you're not as nice as you think you are." He stood. "Thank you for your time, detectives. I look forward to hearing from you."

Well, shit. I swallowed the last of the coffee, and was trying to get my head around Arthur having had a major personality alteration when Taig passed me a folded bit of paper. "For the bin," he said, with a nod. "Evening, Caretakers."

I had no fucking idea where the bin was. Probably filed under 'b'. Listening with half an ear to Arthur chasing them out, I flipped open the torn piece of paper.

Breakfast. Same time, same place.

I scrunched it up, but my brain was whirring. Last time he'd asked me to breakfast, we'd broken some rules, exchanged information we shouldn't have. I was down for that. As for the secrecy, well, I'd find out more later.

Arthur came in, standing awkwardly behind the bench. "I hope that was okay. I know you can put him in his place, but I figured you shouldn't always have to. But. I don't really know." He shifted awkwardly and I felt kind of bad for him. "It was sort of directed at me, too. So."

"I thought it was bloody perfect," I admitted, amused. But he didn't smile at me, just stood there looking exhausted and sad. "That wasn't something you and I chatted about."

"No." He rubbed his jaw. His eyes skimmed away, across the couch and over the cityscape laid out behind the big, sparkly windows. "I contacted some of my exes. Asked for some honest feedback."

Oh, fuck. "You're a brave man."

"I was a driven one," he said, with a shrug. "I guess the potion did that."

No wonder he sounded so defeated. Shit, if he'd actually received honest feedback after the potion had been lifted, when he'd been at a dramatic low...

"No," I said, slowly. "I think that's brave, Arthur. Looking at yourself, actually looking, is hard." And fuck doing that. Seemed like it'd hurt a lot. "I respect that."

His smile was small and bitter. "Yeah. Well. I've got a lot to sort through still."

I glanced at the clock again. "Want to talk any of it over? I don't want to keep you up."

"Can't sleep." He shrugged. "Sorry, I shouldn't have—you don't have to."

"Well, I slept all day." And didn't want to be stuck with my thoughts all night. I went to the coffee machine. "How do I use this thing? I'll be a sounding board for half an hour or so for the price of another cuppa."

He came over. I let him have at it, since he was obviously territorial, and went to flop on the buttery soft couch. He set it in front of me, took a seat on the other side of the U and turned his own cup around in his hands. "I don't know where to start."

"Whatever keeps popping into your brain," I offered. "Or you can throw me your phone, I can read it. But I figure neither of us needs that."

He shook his head, let out a breath. "Okay. Why do women fake it?"

I blinked. "Fake what?"

A quick, unreadable glance. "Orgasms."

"Oh." I sat back and ignored my feelings, the memories that wanted to ambush me. *Beo.* "Lots of reasons. Most of them track back to the fact that guys don't take direction well—either in a situation that's actually abusive, or just fragile ego bullshit." I paused, waiting for him to jump in with some *but I listen* sort of response. He didn't. He just sat, looking confused. "Look. I don't know a single woman who hasn't been coerced, guilted, or pressured into sex at some point. It's an actual thing." He nodded a little, looked back down at his coffee. "Whether it happens with you or not, we all have baggage. Different levels of severity, sure, but all there, all valid. And," I sipped my coffee, shrugged. "It's done with faster if you fake it."

The words sat between us heavily until he let out a long breath. "How do I get around that? How do I…" he waved a hand.

"Communicate?" I thought again of Beo. Brutally I pushed that away. *Look who's a jerk now.* "Practice, I guess. I'm no expert. Enthusiastic consent is a good starting point. It's not about waiting for a 'no', it's acting only if you are freely given a 'yes'."

His brow furrowed a little. "What, so, ask?"

"Yes. It can be incredibly sexy. Also, the way you ask is important." He looked up at me, expression unreadable. "Want me to help you take your jacket off?" I asked, absently.

"I—no, I'm fine."

I nodded, sipped. "Hey, Arthur." I leaned forward. "Can I take your jacket off?"

His expression changed, fractionally. "Um."

"See? Weirder." The coffee was vanishing way too fast. I wondered if he had anything harder.

"So you think it's about communication. Not the mechanics."

Yeah, definitely needed something harder. "Communication will pretty much solve mechanics issues. Knowing basic stuff will help. But remembering life isn't porn is pretty much critical."

He nodded, glancing at the clock, then threw back his coffee like it was the shot I'd been wishing for. "Thanks. Sincerely. I should let you go."

"Too easy." I unfolded myself. "Good coffee, an awesome couch, and no vampires. That's my idea of a great night."

He paused, halfway to the door, and turned to me. There were no dimples. No smoldering looks. But I knew. And my belly twisted.

"Do you want to stay?" he asked me. "I've got shit reviews, but you've been—helpful."

I was a fucking therapist now.

Hot on the heels of the righteous indignation came a wave of compassion that shook me. This guy had just had his autonomy absolutely smashed. Instead of getting defensive, he'd actually taken on what I'd said and was *trying* to be better.

I was pretty sure, in his shoes, I wouldn't be so gracious. And I didn't like that feeling.

He shook his head, turning away. "Sorry. I shouldn't have—I'm grateful for what you've done. The time you've given me. Can I call you a ride? So you don't have to take the tram?"

My bones ached and there was a horrible pain in my chest that I didn't want to think about.

He'd be nothing like Beo.

The hurt was huge and sticky. My limbs were lead but I stepped up into Arthur's space and hoped he couldn't hear how hard it was for me to draw air. We were eye-to-eye and he hesitated, about to step back. Before he could, I asked, "Do you know where the clit is?"

He swallowed. "Yes."

Beo had always waited for a yes.

Beo wasn't waiting for me, though.

I shook my head, trying to dislodge my thoughts. "I'll show you what to do with it." And I reached up, pulled the tie out of my hair. "You're starting from zero, so I'm going to need a fair bit of time to warm up. Just so we're on the same page."

His eyes went to my lips and I refused to think about anyone else. I was a consenting adult. So was he. Fuck the shame and grief. "I... can...should I, um. Kiss you?"

"We're not going in dry, King," I told him, wryly, reaching for his jacket.

He drew back and looked at me, his expression tortured. "You've turned my world upside down."

Yeah, I got that a lot.

CHAPTER 15

THE BACON WAS CRISPY, THE EGGS FLUFFY, AND THE SPINACH IN A frittata. But the detective was missing in action.

I sent off a few texts to Aspen while I ate, taking my time over it. I'd go out, visit her. Maybe crash at Dad's. I checked the time way too often. But I was happy. I mean, I'd be happier if I wasn't benched at work, but, fuck, paid holiday, right? Right.

I had a mouthful of eggs on toast when I saw Taig come in wearing the same bad suit he'd had on last night. The man needed some help with clothes.

He spotted me and slid in opposite. "Wasn't sure you'd get the message. Or still be here." I didn't try to respond, just chewed and waved my fork at him in a *keep going* motion. "We have serious vampire problems."

"No shit," I managed to get out.

He smiled a little. "Been following up on the other district wizards."

I paused, raised my brows.

The server chose that moment to approach. I waited while Taig ordered. He got me another coffee. He was good value. "Nothing concrete. Yet." He shook his head a little, blew out air. "I don't like this."

"So we're sharing bacon and worries?" I asked, offering him some frittata.

"I wanted to touch base with you. I've been pulled off the Amor case." He took a bit of frittata and popped it into his mouth. "Preferential treatment. I'm going to need to be incredibly neutral with you for a while."

"Yeah. Doing breakfast. So neutral." I washed down my eggs with some coffee. "Spit it out, Taig."

"Clint's doing the dirty," he said flatly. "I'm trying to work around him, but it could get ugly. He doesn't like you. I'm hoping that isn't a hill he's willing to die on."

I felt sick but I shrugged. "If he's willing to die, well, I can get that done."

He studied me critically. "Are you okay?"

"I'm great. Slept like a baby after..." kissing Arthur good night when he'd almost passed out "...I got home." And spent almost an hour in the shower. "I'm on paid leave, mate. Best kind."

He didn't look convinced. "I know you've got big things happening in the background, Rory. I'm sorry."

I raised my brows at him over the cup. The coffee was hot and bitter. I was one of those things, too. "Do I?"

He raised his brows right back at me. "Not like you to feign ignorance."

"Mm." The man had the palest blue eyes. I could've drowned in them.

I was so done with drowning.

"Velvela took off," he said, flatly, sitting back. The bottom fell out of my stomach. He didn't know. Couldn't. "I was there, at the hospital, when he visited you."

The kiss I half remembered. The fucking *coward.*

"I'm not saying what happened with Amor wasn't the right thing," he went on, in that neutral cop voice of his. "I understand what you did and I'm bloody glad you were there to do it. But you've dropped a few balls, Rory. And I'm worried."

He was worried. About poor, little, defenseless me.

The fury rolled through me. "Do I look like someone who needs protecting?" I demanded. "Get off your fucking white horse, Taig."

"You're a human," he said, the words hard as mine. "You're a kind one. You could've done a lot of things to Arthur when he was doped up. All you did was look after him. You've got a good heart. And it's hurting now."

I felt nothing, though. "This is a well-being check."

"You killed someone in the line of duty," he said, quiet now. "Your partner left. Either of those things is enough to throw someone's stride off. Together? *Big* deal."

"Cool. Want to explain any of my other feelings to me?" I asked him, brightly. "Or can I go now?"

He said nothing for a moment while the server appeared with his order. "Dierdre's ex was spotted in Port Augusta yesterday."

Port Augusta was in South Australia. South Australia was one state away. He could be here today.

"Fuck."

"We've got people looking for him." He flipped one of his hashbrowns onto my plate. "Your old team is on it."

I considered that. They hadn't caught Amor, but that's because they'd been under a time crunch. She hadn't been too far ahead or I wouldn't have gotten the warning when I had. "But?"

"But we both know who he's coming for." He looked at the food on the plate like it was an enemy. "You get a feeling about this stuff, sometimes. I know that sounds dodgy."

I knew exactly what he meant though. "And what're your dodgy feelings saying?" I asked, picking up the hashbrown because it was there.

"That this isn't good. That I want you to stick close. That I need you functional."

I narrowed my eyes at him. "Wow. Thanks, Taig."

"It could all be dodgy feelings that aren't work related," he said easily. "But I think it's both."

I wasn't doing feelings talk. Not today. Not tomorrow, either. My mind skittered to Arthur and I crushed those memories, focusing hard on the hashbrown in my hand and ignoring the twist of shame. I wasn't making anyone promises here. I couldn't. "I'm on leave. What do you want me to do?"

"Would you take a Retrievals gig if one came up?" he asked me, cutting into his toast.

"For Dierdre? In a heartbeat. I'd be there—leave, Retrievals contract or not. You know that."

"I do. And I don't want that." He shook his head. "We need you for the long haul, Rory. Vampires have moved in. We've held them back for decades." He filled his mouth, shook his head again, looking grim. "The handler for the state says you're technically licensed but not taking work."

He thought the city was about to go to shit. He was probably right. "Who knew Edward was so stabilizing," I said, wryly. And fuck my handler, Bethany.

"It's the power structure," he said, around the toast. "Not the man. It's diffused. All the districts are running around like chooks with their heads cut off. And it's going to be at least a month before they appoint a new wizard. We both know what the government is like. By then," he loaded another sliver of toast. "We *already* have vamps. Faeries will want a piece of pie."

I remembered again the faeries I'd seen. "What're they like right now?"

"Active." He bit into the toast, chewed. "Read your report on that lycan hit you lived through. Good work, by the way."

"We all of us have our skills," I said, wryly. "Mine is living."

"Always said you were the witch I didn't need to worry about," he said, just as wry. "You spotted a fae scout."

"I did."

"Clint buried it."

"Fucking cocksucker."

His brows rose. "That's grossly unfair to people who suck cocks."

"You're right," I agreed, feeling grim. "What else is he burying?"

"And that," he said, sitting back, "is why I'm glad you're here."

It wasn't that huge a leap though. While I waited, I bit into the hashbrown.

"Reports of scouts everywhere. None of the usual hits on residences, businesses. No looting. No brawling. *Scouting*." He took out his phone, passed it over to me. "That's the best I've got right now."

It was a map of the city with about a dozen marks on it. Places faerie observers had been reported.

They were active in my area. Near my coven, too. I zoomed in and identified one near the Playground. "What's the date on that one?" I asked him.

He glanced over. "Yesterday." And then filled his mouth.

Since Beo had up and fucked off.

My belly twisted. I pushed the food away.

I hated this whole situation so much, and there wasn't a thrice-cursed thing I could do about it. So I let out a long breath and rolled my head on my neck. Taig would only have access to areas in his jurisdiction, which limited the data. Still... "If there's one, there's a thousand."

"Yeah."

And faeries were just as bad as vampires. "They're up to something." Maybe he had dodgy feelings about vamps; I had them about this. Nauseous, I propped my elbows on the table. "This can't just be because of Edward. That shit reads like Samhain."

"Don't wish that on us early," he said fervently. "I don't need a dozen rifts opening all over the city. Last year we had a troll out front of the goddamn precinct."

I rolled my eyes. "Trolls are babies."

"They're *big* babies. With very thick skins."

"Well, *I* was working Retrievals last Samhain," I said, unimpressed, cycling out my old coffee, going for the new. "I didn't sleep for four days. I can't even *remember* what we had to do. It was a blur."

He winced. "Yeah. Those times, they're not fun. And they kind of stick with you, don't they? Even when you can't really remember it. Those fragments…"

I sipped my coffee to hide my surprise. Maybe I shouldn't have been taken off guard, though. The guy was a Supernatural Detective. When Retrievals weren't handy, he was called in. "Yeah."

He shook his head a little. "So. Anyway. I didn't want to meet up with you to reminisce. I wanted to give you the heads up. I know your coven is all over the vamp issue."

"We aren't equipped for vamps," I said flatly. "We don't have the charms, the potions, the weaponry or the experience."

"You've got more than that guy," he said, pointing at some random scrolling on his phone across the room.

"He could be an undercover—" I watched as the guy almost knocked over his coffee whilst absently reaching for it. "Yeah, okay."

"Keep your eyes open and your phone on," he told me, seriously. "I don't hate you being home, to be honest. You'll be that much closer to your gear if we need a heavy hitter."

My heart hurt. I breathed through it and didn't tell him I was going to see Aspen later. "I got out of that job, Taig," I said, feeling sick. I didn't want a well-meaning detective pulling me back in.

"Mostly," he agreed, quietly. "And if you ever say no, I won't think any less of you for it. I get it. Tell me now if I shouldn't even mention you to the handler."

I couldn't hold his gaze. My heart felt bruised. It sat, heavy in my chest, thudding away quietly.

This was my home.

It was all I had.

"Call." I threw back the coffee and stood. "I'll be there." I met his eyes, then, hardened my resolve. "And I'll be functional."

Aspen seemed very far away as I strode out into the winter air. I'd planned on catching a train out to Melton, catching up with her for lunch, going out on the town. Making bad choices. I knew I'd probably end up drunk and crying in her arms.

Life was too short.

My feet found their way, somehow, to my siren's place of work. And, hells, I needed a haircut.

She was there chatting to a group of customers when I arrived. And she moved them on very quickly as soon as I was spotted.

"Rory," she breathed, because she couldn't possibly just *talk*. Not when her voice was pure magick. "I didn't expect to see you." And her eyes travelled over me, in my comfy, relatively presentable hoodie and jeans. "Casual day at work?"

The desire to agree was strong. I pushed against it out of habit. "Not working," I said, easily. "Just here for a trim."

"Oh, of course we'll fit you right in," she said, as if she owned the place. And she may as well. "Why, I can do you myself, if you're comfortable with that."

It wasn't like the woman could have me smiling while she slit my throat. Why would I be uncomfortable?

But, hey, she didn't benefit from killing me, especially publicly. That'd be hard to cover up, even for a siren. "That sounds perfect," I lied without a qualm.

She did get me in, and no one even minded after she'd cooed at them. Illegal? Not exactly. Immoral? *You betcha.*

Half an hour later, I no longer had singed hair and my head ached from maintaining the resistance against her lure. I learned nothing except that she was a passable hairdresser. Really, I wasn't on the clock. I could've gone to any number of passable hairdressers. But she was my responsibility, whether I was on the clock or not.

On a whim I sent Aspen a text. *Not heading out today. Feels like a good day to do some cleaning. But when I do make it out, we're finding sexy, emotionally unavailable people to fill our beds temporarily.*

I was almost home when my phone rang. I saw her number and smiled. I had no doubt she had a list of emotionally unavailable bed-fillers to choose from. "What's up?"

"You aren't single!" she almost shouted. "Are you?"

The concrete under my feet became liquid and dragged at me. I strode forward, refusing to get sucked in. "Sure am. Footloose and fancy free."

"Oh, *fuck*. I'm so sorry. That arsehole. I hate him. Are you okay?" She snorted. "Don't bother replying, you goddamn liar. I'll be there soon." She hung up before I could do more than open my mouth to respond. That's the problem with old friends. They knew too much.

I didn't get any cleaning done, but I did flatten my phone doom scrolling. Aspen arrived about midday, sat in my lounge and painted my toenails. I told her a heavily edited version of what had happened.

I'd never explained Beo was a lycan. Since Beo's brother had murdered Aspen's, it seemed much simpler that he was out of my life.

"What a snake," she muttered, angrily swiping some polish off my foot. "It isn't your fault, exactly, that you keep nearly getting killed."

"What?"

She rolled her eyes at me and flicked blonde hair out of the way before fanning my nails. "Come on, Rory, it's not like you deliberately go out of your way to find trouble."

"I know?" I agreed, tentatively.

"But you don't exactly *avoid* it, either," she went on. "But, like, *someone* has to, right? And you're fucking *good* at it."

I tried to figure out if I was being blamed, insulted or complimented. "Yeah?"

"Yeah," she said, firmly. "Arsehole. I hate him and his whole pathetic act. And if he comes crawling back, I want you to make him *beg* for it."

A knife went through my heart. I remembered, suddenly, the paw over my hand. The way he'd stood over us while the building collapsed. His grief when he'd spoken of people he'd lost. "Hurting people hurts people," I murmured, feeling the tears, the overwhelming loss, swelling.

"Yeah, and the other part of that is your trauma is no excuse to traumatize others," she said, flatly. "Don't buy into it, Rory. This isn't on you."

Had there been a small part of him that wondered if he distanced himself from me if some of the damage I'd caused might also diminish? "You know what?" I said, taking back my foot. "I'm done talking."

"Want to shop for a new vibrator?" she asked me with a huge grin.

"I saw one the other day—on a necklace. It was so *pretty* and also super convenient."

There was no way I needed access to a vibrator that regularly. "No." I felt small, sad and pathetic. "How're your parents?"

"Ugh. Mum's renovating the kitchen." She rolled her eyes and followed me into the kitchen, peering into my fridge. "We could make nachos for dinner. I am so sick of hearing about the types of appliances and their various," she waved a hand, taking out some mince. "You don't have avocado."

"Don't I?" I had no idea what was in there. Or what my life was. "We can go get some."

"Yeah. And in date sour cream, too." Tossing it into the bin, she made sure I saw the exaggerated disgust on her face. "But you need to wait for your nails to—"

She broke off as my phone rang. Nic's name flashed across the screen.

I grabbed it, answered, and ignored the way my bestie's brows disappeared into her bangs. "Hey."

"Rory. We're on the wizard who—"

"I know." Deirdre's shitstain ex. "And?"

"We've got their location and we're going in. But Amor isn't a name," he said, the words quiet, hurried. "It's a job title. You're right on the money with the angel, too. Don't think it's the Upper Choir, but it sure as shit isn't the Lower."

Amor was a job title.

She used an illusion.

The spike of adrenaline hit my bloodstream like an old frenemy. "Does that mean there's more than one Amor?"

"Yes. One more, alive, that we spotted this afternoon. I couldn't get clear to let you know earlier. The place is warded to the fucking *nines*. Could use your skills, witch."

I barely heard the second half of his message, feeling sick. "Are they going to come after Dierdre?"

"No clue," he told me, darkly. "I've got no idea how many operatives we're looking at. Where they are. What they're doing. But these people aren't lightweights."

"The one I took out was—"

"One of us, yeah. Went missing in the Northern Territory about five years ago. Presumed dead. The job went south, they never looked hard for her."

I closed my eyes. "Got an I.D. on the other one?"

He snorted. "Yeah right. They're literally identical. Blonde. Great tits. Better arse. Kitted out like a huntress out of some Greek myth and utterly fearless for a reason."

"Thanks, Nic. That's super helpful. Did you catch what cup size she is, just for the record?"

He snorted again. "Fuck you, Rory. I miss you."

"Fuck you, too, Nic," I said, affectionately. "Thanks for the heads up. You called it through to the cops handling the case?"

"Detective Smith?" the disgust he managed to get into those two words made me smile. "It's on my list. I know who gets shit done and who doesn't."

His meaning came through loud and clear. "Well, I'm going to go get some protections in place." That I should've already done, really. "Thanks, Nic, I hate it."

"Yeah, it hates you, too. Blessed be, bitch."

I mumbled some sort of response and hung up, then found Lilith's number in my recents. "Hey Roars," she said, almost immediately.

"Hey. Situation. Amor is a job title."

I heard a chair squeaking in the background. "Oh. Well, that's a bit shit."

"Just a bit." I mouthed *thank you* to Aspen as she set a coffee before me. "We can't ward her."

"I mean, we *can*."

I smiled at the droll correction. "Okay. We can ward her, but it's pointless. I want a tracking charm on her. Is Janet up to it? She's our best at charms, yeah?"

"Hold on." Some rustling. "Janet! Rory needs to know if your tracking charms are as good as your jam."

I hadn't said that, but I gave Lilith full credit for the spin. I heard the discussion in the background and glanced at the clock.

"She says she can do one that's good for seven kilometers. If it's a native stone, she says it'll work indefinitely within that area's boundaries."

Indefinitely was a pretty tall call, but I had no Melbourne stones—that I knew of—and I wasn't in the mood to gamble. My Oma's tracking charm could go Overworld and still work.

I hoped fervently that wouldn't be necessary.

"Thank her and tell her I appreciate it. I'm going to see my Oma. I need her to do me up some others anyway."

Lilith made a noise of interest. "What's her range?"

"I'll tell you when I find it." I tipped some of the coffee down the sink, topped it off with cold water. "I'm going to try to get this to you tonight."

"Okay. Is she at risk this afternoon?"

I thought of Dierdre's competent manner, the way she patiently explained things to her unwell customers. "I don't know. But there's an angel involved. Not a lesser one. If you catch an Amor…"

Lilith blew out a breath. "Take no prisoners."

My heart ached. "You got it."

"No pressure."

"Yeah, no, no pressure. If you speak to Dierdre, let her know I'm on it."

"I will, yeah." And then, brightly, she said, "Hey, *Arthur* could charm her place."

I laughed and farewelled her, then threw my phone on charge and started hunting for socks. "So. Road trip?" Aspen asked, arching her brows. "You can update our playlist as we drive. And I'm definitely buying junk on the way. And the way back."

"Of course." I hopped into the socks. "Reckon Dad will forgive me if I don't visit him?"

She rolled her eyes. "No. Call him, tell him you'll be at your Oma's and that you've been recently dumped. You tick the good daughter box, *and* he'll bring you a lasagna to take home. It's win-win."

I knelt to do up my poor old runners. The laces blurred in front of my eyes. "Yeah. Good plan." And the words weren't thick with tears, either.

Fake it until you make it.

Grimly, I dug out my phone as we left, and ate some humble pie as I got in sweet with Bethany again. I didn't need the Retrievals jobs, but I did need to be in the loop.

Aspen's driving made me wish I'd had some gin before we left. I'd forgotten what a lead-foot she was. We cranked the music and screamed along with it and I found myself fighting tears far too often.

I suspected that was her plan.

When she pulled up out the front of my Oma's place it was just past three. We were greeted at the door with a beady-eyed assessment and ushered in. "Don't let the warm out," she said, as we toed off our shoes by the door. "Don't see you in months. Then you need a charm." She sniffed at me.

"Missed you too," I said honestly, wrapping my arms around her wiry frame. She stood as tall as my breasts and that still seemed odd. I'd watched her battle vampires, faeries, demons and, once, a horde of leprechauns. My heart twisted at the angle of her shoulders, the clouds in her eyes. "Got any rum?"

"Rory got dumped," Aspen called, helpfully, as she vanished in the direction of the bathroom. "He's a fucking coward and we hate him."

Her eyes narrowed. "Well, that explains it."

I didn't really want to know what it explained, but I had to say, "What?"

"That." And she waved a hand at me, turning and pottering toward the kitchen.

I resisted the urge to roll my eyes. For all I knew, the woman *did* see auras. I hadn't seen any proof of it, but, hey, twelve years ago magick didn't exist, officially.

"So. Got some tonic for," I waved a hand at myself. "This?"

She held out her hand and I dropped my cracked ring into it. "No. I'll make you a cup of tea. You don't pour booze into that sort of hole, Sunshine. You'll end up just making it grow."

I wasn't ready for this. How had I thought this would be a good idea? I shoved my hands into my pockets and wandered into the dining room. She banged and crashed in the kitchen. The steady stream of her irritated mutterings was homey and familiar, and that just made it harder to bear.

I didn't have a hole.

Cowards couldn't hurt me.

The glass of the big sliding door was cool against my head. The clouds rolled slowly over the sky, and it was darker than expected for midafternoon. I'd have to encourage Aspen to go a bit closer to the speed limit on the way home. The roads would be a mess.

But I wasn't.

"So," a familiar voice drawled. "I've been asking everyone what LGBTQIA plus stands for. And no one will give me a *straight* answer." I spun, joy rushing through me at the sound of Dad's voice. He held out his arms and I filled them up, curled close. "Hey, now. That's a face darker than those clouds." He smelled like a teacher. They all smelled the same by the end of the day.

I didn't say anything. I didn't need to. He smoothed my hair like he did when I was little, then rocked me back and forth.

And those fucking *tears*.

I forced them back and straightened. "I've got an angel after one of my clients."

His brows rose. "Lesser choir?"

"I wish."

"Got your obsidian knife, Sunshine?" he asked me, worry in his voice.

"No, I threw it out last week."

He pretended to flip his hair dramatically. "I'm a strong independent woman. I can rip angels apart with my personality."

"Finally," Aspen said, strolling in with a glass of lemonade in her hand. "A man who understands you."

"Sorry," Dad said to me, with his biggest, most fake puppy eyes. "I made you, so…"

"That's right. It's your fault." And I poked him under his worn old jacket with the patches on the elbows.

"You never get it right the first time, you know?" he sighed, tucked his hands into his jeans and shook his head in mourning. "Hey, Not-Daughter. Want to be adopted?"

"Mm." Aspen pretended to consider it. "You don't celebrate Christmas. What's in it for me?"

"Well, I know where I went wrong now."

I gave him a nudge, just enough to upset his balance. "Why are you so mean?"

"I'm not mean," he said, pressing a hand to his chest like he was insulted. "I'm Dad."

"When you're all done," Oma called. "These charms are done and the casserole is, too."

"Hi Dad," Aspen said, offering him a hand. "I'm hungry."

I shot her an irritated look. She knew better than to encourage him. But the two of them just laughed and nudged me toward the table. "It's, like, barely even four," I complained as Oma dumped a leek casserole into the bowl in front of me. "I'll just fall asleep if I eat now, and then Aspen will speed all the way home, and I'll end up dead. And then you'll be sorry."

"Will we?" Dad drawled. "Place'd be quieter, wouldn't it, Mum?"

She narrowed her eyes at Dad. "Grow some timing, Gerrard, your girl's nursing a broken heart."

Dad turned to me so fast I just about got vicarious whiplash. "You didn't tell him?" Aspen demanded. "I told her you'd bring her lasagna. Soul food," she said, wisely, to Dad. As if she didn't just want to stuff her face.

"Beo?" Dad asked, gently. "I'm sorry, Sunshine, I know you—"

That was it. I wasn't doing this. "Look. No talking about it or I'm taking those charms and getting back to work. I have bigger problems. There are vampires trying to use charisma on my boss—"

"They're what?" Aspen asked, aghast. "Is that a thing that *actually* happens?"

I dismissed it with a wave of my hand and tried not to think about it. Or about what had followed. "Power vacuum. Apparently, they're a bit like Pavlov's dog when it comes to someone in power being," I jerked my thumb across my throat then picked up a spoon. There was no way I needed this food. We'd had burgers and chips on the way and split a bag of lollies. But if I didn't eat it, Oma would just worry. And it was a lot more nutritious than lollies.

Aspen propped her elbows on the table. Oma cleared her throat and instantly Aspen straightened and sent her an apologetic look. Just like when we were five, and I felt grief rise alongside the nostalgia.

"Vampires, huh," Dad said, colossally unimpressed. "Cool. You've got spare wooden spoons?"

"I'll get you some charms," Oma told me, firmly. "Before you go. I've got a good slowing and anti-slowing pair so you can do some time shenanigans. And they're pretty."

I didn't want to go home with everything and the kitchen sink. "It's fine," I assured her, earning a dark look for speaking with my mouth full. "I probably won't see any action anyway, since I'm on leave."

"You're what?" Oma demanded. "When? How?"

I opened my mouth. Shut it. "I…"

Dad put down his spoon and sent me a level look.

"How's *your* work going?" I asked Aspen brightly.

"Oh, you know, leading horses to water, watching them not drink," she responded in kind. "I had a run in with my annoying middle manager Kevin today—"

"Nope," Dad said firmly. "Spill, Sunshine. Stress leave again? Are you okay?"

My belly tightened. "Not that sort of leave," I said, reaching for patience and instead filling my spoon. It was close enough. "Administrative. I cut a witch's throat before she summoned her angel buddy. The detective on the case hates me."

"Mm," Aspen said, licking her lips. "This is delicious, Oma Iris. Not even this disgusting conversation could ruin it."

"Angels and vampires," Dad said, slowly. "Anything else stirring?"

"Got some faeries," I admitted, grudgingly, and watched as his eyes narrowed. Dad always had a thing about faeries. "Acting weirdly. Taig —a detective I work with, sometimes—says they're giving the vamps a run for their money."

Oma and Dad shared a glance and I could just feel the overprotectiveness oozing from them. "I thought this was supposed to be a safer job," Oma said, swelling with her disapproval.

I smiled wryly and wagged my spoon at her. "Me too. Took a pay cut and everything. This actually *is* good. Did you grow the leeks?"

She narrowed her eyes at me. "Who's working the angel case, if you've been given the boot? They wouldn't have many Retrievals trained witches they can get in to do their dirty work—especially without dropping some cash."

She wasn't wrong about the second half of that, so I didn't bother correcting her about the angel being only important because of my client. "Nic." I glanced down, dug into a dumpling.

The silence stretched out. "Nic? That one you were sleeping with?" Oma asked, raising her brows. "Frankie's boy. He was always a hothead."

I sighed. "Yes, Oma, Frankie's boy who I slept with." And so he would forever be known.

"He's okay," Aspen said, with a shrug.

"For a wizard," I put in, and saw Oma grin.

"I resemble that remark," Dad had to say, of course, as he puffed up his chest.

"Yes," Oma agreed, blandly.

"We know," I put in, out of long habit.

Aspen giggled at us. "Hey, Solstice soon. You going to the big shebang in the city?' Dad asked me. "Of course you are—it's basically court ordered, isn't it, for you?" Before I could even respond, he'd turned to Aspen. "And how're you?" He sent her a wry smile. "Last time I spoke to your dad, he mentioned you were considering going competitive again with your kickboxing."

"Oh, I'm doing *one* display fight," Aspen sighed. "It barely even counts. I'm retired. I like food too much. But Nina's got a big fight, and her name isn't really known yet." And she picked up the conversational gambit and ran with it, kept it up until we opened the door and dashed out to her car through the rain. Loaded down with dried fruit soaked in sherry, potions, poultices and the charms I'd come for.

"You *so* asked for that," she said, putting her hand on the back of my chair and twisting as she reversed down the drive. "Anyone else would've just been like 'oh yeah life's good, saw a movie last week'. No, you're all like 'I cut a witch's throat'. Jesus, I love you."

Confused and tired, I let my head fall back and shut my eyes. "Don't speed. It's wet."

She snorted. "Says a woman who goes toe-to-toe with supernatural beings for shiggles."

"Cash," I corrected. "No shits or giggles accepted as payment. Speed limit. Or I'll call my cop friends."

"You would, too, you sly bitch," she said, admiration in her tone. "Hey. You mentioned a detective, when you first moved to Melbourne. Sexy voice. Is he your friend?"

"You have an excellent memory when it comes to my sex life."

"Oh, so you went there?" she flipped the music on to a modest volume.

"No."

"No?" A finger poked my arm. "Not sexy after all?"

My mouth was dry. Yes, he was. I could still remember the feel of his fingers in my hair. And it hurt.

That was the last night I'd been with Beo.

"Hey. There's a movie coming out," I tried, weakly.

She snorted. "Message received. We should book in some festivals for the summer. I think there's one out the other side of Geelong."

"Oh yeah?" I couldn't think that far ahead. I didn't have to. I'd just…coast. And stay functional. "Who's playing?"

By the time we got back to my place it was eight and I wanted nothing more than to fall into bed. Instead, I flicked Lilith a message, did the rough handover of the half of the tracking charm and refused to give her my part of it.

Lilith took it with grace, but not without some 'duty of care' and 'if Arthur hears about this' sort of mutterings.

If anything happened, I wanted to be the first to know.

Deirdre was *my* witch. And that meant a lot more than the rules.

CHAPTER 16

WITH ASPEN SETTLING IN ON THE COUCH I CURLED UP IN BED AND tried to turn off my head. Instead, my thoughts spun in loops.

Beo.

In his *bones,* was I? Or just on one of them?

My phone said it was almost witching hour. I sent a message to Arthur. Just checking in, seeing if he was okay. It was just the kind thing to do, really.

I lay there, staring at my screen, watching the message stay unread. He was asleep like sensible people. But he'd said he couldn't sleep… He was feeling better, though, obviously. Good for him. I hoped he held onto some of what he'd learned. I hoped he figured his own way forward.

I hoped he remained an oxygen user, not abuser.

My phone's light timed out. I fell back onto the pillow.

And then felt it. The weight of magick.

My heart squeezed in my chest as I went to jackknife and pressed against the invisible field over me.

"Khamuel guide you," a voice murmured over me. Hands on my jaw. I could feel the bitch's nails and couldn't move, couldn't even open my eyes. Terror pounded through my veins and I was stuck.

Spells clawed in my brain but I had no wand. "May He find you. May the light swell inside of you." Something sweet and liquid against my lips.

If this bitch was love potioning me, she was going to feel the fucking *ocean* of rage—

"May you embrace the calm and love. May you walk the path of Light." And there was glee in her voice.

I focused, hard, on the spell on me, and felt the edges of the ward.

I knew the spell. Immobilization. I was proficient, but I didn't know it inside out, back to front, down to a molecular level the way I did the Impenetrable Ward. And I had no *wand.*

Then I heard the click of a light, followed by rapid movement, grunts of pain. The sound of a body hitting the wall.

Aspen.

Oh, *fuck.*

My heart broke.

The smell of blood. Shattering bones. The sunlight warmed my skin.

I couldn't—

Breathe—

Thuds. Grunts. A hiss of pain.

No. No.

Not Aspen.

I fought. I couldn't cast or even speak. Couldn't even look. But I fought with every cell I had. If she wavered—if it even *flickered*—I wanted to be up and moving. I could hear them in the hallway, now. Smashing plaster, grunts of pain, a shout of fury.

And the afternoon sun.

Oh, fuck. *The afternoon sun.*

Smashing glass, somewhere. My lungs weren't working properly or there was no air or *oh fuck.* If something happened to *Aspen—*

"Rory!"

I could have wept, had I been able to.

She talked to me. The words tumbled, nigh unintelligible. I felt her weight on the bed. Her fingers at my throat. "Better be alive you motherfucking shitfuck bitch of a hardheaded arsehole," I was pretty sure I made out.

My hand was grabbed and pressed against something cold. A moment later I heard, from far away, Lilith's voice; "Rory? It's almost midnight."

"This isn't Rory. It's Aspen. There was a witch in here tonight and Rory's not moving—"

I couldn't hear the response but I felt the adrenaline ebbing away in my bones.

In my bones.

Shit, I had a good friend. I recognized the instructions she gave to emergency and let it wash over me.

She was okay.

We were okay.

Elders. I could feel my body vibrating. The stress. The strength. The fucking *spell.*

Ripping fabric, ragged breathing. My world existed through sound and smell. Was she okay? She had to be okay. She was here, talking. That was okay.

Lay down, Aspen, I wanted to say. *Put pressure on it and lay down. Wait.* But she left. I heard every uneven, heavy step she took. I heard her misstep or stagger. And I tried not to borrow trouble.

Aspen wasn't a witch. Oh, she knew a few spells, but not enough to get the qualifications. But she was magick with her fists.

When she returned I could smell blood. *Sunlight.*

But. I. Couldn't. *Move.*

Time crawled. I heard her muttering curses. I heard her breathing, too hard, too fast. I measured time by her sounds.

And Brandon was in my head. Her brother. The way he'd shot me a cocky grin that afternoon and given me shit on principle.

The way he'd never come home. The empty seat at Christmas. The birthdays mourned. The meals he used to love. The quiet in his aftermath. And I hadn't saved him.

And I hadn't saved her.

Running steps. "Hello?"

Lilith.

Relief washed through me. "In here!" Aspen shouted.

"Elders," Lilith breathed. "Keep the pressure—don't get up. Has she—"

"No, she hasn't—"

"Don't move," Lilith barked. "You called the ambos?"

Aspen was hurt.

I was hurting.

A hand on my throat, then my forehead. Cool and strong, I could smell Lilith's skincare, the wonderful, safe smell of my friend. "Rory. Shit," she muttered, and I wanted to cry, to just curl up and sob. But I had this horrible feeling that even if I could, the tears wouldn't come. I was a desert.

Movement around me, rummaging noises. A cool metal shaft was pressed into my palm. "If you're in there," Lilith said, "you've got your wand. I'm going to try to figure this shit out. Feel free to join me."

I tried to find the words for a spell but they swam and slipped. I wanted to scream. "What's wrong with her?" Aspen whispered, into the heavy darkness that was my world.

"Some sort of spell is all I've got so far. Curses aren't my thing." I felt the bed shift beneath us. "Shit. I might need to call in Arthur and I *know* she's going to be ropeable if that jerk wad sets foot in her bedroom."

My belly writhed. I gritted my teeth and hardened my focus. I knew the spell for the Immobilizing Ward but couldn't quite find the counter spell.

"She's okay, though," Aspen breathed. "She's going to be okay."

"Probably," Lilith said, neutrally. "More okay if I don't have to call a wizard for help."

Aspen's too-high, too-loud laughter sent a wave of relief through me, and the fear began to ebb.

The words floated right there, finally. I gathered them up with relief. *Engine light or no, go go go.*

The spell disappeared. I could feel it like pins and needles on my skin. No fucking wonder I couldn't remember it. Coming up with spells when you were seventeen was a bad idea.

My eyes opened.

"Aspen." The word was hoarse as I sat up and pulled blankets and Lilith with me. I grabbed Lilith's shoulder in gratitude as I scrambled over to my friend.

She was sitting beside the door, wooden spoon in one hand, kitchen knife in the other. And there was a puddle of blood under her.

My heart twisted and I couldn't breathe.

"It's fine," she said. "Pretty sure. I'm still totally lucid. Right?"

"Right." I pressed a kiss to her forehead and felt tears burn my eyes. I tasted, on my lips, whatever I'd been forced to drink. "Bitch Immobilized me," I shouted, on the way to the kitchen, hitting lights as I went. "Poured something down my—"

"I'm here." Lilith's voice right behind me made me jump. My heart skittered frantically. "You got something to stop the bleeding?"

"Yeah." I shoved aside spices and grabbed the tub of magickal first aid powders, balms and salves Oma had given me, dumping the whole lot of it on the bench. "It'll be labelled 'cuts' or something like that."

We dug through jars, bottles, and little plastic containers until I found the right one. It wasn't much, but it was made by my Oma.

Aspen was exactly where I'd left her. "Does this mean I'm more badarse than you?" she asked me as I fell down beside her.

My hands were shaking so badly I didn't trust myself with the twist top lid. I thrust it to Lilith. "Yeah," I agreed absently. "Where are you hit?"

"Leg." She snorted. "Bitch was going for the groin."

My blood ran cold. "There are major arteries in the groin, Aspen."

"I *know* that." She rolled her eyes at me. "Jesus. The point was, she didn't get anything important. And I'm a badarse. I want that in writing. I beat a witch assassin. I'm going to put that shit on my *socials*."

Lilith offered me the open jar. Who needed a man when I had my witches?

"Give me that, big shot." I took my jumper—fuck, another hoodie gone—from the cut on Aspen's thigh.

It wasn't good, but it wasn't mortal. "You're replacing those leggings," Aspen said through gritted teeth as I took a handful of the gritty powder and applied it by the fistful. "They had pockets."

"Now they have ventilation." I assessed the wound as the flow of blood halted. It shouldn't have accounted for all that blood. "Let me see the rest of you."

She had five more gashes I identified and treated before my brain kicked in.

Deirdre.

I stood, remembering the pattern last time, passing the jar back to Lilith. "Look after her," I ordered. "I have to go check on Dierdre."

Her expression hardened. "Roars…"

"Amor isn't coming back here," I said flatly. "She didn't want me dead, or I would be. She wanted me distracted."

"Fine." Lilith dug out her phone. "I'm calling in backup for you, though. You don't know what she gave you."

"Ten bucks says love potion." I shrugged it off. If I fell head over heels for a random on the tram, I'd deal.

I had shit to do. Feelings wouldn't get in my way. And, anyway, it couldn't be any worse than my last relationship.

CHAPTER 17

I'D *ALMOST* GOT TO DIERDRE'S WHEN A PATROL CAR, WITH LIGHTS AND sirens, pulled up beside me. Two uniformed officers climbed out, drew weapons. "Aurora Gold!" They shouted, as if I hadn't just jumped off the last tram and stopped to cross the road.

"What?" I demanded, waiting for a car that hadn't stopped to let me cross the road, the way they were supposed to.

"You need to come with us for questioning."

They had to be joking.

I didn't bother glancing at their guns. "Seriously?" I demanded, jogging over the now-clear road. "There's a witch up there who could be—" I broke off as a van pulled up and officers climbed out. They were looking in my direction, armed in tactical gear.

I recognized the we-can't-get-Retrievals swarm and felt sick. *Seriously. Me?*

My eyes went up to Dierdre's building. Her windows were on the other side, but...

They hustled into position around me. I drew a deep breath. My two options stretched out before me.

Drop a ward, soak the first round of gunfire, let them deal with the ricochets. Who the fuck brought a gun to a magick fight? I'd activate my Blowback Charm and knock them all off their feet, out of my way. I'd be up the stairs in moments.

Alone. Unsupported.

Or I went along with it. If Amor was up there, she'd either annihilate them all with a single sweeping spell or, if she wasn't feeling like being flashy, maybe just use the same strategy I planned. Minimal damage, maximal fuck you.

And I'd be sitting down here banking on the fact that this swarm of angry law enforcement hornets could at least radio for help before they went up in flames.

I closed my eyes, my head spinning. They were shouting and my heart drummed in my ears, drowning the words out.

Amor was there; I threw the dice, see if I came out on top.

Amor wasn't there; I sent up the alert.

It was the next part that was hard. Staking Dierdre out. Waiting for Amor to make a move. Hunting her back to their nest. Burning it.

That would be much harder to do if I had a target on my back.

I lifted my empty hands and stepped in a puddle of water that had gathered between the old bluestones that made up the gutters in this part of town. Of course. "Put your wand on the ground!"

Seriously? I shot the guy who shouted that a dirty look. "I'll come along for a drive." I kept my hands up. Without my wand in hand I'd absolutely eat any bullets that came my way and fucked if I was going along with that. "Cuff me. I don't care. But send the rest of this crew upstairs to check on the witch in unit three."

They secured me in the back of the car. I saw looks exchanged as they tried to figure out whether to push me about the wand.

If they did, and if Amor was around, we were *all* toast.

I kept it to myself and played it nice. Who said I couldn't be fucking diplomatic? The car left with me. The others stood around, radioing for instructions. I watched them grouped like clotted blood. And I hoped.

Aspen had messed up plenty of folks in her time professional kickboxing and amateur brawling. It wasn't impossible that she'd done real damage to Amor.

I didn't love the odds.

Into the precinct I was hustled, in cuffs, again. They hadn't gagged me. If I was a gambling woman, I'd bet it was because they didn't know how to secure magi, not because they knew it was pointless with me.

The receptionist saw me coming and held a carefully neutral expression. I didn't miss the way she reached for the phone, though. Someone's heart was going to be served up tonight and I was feeling hungry.

The interview room was different to the last one I was in. I was left to sit and trust the shitheads around me to do their jobs.

When the door opened to a fresh-faced Clint with a sergeant in tow, I was utterly unsurprised. "I trust measures have been put in place to protect Dierdre Summers from Amor and her ex."

"I'm not at liberty to discuss that situation." He settled down opposite me.

Arsehole. A simple, 'we'll do our job' was the normal response.

"You are, actually," I said in a friendly way as I shot him a smile. His heart was first. "As Dierdre's case manager, I'm allowed to access information on her. Even on administrative leave." I didn't know that for sure, but if *I* didn't know, I'd bet he didn't, either.

His smile was thin. "That's a bridge we'll cross when we come to it. We need to discuss a separate matter. A woman was wounded in your home tonight. Is there anyone who can verify your whereabouts or actions during this time?"

He couldn't seriously hope that'd stick. "Sure. The woman who was sliced up can."

He wasted my time. I suspect he enjoyed it, too.

Time ebbed. They left and I stood to stretch as best I could around the cuffs, which didn't slow me too much. The heat in my muscles, the fatigue of the day, the low after the adrenaline all went with the territory. I had no idea how long had passed before I heard a conversation in the corridor outside. No, not conversation—*disagreement*.

Anticipation fizzed under my skin. I heard Taig's voice, always so calm and measured. But there was a power in the man's words.

So much for playing it neutral. And, shit, I didn't even care. That was never a me problem.

Clint's voice was louder. I made out "standard protocol" and "favoritism". And then it dipped down and I could barely hear their voices, much less make out the words.

No way Taig had backed down. Knowing Clint was getting served made me want to laugh.

If it cost me Dierdre, I'd eat his heart *publicly.*

My feet had started to ache as quiet descended again. I fell down in the chair, blew a strand of hair out of my face, and waited.

Eventually the door opened. Uniforms came in, took off the cuffs. Their painfully neutral responses, the "we need to gather more information, but it seems that you're in the clear" bullshit smacked of political maneuvers.

I was taken to the hospital for a tox screen and was allowed to use my phone. It made sending up the alarm for Dierdre and Lilith much simpler. It was two in the morning, though. I didn't expect much.

There was a missed call from Bethany, but my return call went through to her message bank. Non urgent, then. So I sat around for a few more hours at the cop shop. At least they gave me coffee. Bad coffee, but, shit, I wasn't turning it down.

When I saw Taig he was wearing the navy suit that made his eyes look dull. That suit was a crime. He was with one of the sergeants I'd seen that night who may or may not have been a douche canoe. "Officer Aurora," Taig said, nodding. "This is Sergeant Greene."

Ah. So I was wearing my Retrievals badge now. And hadn't I met Greene once or twice? "Morning," I drawled, watching them take a seat at the table I'd been plonked in front of in a little waiting room with comfy chairs and shitty coloring books.

"I understand you're here regarding the matter of Dierdre Summers," Taig said, putting a file he carried onto the table. "I thought I'd chat with you while you're here about a contract that's come up. I spoke to your handler, but she wasn't able to get hold of you earlier."

He slid the contract over to me. To actually *see* a contract ahead of time was almost unheard of. To have it printed was a whole level of organization I'd encountered…once? Maybe twice.

Retrievals had to be responsive and flexible. Rarely did we have time to get *organized*. I pulled it over. There was blood on my hoodie from Aspen. None of the arseholes had told me how she was, but she'd be fine. Eventually. And Lilith had her.

I skimmed the details. "Vampire." And the summary jumped out at me.

Using charisma on a District Wizard.

"This is out of your jurisdiction, Detective." The address wasn't Arthur's. But it could've been.

"I'm being called in as part of the task force," Taig acknowledged. "As is Sergeant Greene here. We can't get a full Retrievals team."

No. Nic was bogged down with Amor in another state; he did most of the Victorian stuff. I skimmed through the known information again. Lone vampire, probably. Suspected part of a network. No mention of how old they were or whether they were gingko'd up.

Even a lone vampire wasn't a joke. Going in unprepared would pretty much always go badly for us.

"Strike this morning." In a few hours. I had time to get kitted up—if they let me go. I took the pen he offered me and signed without glancing at the rates. Melbourne wizards were being picked off, just like I'd thought.

Being right really was a curse.

"I understand your bloodwork is back," Taig told me, as I set the pen down. "You're under the effects of a Love Potion."

I raised my brows and thought back to who I'd seen first. I sure didn't feel like a puppy. "Well, I'm functional, anyway. Does it have legal ramifications?"

"Could," he admitted. "The contract came through before the results did, so I didn't have the opportunity to check."

"A later problem," I said, dismissively. "I'm suing no one's pants off. Maybe the potion fizzled. Regardless—I need to kit up. Am I free to go?"

The sergeant shifted a little in his seat, glancing at Taig. "Perhaps a statutory declaration," Greene suggested.

"Wouldn't hold up if the contract doesn't," Taig said, standing. "Rory says she's okay, then she's okay." And, the subtext; they needed me.

"I'll write something that says I'm aware of it," I offered, because the young guy was a bit hesitant. "Won't hurt."

"Sergeant, can you see that's sorted? I'll make sure Officer Gold is free to leave. We're in a time crunch," he explained to me.

"Got it." And he had to deal with Clint. I kept my smile to myself and waited for wheels to turn.

Half an hour later I was off the tram and headed up to my apartment. It was being processed by a few police who weren't stoked to have me stomping through, but I was allowed to get my kit.

Vampire. I knew how to deal with them.

I put on my Lupetec armor at home. I thought of Beo and I hurt.

Grimly, I took off my standard charms and swapped in combat ones. My weapons belt settled, a heavy, reassuring weight on my hips that I spun so the wooden knife was the easiest to reach, then added the vampire specific rope I had, made of braided lycan hair and studded with sharp pieces of wood that reminded me of Amor and her arrowheads.

I still didn't know how Aspen or Dierdre were doing.

I shoveled food in my mouth, ignoring the cops giving me serious side eye, slammed down a coffee, and grabbed some snacks to travel with.

South-East Melbourne Coven wizard was the victim. I considered asking Arthur if he knew about his colleague being vamped but figured it was better not to muddy an already probably quite muddy investigation.

The police station in this part of town was the same generic layout with the same vibe that was probably supposed to be calming but came across as soulless. I dusted salt from the nuts I'd been eating off my chest as I walked in, then grabbed my headgear as I approached the front desk. I stuffed hair on top of my head as I walked. I probably should've been doing something with it instead of eating, but... fuel. And snacks.

"Hi," I said, to the guy behind the reception whose eyes kept going back to the rope coiled around my left arm. "I'm—"

"Aurora," he said, with a nod. "Retrievals. I'll take you through. The team is gearing up."

I was guided through a long, boring corridor full of closed doors to the break room where talk and the smell of coffee was coming from. And though I wasn't openly stared at much, there was a definite lull in conversation.

I skimmed the room. Uniforms. Armored vests. Wooden batons. Helmets. About thirty of them, and I spotted Taig in their number near the coffee.

Instead of going to him, I ignored the quiet and went to where some helpful cookie had stuck the building plan up on a whiteboard. Off center.

Six levels of luxurious apartments. Of course, a wizard had a delightfully spacious apartment in a city where most of us could barely make rent. I tucked the last few tendrils of hair up under the headgear as I let my eyes wander the plans, then the actual apartment in question.

"We don't know where she'll be." I glanced up, found Greene beside me, offering coffee.

I eyed it off. Satisfactorily black, but... "is that sweetened?"

"O'Malley made it," he said, with a shrug. "Said he thought you might need it. You've had a big night."

And it was going to be a big morning. I took the coffee, trusting Taig to know I was sweet enough. "Any idea how old she is?"

Another vested, armed person appeared at my other side, a woman with lines carved deep in her skin and blonde flyaways that made her look frazzled despite the calm expression. "None. But we know she's part of a coven."

"So. Could be multiple." The thought didn't please me. "You in charge?" I asked, as Greene melted away and left me holding a chipped mug of ambrosia.

She offered me a puffy, firm hand. "Richardson. I'm glad O'Malley got you on board. We don't think there's more than one on site." Her eyes were steady as she looked up to meet my gaze. "But we know what one vamp can do when cornered."

And she did. It was in the thinning of her lips, the lines around her eyes. "Shame the government doesn't want to increase Retrievals numbers, isn't it?" I asked, by way of agreement.

"Shame they don't do a lot of things," she shot straight back. "I want you up front."

"Perfect." Fuck, I hated this.

I was the rearguard in my team. Nic, Bang, Vix—*fuck. Vix.*

But in this team…well, we'd hope a rearguard wasn't needed. "You mostly covering the street exits?" I asked, eyeing off the people who were as trained as law enforcement could be to deal with supernaturals. They'd have experience. The chaos of Samhain, with rifts opening everywhere, with the flood of violence, they'd seen plenty.

That was different. That was tactical risk minimization. Get in, close the rifts, identify the threats. Everyone was going everywhere. Supernaturals trying to get into hidey holes. Us trying to keep tabs and hope Retrievals came in to mop it up.

This was going into a nest. This vamp knew the lay of the land. She had a target and a network behind her.

"We'll have people in these spots." Her finger, nail bitten to the quick, tapped firmly on the various points. "I've got a core group going into the residence. We want the family safe. We need to know what's driving this."

"Family." I looked at her, raised my brows, waited.

"Wizard, witch, two kids."

Fuck. Kids. "Pets?"

"Not that we know of."

Cool. No dogs. They could complicate situations. "Am I going in hot?"

She considered the layout before us, her hands on her sturdy hips, and chewed on her response for a while.

That was a yes, but not officially.

"There's an issue with that. She's legally, theoretically, registered. The ink is wet on her paperwork, and we're investigating exactly *how* it went through. She came down from Sydney, though, so..."

So it'd be months, if not years, to get to the bottom of this. For now, she had the protection of a legal citizen.

I rolled my shoulders, felt the weight of the wood-studded rope that was an all-purpose vamp trapping tool. "I'm a bit overdressed, then."

"Paperwork didn't say whether you did or didn't have kill orders," she said, flatly.

I cast my mind back, felt a smile tugging at my mouth. *Well, shit.* "Well played," I murmured, amused. *Many a slip twixt cup and lip*, my Oma would've said. And some slips could be handy. The bonus; Bethany would be *pissed* that had got past her.

I sipped my coffee while I pulled out my phone. I had a few texts from Arthur. Was I okay, what was going on sort of stuff. I sent off a quick response. *On Retrievals contract. Unrelated. Look after Dierdre.*

I got a response almost immediately. *Sitting at her bench with a cup of tea right now. She says hi.*

One less worry. I let out a long breath, opened up maps and sussed out the street view of this place. Blueprints were fine, but I had time to kill. And a vampire.

"What're you thinking?" Richardson asked me as I held up the phone, eyeballed the way the balconies of this wizard's place perched over the road, the parking building over the road. Shit view, really. Probably was a park when he bought it. I flipped it. The other side would have a nice cityscape.

"She's protected from morning light," I said, looking at the position of the windows, trying to get my head around it. "I assume that's why we're timing it like this. To use that to our advantage."

Richardson tipped her hand one way, the other. "I hear they're warier in the day. We thought we'd hit a bit before that. Give her minimal time to clear the area, but try to get in before all the defenses are up."

Shit, she *was* on the ball. "Good call." And if she was thinking this woman would get away, she really did know how dangerous she was. "I don't like this." I waved a gloved finger at the car park. "A juiced up, century old vamp could make that, I reckon. We got people over there?"

Her eyes narrowed. "No. That was O'Malley's call. I figured it could be a possible exit."

If Taig was consulting, he was more than just another person in a vest. *Interesting.* "Street?"

"That's a six-story drop," she said, with an amused snort. And then she looked at my expression. "Surely, not."

I put my phone away, thought hard about what I'd seen. "I don't know. I wouldn't gamble on it."

She muttered something unhappily, then turned and barked, "O'Malley!"

I didn't follow her gaze while I weighed my options. If I went in with the first push, I could lock down those windows, but then I'd be useless for casting. If I waited until she made a move, I could lose her. Vamps were slippery.

And if I lost her…well, she'd find the teams positioned below.

This was why Retrievals wasn't a one-woman show. *Elders curse it.* I took a generous swig of the coffee and smelled him before I heard him, the sandalwood of whatever he wore working its way delicately up my nose and wrapping around my tired brain. "Problem?" he asked.

"Gold's asked if we have people on the street. We got a weak point." And her stubby finger struck the blueprint squarely.

I half turned, met Taig's eyes. "If she can make that jump, there's no team we can put together who can stop her. So, no, we don't have people there."

He was right. Fuck. "Good call." I let out a breath. "I'll try to make sure she doesn't, then."

"We look after us first," Richardson told me, flatly.

"Don't worry," I told her, finishing off the coffee. "I'm good at that." Despite what some people might say.

And, to my surprise, a grim little smile appeared on her face. "That's what I hear."

Beside me, Taig just sipped calmly at his coffee.

CHAPTER 18

THE PRE-DAWN DARK WAS MADE WORSE BY THE HEAVY CLOUD COVER. I followed a brawny guy, who went by Pickle, into the building as the other teams filed through, positioned at tactical points that I didn't worry too much about.

Taig was right. If she got past us, they were fucked.

The four other 'best of the best' options included Greene, who offered me a stick of gum as we went up the millions of stairs. I hadn't done this shit in so long my thighs were feeling it by the time we reached the sixth floor. Taig was down one end of the corridor, controlling the elevator. Richardson had the other end and the stairs. They'd bolster us if we needed it. But too many people in a small space would just lead to chaos.

I pulled down the headgear and made sure it sat properly over my neck as we approached the door. I'd been vamp bit before. It wasn't a sensation I'd care to repeat.

"That's bulletproof, right?" Greene murmured.

"Right."

"I hear you fight in close quarters," he explained, softly. "Not planning on shooting you, but…"

I nodded, resettled my right glove. My wand was loaded into the wrist of it. No chance of losing it. Not unless I lost my arm, anyway. It didn't get in the way if I had to use my hand, either, but it sure as hells wasn't comfortable.

They looked at me as, at either end of the hall, we were given the signal to move. I took a breath and gathered the words and power. *Silence is golden and so is stealth.* The Silence Ward settled into position like a blanket over the door and I gave the nod they were waiting for, stepping back.

The big black key was brought forward and I shrugged the rope off my arm, looped it loosely in my hand as the woman with the battering ram lined up her target and swung. Nic's forced entry spell was neater and had more applications, but the officer must've known what she was doing, because the door ripped open first swing. She tossed the key aside and it landed with a thud that wouldn't travel further than my ward.

Secure the family. Secure the vamp. Those were my orders.

There was nothing more secure than a dead vamp.

I shrugged the loose loops of rope back up onto my shoulder to free up my hands. I wasn't *technically* going in hot. Pulling my knife at this point wasn't *technically* allowed.

So I just made sure it sat loosely in its sheath.

"Collapsing the silence ward," I told them out loud. "In three."

Nods. I counted down, felt the rapid beating of my heart, the desert in my mouth. *As I will, so shall it be.*

They moved into the room and Greene, beside me, sent me a grim look, tapped his ear with its black comms set. *Made*, I think he mouthed.

My heart rate doubled. If she knew we were on the way, then she had security of some kind.

The house was silent. Light spilled out into the darkness from the lounge. That room had the biggest, most problematic window. And it wouldn't get morning light for a few good hours.

My stride lengthened and I matched Pickle's pace. The family *could* be asleep. Or they *could* be dead.

The vampire was the standard supermodel build with cascading blonde curls. And she was putting down a phone when we walked into the longue. Backup was on the way.

Clock was ticking.

The family was seated around her, gazing at her like kids at an all-you-can-eat dessert buffet. Alive, but obviously drained.

Pickle started to say something. I'd got the brief. I knew what was supposed to happen. And I also knew we did not want to be fighting her *and* her backup. "Stake your hand, now," I said, over top of Pickle. "And get into cuffs. Or I'll stake something more precious."

She grinned at me, glanced up at the clock, and grabbed the girl closest to her in the blink of an eye. There was none of the wind I associated with those rapid vamp movements, but the way she blurred, the speed in which she moved, told me a few things.

She wasn't more than a century, probably. She wasn't ginkgo'd up. And she couldn't make the leap out the window.

I breathed and sent magick into the charms at my ears. Time slowing burned like ice. Immunity from time spells burned like fire. It wouldn't be enough on an old vamp, but with her...

Heart in my throat I dropped an Impenetrable Ward around her. Power roared in my veins. Around us carpet exploded in slow motion, dust and wool particles erupting in a perfect circle encapsulating her and the girl. And I went hard.

It was the only way to go.

She shoved the girl between us in a move that would've worked if I hadn't slowed her down. As it was, I had to go high, rope taut in my hands, the wood biting me through the gloves. She ducked away. I'd known she would. But incapacitating her wasn't the real goal.

I grabbed the girl. Her eyes widened slowly as she struggled to track my movements. My fist, weighted with rope and wood, I drove toward the arm imprisoning her.

The vamp let go. And, keeping my hand on the girl, I shoved her out of the circle to safety. She flew through the air like a ragdoll, free. No one and *nothing* could leave or enter my ward as long as I drew breath without my say-so. She was safe. I pushed off with my back foot, trying to follow her.

But I was grabbed.

I was slammed into the floor.

Stars. Pain. The vamp, over me. Teeth bared. Stinking hair in my fucking face. I struck out, not to hurt but to get leverage. She was steel. She was diamond. I wore a blow to the ribs, the force of it dispersed by my Lupetec. The rope tangled but I dragged it over her face and she fell back, blood welling slowly. Movement, around us, like everyone else was underwater. So slow and graceful.

I followed her. On my knees. Grips, air, rope, untangling, flowing. I was thrown off and hit the ground again. Charms at my ears, burning, *burning*. Had her in my guard. Just. Needed. To. Get. The. Wood. In. She grabbed it, tried to throw it. Instead of fighting I let her have one end and threw the other over her while I bridged and caught it, somehow.

Fucking hand-eye coordination. *Thanks, Dad, for the cricket lessons.*

Purpose screamed though me. Sounds, from outside the ward. Roaring, too. I pulled the rope tight and threw her over, drove my fist into her face. Felt the give of bone. *Crack. Smash. The smell of blood.* She didn't have her magickal strength when she was skewered.

A noise. A bell being struck.

I looked up.

Pickle slid down the outside of my ward, his helmet askew, vest torn. In his wake, blood trickled down the invisible magickal barrier in slow motion.

The cracking of bones. The spurting blood. Afternoon sunlight and the earthy smell of the bush.

Behind him, chaos.

Lycans.

CHAPTER 19

I DIDN'T HESITATE BUT DROVE MY FIST INTO THE VAMP'S FACE WITH ALL the strength adrenaline and a half-arsed dedication to my gym program could give me. She went limp. For now.

It'd have to do.

I pushed up and collapsed my ward. The charms at my ears. *Burned.*

And I needed them still.

The woman who'd been the crack shot with the battering ram was raising her pistol. Slowly—too slowly. And they were using wood-tipped bullets in modified guns. Useless.

Fucking. *Lycans.*

I drew my silver knife. The lycan was going for the woman. It was slower than me with the charm working. My good old kitchen magick spell, repurposed, filled my mind. *With this blade I cut you three by three from top to tail.*

Lycan filet.

I ran through the chaos. And I took it with me.

The sound of breaking bones.

The reek of blood and shit.

The terror.

The panic.

The sunlight.

A lycan hit me as I got into the corridor, drove me into a wall, then through it. My spell crackled and cut. I fought out from under it as it twitched. I was surrounded by the bark of gunfire.

Taig at the elevator. Richardson at the stairwell.

No way a lycan pack rode the elevator.

Vamps, too? Are there vamps? My heart skittered, faster, faster. Riot shields. Rifles. Useless. I saw the barricade between the stairwell. Saw Taig. It was his doing. Reached for my magick. Leapt, fumbled the spell, found it. *Gravity sucks but I sure don't.* I leaped over their heads, struck the roof, and barely felt it. I could feel my charms though, burning into my skull, the time warp magick bleeding away as they seared me.

Shit wasn't going to last forever.

Richardson was on her back, firing at the underside of a beast who had no fucks to give. Blood on the walls. Arcing sprays of it like some sort of dystopian art. Bodies like an apocalypse.

I lifted my knife. A lycan hit the edge of my charmed area and went from running in a horrific blur to just a quick dash. The pain in my ears, in my skull, was getting more than real. Something hit me in the back and knocked me aside the same time I sent my spell out. I staggered. *Shot. Fucking cops. Trying to save their fucking arses and—*

The agony from my ears was radiating into my skull. I couldn't hold it. Couldn't keep it up.

Lycans. Gunfire. One went down, crashed through a wall. Screams. Sirens. Someone had silver bullets.

Thank fucking fuck. I cast. Again. Again. Felt the words slipping. Again. Hit, by one. Jaws. Drove the knife into the roof of its mouth. Felt the rip of its teeth on my arm. Lost the knife. Got myself out. My head. Pounding. Pounding. I couldn't. Another, leaping over us. The corpse of its packmate.

Beo wouldn't have done that.

Would he?

CHAPTER 20

I DEACTIVATED THE CHARMS ON MY EARS AND THE CHAOS, THE movement, the roar and bark of gunfire. The *stink*. Who would've fucking thought *smell* would be delayed?

Nice work, Oma, I thought hazily. *Good charm. Top shelf. Get me another.*

Bones. Splintering.

Afternoon sunlight.

I shook my head, forcing myself to my feet. Crawling through the carnage I ripped my silver knife free. The beast twitched and I set my teeth against the roar of adrenaline that coursed through me in response. The adrenaline would ebb. Shit couldn't hold me forever.

"Behind!" came a shout, the word reaching my pain sodden brain. "Behind!"

The barricade exploded like a popped cork. *Vampire.*

Charms. Reactivated.

Agony.

In.

My.

Skull.

The wooden knife slipped in my blood. She had the girl over her shoulder and still looked gorgeous with her nose all fucked up.

I didn't try to cast. She hadn't seen me. She was too focused on the stairs and getting out to pay me any mind.

Yeah, poor baby vamp couldn't make the jump.

I pushed up. My legs. My fucking magnificent legs. They listened. They did it. I went, hard. Like always.

Into her.

Into the wall.

Didn't. Bounce.

I saw the recognition, the hatred, in her eyes. And I drove the knife in. It slid home. And I felt it break. The force of it, the jarring sudden change in direction of my wrist, sent pain spiraling up my arm. That shit could take a number, though, because it was nothing next to my head.

Laughter bubbled up in my chest. Splinters are the *worst*. Dad always told me so. Hope she had a set of tweezers and a steady fucking hand. Or not.

Her guts met my knee and I felt the wall give behind her. She bared her teeth, twisted her head—toward the girl.

I smashed my elbow into her mouth. The reek of burning flesh filled my head and I knew it was from my charms and that was my meat that was no longer rare. *Fuck.* How deep was the brain? *Fuck.* I grabbed the kid again and ripped her free.

A lycan was descending on us. I collapsed, coiling around the kid, hoping. Hoping.

We were knocked along the ground. I kicked off, steered us, like some sort of frenzied pinball, through the dead and dying. The girl's eyes were huge and terrified.

But alive.

Afternoon sunlight. My heart in my throat.

I cancelled the charms, staying there, on my hands and knees, trying to breathe. Trying to breathe. The pain. Nausea. Like icepicks. I forced myself up. Up. The plaster of the wall was cracked and covered in a mist of blood. I reached for a spell. The words. Ducked. Wove. In my head. I looked up. The barricade was down. People were helping colleagues up.

Dust, settling. It was over. I fell against the wall and breathed. *Sunlight on my skin.* Tears soaking my mask.

CHAPTER 21

back to their hidey hole. Weather favored them. I didn't care. Bitch had half my knife lodged between her ribs and, shit, that felt good.

My arm wasn't too bad. I ignored it. Did my job as backup battlefield medic. That's what I'd been, a witch of all trades. And, apparently, what I still was. Master of none.

This was why they had Retrievals *teams*.

I was all but shoved into the elevator, into the van, into the precinct, into the break room. I guzzled coffee. Some arsehole put milk in it. It was so bad and I didn't care.

My hands shook. I stood at the sink. Talk, shock, and horror rose and fell around me. I was pummeled by the rise and fall of the breakdowns happening around me, the conversations recounting waves of horror. I rinsed my arm under the tap of the big, communal sink half full of coffee cups and watched the water in them turn pink with my blood. Probably an occupational health and safety concern. But not mine.

My coffee cup was taken, the last of the dregs tipped out. When I glanced up the room lurched. Taig was there, sweat making the tawny hair on his head darker, the greys brighter. His eyes went to my arm and narrowed. But he just went over to the big urn on the wall that kept a police force worth of water hot and filled my cup. Added the coffee powder. Who added powder *second?* I watched, hypnotized. He came back over. Topped it off with cold.

"You're good at that," I said, and the words were a bit slurred. "Coffee. Making coffee."

"I'm good at a lot of things." That low, sexy voice or the hormonal roller-coaster made my mind go to all the other things he could be good as he offered me a cup. "Media's requesting you. Richardson is stalling them."

"Better keep them stalled," I said, tiredly. The mug weighed as much as a lycan. *Breaking bones. Ice in my veins.* I breathed. No way was I functional enough to do much more.

"She will. Had to give 'em something, though." He shook his head, his mouth a grim line. "I told them we needed a team."

I tried out a smile but it felt bitter. "Saying I'm not enough?"

His eyes zeroed in on me and seared me to my soul. "Never."

My breath caught. My head spun. My heart thudded heavily.

"Come on. We can get basic first aid for that." For a minute I thought he meant my wild overreaction, but his gaze went to my arm. "Actually, you wait here."

I didn't bother to reply. I hadn't been strong five minutes ago. I was putty now.

Boneless.

The agony was immense. In my head. In my arm. In my ribs. In my knee. In my heart.

I lifted the coffee and some of it spilled down my front because who was coordinated, right? Black was the best for hiding spills. And blood. No one would know.

I walked over to a nearby chair at a table full of discarded cans of soft drink and fell into a chair. My coffee left a brown smear on the tabletop.

The arm injury meant my top needed to come off. But I just sat there, feeling the enormity of the task. I had to get my exhausted, battered arse home. Maybe I should do that first?

The options spun before me. I dug my phone out. The screen was cracked, but it still turned on. Just like me.

Approximately a million notifications pinged. I swiped them away so I could open up messages. Blood, watery from the rinse I'd given myself, fell on the table. More OH and S concerns for someone. *Lilith.* I needed Lilith. But when I scanned her texts the words just danced meaninglessly in my brain. I tapped reply. *Words. Come on.*

I could just call a taxi.

She'd skin me for not calling her, but, hey, later problem. *Central police precinct*, I managed to type. The next bit was harder. I should be polite. Not too...abrupt? Demanding? The only words that came to mind were 'extraction required', though.

Taig sat down opposite me. I squinted at him. "Extraction required. What's that in," I looked at my phone. "Human talk."

"Come get me," he offered, opening the big, bulky case of bullshit Western medical first aid. "Want me to type it?"

I considered the tub. I'd probably used the best of the kit Oma made me on Aspen a few hours ago. *Fuck, what a day.* "Yeah."

Fucked if I was going to hospital. Not when I knew what their emergency room looked like right now.

I started working at my belt. He reached over, tapped a few words into the phone, sent the message. "That wasn't broken this morning, was it?" he asked me. "Your phone."

My belt fell heavily on the floor. A few people glanced over. I barely noticed. "Yeah."

"Yeah, it was broken before we went to save the family?"

"Yeah, it was broken this morning, during that." Why did he have to talk?

"I'll put it in as an expense."

I shut my eyes and started working my arm out of the sleeve but had to stop, open my eyes, and pull off my glove. My wand rolled in front of me, freed. "Get me a new top. This one has teeth marks." I had insurance.

He didn't say anything, just got out little tubes of salve and the gauze. I managed to get my arm out and didn't care I was showing some skin, just flopped there while he silently treated the wound. "It'll need attention," he told me, when he was done. "That'll hold you."

"I like being held," I said, my mouth working independently of my brain.

"Reckon we all deserve it, after that," he said, quietly. "You saved a lot of lives."

Sunlight on my skin. Bones breaking. Blood. Arcing. Pump, pump, pumping in time with his heartbeat.

Brandon.

The vamp could've taken her hostage and gotten out of there. Kid would've died, sure, but she probably would've been the only one. If I'd just let her go, that's what would've happened.

The idea was agony.

Sensible, but agonizing.

My phone rang and I flinched as the noise pierced my sensitive skull. I needed to treat my burns. Elders, I needed my Oma.

"It's Lilith," Taig said. "I'm going to get it if you don't."

I just nodded and considered trying to get my arm back into the top. It was wet. Too much work. They could all just admire my right breast in my comfiest t-shirt bra. Or Taig's skill with medical tape. No fucks given.

I didn't try to turn his words into something that made sense, just wondered, dimly, how close I'd come to melting my brain.

Warmth, on my arm, then scratchy fabric that smelled of sandalwood. I opened my eyes. His shirt, was draped over me. The t-shirt he wore was sweat soaked. I closed my eyes again. Noise was everywhere, hammering at me.

My phone rang. He answered. The words meant nothing. My elbow was taken. I grabbed my wand out of long habit, a fistful of other stuff. There was coffee in my cup, still.

Shit was bad when I left coffee behind.

The sight of that roused me, a little, from my daze. I stood without support, folding the shirt over my body.

A thought occurring to me, I stopped in the hallway. "My belt."

Taig lifted a hand. My belt dangled from it.

"You're a gem."

"I'd be a dead gem without you," he said, casually, grabbing the door for me. The words smashed into my skull. I breathed through the pain. "Richardson will chase you for your report."

"No, she won't. I'll get it to her before she needs to." And she'd have plenty of admin to wade through in the short term.

He opened his mouth to say something but I held up a hand, my heart in my throat. Ahead of us in the hallway, the girl I'd ripped, twice, from the clutches of the vampire clung to her mother, with two stony faced officers behind.

"I don't want to go in by myself," the girl was saying, her hands white-knuckled on her mother.

"We won't be long," one of the officers said, opening the door.

"Can't we just—" her mother began.

"It'll be fine, won't it, Eliza?" the officer said. "Come on, now."

Taig stepped into my line of sight, his hand under my elbow, and propelled me a different way.

But my heart was left behind, bleeding.

That kid was about to be re-traumatized. I knew it. She knew it. Her mother knew it. Because of...what? Protocols to stop parents coaching kids? I felt sick. She'd been through enough. More than enough. What she'd seen knocked out people working in the field. She was a *kid*.

"That's bullshit," I whispered, horrified to feel tears burning my eyes. "That's such bullshit. She needs..." I didn't know what she needed. Fuck, I didn't know what *I* needed.

"Yeah, it's bullshit," he agreed, grimly. "They do say all cops are bastards."

I shot him a quick look, disoriented. "What?"

"We aren't," he went on, still quietly. "But our system, and what we stand for. It makes us act like it. And, as you know, plenty are very comfortable with that." He dropped his shoulder to open a door. "Lilith's out here. Keep your head down, you should get out without anyone noticing."

Still disoriented I followed him out the door and into the sunlight.

In the reception area, a camera crew and news anchor waited, with another few out on the footpath. My mouth went dry. Lilith fell in beside us, putting herself between the cameras and me.

I wanted to cry. Forever.

Lilith said nothing, just unlocked her car and went to open the door for me. "I got it," Taig told her. "Get her out of here. They don't have her face. Yet." And he reached out to open the passenger door.

The world was spinning. Breaking. He was reaching for me. And it felt so good. So natural. I reached back and fitted into his arms.

His embrace was a little awkward. "Sorry. Was just…your belt. I was just putting it down. Had to, ah, reach around you."

I heard my breath shake. "Then put it down." A solid thunk from the car door shutting as Lilith climbed in. But his arms settled, firmer, around me, unhurried. I was hugged. The afternoon sunlight. That was why I was shaking. "It was you. With the silver bullets."

"We all had them."

He didn't deny it, though. I'd put money on the fact that he'd had them loaded when they were needed. And I hated it. I hated lycans.

Some lycans.

"Get home, Rory," he murmured, easing back. "Rest. Call me, if you want. I'll be around."

I didn't have a choice—I almost collapsed into the car. "She pulled out all the stops," he said, leaning in slightly with a hand braced on the roof of the car, his words directed at Lilith. They hurt my head. I just sat back and fumbled with the seatbelt. "It cost her. You okay with the aftermath?"

"Yeah," Lilith said. "Thanks, O'Malley. Just her arm?"

"There'll be more," he said, the words matter-of-fact as he straightened. "But she's in shock."

"Fuck you," I muttered, and was humiliated to hear tears in my voice. "I'm right here. My head hurts. I fucking hate lycans."

Lilith's brows rose as she started the car. "First time you mentioned it."

"Shut up, witch." It was a plea. I cringed as Taig closed the door, rapped twice on the roof. Why did people do that? And his shirt smelled like gunpowder and fear. But holding him felt good all the same. I curled up, put my hands over my tender ears. The charms had to come out. I hadn't looked at the damage and I didn't want to. Maybe I'd just call Dad. Oma. They'd bail me out.

Aspen was asleep on my couch when I got home. My broken window had cardboard stuck over it, but the debris was gone. "I took photos," Lilith told me as I looked around dully. "For insurance."

I didn't even care. "You're amazing," I managed, somehow.

"Yeah, that's me. Shower, or bed?"

My head swam. "Bed. I need healing. Later."

She walked with me. "I can get Bernie. She can do it while you sleep."

The thought made my skin crawl. It also made sense. Less time spent in recovery. "Dierdre?"

"Totally fine. Amor's in the wind. Aspen's got a mean streak, doesn't she?"

I struggled to follow. "What?"

"She ripped into Clint."

Tension ebbed away. I could imagine Aspen giving Clint the sharp side of her well-honed tongue. Falling down onto the bed made pain lance through me. I didn't hear what Lilith said. How did my *jaw* hurt? My *teeth*?

"...your love potion," Lilith was saying, the words calm as she tossed my shoes aside.

Love potion. I was loved up. "I don't feel love drunk.".

"Maybe you're just not into me?" she asked, teasingly.

I opened one eye. "Sorry, but I'm straight. Proof sexuality isn't a choice," I added, curling up in my doona. "Bernie."

She said something half amused and half exasperated. I listened to the rise and fall of her voice, content. The sound of my wand being set beside my bed was reassuring. Trust Lilith to know.

The pain was there, a huge, snarling beast. But I couldn't quite get up to take anything for it. When Bernie arrived, smelling like vodka and lollies, I felt her magick with relief.

It beat the afternoon sunlight.

Lilith stayed with me until I was on my feet. Aspen stayed longer, eating junk food and binging our favorite shows from when we were teenagers, talking about happier yesterdays.

By the time she left, I was more than ready for my own space. I'd only just waved her off when my phone rang with an unknown number.

I eyed it off warily as I brushed some nacho dust off my hands from the plate I'd been stacking into the dishwasher and answered with a cautious, "Rory."

"Hey. It's Zane."

My heart did a slow roll and I wondered if he could hear it through the phone. Zane meant Beo. "Hi, Zane." Was Beo okay? The words crowded my mouth, suffocating me.

"I've got a few boxes of your stuff here," he said, the words hesitant. "I, ah. Can't fit them on my bike, or I'd offer to drop them off. And I don't have anyone to help me carry them."

I tried to sort through all of that and somehow breathe. "Aren't you in New South Wales?"

"No. I'm staying. Keeping the territory." He sounded a little puzzled. "Didn't you… get the transfer info?"

I hadn't. I could've looked, but I hadn't bothered. "Why didn't you go?" Then it clicked. "You're defending the rift."

I could almost see him shuffling his huge feet. "I, ah."

"*Alone*, Zane?" I demanded, horrified. I knew the shit that came through those rifts. "Really?"

"I've applied to foster some young lycans," he offered, sounding for all the world like a child caught with his hand in the cookie jar. "I'm Alpha, now."

I closed my eyes on the bombsite that was my kitchen.

Beo was gone.

But Zane wasn't. The world kept turning. I had a job to do, and he was one of mine.

"Look, I'm not working right now," I said, my brain slowly ticking. "I can't monitor the situation myself. But you've got my number." And that meant Beo had given it to him, rather than deal with me directly.

Fucking *coward*.

My heart broke.

"Yeah, well," he cleared his throat. "I've got some friends helping out, you know?" I didn't, but the less I knew, the less I'd have to lie about later. "Anyway. Um. Couple boxes. They're totally fine at my place for now, but if I get approved to foster…"

His apartment wasn't tiny, but it didn't have a lot of extra space. "Yeah. Sure. I'll come get it." I couldn't call Aspen, even if she was twenty minutes away. Not to go get my stuff from a lycan. My car was depreciating in dad's garage, a good two and a half hours to the west in Ballarat. "I'll see what I can do, but I don't have wheels. I'll call you."

"Yeah. Sure. No worries. No rush, like I said." He cleared his throat. "Sorry, Rory. About…"

I waited for the swell of rage, but I just felt hollow. "It's fine." It'd be fine. "I'll call you, okay? Set up a time."

"Yeah. Sure." He was quiet for a moment, then, "I'm free until six, anyway. I'm taking the classes, now."

Hellfire, the guy was basically stepping into Beo's life. Had he always lived in his shadow? Or was it some sort of sad hero worship? "I'll do what I can. How many boxes are we talking?"

"One big one. Two smaller ones."

How in the ever-loving fuck had I left that much shit there? "Okay." Definitely not a tram job. "I'll, um. I'll try to organize something."

Lilith had wheels and no trauma involving lycans. I hung up and reached mechanically for the stack of plates I'd been loading into the dishwasher. Lilith would be working. She'd also be happy to help out. And, fuck.

Fuck.

I took a breath. First, dishes. My head still ached but I had to follow up with Arthur, see when I could get back to work. Thrice cursed Clint had slowed me down long enough.

Lilith was as willing to help as I'd known she would be. I paid for her to fill her tank on the way, ignoring her protests. What else could I possibly do to acknowledge the fact she shuffled her work day around me without a second thought? I didn't deserve her. Or maybe she didn't deserve me.

The boxes weren't too heavy. They fit into the back of her sedan, crushing a velvet jacket she didn't seem concerned about. Zane carried them, then stood, a big, blonde lump with his hands in his pockets, looking uncharacteristically awkward. I waved goodbye, went to get in the car, and didn't talk shop.

Then couldn't. Just couldn't.

He was still mine.

I climbed back out of the car idling illegally behind someone else's carefully parked ute and walked back to him, reaching out for a hug.

Strong arms folded me in his chest in a way that was so familiar it was almost the same.

But he wasn't Beo.

"I've got your back still," I promised, into his chest. "You aren't alone. Okay?"

He held me tighter. My ribs creaked and tears burned my eyes. I didn't let them fall. "He couldn't bring them down on you, Rory. He couldn't. I'm sorry. I'm sorry for you both." I had no rage and no buffer, so I just held on as he let out a long, unsteady breath. He eased back before I was ready, but I forced myself to let him go. It felt like ripping off a bandage. "Thanks, Rory. For being here. For being you."

Shit, it felt big. More than just a changing of the guard. And my heart hurt. "Call me. Promise."

"Yeah." He touched his forehead to mine. "You're a good witch."

Good was subjective. The sunlight felt more like afternoon than morning despite the time of day and I hurt. My *bones* hurt. "You're okay, yourself." I stepped back, gave his giant arm a bit of a rub. "See you soon, Zane." He nodded and swallowed. "And wear your damn helmet," I added, just to lighten things.

His smile didn't ease the hurt. I turned, blinking the sun from my eyes, and jogged back to the car.

A few weeks ago, I'd defended his pack right here on this street. They'd replaced the broken signs and swept up the shattered glass.

Buildings around were in various stages of repair, with windows still boarded up, walls still sporting cracks, fences still flattened. But there was no blood on the road when Lilith merged into the traffic and turned us homeward.

She put on a pair of sunglasses against the glare of the light on wet bitumen. "You okay?" she asked me.

"Yeah." I was totally fine. "I mean, it isn't like I've just, you know, been put on admin leave for doing my job."

Her brows gave a sarcastic little quirk and she shook her head. "Yeah, that happened."

"Not like I cut a woman's throat, what, a week ago?"

She turned down the music. "Six days. Does she count as a woman if she's possessed?"

I remembered her hair in my hands and the way I'd tipped back her throat. Deirdre had been hiding in the shower. I remembered the texture of the carpet, the generic painting smashed behind her. "She was a woman," I said quietly. "Probably just like us." I picked at a hangnail. Line of duty. Whatever. Shit, it wasn't the first time. *Blood, pooling. Bones, breaking.* "And I got my arse kicked by a vamp three days ago."

"Pretty sure it was the lycan pack," she offered, warily.

"Who were there because of the vamp," I shot back. "Who just mauled their way through all those fucking cops like they were paper cutouts."

"Rory," she said, doing a quick head check before merging, "you did the best you could."

"Yeah, and that kid. Being dragged off." I tried to breathe. The grief. Fuck, the *grief.* "I don't know. I don't know if the other wizards in power are *all* vamped. I don't know if the faeries are in it to win it too. I don't know if Amor is *right now* on Dierdre's door, and I've got a box of shit I didn't know I'd even left at a bloke's place I'll probably never see again and I," I sucked in air, put my hands to my face. *Tears. Burning, scorching.* "I'm a fraud, Lilith. He knew it." And the horrible, sick truth of it was agony. The words were so quiet—broken. I didn't recognize them. I didn't recognize myself.

Her hand rested on my thigh. "He was scared."

"He was a *coward*." But the words were a sobbed plea for validation. And a lie. "Oh, shit, Lilith." And I couldn't breathe. Couldn't. Around the pain. The tears. "He said." *Air. Agony.* "And. And I."

Her hand squeezed on my thigh. The car stopped. I didn't see. Couldn't. Anything. "Come here, witch," she said, kindly, and I just fell into her arms. Just wept. All the grief. All the loss. It was too much.

She rocked us. The gearstick drove into my hip and reminded me of him. Of Beo. Of when he'd held me, of how he'd been so undemanding and kind. She smoothed my hair and held me close. I was caught in the flood, lost in the flow of Melbourne traffic inside the bubble of Lilith's friendship. The grief was ripped out, but it was a bottomless well.

My bones were broken.

She passed me tissues and flipped off someone who leant on their horn, I think. I couldn't talk. Couldn't tell her. What it all meant. How it all was some sort of huge force inside me I couldn't control. Couldn't ride.

I was drowning. But a small part of me knew we wouldn't go under if I could just hold on to her.

CHAPTER 22

I cried myself to exhaustion. She tucked me in on the couch and set hot chocolate beside me with my phone. I couldn't keep my swollen eyes open. "I'll be back," she promised. "If you're okay for a few hours."

What the fuck was I going to do? I just nodded, pathetic, and huddled lower in the blanket, listening to the silence of my apartment offset by the chaos in my head. There was nothing I could do except sleep.

When there was a knock on the door, I assumed it was Lilith. I mopped fresh snot off my face and tossed the tissue on the way to get it.

It wasn't Lilith. Arthur, impeccable in his three piece and holding a couple of bags, looked at me with compassion. "Um. Brought you some supplies. I heard what happened."

My mind went straight to Beo. "How?" I asked, the word rough.

"Reports go through me." He offered me the bags. "The cure is almost worse than the disease with love potions."

I looked at him, lost. "What?" I stepped back. Fuck it. Why not. Arsehole boss turned good. All it took was a bunch of hormones. Who knew? Who cared?

"The come-down from the love potion," he said, following me in with just a quick, furtive glance around. "Lilith said…but I know how it feels. So." He set the bags on my mostly clean bench, started unpacking them. "Feel free to crash. I'll just put this stuff away." He glanced around again. "Somewhere."

Even knowing he'd probably be trying to file shit alphabetically in my mayhem-driven system didn't amuse me. "I haven't had any potions," I told him, dully, watching as he put some fancy tissues in front of me. The sort for noses that had been sandpapered by frequent blowing. That was…weird of him.

He paused in the act of pulling out some fresh berries that would've cost a bomb this time of year. "Uh—okay." He was studying me. "Then why are you all." He waved a hand at his face.

I seriously considered punching him. A good gut punch. The mental image brought an inkling of satisfaction with it. "Because I just got my shit back from my boyfriend, you insensitive jerk." But the words held no heat, just exhaustion. I took the strawberries from his hand, popped the lid, and plonked myself down on a stool. "Want one?"

He gave me serious side-eye. "I didn't know you had a boyfriend."

I rolled my eyes at him. "Why would you?"

"We slept together, Rory," he said, and there was a bit of steel in his tone that went straight to my spine, making me straighten.

"Yeah." I bit into the berry. "And I mostly didn't think about the fact I was newly single and you were—" I cut myself off, disgusted, looked down at the berries. "Fuck."

He went back to unpacking bags. They rustled in the silence. Plastic and cardboard rustled against my bench. The bottles chimed as the fridge door opened. I had a good selection of sauces I couldn't be bothered using. And I just felt sick.

"Sorry," I managed, and bit into another berry. "It's not on you."

"Well. I guess knowing where we stand is good." And there was some chill in the words.

I deserved it. "Yeah. Well. Not like we talked about a future, did we?" I shoved the berries forward. A bag of nuts got pushed into some protein pancake mix. I didn't know what protein pancakes were and I didn't want to. "Have one."

He shook his head, taking some sort of green juice and putting it in the fridge. "No, thanks." He exhaled slowly. "So. You're still under the effect of the love potion."

I shrugged. "If I ever was, I guess."

He paused again with a bundle of deli meat wrapped in white paper in his hand. I peered at it with mild interest. "What do you mean? Your bloodwork showed it."

I shrugged again, eating another berry. They weren't a patch on Oma's, but better a berry in the hand than a punnet in the future. "Well, I didn't feel it."

He stayed standing there with the wrapped meat in his hand, his eyes fixed on me. "Who did you look at first?"

Casting my mind back took some doing, but I got there. "Lilith." I bit into the berry.

"I've done some research." He put the meat down on the bench, studying me intensely. "Love potions should work. Always."

Around some masticated berry, I said, "Unfortunately, I'm straight." At his confused look, I just shrugged. "Romantic love isn't the only sort of love, Arthur." It must take skill to grow berries with so little flavor. I looked through the punnet, disinterested. "I loved Lilith already. Guess that conquers all." The idea probably should've amused me, but right then, it felt a bit hollow.

He looked at me with the guileless expression of a child. "Are... are you joking, or serious? I can't tell."

My heart ached for him, just a little. He *was* being kind to me. So I said, "I'm serious. Didn't mean for it to sound flippant." I didn't apologize, but it was a near thing. Maybe Arthur legitimately didn't understand loving friendships. It said sad things about what society expected of men, really.

He shook his head slowly. "Wow. Okay. Well, I guess we don't need to worry about the come-down, then." He looked at the could-be-salami package between his hands as if he'd never seen it before.

Clearing his throat, he picked it up and took it to my fridge. "On the topic of Lilith, I have a problem I'm hoping you can help me solve."

"Oh, yeah?" I grabbed another berry. It had a dark bit on it that looked suss.

"The pins for the Solstice ball arrived a few days ago. I haven't handed them out, because…*legally*, she's on the male list. But I have an idea." I raised my brows and discarded the berry, because life was too short. "I got another envelope, renamed it, but those pins are worth a mint. They didn't give me spares. I can't swap it. If I give her a guy's one…well, I wondered if you'd be fine to wear a male mask."

I stopped perusing the dwindling pile of thanks-for-the-memory strawberries, focusing in on his earnest expression. "What?"

Judging by the dark look I got, it was the wrong reaction to his grand plan. "It isn't my fault, okay? I'm trying to figure it out, but everyone I speak to is just running me around in circles. She has to wear a mask, it's a thing."

Who the hells thought a masquerade Solstice celebration was smart? I'd forgotten it was even a thing, but now I thought about it, Lilith had been less excited than usual about the compulsory social bullshittery.

"So as long as you don't mind, no one will care if you do the switch, and she won't have to feel like shit."

"Or," I began, thoughtfully, "we could *ask* her?"

He half-laughed, but I didn't smile. "Wait. Seriously?"

I raised my brows. "Yes. Seriously." Surely that wasn't even a question. "Meanwhile, get the fucking mask policy changed, you useless wizard."

He winced. "I'm working on it. It'll take a few months. Nothing happens fast. I've drafted a proposal."

Surprised, I turned back to the strawberries. "Really? Consulted relevant stakeholders?"

His brows gathered. "No. But—" he stopped to think. I could just about hear the squeak of cogs in his head. "I'll have to clear it with the council, send out an invitation to the Covens. Get feedback." He ran a hand through his hair. "Shit."

My heart sat a little lighter in my chest at his somewhat stressed expression. At least he was stressed about something relevant. "Meanwhile. Vampires."

His frown deepened. "Yeah. Vampires. And you're out. I've been campaigning to get you back." He glanced at me. "Maybe some time isn't bad, though."

I raised my brows. "Gonna tell me I'm too emotional?"

He opened his mouth, then closed it and cleared his throat. "I should go. Got a meeting with the council tomorrow. Need to prep."

"Council?" I asked, standing.

"Wizards," he explained. "First one since you pulled that stunt—" he stopped. Shot me a quick look. "I mean. Did the, uh, Retrievals contract. For Vincetto."

I connected the dots. Vincetto must've been the wizard and his family. "That should smooth the way."

He shook his head briefly. "No. They're crying conflict of interest."

"That's trending right now," I muttered, sad and irritated. "I hardly ever take contracts."

"Just two that involve wizards in power," he pointed out, grimly, heading toward the door.

"You're shitting me," I said, horrified. "They're pulling that?"

He jiggled his keys, waiting for me to open the door. "They're trying to."

He was backing me up.

That was even weirder than puppy-eyed Arthur. I shook my head slowly. "I want to speak to them."

"I don't think that's a good idea," he said, in his smooth, middle-manager way. "You don't know these men, Rory."

Oh, but I did. I knew them better than they thought and far better than they wanted me to. Fury started to bubble. If they were trying to pull conflict of interest, I was going to be forced to give up Retrievals work.

I thought I'd wanted that. I did, still. But...

I thought of the girl, Taig, the cracking bones, Richardson, on her back, firing fruitlessly at the underside of a lycan. Pickle sliding down my ward.

They fucking *needed* me.

"Send me the meeting details," I told Arthur flatly.

He opened his mouth to argue but snapped his jaw shut. He was gritting his teeth and that self-restraint stirred something deep in my belly. "You aren't at your best."

"No shit." I yanked open the door. "And I'm still good enough to take them all. Get me in, Arthur."

CHAPTER 23

PROTEIN PANCAKES WERE FINE WHEN YOU SLATHERED THEM IN SYRUP and ate them with a side of righteous indignation. Arthur was *so sure* it would only backfire if I went in all guns blazing and even knowing in my bones that polite discourse with oppressors gets you politely oppressed, I'd somehow let myself agree to play his game. Once. Just once. That was all he got. And, shit, maybe a demonstration would show Arthur what the world really looked like.

I got an update from Nic so I knew he was still alive. I called through my report to Bethany, touched base with Dierdre off the books, and followed Arthur's advice to wear something feminine, much as it pissed me off.

But I wasn't burning bridges today. I was helping wheels turn. Pushing shit uphill. Pick a metaphor.

Anyway, my wheels would go uphill faster with some pushing. And today that involved getting out the soft green dress I'd worn once in two years because it seemed to generate its own body odor. Cheap fabric was such bullshit.

Taig called while I was avoiding the worst of the rain under a store's awning while I waited for the tram. "Hey."

"Hey yourself. A little bird told me you're pleading your case to the local wizards." I heard the complete lack of emotion in his voice. "Thought I'd give you the heads up. We know one of them is charisma'd. And you're in the *threat* category."

"Too fucking right I am," I muttered, and a middle-aged guy hurrying along froze about a meter away, staring at me, disgusted. "I'd kiss your mother with this mouth," I told him and puckered dramatically.

He moved along.

"She'd probably soap it," Taig said, amused.

"Oh. Not you. Generic passerby." I saw the tram trundle to a stop at lights on the other side of the intersection and timed my dash across traffic. "Who's dirty?"

"Is that for me, or your passerby?" he asked, and there was laughter in his voice still.

"You."

His voice dropped, became lower, but no more serious. "Well, I'm in public, but..."

He startled a laugh out of me. "Hellfire, Taig, you knew what I meant."

"Bart Griffiths." And he sounded serious, now. "South Melbourne coven. Don't know how they're getting at him, yet, so you haven't been called in. You don't know anything."

My heart ached. I wondered if he could lose his job for this. "My lips are sealed."

"I trust you." There was a blast of crackling from his end. "Sorry. Windy today. You got someone watching your back?"

I rocked as the tram moved along, dinging every now and then, the familiar back and forth of commuters and the rustle of umbrellas a strangely comforting environment. "Yeah," I said, kind of surprised when I thought about it. Because Arthur was in my corner. Sort of.

Against vampires trying to—what? Organize our bureaucracy?

"Also hearing an interesting rumor or two," he said, and the words were so quiet I had to work to hear them. "About a *very* old vamp who's transferring."

Unease trickled up my spine. Babies I could nail. Ancients were another thing. "Keep talking."

"Can't. Haven't seen the paperwork. Just know people, who know people who, who know people who are scared. Could be nothing."

His tone said he didn't believe it. I had respect for Taig's instincts. "How old are we talking?"

"Word is he's been traced back to the seventeen hundreds." *Fuck.* I glanced absently at the stop number as someone else boarded, held the information in a small part of my brain. "I've heard a lot more, too. Don't know if any of it is true, but there's definitely something happening."

The unease spread. He was very right about that. "Hey, Taig."

"Mm?"

I tucked the phone up closer to my still-tender ear. "You've been to the Solstice bullshit before, right?"

"Yeah. Required attendance for anyone working in the magi field." And that was it.

My mind spun as my body rocked. "I'm thinking about it," I said, slowly, feeling sick.

"About…not working in the field?" he asked, just as slowly.

"No." I tried to remember the specifics. A quiet park somewhere. Outdoors, but with marquees or whatever they called them, those big arse, fancy tents. Probably bows on the chairs. If there were chairs. Shit.

"Want to go together?" he asked, casually.

"Yeah." Because there was a sense of dread somewhere in the pit of my stomach. "Maybe. You keen?"

With laughter in his voice he said, "Sure. Just let me know if I'm your date, your backup, or your guide, though. Helps avoid awkwardness."

Oh, fuck. Yeah. Woops. "Backup. Masquerade ball, all the magi gathered in the middle of nowhere—"

"It's behind the Royal Children's Hospital. That's the opposite of the middle of nowhere." But there was a hint of curiosity coming through. "Keep talking."

I glanced up, gauging how close I was. "Can't, gotta get off in a few minutes. But. Anyone else I should keep my eye on?"

"All of them," he said, dismissively. "But nothing specific. Call me when you're done? I'd value your opinion."

"Sure. Don't hold your breath though. Wizards talk forever."

"Amen," he agreed easily. "Good luck, Rory."

I wasn't going to get to do much, though. The goal was to make me look as least conflicting as possible. *Conflictual? Conflicted?*

Fuck. I was so screwed.

I stepped in a puddle climbing off the tram and my painfully cute heels offered me no protection. I could all but *feel* the water gleefully travelling up the boring beige stockings I'd bought specifically for this occasion. With an arm over my face to protect my very minimal makeup from the drizzle I dashed across the road and started to trudge.

One wizard; known vampire fodder. One more; recently rescued. Arthur. That was three out of five they'd had a swing at that we *knew* of.

And Amor was in the wind.

I kept my eyes on the path ahead. As Taig had said, it was a windy day today. I didn't want any long-lost witches blowing in.

Why the fuck had she gone after me? Revenge? It wasn't like I was still standing between them and Dierdre. Officially, I'd been kicked off the case. Lilith and Arthur were greater threats to whatever morally corrupt scheme they'd hatched.

I didn't need to double check the number at the front of the building. *North Melbourne Coven* was emblazoned across the front window in heavy lettering. It had probably been some sort of three-story office space at some point. Now it was all witch, down to the huge window planters overflowing with somewhat dejected herbs and the black cat curled up on the couch in the reception area.

How come *we* didn't get a reception area?

Our cat was cuter, though. And wanted to eat the rich.

A man stood smack bang in the center of the reception room, an espresso mug in his hand and the serene aura of unshakable power—said dickhead vibe made me confident he was a wizard.

Maybe I should start up some sort of side hustle. *Can spot arseholes after point-zero-one seconds. Aura reading by Aurora.* Ew. No.

"Rory," he said, smiling and offering me a hand. "Jerome Hamilton. Welcome to my coven."

His coven. Sure.

I put my hand in his and felt the callouses from wand use. It surprised me, a little, that this old relic in his fancy suit with his miniature coffee did work. "Pleasure to be invited," I said, glancing down at the hand in mine. Diamonds. He was charmed to the nines.

"We both know you weren't," he said, amused, as he released my hand. "Arthur's been campaigning for you."

I met his eyes and bit back the responses I wanted to make. Instead, I just said, "He's a good wizard."

"He is," Jerome agreed, making no move to lead me to wherever we were supposed to go. Or offer me a coffee. I could deal with mini coffee. The cute cup would match my cute shoes. "But he isn't the best diplomat."

I raised my brows. "Aren't we on the same team, Jerome?" And, shit, I was polite.

His smile was not at all warming. "The witch who brought down the High Wizard, not understanding there are competing interests at play?" he clicked his tongue at me and shook his head in disapproval. "You'll have to do better." He stepped back, waving a hand at a set of stairs. "But I trust you know how. Up the stairs, first room on the right."

I walked past him, that warning ringing in my ears and a sick weight in the bottom of my belly.

The first room on the right was well lit but not from any source of sunlight. The whoosh of ducted heating kicking in was my greeting; a table of four wizards, complete with name plates, dominated the room. One beige wall was taken up by a gigantic image of a mythical wizard holding off a demon and a whole sea of nasties with what looked like the Homefires spell. I mean, Homefires was great, but I'd been there. It didn't look half so pretty in real life.

"Good morning," I said brightly, taking the one seat without a name plate as Jerome shut the door behind me. "Thank you for having me today."

"Aurora Gold, this is Samuel Brown from West, Bart Griffiths from South, and Vincetto Delerenzo from South East. You've met Jerome?" Arthur asked, as said slimeball slipped into his seat. Not waiting for me to respond, he said, to the table at large, "Aurora is keen to return to her work. Being a witch down, given the climate right now, is a major issue, and as a diligent worker, she's—"

"The climate is exactly why she can't return," Vincetto said, sitting back. I barely remembered his face. I wondered if his kid was doing okay as his eyes went to Bart, over the table.

Bart resembled a side of pickled pork left too long in the pot and there was something very cold about his gaze that made me wonder if I'd bother taking a contract if it was just to save his hide. "We aren't here to be judge, jury and executioner." And he reinforced these words with a firm nod of his head. "We need to separate Caretakers from any form of law enforcement."

I kept my mouth shut. He wasn't technically wrong. I was a pretty good executioner, though. And not the worst judge or jury.

Samuel frowned at Bart. "The vampires are a very real threat, and we have a very real weapon, right here. Why not use it?"

Arthur cleared his throat. "Aurora is a witch, not a weapon, Samuel, however I think I take your meaning."

"What say you, witch?" Jerome asked, setting down his espresso cup beside his laptop without looking at me.

I wondered if they'd taught him to talk like a dirtbag at Self Important Arsehole School. "I've taken two Retrievals contracts in the past twelve months," I said, perfectly polite. "I do not actively seek employment in that area. I'm known to Victoria Police, it's true, but I don't take contracts directly from them." I mean, I had, but only for expediency. "They contact the Retrievals handler, who weighs need against resources. I'm a resource." And I didn't look at Vincetto. Fucking wizards. "My focus is supporting the vulnerable. I take my job as a Caretaker seriously."

"Aurora hasn't been part of a Retrievals team for quite some time," Arthur agreed, turning back to the table. "The jobs she has taken only strengthen her connections to our community."

Samuel was nodding. "And someone who can deal with vampires and lycanthropes when the chips are down is good to have on the books."

I folded my legs, feeling sick, and waited for the rebuttal. "Caretakers have a lot of information at their fingertips," Vincetto said, shooting me a look of disdain. "Aurora, you leveraged that against Edward Van Der Holst."

Fucking right I had. And I'd do it again.

"Which was, of course, the right thing to do at *that* point," Bart cut in. "However, that sort of power—and the division of loyalties—isn't viable in the long run."

Jerome, up the end of the table, met my eyes as Arthur said, "Aurora's role in uncovering Van Der Holst's corruption is one we *all* support." And the statement was most definitely a threat. "As do the media." I kept my brows from rising. How come *he* was allowed to push his weight around? "The issue isn't Van Der Holst *or* conflicts of interests. It's the death of a woman who had been moments away from summoning an angel, and whether we feel that Aurora needs to await the results of the police investigation."

"That's just the symptom of the problem brought about by the actual underlying issue here—her conflict of interest," Vincetto said dismissively. "We cannot have this as a precedent to allow other such breaches."

The cycle kicked off again. Jerome picked up his espresso, swirled the contents of the cup, and let it continue.

Two on one side. Two on the other. And there Jerome sat, just watching me, amused.

Fuck.

I listened. I wasn't invited to speak again and I probably couldn't have even if I had, because they were all so keen to convince one another of their arguments. So I sat there, nonthreatening, low conflict little old me, and waited it out.

Jerome eventually cleared his throat and stood. "Perhaps we should meet again in a few days' time, ladies and gentlemen? Aurora, if you'd wait downstairs, I'd like to consult you on a separate issue in your capacity as Retrievals Officer." Unease climbed up my spine to wrap around my throat. "Gentlemen, when should we five meet again?"

The handle of the door was cold. My stockings had dried a little, but my shoes were still soaked. I walked downstairs, sat on the couch, and let my mind turn.

Retrievals? I'd put money on the fact that this arsehole had vampire problems. And that he was about to use my tenuous position to force me to do something I didn't want to do.

I sat back and the cat on the couch stood and showed me its butt-hole. I wasn't sure if that was approval or not. I could be cleared next week. Multiple Amors meant multiple opportunities for them to call on an angel. Even if Nic witnessed what I had, identified it, reported it, that'd be enough. Shit, I wouldn't want them to have to actually *deal* with even the echo of the being that a possessed person could call on.

On the other hand, the situation could settle. And there may *never* be enough evidence to get Clint off my back. Then I'd have to wait on the mercy of the new District High Wizard, whenever, whoever, however that happened.

I figured the odds were unfortunately pretty good I'd have evidence of angelic threat before the month was up. I also knew firing me right now, after I'd caused such a ruckus with Van Der Holst, would be a very bad political move. 'Oh she was super anti-corrupt earlier but now turns out she's corrupt ha-ha promise we aren't just singling her out' wasn't going to fly with the voters. Especially not after I opened my big mouth. This was a government job. The Minister of Magi didn't want to look any worse than he already did. I was relatively safe.

Annoyed, delayed, but safe.

But it never hurt to hedge my bets, did it?

They filed out in pairs. Arthur and Samuel stopped, shook my hand. "We need you," Samuel told me, and there was an intensity to his gaze that made the hair on the back of my neck rise. "The city is rife with vampires and lycanthropes. We need witches like you to stand against that. Thank you for your service, Aurora."

I was reminded of the picture up on the wall of the idealized wizard standing against a flood of darkness with just a flashy kids' trick. Fucking wizards. Everything was about them. Even in actual fights for actual causes, they made themselves the heroes. "I'm just doing my jobs, Samuel," I said, calmly. "But thank you for your kind words."

"Humble, too." He nodded in approval. "Blessed be, sister."

"Let me know when you're free," Arthur told me, as Samuel released me and stepped back. "Today, preferably."

I raised a brow at this, then smoothed it quickly when I heard Jerome coming down the stairs. "Sure."

He nodded firmly. "Be careful," he murmured as he moved past me.

I didn't even roll my eyes. Who the hells was I?

"I've got a meeting next in your area," Jerome told me with a glance at his watch. "Perhaps you could ride with me so we can talk and travel?"

I resettled my bag on my shoulder, fell into step beside him, and was guided out front to an idling car. I hadn't seen a single witch, just a cat. Interesting.

Jerome opened the back door of an oversized car and ushered me in. "I employ a driver," he said as I did a quick scan for anything that should be concerning me. "Allows me to work during traffic jams." The rest of us just employed public transport, but sure. I climbed in, slid over the leather seats to the far side.

"Usual, sir?" the driver asked, watching his side mirrors.

"Thanks, Xander. We'll need to drop Ms. Gold off, too, perhaps at the Melbourne East Coven?" He checked with me and I nodded. It was closer to home than this was, and Arthur said he wanted to see me. "If you wouldn't mind, Xander could drive you after I'm at my meeting." It wasn't a question. He took his wand and murmured a spell. A privacy wall appeared between us and the driver.

He thought he had me cold.

I watched him, curious. I was uneasy, sure, but what could this guy *really* do? Nothing I couldn't fight.

"I hope you don't mind, the consultancy was more or less an excuse," he admitted, settling back, ankle over his knee, arms spread. Taking up space. King of the car.

My belt was buckled. I resisted the urge to dig out my phone and send a few texts just to piss him off. "I assumed."

"We *are* having an exceptionally old vampire transferring," he went on, as if I hadn't spoken, "but it's being managed by Retrievals."

The word *real* was inferred there ahead of Retrievals. "That's good," I said, blandly. But mentally I ticked off Taig's rumor as fact. 'Exceptionally ancient' wasn't a precise term, though. And damned if I was showing him I was interested by asking more.

"You've now seen the situation," he said, calmly.

"I don't need a unanimous vote, do I?" I asked him, just to make sure. And I'd double-check his answer with Arthur later.

"Just a majority." And there was just a hint of amusement in the words. "You're a smart woman. You know you're on your knees, now."

I considered that. I'd been on my knees plenty of times, and when shit got real, I'd often go there out of choice—to fight. "I should probably address the media requests I've been receiving since the last job I did."

Where I'd saved Vincetto's family. And a bunch of cops. And that was *already* known to the media.

"That would be excellent," Jerome agreed, idly. "Clear up any misconceptions about poor Vincetto still being under the influence of vampires. Of course, having media involvement in most of our doings would be a lot more difficult." He just tilted his head ever so slightly, watching me like a bug. "But I'm sure you're right about this particular time."

I got the inferred threat and didn't bother to hide my amusement.

"Let's cut the dancing, Jerome. You tell me what you want, I'll tell you what I'll pay to get it." Everyone knew you could catch flies with honey, but a hollowed-out corpse also worked, and I didn't mind which way we went.

Arthur was going to flip.

He shrugged a little. "It'll be a bit of work for me to deal with the council. Agreeing to reinstate you will mean discussions, paperwork. Annoyance. I'd consider some stress relief a fair trade." He held my eyes. "And you are already on your knees, Aurora."

Well, the gum was safe then. I popped open my bag, took out a stick and unwrapped it. My belly was a massive knot and that was just fine. "Just to clarify. You want me to suck your cock."

"That isn't what I said. There are many ways we can make one another's life easier."

Yeah, just in case I was recording this. But his eyes were on my mouth as I slid the gum between my teeth. I was happy to lick the boot, damned if I'd deepthroat it. "Cool. Well, to clarify, I'm actually not on my knees." I folded the gum wrapper neatly. "I'm on the ground. And it just so happens that's where I fight best." I tucked the rubbish into my bag. "What I'll offer you is that I'll forget about this conversation and provide my expertise as a priority to you and yours for the remainder of the year." I cocked my head, kept on smiling at him. He had a hard on and he wasn't even trying to be subtle about it. Climbing into his lap right now was tempting. I could do a lot of damage to that dick. And his genitals, too.

His brows rose a little. "Arthur speaks about you as a loyal witch. Your job is important to you."

I felt the laugh bubble up in my chest. "Sure it is. It's my life. I would *absolutely* go back to my Retrievals team—who, by the way, have requested me numerous times, including this morning—and use that work to fund an unfair dismissal case." I sighed and he could make of that sound what he wanted. "The timing of this would be very inconvenient, too, what with Van Der Holst and Vincetto being compromised." I met his eyes squarely. "And who knows who else could be dirty. Right, Jerome?"

He raised a brow. "Are you threatening me?"

I considered it. "I mean, you could buy a *lot* of masturbation sleeves or hours with a quality sex worker for the cost of fighting an unfair dismissal, couldn't you?" His eyes were diamond hard and mean. "Oh, look. This is my stop. You going to give Xander the nod to let me out here?"

He didn't glance out the window. "I don't believe this discussion is finished."

"Well, that's the thing. I do." I undid my seatbelt, my keys and wand in my hand as I steeled myself. "Just as an FYI, mate, I've jumped out of helicopters way more times than you've successfully convinced vulnerable folks to dick ride you, so I have no qualms with making a scene right now and throwing this door open." Maybe just a few. A helicopter was light years away from a car in traffic and my armor was a wafer-thin dress.

"You have a revolting turn of phrase, Aurora." And he ended the spell. "Xander, please stop at your earliest convenience. Ms. Gold has another appointment."

"For what it's worth," I said, taking out my phone. "My offer stands until," I checked the time. "Tonight. Make sure I'm at least BCC'd into any correspondence today if you'd like to take me up on it."

He said nothing as the car stopped. I glanced out, saw the tram beside us. Close enough. I opened the door, climbed out into the rain and, heart in my throat, dashed toward safety.

CHAPTER 24

I FOUND MY WAY TO A PLACE THAT SMELLED LIKE AMBROSIA AND GOT myself a coffee. My hands were shaking.

I didn't want to go back to Retrievals.

No thrice-cursed way was I getting on *that* ride, though.

My coffee arrived as I was staring at my phone. I sent Lilith a text first, knowing she'd be waiting. *Went badly. Don't call now. Tonight, yours? Will bring junk food.*

The response landed almost instantly. *Sure. Also happy to eat out. Night before battles are great times to feast. Choose later. Xo*

I loved my witch.

The air I drew into my lungs was warm and rich with spices. I wasn't hungry, but I should've been. The words on the menu blurred in front of me. Who else had I promised to check in with?

Arthur. Elders, I didn't want to tell him what had gone down. He'd white knight for sure. And if I didn't tell him, he'd lose it at me for undermining his efforts. Which, I had to admit, weren't small.

That pretty much left Taig. I remembered the throwaway remark Jerome had made about a vampire. Now we knew where said vamp was landing. It was something. I sent him a quick text. *Call me.*

Then I breathed. I felt the seat beneath me with its generously stuffed cushions, the cold surface of the beautiful wood table beneath my hands, the wet of my shoes on my feet. I knew better than to try to be small to be accepted. If people didn't accept you when you were you, they wouldn't really give a shit about you any other way, either.

Grimly I glanced at the menu and forced myself to read. Duck fat potatoes jumped out at me and I wondered if I could get it down even if it was as good as it sounded.

My phone rang. Taig's name glowed on the cracked screen. I answered and he said, "Good, bad, ugly?"

"Ugly."

He grunted. "You okay?"

"On a scale of garden variety annoying wizard, to wizards who could fall into a pit of lollipops and still end up somehow sucking their own dicks?"

"That good, huh? I haven't taken lunch yet. I can meet you."

I glanced back down at the menu. Eating with someone seemed a lot less daunting and it would mean I could tell him the very little I knew. Little bits of information added up. "I *am* at a place that has duck fat potatoes. And good coffee." And it wasn't just to help me out. This was his job, after all. I was basically an informant.

"Coffee and potatoes went without saying," he told me, amusement in his voice. "Where are you?"

"One of the amazing smelling restaurants on Lygon Street. I'll text you the name once I figure it out." I ran my eyes over the bar. "Thanks, Taig."

"See you in about fifteen."

I put my phone down, tried to read the menu again. Failed.

A rush of rage would've been nice. I could've called Aspen, ranted at her. She would've been great. I could've called Oma, got all the dirt on Jerome. Or at least fifteen minutes' worth. But instead, I just sat there feeling like shit and scrolling through social media.

Taig arrived, brow creased lightly with concern, just as I was considering getting into an argument with a random person who'd made a *not all men* sort of comment on social media. "Lost your jacket?"

"I'm being feminine, as per Arthur's demands."

His brows rose fractionally. "Jackets are gendered?"

"Mine are all toast or clash with the dress."

His brows rose further. "Dresses are gendered?"

I felt a smile tug at my mouth, but it was sad. "Are you going to offer me *your* jacket, or just sit there being sanctimonious?" And I really *was* cold.

He shrugged out of the big, sensible jacket, passing it over carefully. "I want that one back. It's good for these just-above-freezing days we're having."

I stood to scoot into it quickly with a sigh of relief. It held his warmth and some of the sandalwood I associated with him. "Yeah, I'll give it back when you go. Of course."

"Keep it. It's too cold out there. Tomorrow. Whenever." He glanced at the menu. "Step or two above our usual hole in the wall. Nice choice. But you can't go wrong on Lygon Street." He poured us both a water absently. "I could take you for gelati when the weather gets a bit better. There's a great place just a few doors down."

My heart squeezed. That wasn't an absent offer. "I was just sexually harassed by a dude in power, Taig."

The menu drooped in his hands. His jacket wasn't huge on me, but I felt like a kid, suddenly. "I'm really sorry that happened, but I'm glad you told me so I don't put any more moves on you at a time like this."

The feelings swirled, big and potent. I breathed. "I like your moves."

"Good. I've got plenty for you, when it's appropriate." He set down the menu. "What can I do right now to help you feel safe?"

Shit, the man was a cardboard cutout of perfection. I pulled back, taking the glass of water with me. As shields went, it'd do. "I'm fine."

"Yeah, well, that checks out." He glanced up as a waiter came over, held up two fingers to ask for more time. I *hurt.* The glass was cold as I lifted it to my lips.

"Want to tell me about it?"

"It was pointless," I said, wishing I had the armor of fury to pull on. I just felt tired. "This is why we don't *ask nicely* for shit, you know?

People are like," I dropped my voice and put on my best Chad face, "'If you just asked nicely people would be much more likely to listen.'" I sighed at the glass of water, rubbing the Chad away. "And that's just not it."

Taig nodded slowly, studying me closely. "You don't usually bother playing by their rules."

"No, I don't," I agreed, feeling suddenly very small. "They're playing with a stacked deck with rules that favor them, so why would I?" I took a sip of water, but it didn't wash away the taste of bile. "Anyway, maybe Arthur will learn from it, at least." I shrugged it off. If it took an active demonstration to prove that, well, maybe he'd see it. "And as for the wizard who tried to corner me." A lump in my throat silenced me. The water let me wash it away, at least. "I promised I'd forget about it if he played ball today." I blew out a breath, let my shoulders drop. "And take it to the top if he got me fired."

His face was perfectly neutral. "Want to put in a report tomorrow after he doesn't agree to your terms?"

"Maybe." I shook my head but it didn't clear any. "Anyway. That's a later problem."

"I'm not on tomorrow," he said, quietly. "Unless you tell me you're coming in. Then I'll try to swap shifts with Clint."

I waved that away. "No. Let me sit on it. And we have internal processes I'd need to look into, too. But considering what I pulled out against him…"

Taig shrugged. "Doesn't matter." Then he glanced down at his glass. "Okay, it might matter." And he let out a long breath. "I'll be in your corner, though. Whether you make it official or not."

I found his foot with mine under the table and gave him a nudge. "Hey. Not that big a deal. But he mentioned an 'exceptionally ancient' vampire coming onto his books."

Taig met my eyes, his narrowed with concentration. "Which one is he?"

"Jerome Hamilton. He's North."

"Don't know him. Yet." He took out a notepad, scribbled something. "Good to know where this ancient is landing."

"Thought you'd be glad to have that snippet." I finished the water to wash the conversation away. "I'm having whatever those potatoes come with. Know what you're getting?"

"Disillusioned," he said, wryly. "With a side of gnocchi."

"Hey, that's what I had for dinner last night," I said brightly, enjoying the humor that lit his pale blue eyes. The way he looked at me warmed me in a way the jacket hadn't quite managed. I almost pulled back again, almost picked up my glass. I didn't. But I couldn't quite reach over the table to seek out the hand I knew he'd give me. So, I sat there with him, feeling warm and safe in the little pocket of bullshit free peace he'd somehow managed to carve out. "Maybe by summer I'll be down for gelati," I offered, then wanted to snatch back the words.

His smile deepened. "They've always got it. Tomorrow, this summer, or in ten years' time, pretty sure we could grab a gelati at Lygon Street."

My head spun at the enormity of that offer. I glanced at the menu, flipping to desserts that I couldn't read. "Know anything about Samuel Brown?" I managed, somehow.

"Whispers. Nothing concrete. What've you got?"

We talked. Ordered. Talked. Ate. Talked. He offered to drive me to my coven, since it was on his way back to work, and made it...easy. He'd brought his personal car, not a patrol car, and there was something about the blast of music that came on when he started it up, the sunglasses on the dash, the half-empty water bottle on the ground at my feet, that made me feel like I'd just been invited into his inner sanctum.

It was a nice place to be.

"Got plans tonight?" he asked as he eased into traffic. "That isn't a move. I'm checking in, here."

Sitting there in his jacket, in his space, I felt my heart shiver. "Last guy who got concerned about me ended up an arsehole."

"That takes time to process." He glanced over at me fleetingly, back to the road. "I'm not going to lie and say I don't care what happens to you, but I know you can handle yourself. And not just when you're sticking ceremonial knives into the throats of lycanthropes." He shrugged. "Still. No one gets through alone. No one should have to."

If I hung out with him much longer my teeth would start to rot from all the sweetness. I kind of wanted one more bite, but I knew I couldn't keep it up forever. "You do know I'm a heartless bitch."

"I know you've got a rep," he said, amused. "Looked into you when you knew things a wet behind the ears witch shouldn't."

Unease skittered up my spine. "Oh, yeah? What's my body count at, Taig?"

He shot me another glance, this one amused. "You trying to piss me off or scare me off?"

"What'll come first?"

He reached up, rubbed his jaw. "I don't scare easy. I'm already pissed off, but not at you. So." He tossed me his phone, unlocked. "You don't wanna talk, that's fine. DJ."

In the music app I scrolled through his recently played. I knew most of the songs, liked a lot of them.

Fuck.

"Any news on Amor?" I asked, trying desperately to get back to somewhere comfortable and familiar.

"I haven't looked at my work phone since I left the office when you messaged. I'll check work emails when we stop." He settled back. "Are you down for an early morning raid tomorrow? If, hypothetically, there's a wizard who's been charisma'd?"

"This wouldn't be the one I don't know about?"

"Couldn't possibly be."

"Cool. He can eat a dick. But I'll be there to save your arses. Hypothetically." I turned on something heavy and hard. "My shirt still has chomp marks. And—shit. My wooden knife. I haven't replaced it."

He didn't look away from the road, but I saw a frown crease his forehead. "Can I help source something tonight? It's likely we'll move tomorrow, we're just waiting on clearance. Richardson is driving again."

I liked Richardson. "Can you whittle?"

He glanced at me with raised brows. "You serious? Your foci is just a chunk of wood that, like, you've cut down and sanded in a knife shape?"

With my tongue firmly in my cheek, I said, "Well, I did dance naked in the moonlight whilst sanding it."

"Sounds risky. You don't need grit in sensitive areas." I felt a smile tugging at my mouth. I was slipping all too easily into the rhythm and pleasure of his company. "Make sure you wear eye protection," he told me, blandly. "Next time."

"Yes, Detective." I slumped down in the seat, propped a knee up on the dash and nosed through his music. "You need some charms for tomorrow?"

"I'd never say no," he told me. "But I can't carry half the shit you can."

I glanced up from his phone. "You've gone *that* deep into my file?"

"Good thing I did, too, or you'd have been forced to justify how it is you came to access it. Those time controlling charms you just casually popped the other day got some attention."

I winced. "Shit. Nothing casual about it. I *still* hurt from that."

"Yeah? Well, you made it look pretty easy." He turned up the heat a bit with an absent flick and I remembered those strong fingers in my hair. My blood warmed and it had nothing to do with the increasing temperature of the air. "Someone with fancier words than me said 'graceful'. Or 'elegant' or something, I can't remember."

"Huh. Greene's a sweetheart. He's going to get dead if he isn't careful."

He shot me a fast look. "He likes you. He's a good kid."

I snorted. "Fuck off, Taig."

"What?" he asked. "He does and is. Not like I've got a monopoly."

"Yeah, and you know damned well I don't go in for *kids*."

He scratched at his jaw again. The rasp of stubble against the skin of his hand made me wonder what it'd be like against my chest. My thighs. *Shit.*

"Anyway. I'll try and help him not get dead." He did a quick head check. "Interesting, though. You didn't mention it isn't the fact he's a cop that concerns you. Good to know."

"Don't take it to the bank," I told him, amused, and changed the song.

"Wasn't where I was thinking of going," he told me lazily. "Want a coffee before we land? Drive through place here isn't the worst."

"Mm. No. I want to hear what's in your work emails." I thought of what was waiting for me at the coven.

The conversation I'd have to have with Arthur.

"Actually—" I cut off what I was saying. He was digging in his pocket. "What're you doing?"

He pulled out what I recognized as his work phone, unlocked it with his thumb without looking at it. "Keys to the city," he said, amused. "Here. And *I'm* getting coffee."

I took it, mildly stunned. "Pretty sure this is super illegal."

"I know it is." He took the exit off the street a bit hard, wincing as he scraped the bottom of the car on the gutter. With an apologetic pat on the dash, he guided it into the drive through. "Gonna get me fired? We can go private together. We'd be rocking PIs."

My head spun as I looked at the tiny, compact phone in my hand. "Um?"

"I want it to be super noir. How do you feel about trench coats and hard lighting, Rory?"

"Oh. Yeah. I'm, ah." I cleared my throat. "Wait. Aren't I the femme fatale in this fantasy?"

"No. I want that job. You're the hard bitten, gritty get shit done one. And you have to wear the hat." He stopped at the speaker. "Can I have a large latte?" And he looked over at me, brows raised.

I leant over. "And a long black, thanks," I said, loudly. "Regular." I could smell him. I pulled back, hard, tossing his phone back. "I hate hat hair. You tell me if there's something I need to know."

"Fine. We can both be femme fatales. I can share." He eased forward in the queue and, once we were idling, glanced at the phone.

I looked out the window. The man was way too smooth, and this was far too comfy. He wasn't going to be half as simple to be involved with as he made out. Not when he had me all but eating out of his hand, even now, with all the shit going on.

"Got an update," he said, and the words were neutral. "Your old team was on the Amors. They followed them back to their den."

I knew that, but something about his mannerisms made alarm trickle up my spine. "And?"

He wasn't smiling. I felt the world dropping away. "They've gone dark."

Ice went through me. *Afternoon sunlight.* But they weren't dead. In my haste to sit up, I banged my knee on the dash. "What? When? I spoke to Nic this morning at eight. No news was good news."

"Sent a call for backup at," he glanced up, eased forward about a meter in the queue. "Ten thirteen. Went dark at ten thirty-two."

I fell back, feeling sick.

If they'd gone dark it meant they were in serious trouble. You didn't cut off all communications lightly. The only reasons were if they had to go underground to escape pursuit...or lay a particularly dangerous trap. And if they'd called for backup...

"What was the backup call for?"

He passed the phone over silently.

The email was an automated one. No specifics. Just a 'this may be relevant to a case you're on'. The request for backup was exactly that, nothing more or less.

It didn't tell me if those words had been whispered, screamed, or sobbed. It didn't tell me if they had their back to a wall or were on the run. My chest was tight. I'd been there. Done that. Twice. I'd walked out, twice.

Not all of us had.

I tried to piece it together. Nic's nonchalance earlier on the phone. He'd hit on me in the same way he always did. Said nothing new. Knew nothing new. Then this call for backup. What was new?

I glanced back at the email and the ice in my veins seeped into my bones. "Bang sent up the call."

"Not the usual MO?" he asked me, easing forward a bit further.

"No. Nic's job. She's third in the chain. It means..."

"They couldn't," he finished, quietly. "But there's a lot of reasons for that." The sound of the warm air pumping into the car sounded like the rush of air before a projectile. "I guess you know enough to know what to worry about."

I dragged in air. *Vix. Brandon.* They were the tip of the iceberg. "Angels aren't something to play with, Taig."

"I believe you." He eased forward a little further, digging out his wallet. He must've paid, but I only registered as he turned and tossed the wallet into the little spot in the console host to half a packet of antihistamines. Before I could do more than open my mouth to object he shot me an annoyed look. "I can buy you a coffee, Rory."

There was a lump in my throat. "I don't know—if Amor could be on the move, or what's his face, the ex—"

"No pressure about tomorrow. We've done it without you all this time. We can do it again."

Pickles sliding down my ward, the dripping blood. *Broken. Dead.* "I'll go. But I won't take point." I couldn't afford the injuries. Not now.

"You don't have to decide right now," he said, calm as the eye of a storm.

If Dierdre's ex was on the move, if they'd managed to pin my team down…I knew where Amor would end up. I knew what it'd look like.

I'd never fought an ancient vampire. I'd heard stories, though. Read a report or two. And those vamps hadn't been around since the seventeen hundreds. Rule of thumb with vamps; if you could track them for one year, they'd been there for ten. My brain couldn't do that math, much less extrapolate that potential power into reality or plan for tomorrow.

But I knew what it was to go dark. I knew what my team were facing. Not the nitty gritty, but the overall. *That* I could picture.

And if I had to choose between a police task force and Dierdre, those cops were toast.

Taig was one of them.

My head spinning, I struggled to breathe. There would be lycans. He had silver bullets.

Brandon had too.

"You going to vomit?" Taig asked me, bluntly, as we eased forward. The words overlaid the sound of breaking bones that echoed in my head. My heart. *The spurt of blood.* "Maybe," I lied, because it was easier. Because I knew what he'd do.

Sure enough, he thrust a vomit bag into my hand and reached over, double handed, scooped up my hair. I felt every shifting strand as he neatly fed it into one of his hands, then twisted it comfortably around his fist. Something about that tension felt comforting, so I stayed there, over the vomit bag, as he eased the car forward one handed and held my hair with the other.

He kept me anchored.

The warmth of that hand, the tension, felt good and real and wholesome. Maybe I could have my cake and eat it too. Be there for Taig. Be there for Dierdre. I had no idea if and when Amor and Co would land. I *did* know what the police going in without magickal expertise would look like, even if I couldn't scale a truly ancient vampire's power to my experiences.

Pickles sliding down my ward. The bark of gunfire. Blood sprayed over cracked plaster, semi-caved in walls. Bodies, twisted and tossed aside. I could *hear* the sound of Taig's bones breaking, and maybe I did need the vomit bag after all. Because those silver eyes with their beautiful grey flecks would be as cold as the blood in my veins in minutes.

"Breathe, Rory," he said from beside me.

I struggled to do as he said. There was a slight tug as he leant away from me, his arms both at full extension as he took the coffee. I'd tricked him into that contact and it made me feel cheap, but I didn't tell him it was unnecessary. Even if I did puke, it wouldn't be the first time I washed vomit out of my hair.

We moved forward a short way and I felt the car come to a halt. "We're okay. Got us a good park. Some passable coffee. We're about three blocks from your coven."

I nodded and the grip on my hair eased a little. Without thinking, I slapped my own hand over his to keep him there. The window buzzed up and I sucked in warming air. "Want my other hand?" he asked, so calm, so relaxed.

I wanted so much more and it made the nausea spike. I breathed through it, clutching the vomit bag.

I couldn't do this. It wouldn't work.

I let his hand go and he, in turn, released my hair slowly. The sensation of those strands shifting was both familiar and strange as curls fell down to curtain my face. I let the bag fall away and dragged air in deep.

"Want to talk about it?" he asked me quietly.

"No." I shook my head in case the word was as indecipherable as the thoughts, the feelings, the whirlwind in my heart. "I didn't leave the team because I wanted to." I squeezed my eyes shut and wanted to snatch those words back. "No. I don't want to talk about it."

"I'm not judging you," he said, quietly. "Like I said, I've done some digging. Your file wasn't bedtime reading."

Oh, fuck. I couldn't look at him but I wanted to cry, right then. Totally fall apart. Just climb into the footwell and howl like a wounded beast. "Don't rely on me, Taig," I managed to get out, somehow. Because I couldn't bear the thought of his bones splintering in the afternoon sunlight, too. "I can't keep you safe."

"Sounds, to me, like you're taking a lot of responsibility there," he said, with a sigh. Into the silence, his seat creaked. "Things go wrong. They go wrong when I'm there. They go wrong when you're there. We just try to minimize the shit that hits the fan, Rory. That's all. And we aren't perfect." He had no idea, though, exactly how *far* from that I was. "Neither is this coffee. Try yours. Tell me if I should take this swill back."

I knew what he was trying to do and couldn't fight against it. Sitting up, I nursed the coffee as rain fell against the windshield, a slow, steady, soothing sound that felt right and good. "I mean it, Taig." I couldn't look at him. I was so small, so brittle. "You've seen me do okay. I don't always."

"Yeah, well, you didn't introduce yourself as a hero, so." He held out his hand and I couldn't put mine in it. It fell away and sat between us, an offer. My bones ached. "All that shit aside, Rory—I've seen you at work. You fall apart at the end. That's pretty much what the end of a shit show is for."

Bones, breaking. I swallowed around the tears in my throat. "I think the lycans that day. Seeing that. Knocked me around."

"Yeah, well, you'd know what it is that's eating at you." From the corner of my eye, I watched him take a sip. "Reckon the rest of it wouldn't be nothing, too. Not like your job is at risk. You've had a woman break in and drug you during your sleep. You've got a shit-head detective all but fabricating evidence, and you've killed a woman while her victim sobbed in the next room."

I closed my eyes. "Okay. That does help, strangely."

"I can go on."

I laughed and the sound was strange, brittle. "Shit, me too."

"But, hey. You've got a different shithead detective in a cozy car, a hot coffee, and beautiful weather."

This time the laugh didn't sound quite so brittle. "Don't insult my favorite detective, you jerk. He's the best at holding back hair I've ever met."

Rain drummed against the roof of the car. Into the quiet, Taig said, "I do believe that is the first time *anyone* has *ever* listed that as a skill."

"When your hair is basically a natural disaster waiting to happen, it's a priority," I promised fervently, and sipped the coffee. The pain hit before the flavor did and I winced, pulled it away. "Fuck. You weren't joking about the temperature of this."

He offered a hand for the coffee, put it back in the cupholder. "Wouldn't lie to you, sweetheart," he drawled, and I couldn't help but glance up, meet his eyes. "Cut yourself some slack," he said, the lines on his face carved from worry making him look strangely beautiful. "The world will keep turning if you step back. And considering how great I think you are, that isn't a small statement."

The shame was real and alive and huge and I could feel it pulling at me. I didn't want it. I needed something to hold on to. "Want to kiss me better?"

He cocked his head, just a little. "That was not the vibe I got from you earlier."

It grew fangs. The guilt was black and hot and huge. I looked away.

"Sorry." I couldn't hold on to him. I knew I couldn't. I couldn't hold on to *anyone* good.

"Me, too, because the answer is absolutely yes, when the time is right. And as stunning as this weather is," he sighed, "I don't really want to complicate something that could be pretty amazing before we can get it going."

I nodded, wiping my face. "Yeah. You're right." I so badly needed to get out of there. Get away. Get control. "Look, I should get to my coven. Figure out what my position in this clusterfuck is."

"Sure." He reached toward the ignition. "We can always take some more time out the front if you need."

I did not need any more time alone with a man who was far too good to me. I'd had my bones hollowed out. I didn't need to have my heart broken, too. Again. "I'm good, Taig. Really. And, hey, I need a new knife." I glanced over and saw he was still watching me with that sharp-eyed expression. He saw too much and I drew on my armor, raising a brow. "*Can* you do any woodwork?"

"Not the sort you're looking for," he answered, blandly.

CHAPTER 25

SITTING WITH MY WITCHES, SIPPING MY COFFEE, HEARING THE EXCITED swell of information around me as they caught me up, was fine. But I wasn't all there and I knew it.

When Arthur got back from wherever he'd been and saw me, he did a double-take then waved me up the stairs. "You aren't supposed to be on premises," he told me, ushering me into the office.

"I didn't get the memo." I fell into the chair opposite his big, self-important desk, then blinked. Where the old school map of Melbourne had been on his wall, there was a map of the region with the First Nation landmarks and names.

He passed me a coaster before I could set down the coffee on his desk. "What did Jerome want?"

I hadn't thought this through or planned it out, and my options whirled before me.

"Hold on. *Words or whispers, scream or shout, no sound within will make its way out.*"

He rhymed. Of course he rhymed. I watched as he draped his jacket over his chair, the movement one of long habit rather than temperature requirement. Our coven's crappy old gas wall heater sure didn't make it comfy.

"He wanted to talk to me about an ancient vampire they're getting on their books," I heard myself saying.

Arthur looked over at me, brows raised. "That's it?"

"No. But I'll talk about the rest later." I stood, pacing. Carpet was rough beneath my heels.

He was saying something, and the words were far away. I didn't want to get into it. Not now. Maybe now. "Arthur," I said, over top of whatever he was saying, "Bart is vampired."

"You don't know that for sure—"

"Yes, I do. I'm probably doing a Retrievals job tomorrow morning." I didn't watch his reaction. I needed to take control. I couldn't fall apart. "Everything's falling apart. I think we need to seriously consider how we can manage the situation." I'd meant to ask Taig. But I already knew the answer.

"We can't do more than we already are."

I threw my hands up. "You've got vampires picking off high ranking wizards, Arthur! We don't even *know* what the faeries are doing in town, but we know if the vamps are making a play then the faeries will try to beat them to the punch." He wasn't listening. I could see it in his face. "One hit, if they timed it right, and the whole *state* would be theirs for the taking."

"Perhaps, but we're stronger than they know. They'd have to be foolish to try anything."

I felt the bubble and roll of anger through my veins and reveled in it. "No, they'd have to be *organized*. And they are, Arthur. Better than us."

His eyes flashed and jaw tightened. "We need *tradition*," he said, climbing to his feet, his face all splotchy and red the way he always got around me. "We need each other, Rory! Elders take it, woman, you cannot rip the *entire community* apart!"

I got up in his face, smelling his aftershave. A kick of something hot and powerful hit me low in the guts. Blew on those embers, igniting them. "Can't I?" I asked, quietly. "You going to stop me?"

Through thin lips, he said, "If I have to."

The rush of conflict or desire, I didn't care which, burned brighter.

It was mine. I could control this. "Do tell, oh Head Wizard, how the hell you're going to keep it from the media. From the ears of the people impacted."

His jaw tightened. "You want me to gag you?"

I bared my teeth. "Try."

"You're not a cold-hearted bitch," he said, quietly, furiously. "You can't push this agenda. It'll hurt us all."

"You know what hurts, Arthur?" I raised a hand to shove him in the chest and he fell back half a step. Shock flickered on his face, filling me with satisfaction as anticipation coiled. Here was a game I could win. "*Losing people you love.* You know what hurts?" I went to shove him again and he grabbed my hand so hard pain lanced down my arm, and I wanted to laugh. He had no idea. None. "Listening to the sound of them *dying,* Arthur. *That hurts.* Fuck tradition!"

"You're upset," he said, tightly. "I don't blame you. But you can't hurt others just because—"

I ripped free of his hold, felt the burn of his fingers on my wrist, the burn of something dark and wicked in my veins, tightness in my chest, and wanted to howl with the emotions that rolled through me. "Don't you *dare* tell me what I can and cannot do, or by the Elders, I'll make you eat every. Fucking. *Word.*"

He was all but quivering with fury and I loved it. My heart was racing behind my ribs like a rabbit but it wasn't fear.

"You need to leave."

"You're right." I didn't move, though, or drop his gaze. I wasn't done. This was *my* show. "I'm going to the next wizard council shit-show, and I'm playing by *my* rules this time. And you're going to invite me."

"Why?" he demanded, throwing his hands up. "So you can under-mine me?"

"So I can *reinforce* you, you big lump of misunderstandings!" And I went to shove him again but grabbed his shirt instead. The thick luxurious fabric was tight in my fingers. Buttons strained beneath the force of my hands as I reeled him in and felt his body fit against mine neatly. "Fuck you, Arthur," I said, against his mouth.

"What—"

"And fuck me," I demanded.

I was in control.

He pulled back a little and I let him, forcing my fingers to unravel. Fury and wanting rolled through me and I tipped back my head, breathing it deep.

"What the hells?"

He needed a *roadmap.* "I want to have sex with you," I said, tightly.

"After you've been a total—" he cut himself off. "When you're so upset?" he amended, the words coming out from between his teeth. "If you think I'm going to agree to your ridiculous idea just because—"

"I think you'll agree we can blow off steam and go around after." I watched his gaze flicker over my body, and heat roared in the wake of his attention. Wanting flooded through me, and all my go to zones lit up like a casino after dark. I felt *alive.* And maybe he would, too. "Lock the door, King, if you want in, because I just want to be bent over your desk right now. Or I'm going home to do it myself."

His mouth opened, then closed. With jerky movements he turned and went to the door, but hesitated there. I felt my heart beating in my chest, the peaks of my nipples aching for attention. The craving to feel the slip of fingers over my core. I hungered. The heavy beat in my body, low in my belly, deep within, was a beautiful song.

"You're trying to use me," he said, quietly.

"Yeah, to get off. I've already told you what I'm doing. I don't bull-shit, Arthur."

Hand still on the doorknob, he looked at me like he hadn't yet decided if he was going to kick me out or lock us in. I folded my arms and raised my chin. He didn't know yet. But he was mine. Right now, he was mine.

The lock clicked into place.

A rush of satisfaction went through me, the forerunners making me shiver. I turned and planted my hands on his desk. "You want me to take your dress off? Help take your dress off?" he asked, the words rough and irritated, like he'd just figured out what I'd already known.

"Really?" I demanded. *"Really?* It's a *skirt,* Arthur. You *lift* them!"

His hands were hard on my thighs. My breath caught, then escaped. The room fell away as cold air washed over my backside. "You said there was an order. I can't reach your clit well from here. Haven't touched you."

The words were jarring. I didn't want to think or reason right then. "I want you to pull my stockings down," I told him, making sure the words were clear. "And *fuck me.*"

His fingers bit into my hips.

"Right now."

I shot him a look of pure fury over my shoulder. "You've got a nanosecond to—"

My stockings tore beneath his hands. Laughter and satisfaction got tangled up in my throat, and my cackle of glee turned into a moan as his fingers dragged down my skin and bit into me. I pushed back, felt him hard behind me. He was fumbling with his belt. The beat of gnawing need in my skin, in my flesh, was all I knew. His fingers slipped and slid over me. Hot, hard shafts of delight speared through me. My breath caught. He wasn't careful or gentle. The pressure was uneven, irregular, as he shifted behind me and I heard my own breath, my own ridiculous reaction. *More.*

Lips, on my backside, then teeth. I hissed in pain, felt the laughter again, strangled. His fingers moved and I moved with them, ravenous. His hand on my hip, then my waist. I wanted more. Hungrily I pushed back into him, demanding he give me what I wanted. My heart roared. I leaped into the fire head first. I took.

His fingers left but before I could turn and rip him apart, I felt him pressing, pushing, nudging at me, seeking entry. I drove myself back, filled myself to the brim. Heat and hunger and *more.* His hands were hot and hard. I arched, feeling the rush of lava. The air was gone. Waves of furious hunger took me so hard it *hurt.*

"More," I demanded, between my teeth. "Now."

He clung to me like a drowning man. The desk beneath me blurred. Hot, fiery lances of heat seared me. Those fingers bit deep into my flesh and the laughter in my chest was burned to ash.

My head dropped almost to the desk as flesh slapped, and I sought more. The right angle. The right pressure. His thumbs, pressing. His rapid, irregular breathing. I flexed and held. I took, consumed, devoured. There was a flow but no ebb. Just the build, the climb. We clawed, fought, and struggled our way to that edge. And then we rode it hard, gasping, clinging.

It ripped through me, the rush, the glory, the sheer *power* of it tearing a cry from the bottom of my soul as the heat flooded every fiber of my body pulsing with fire.

I heard his choked sound. Shock, maybe. Probably. And I took that, too, as I flexed around him, forcing him to *work* to withdraw. Laughter bubbled in my throat as his legs collapsed and mine did, too. Somehow, I grabbed the desk and managed to keep us both upright.

He lifted away from me, sweat on his brow and his chest heaving like he'd run a marathon rather than steal two minutes. With wide, shocked eyes he stared at me.

I kissed his open mouth. "Don't get used to it," I told him, breathless still. I couldn't quite wish it away, not when I felt so good, but I wasn't going to lead him on.

He blinked, then looked down at my stockings, pooled around my feet. "I...did I hurt you?"

"Only my impatience." I toed off the shoes before kicking off the stockings. "Throw me some tissues, King. I gotta get home."

"I...just like that?"

I paused as guilt reared its ugly head. "Yeah? You want to cuddle? I can cuddle."

"I—no. No."

Once I'd finished what I was doing, I went to where he was fumbling with the unopened box of tissues on his desk and put my hand on his arm. "Hey. Thanks."

"Yeah. Sure." He cleared his throat and popped the cardboard open, then offered it to me awkwardly.

The box I set aside. My stomach ached, but I fitted myself into his arms. His heart was kicking and writhing and heat radiated off the man. My heart hammered, too, but only from exertion. "That wasn't fair of me," I admitted, letting my head drop onto his shoulder.

"Probably not, no."

"We aren't dating."

"Got that." He held me, though. His arms were nice. It felt okay. I could see, out of the corner of my eye, the clock. Four fifteen. I could get the four twenty-seven tram if I didn't get too caught up. It was a few minutes' walk, comfortably doable.

"That went way outside of what I expected."

"Me, too, if it makes you feel better." I pulled back, pressing a kiss to his cheek. "Thanks. Sincerely. It felt good. I feel good. I need a shower, warm, cozy clothes, and a bucket of ice cream."

"Is this more 'my boyfriend broke up with me' stuff?" he asked, his eyes narrowing.

I felt like I'd been punched. "You're not supposed to ask that out loud, Arthur." I grabbed a few tissues. "And no. I'm a mess, but not specifically that flavor of mess this minute." *Right? Yeah.*

I cleaned myself up, sorted out my hair as best I could, stuffed the stockings in my bag. I hadn't picked him as the clothes tearing type. "You've got style, King."

"Do I?" he asked, and he sounded a little amused, now, and more than a little worried. "Should I be organizing some sort of counselling for you? You've been in some rough situations recently."

I tried not to think about that. "That's a kind offer. Maybe. I'll get back to you, okay?" I shouldered my bag, stepping into my shoes.

"Make sure you look after you, too, King," I said, hoping the words sounded nonchalant as I tossed the tissues in the bin on my way to the door. "You're kind of important." I reached for the door handle and shot him a quick, loaded look to be rewarded with the flash of dimples. We were both smiling when I left.

My smile didn't last more than two steps.

I got the shower, the cozy clothes and, hollow, I headed to Lilith's.

"So," I said, when my chicken nuggets were done and we were deep in the cute farming game we played together, "we need a plan."

"Plan?" she asked.

"Vampires, faeries, yadda yadda—shit's going to go down." I kept fishing. "Hey. Did you milk the cows?"

"Yes I—shit isn't going down, Rory. You're listening to too much true crime."

"What? Yesterday you forgot them. The cheese is worth a fortune and I want to upgrade my damned fishing rod already."

"Not the game, Rory. Pause, curse it."

I sighed, tossed my controller on the couch beside me. I couldn't tell her that I'd slept with Arthur. I didn't think she wanted to hear how low my standards and mental health were. "Also, you've been assigned a bloke's mask for the masquerade. I'm happy to swap, if you want. Got a cool idea that'd match with it. Or not. Your call."

She looked at me as if I was speaking another language. "Solstice. You're asking me about solstice?"

"Yeah. How do you want to do it?"

Her expression was tortured. "Rory, we've been playing for twenty minutes and you ask me *now?*"

I checked my watch. It had been almost three hours—typical gaming. "Guess so. You can tell me later. I don't mind. Figured you should have a say."

She swallowed. "Well, if you have a plan. With the mask. Sure. Thanks."

"Too easy." My plan was to make up a plan, but whatever. My heart sat lighter all the same. "I think something weird's going to go down, though."

She rolled her eyes, then paused for a moment to study me. "Why?"

"First thing's first, what's news on the street? Vamps, faeries. Hit me."

"Hit you *now?*"

"Nugget powered," I told her, tapping my head.

She rolled her eyes hard. I had to admire her dedication. "Okay. Fine. Um. Vampires? Got whispers of something big. Someone big. A group. I don't know. We're flat out keeping up with everything. We've split your caseload. We're doing hourly checks on Dierdre, rotating it."

My head spun. "You are?"

"Yes?" she looked at me like I'd just asked if the sky was blue. "You

aren't reading your emails? Hourly status reports. It's a *bitch* to organize." How had no one mentioned this when I'd been there that afternoon? "It's police ordered. Isn't it?"

I shot her a pitying look. "Clint's overseeing her case now."

"Oh," she breathed. "Oh, fuck. Wait—then…"

"Arthur."

Her brows gathered. "No way. Although…could be duty of care.
That'd get him going."

I remembered the hands on my thighs. I knew how to get him
going. It made me feel sad. "Maybe. Doubt it. We've had bad shit
happen to clients before."

"True." Her frown deepened. "This is weird."

I laughed as she went to make coffee. The mug she pulled out for
me said *I think I seized the wrong day.* Lilith understood the universal
rule about mugs.

I sat on a stool as she moved around slowly. "Okay. So. The guy is
actually working. He's taken on half your caseload himself and divvied
the rest up. He makes sure we can all do the check-in, monitors it,
does more check-ins himself than we do each, to be honest. I assumed
someone was riding his arse."

"Not guilty of that," I assured her, holding my empty hands up.
Before she could question me, I offered, "There's an ancient vampire
in town. Or about to be in town. Lots of attention from various
agencies."

"No shit?" Her eyes sharpened. She dragged her purple hair back,
looped it up in a messy bun that was casually elegant and impossible
not to admire. "Seems like a pretty big coincidence that Arthur and
that other wizard were vamped right before some bigwig lands."

"Yeah, that's what I'm thinking. Also, there's a third wizard. I'm
probably going to be up early staking a vamp tomorrow with Taig."

She sighed. "And you're here, drinking coffee and telling me *I*
forgot to milk the cows."

She wasn't wrong, so I just waited on my cuppa.

"Bitch. You owe me some hours."

"Done. Tomorrow. You got me."

She grinned at me. "Vamps?"

She considered it for a moment. "I've heard some rumors. Docklands is a hot-spot, apparently, but I figured it was bullshit." Absently, she added, "I wonder where this ancient is living?"

"Yeah," I agreed, then tried not to think about calling Nic. Getting the scoop was hard when they were dark. "I'm feeling nosy, Lilith."

She froze, mug halfway to her mouth. Suspicion looked good on her. "I am *not* going after vampires for funsies."

With the bench taking my weight, I dragged my coffee toward me. "What about for…" I dropped my voice dramatically. "The greater good?"

She snorted. "No."

I sighed. "You know if this was a movie, they'd totally attack us at Solstice."

She let out a long breath. "Yeah. Good thing it isn't. Although we'd probably have much hotter clothes." I considered that and she must've, too, for a minute, before adding, "On the topic of the ball, though, Deirdre's mentioned she's keen on going."

My heart froze. "No."

"Yeah, well, that was kinda my reaction too," she said, wryly. "But Arthur had already said yes. Connection, or some shit, something feel good. Again, I thought it was police pressure…you know. We can't *order* her to stay home."

I felt sick. "No, but." She was a smart woman. She knew she was in danger. Why the hells would she stick her neck out?

"So." She cleared her throat. "I guess that's another factor in whatever scheme you're cooking."

I turned away, hurting. I couldn't keep her safe there.

"I need to talk to her."

"Sure," Lilith agreed, amused. "I've got four check-ins tomorrow. Pick your time slot."

Her somewhat messy, very cramped kitchen swayed. Too many things to juggle. This was all too neat. Was Tobias—hey, I remembered shithead ex's name!—in league with vampires? Faeries? She'd had fae substances. Faeries were present but not making a move that we knew about. But they were up to something. Would they hit her at a gathering? Surely, not.

So far Amor had chosen non-lethal methods out of preference ,and then gone hard if she was pursued. They. They were pursued. Standard Retrievals MO. I tried to flip it, and think about Dierdre as a target. Focusing on defense was getting me nowhere. I'd been putting out fires and minimizing risk. What was I, *Arthur?*

How would *I* deal with Dierdre?

I'd just fucking wait. Wait until the furor had died down, until no one was looking and the cost of surveillance got too high. People on the ground got bored when nothing happened. They bitched. People above got annoyed when the invoices kept rolling in. They bitched. It'd be one week, maybe two, and then we'd have to go to two hourly check-ins. Maybe twice daily. Shit, I doubted they could maintain it for two weeks, really.

If I was in their shoes, I'd be bunkered down somewhere for about a month. After this long, it hardly seemed to matter. Life would settle into the normal rhythms. No one would be looking.

And then another stunt like her arrow that went into Arthur... except with Rapid Decay. And into me. That's what I'd do. I was a risk, now. They knew it. They'd waltz in, grab her, and vanish. Maybe even go Overworld.

A lightbulb went off. *That's* why Amor hadn't been there in the warehouse. She'd been getting rift juice ingredients. They'd been about to make a jump. But they couldn't make it without Dierdre. Had they asked what she needed? Had she lied? Had they lost something, miscalculated, needed emergency supplies of something?

Were they working with the vampires? The goals seemed entirely different—unless they were just benefitting from one another's chaos. Spreading us thin.

I felt sick. If I was Amor—If I was Tobias—

I would *absolutely* make promises to vampires to stir shit up. Worst case, distraction. Best case, conveniently placed allies who helped reduce that month-long wait period to just a few days.

And it would've worked already, if not for Arthur. The cops had pulled surveillance. Retrievals were—

My heart hurt. Had they been lured out? Fuck, were all the vampires, all the callouts—were they *deliberate?* Surely, not. The scope was...

"I know I need to clean my stovetop, but it isn't *that* bad," Lilith said, and there was a bit of worry in her voice. "Dierdre will be okay, Rory."

"Yeah." I tore my eyes away from where they'd been stuck on Lilith's medium-sized, favorite gas burner. My head hurt. It didn't explain the faeries. It didn't explain the angel. The angel would have their own goal. But Dierdre fed that, so maybe it made sense. So— faeries.

Once again I had to ask. Who sent the fucking *faeries?*

I met Lilith's eyes, feeling sick. "I think we're in trouble."

CHAPTER 26

Jogging in place as I waited for the pedestrian lights near home I flicked Oma a quick message. *Angel. Smells like roses. Khameul. Know anything?* The light turned green and I made my way across, avoiding a couple of blokes huddled together to avoid the wind.

The music pumping through my headphones died and I heard my phone ringing. I waited until I was over the road to answer. "Hello, Oma."

"What's going on?" she demanded.

"Wizards are shitstains," I told her, as I kept my feet churning. Icy wind and the damp air stung my throat and burned my eyes.

"Not all wizards," she said, and there was mockery in her voice.

I laughed. "And not all fourteenth century rats."

"And yet," she agreed, delighted. "Oh, I like that. I think I'll embroider that on a tea towel."

"Thanks. I stole it from Dad," I admitted, a bit breathless. "Talk. I'm jogging."

She cleared her throat. "You can't walk, can you? The wind sounds *terrible.*"

I glared at the clouds. It was going to bucket any minute. "On a

233

deadline. Gotta get home. Just a quick jog." Elders, sometimes family was annoying. "Hit me, Oma. I'll mute myself so no wind noise."

She sniffed. "Fine." I found the right button. The screen didn't like my cold, damp finger, but I made it work. And around the sound of my own breathing, the murmur of the city around me, I heard her say, "So, angels. Basically, the same as demons, just what they're selling seems better on the surface."

Shit, I knew that.

"Single-minded devotion to even the best of ideals isn't ideal," she said, wisely. "You'd know that, though." I did, yes, and gritted my teeth as I glanced up and down the road, ran alongside while I waited for a car to pass, then cut over. "Yours is mid-tier. Hasn't been seen for a few centuries."

I wanted to ask its goal, its driving desire. I didn't, just picked up my pace. Two blocks. Then Lilith and Deirdre.

"It's all about love, from what I'm reading," Oma mused on the other end. Around the whistle of wind, I could hear her mouse click-ing. "Nasty."

I thought of the love potion, the warped Cupid-esque fantasy. It fit.

"It'll target folks with an abundance of love—but not, you know, healthy respectful love."

"Obsession," I said, grimly, thinking of Dierdre being stalked. But she couldn't hear me.

"It wants everyone to just love each other. Got a recount here of some sort of massive event. Isolated location, hundreds of people, *giant* orgy, maybe." She cleared her throat. "I hope it was a giant orgy. And then everyone killed themselves out of devotion to their leader. Because nothing says true love like self-sacrifice, right? But, hey, it was like three hundred years ago. I'm hoping it was just a giant orgy. Death by orgy, that's not the worst way to go. As long as they all had decent hygiene." She fell quiet as I ducked into my building out of the wind and the relief was huge. "Hm. Okay. So. Most of these are pretty dull. The world could use more orgies, I reckon." She sniffed loudly into the phone and I struggled not to laugh. "Generally it's someone gets obsessed with someone, who's obsessed with someone else. Jealousy leads to conflict leads to everyone ending up dead because therapy wasn't a thing. Honestly, Sunshine. More orgies, less obsession. Is that so much to ask?"

I grinned and dashed my dripping nose on my sleeve as I started up my stairs, fumbling for my phone to unmute myself.

"You'd think a love angel would be pretty shit hot, wouldn't you?" she said, absently. "You'll want a major banishment spell if that thing pops. Ideally, just kill its puppets before it comes to play, there's a girl."

I hit the button to let her hear me. "Any specific weaknesses, management strategies?"

She snorted. "It's an *angel,* Sunshine. Hit its images with obsidian, you might get some breathing space. Give it what it wants and it'll chill its beans. You'll end up enslaved, but, hey. That's a form of management, right?"

I found the light switch and flooded my unit with the synthetic glow. I didn't really know that it was. "I suppose?"

"Great. So. To recap. Kill minions first. Ask questions later."

I loved my Oma. "Got it." But the rest was interesting.

I had to draw Tobias out. I had to control the situation. I had to buy some breathing space.

What would draw him out? How could I control it?

Taig hadn't responded yet. I changed, feeling like the answer was *right there.* The tram ride was lulling, but not enlightening.

Lilith met me in the parking basement of Dierdre's building. "Hey. You look frazzled."

"Frazzled?" I repeated, amused. "What the hells is *frazzled?*"

"You." She dug in her bag, pulled out a packet of lollies. "Suck it."

"That's what I told them," I agreed, grimly, taking the lolly with pleasure.

She shot me a grin, shouldered open the door, and led the way along the corridor to Dierdre's apartment. "How'd they like that?"

"Who cares?" I waited as she lifted a hand, knocked.

Before she could respond the door was opened and Dierdre's face lit up. "Rory! Lilith!"

I stepped into her open arms and returned her hug, feeling the energy of the woman. "You look so happy," I said, a little shocked. And when she stepped back, waving us through, I spotted a multitude of little changes. Hair. Brows maybe. "Oh! Nice nails." Classic, pretty. Suited her. I'd never seen her with her nails done, though.

She beamed. "I'm so excited, Rory. Did Lilith tell you?"

"About the Solstice?" Lilith asked her, ignoring my pointed glance and shooting Dierdre a smile as she went to the cupboard, took out mugs. "Yes please," she said, as Dierdre held up the mugs in invitation.

She didn't even ask me; just assumed. "I am actually so excited. I didn't realize quite how much I'd missed the idea of going out and having fun. And Arthur's been so supportive." She shot me a look. "He's my bodyguard for the night." And there was color in her cheeks and a lightness to her step I wasn't used to.

"Is he, now?" Lilith asked, idle curiosity in her tone.

I glanced over again at that gentle probe. Her expression was as bland as the words but she caught my look and, as Dierdre turned to make cuppas, cocked a brow at me. "Oh, well." She fumbled a spoon. "I was saying how horrible it is, being locked up all the time. I haven't been to work, barely go to get groceries." She shrugged like it didn't matter, but there was a bite to the words, a frustration, that I hadn't factored in.

The trap was only good if the bait stayed put.

I wandered over to help her transport drinks and took the biscuit tin she passed me with a murmured thanks.

"There are factors you don't know—" I began, grimly.

"Hey, Rory," Lilith said, brightly. "We're going. *We* could go with Dierdre."

"Oh, I couldn't do that to you," Deirdre said, instantly, and the saucers in her hand rattled as she took them to the bench. "You help yourselves. No, I don't *want* to be an inconvenience, but he offered, and..."

And she'd been isolated long enough.

"Well, we're offering. Aren't we, Rory?" And the last was pointed.

Fuck. "Yeah." Not like I could say, 'No, stay home where it's safe'. It wasn't. I remembered her cowering in the shower, the way she'd sobbed as I fought Amor, the soundtrack of combat warping. My heart ached. "Yeah, three is a good number."

Deirdre flicked me a look on her way across the kitchen to the kettle, pouring water into mugs, brewing drinks. "It's okay, Rory. You're not even at work at the moment. And I'm work. So please, don't feel obliged. I don't want to be a burden."

My thoughts ducked and wove. Lilith took a homemade jam drop biscuit and plonked it loudly on my plate. Then she shoved it along the bench, making it scrape the whole way. "Try one," she told me.

I shot her a quick look, trying to figure out what the hells I was doing wrong.

Silence stretched out. The pale little biscuit was wonky and had cracked from Lilith's force. It looked wonderful. I knew it did. But I had no appetite, suddenly.

How the fuck could we actually keep her safe? We should have a guard on her *especially* tomorrow night, when everyone who was anyone was going to be interested in socializing and free champagne. Maybe Arthur was right. Keep her close, keep tabs on her. Would they expect it? If it was me, I wouldn't make a hit then. *But the vampires?* Shit, it was a golden opportunity for *them.* And that would bring chaos. Chaos would give shitstain ex an opening.

"Are...are you okay?" Deirdre asked me.

A sharp sting in my leg from Lilith's swift, silent kick made me work to keep my expression blank. "I'm not the best," I admitted, still unsure what I'd done wrong. "I, ah, broke up with my partner." It was true. And it'd do. "And, you know." I had no idea if she *did* know what Clint had done, the reason I was on leave.

Her expression softened, though. "Oh, Rory." Another biscuit was added to my plate, gently this time. "What happened?"

"The usual," Lilith sighed from beside me, saving me from having to figure out details. She was probably trying to avoid me putting my foot in my mouth. My heart swelled at the easy, protective phrase, at the way she caught Dierdre's compassionate look, returned it. She gave me a buffer.

But, fuck it. "Not really." I took the coffee and remembered the night before it'd gone south, how he'd held my hand and my bones hadn't hurt so much. "I usually get the 'you're too much for me' thing." Why not? She'd been honest with me and I had no horse in this race.

"That's their loss," she told me, firmly, and perched her elbows on the bench, peering at me with both compassion and curiosity. "Men are jerks." The phrase was almost tentative.

I shrugged a bit, gave in to the weirdly nostalgic feeling. "My Dad used to say, 'You're not too much, they just have the emotional maturity and communication skills of a peanut'."

Lilith's face cracked in a grin. "He's not wrong."

"It happened often enough he cut down on the words," I admitted, wryly, for Dierdre. "Became, 'They're too small'."

She smiled, and there was so much sadness in her eyes, but also something that looked uncomfortably close to respect. "I like that." Then her eyes widened. "It isn't—wasn't—Detective O'Malley?"

I froze with the biscuit I'd just picked up halfway to my mouth. Beside me, Lilith coughed. "What?" she demanded of me.

"No!" I put down the biscuit, but felt remarkably—seen. It wasn't comfortable. "No," I repeated, adding a bit of laughter to it to deflect. To avoid. "Nothing between Taig and I," I told them both, and took a bite of the biscuit. I even made a noise of appreciation as it coated my tongue and teeth with ash. I knew it'd be great.

But I wasn't.

Deirdre sighed and shot Lilith a look to share in her disappointment. "They were very sweet together." At Lilith's wide-eyed look, she said, "Oh, nothing, um, *personal*, you know. Just the way they kind of... worked. They looked almost like a comfortable old couple, you know?"

"Oh, so now I'm *old*," I said, deflecting with a laugh. My heart ached. I remembered sitting in his car, just he and I and the sound of rain. "No, it wasn't Taig, nothing to see there." I let out a long breath. "You don't know my ex." The coffee mug was warm in my hands and featured a picture of a cartoon kitten rolling in flowers. Cute. Deirdre knew how to do mugs, too. I held it up. "This is adorable."

I didn't miss the quick look Dierdre and Lilith shared. "Dude was terrified of her work. Total coward," Lilith said, dismissively.

But he hadn't been a coward. Not really.

"*Oh,*" Dierdre said, her eyes huge. "Oh, no. I get it, like. It's a lot. What you do. But still, he would've known that. Wouldn't he? From the outset."

She was right. I frowned. "Yeah," I said, slowly. But he'd always managed the risks. Escorted me home if I was vulnerable, checked in, hung out. What was different, now? Was I looking for an excuse, or had something extra happened?

Was it the faeries?

I shook it off. "You know what?" I set down the biscuit. "You're right. He knew what he was in for. Like, he *really* knew." And he'd said he was fine with it—supportive, even. "So, screw it. Let's go out tomorrow. Celebrate being us."

Hope and fear danced across Dierdre's face. "We could."

"We *will,*" Lilith said, firmly. "I've got an amazing new underbust skirt to layer. I'm going to be hot *and* warm."

"Bitch," I muttered, thinking of my options. "We should get ready together."

"Oh, you don't have to…" Deirdre trailed off. "But, if you *want* to," she said, her voice a little tentative.

"I'll have to go home and shower first," Lilith warned us.

I waved a hand. "Yeah. All that stuff. But hair, makeup?"

Deirdre's eyes were shining as she looked between us. "And," she cleared her throat. "I've got a, ah, police escort. To the venue." She shot me an apologetic smile, and I knew exactly which Detective she meant. "Sorry. It wasn't, um, on purpose. He volunteered," she explained. "He's very kind. After they ended their surveillance he'd stop in every day after work, have a cup of tea, tell me about his day." She sipped her tea. "I ran out of," she waved one manicured hand at the biscuit tin. "Flour and so forth, and had felt a bit too flat to go shopping. I felt bad I couldn't offer him anything much. The next day he arrived with groceries for me."

Oh, shit, my heart. "Way too old, though," Lilith mused.

Deirdre's brow furrowed. "He isn't. Is he?" And she looked at me. I held up my hands in surrender, tried desperately to deflect. "He isn't," she said, firmer, to Lilith. "I think he's just had some, um." She paused, searched. "Experiences."

"Dog years, you reckon?" Lilith asked, thoughtfully. "Maybe. Still, Roars can totally go for someone young, hot, *and* emotionally mature."

"Oh, of course," Dierdre agreed. I couldn't figure out if I was going to laugh or groan, and ended up doing a weird mix of both. Her eyes glittering mischievously, she added, "He *is* lovely, though."

"Feel free," I told her, waving my hand. "The man's too much trouble for me." I melted like wax beside a flame whenever he was around. That was dangerous. "He's too…" I searched for the words.

They waited silently and my brain just short circuited.

"I'm actually totally cool being solo," I somehow managed. "Girl's night tomorrow. I'll bring something to nibble on. We're going to party." And if that involved dancing with some vamps, well, it wouldn't be the first time.

We hung out, helped Dierdre narrow down her outfit. And on the way home, Lilith cut her glance across to me and arched her brows.

"Detective O'Malley?"

"Complicated." Had I asked him to sleep with me? Pretty sure I had. It was fuzzy. "Not touching it." *Shit, no.* I'd be a puddle at his feet in about five minutes if he actually tried. "Also, brokenhearted."

"Fair."

She made a noise of agreement. "Are we *allowed* to do this? With Dierdre?"

"Probably not." I pulled my jacket closer as she turned down my road. "Don't try to park. Thanks for bringing me." I paused and looked at her. Properly looked at her. Her purple hair was all messed up from a day's worth of wind and neglect, but her makeup was impeccable, and her hands relaxed and capable on the wheel. "Thanks, Lilith. You're amazing."

She shot me a grin that faded when she saw my expression. "Are you okay?"

"Yeah." I was. Kind of. "No. But I'm circling closer. I think."

"Ice cream?"

"No." I wanted to lean over and press a kiss to her cheek. But she was busy double parking. "Text me what time you're arriving."

"Yeah, sure," she said, distracted. "Wait—where?"

"Dierdre's." Winter air rushed into the car as I opened the door. "Love you, witch," I half-shouted as I hauled myself out of the warm, slamming the door behind myself and bee-lining it inside.

My apartment was warm and cozy. I rummaged through the fridge but just felt lost.

When my phone rang, I answered it with only a quick glance at Arthur's name. "I hear you visited Dierdre," he said, with no ado.

"Did you?" I asked, giving up on food for now and going to my bedroom. I cast my eyes over the section of formal wear. Evening dresses were *not* suitable for being outside at midnight in the dead of winter. "Want to bring over some Chinese?"

"I—what?"

"Food. I have nothing interesting."

He was quiet for a moment, then said, slowly, "I do have to give you the mask, illusion charm, and your official invite to the Solstice."

"Cool. So. Come over, bring food."

He was quiet again as I assessed my jackets. I had a lot, but were they *formal*? And would they go over any of my dresses?

"Okay. Sure."

I pulled out one of my better suits. It was cut amazingly, but was grey. I didn't feel like grey. "You're wondering if I'm trying to dodge the issue."

"Yes."

"Of course I am. I broke the rules. You don't need to *know* I did, though. Right?"

"I already know, Rory."

I rolled my eyes. "Play along, Arthur."

"Are you trying to use me, Rory?"

I sighed at him and pulled out another suit. Black. Severe. Maybe? I could add some sparkle, some heels. And I'd be warmer. Slightly. "Hate to break it to you, King, but this is pretty much the dance we've *always* done. Nothing new to see. I'm just honest with you now." I considered the suit again. "I've got a bloke's mask, right?"

"Yes. That's—you said that's what Lilith wanted. I swapped it."

"Good." I considered the suit, an idea forming. Why the fuck not? "Come over, tell me off, you know you want to."

"Is…" his voice dropped. "Is this…a thing?"

I considered feigning ignorance and figured it'd just tie the poor guy in knots. It'd be funny, but cruel. "Maybe."

"Because…you didn't mention you were into…"

"Oh, no, not *that* sort of 'tell me off'. Like, rant and rave while I eat." I tossed the suit on the bed. "Then maybe sex after, if we feel like it. Or maybe not. We're adults. We can choose. I'm going to hang up now Arthur. See you soon."

"I—okay." He cleared his throat. "I'll, ah. See you soon."

I tossed my phone on my bed, wondering if I wouldn't be lectured as hard as I might've been had we not got all that out in the open. Well, maybe I wasn't a communications master, but things were usually simpler when you were honest.

My shirt and hoodie came off together. Was I a hypocrite? I took the jacket off the hanger, pulled it on, wandered into the bathroom. *Maybe.* But I didn't like to dwell on my own shit.

Therein lay darkness.

I turned and considered. The bra would have to go, but that was fine. I'd pack a shirt in case I wasn't feeling brave. Problem solved. He hadn't asked what I wanted for dinner. I checked the time; it was too early to be this hungry.

When Arthur came to the door he had coffee and a bakery bag in his hand that did *not* look like dinner. I looked at it warily. "That isn't Chinese."

"No." He passed it over. "But I didn't know what you wanted, and we've got time to go out so you can choose."

I took the bag, my heart sinking. "Arthur, we aren't going out to dinner." Because I knew what that would make him think.

He shrugged, passed me the coffee. "Fine. Then I'll go pick it up. Whatever. Rory, you can't be breaking the rules all the time."

I took the cup and went inside, peering into the bag. Cinnamon donut. Classic, safe, and appetizing. "I know."

"Do you?" he asked, frustrated. "Because you aren't *acting* like it. We don't have different rules for you."

"No. You have bullshit rules for everyone," I agreed, sagely, fishing the donut out. It was warm. "Oh, wow, is this *fresh?*"

"Yes," he said, sulkily.

I shot him a smile. "Thank you."

He looked a little uncomfortable. "It's fine. You're supposed to apologize, I'm pretty sure."

"Why?"

Color crept up his cheeks. "Because you did the wrong thing, and now you're asking me to *lie* for you."

I shrugged then bit in. Finally, my taste buds were working. I sighed in pleasure. "I'm asking you to *omit*. You know. Look the other way. Plausible deniability, King."

He stood awkwardly in my kitchen, deflating. "I can't keep doing this, Rory."

"I know." And I did. With a sigh, I straightened. "I'm sorry I made you uncomfortable. I'm not sorry I broke the rules, because it was good to see Dierdre. But I'm sorry for the cost to you."

His thoughts all but swirled over his face. "That's...it?"

I shrugged. "I wouldn't do it unless..." I hesitated. "Look, maybe it wasn't *strictly* necessary. But I'm worried about her attending Solstice. You were going to be her guard?"

"She deserves to be safe when she leaves her house," he said, back to being sulky. "O'Malley and I organized it."

Inconvenient, but sweet of them. And where the hells *was* Taig? I glanced at my still silent phone. He would have news on Nic. "Well, we've organized it, too. We're going to be with her."

A bit of relief flickered over his face. "You're coming to the Solstice?"

"It's basically a royal command performance," I muttered around the donut. "Yes, I'm coming. And I'm going to dance. With Dierdre. So, you can." I waved a hand. "Chill the fuck out and guard the perimeter. Or whatever."

He let out a long breath and wilted against the bench. "Thank you."

That wasn't what I was expecting. "You into her?'

Horror made his mouth into a comical O. "What do you *take* me for? She's a *client!*"

Ah, of course. "Pretty, though."

He looked at me like he'd never seen me before. "You wouldn't."

"Wouldn't what?" I asked, licking sugar and cinnamon off my fingers. I was still hungry.

"Wouldn't sleep with a client."

Had I thought something earlier about honesty? "No. I didn't ask if you were sleeping with her, though. You can be attracted to someone and not act on it." I shot him a look. "Right?"

"Of course," he said, like it wasn't a thing millions of people seemed to forget all the time. "What do you want? I'll go get it." And it was said through his teeth.

I raised my brows. "Forget it. I'll feed myself. I can do that."

"I—you can't say you do want something, then change the whole plan on me."

I should've known that was coming, bless his cotton socks. "Can. Did. Anyway, you brought me something. Thank you. Plan complete. You done telling me off?" Because there wasn't much point in me apologizing to the big buffoon when we'd be doing this dance again, probably daily, for the foreseeable future.

He opened his mouth, then closed it. If I ever got a goldfish, it was going to be named Arthur. "Yes," he said, finally. "I think we understand one another."

I sipped some coffee, considering that. We were getting there, and that surprised me. Still, I wasn't going to tell him that the coffee was damn good. I didn't think it'd make him happy, not when he wanted to tell me off. "So, charm?"

He dug into his pocket before putting an envelope on the bench. "Then we're finished, I guess."

"I guess," I agreed, considering the rest of what we could get up to and whether I actually could be bothered. It was pretty cold, even inside.

He didn't move, though. "About yesterday."

I wanted to sigh, but if I'd stopped to think for a nanosecond I would've known he'd need to talk it out "It was consensual fun."

"Yes, but…I don't want to be…at work."

"Me, either."

His eyes flashed. "You *literally* told me to fuck you."

Shame made my mouth dry as a desert. I washed it away with some coffee. "Yeah, and I shouldn't have." Screw all this apologizing. "I was a mess. Okay? I'm sorry."

"Was."

All my muscles locked down over the flinch I refused to show. "Okay. Bye, Arthur."

"Wait—I'm sorry." He blew out air. "I'm sorry, Rory. I'm working on trying to leverage the mental health supports in place for law enforcement in the supernatural field. There isn't much, but if we can piggyback off it…but we don't right now have, you know, free counselling or anything." He shrugged awkwardly. "I'm sorry. And…I'm sorry if I've made it harder. On you."

My annoyance faded and I was left feeling tired. "It's fine, Arthur. It's just a lot."

"Yeah, I know."

He really didn't. "My Retrievals team went dark. My old team," I amended, feeling kind of sick. I shrugged it off, took another swallow of coffee. "I don't want to talk about it."

"I…don't know what that is. But…okay?"

He was trying. So very trying. But also kind of sweet. And better than more housework or couch time. Idly, I swirled the coffee in my cup. Maybe he didn't want to be alone, either. I couldn't really blame him for that well-aimed barb. Not when it was true. So, by way of apology for my reaction, I offered, "Want pizza? Local place doesn't charge too much for delivery."

He looked toward the door as if lost. "Wasn't I going?"

Did I really blow so hot and cold? *Yeah, I do.* "You can go. You can stay and eat junk. I don't mind." I resisted the urge to twist my hair around my finger. I'd kicked that nervous tick when I was a kid and no weekend warrior with puppy eyes was bringing me undone. Especially not one who needed a roadmap to do so. "If you stay, I'll probably end up offering to climb in bed with you, which you might not really want to do again, but there's no pressure." There had been, the other day. Against the desk. He'd hit the right spots at the right time. If I could just remember that, I'd be okay.

"You want that?" he asked, hands in pockets, like a kid checking if he can have a second serving of dessert. "Tonight?"

I couldn't help but smile a little at his interest. "I think so. Not as much as I did yesterday. But that was good enough that thinking about it…"

A smile touched his mouth. One dimple. Two. "Yeah."

Heat stirred. I wasn't *that* hungry anymore. "Shame about sex at work, hey? That desk had a great angle."

He glanced around. I saw him eyeballing my kitchen table. "How high is your bed?" he asked.

"Not that high." I stepped in close, tipped my face for a kiss. "We could experiment."

"Yeah," he said again, against my mouth. "I've got some ideas. And we could do a Share Spell."

"Mm." I ran a hand up his chest. "Sharing might make experimentation a bit tricky."

He frowned a little. "You're right. I'd get caught up if I could feel both of us."

I didn't really want to debate the merits of sex spells right then. "You're wearing a lot of clothes."

"We both are." His hands settled on my hips. "What would you like?"

"Um." I tried to think ahead. Couldn't. "Naked time. Lots of touching."

His breath was warm as he nuzzled my ear. "I want to touch you. I liked that, the first time."

I tried not to remember the awkward training-wheels sex we'd had. "Yeah." Surely it wouldn't be like that. "I have my toys." Backup plan, best to flag early with this guy.

"You can show me how to use them," he offered, smoothing his hands up my back under my jumper. "I like the idea of being able to fuck you for hours."

My brows rose. "Hours?" I guess it was almost Solstice. We had a lot of night.

He hummed in the back of his throat. "You came three times, that first time. Only once yesterday."

I didn't tell him the once yesterday had felt a whole bunch better than those three awkward times when I'd had to keep ignoring the fact he wasn't Beo—still wasn't Beo.

"I'd like to see how far you can go." He brushed his lips over my cheek and I focused on that feeling. "Before I do."

I remembered exactly how excited he'd been the first time. How grimly determined to hang on. Kind of cute. Kind of annoying. "We can always have a break, eat, go round two."

His breath shook. "I can definitely help if you're hungry."

I tugged his shirt out of his pants and started working on his buttons. "Start the engine before you try to get to third gear, King."

CHAPTER 27

ARTHUR PUT DOWN HIS PHONE VERY QUICKLY WHEN I CAME INTO THE room with the leftover pizza. I passed the half-empty box over and he fell on it without murmur about his diet. My sheets were going to need a soak after this and with contentment humming through my limbs I didn't even care.

"We're like petrol and fire, you and me," he said, around a mouthful of loaded pizza.

I glanced at the time. One in the morning. "Oh?" I didn't know if he was looking to stay, but I was done.

"Like, I thought…after the first time. You're kind and gorgeous and fierce and loyal. I admire you. Respect you."

I eyed him off, amused. "I can hear the 'but' there, King."

He sighed, looked at the congealing food in his hand. "I thought, hells, maybe I could love her. Really love her."

My heart squeezed with guilt, dark and inky. "Nah."

He met my eyes, his handsome face full of regret. "You're chaos, Rory. I…I don't know what to do with you. You treat rules like…like guidelines."

And that was because some rules weren't moral, and fuck legal but immoral shit. I pressed a kiss onto his beautifully sculpted shoulder. I felt nothing but lingering shame. Had I taken advantage of him? Probably. I hoped I'd given more than I'd taken, though. "We can be friends, Arthur."

He looked away. "I don't think I can separate it like you can. The physical and emotional. I keep wanting more. But…"

"More with me wouldn't work," I offered, gently. And, anyway, it wasn't on the table. But I figured pointing that out wasn't kind, especially not to the guy who put 'King' into overthinking. I resisted the urge to cuddle into him, keeping my regret to myself.

"It wouldn't. And I hate that. But I think…I think if we tried to make it work, I'd just live in constant anxiety. I think I'd resent you." He let out a breath. "I'm sorry."

I gave in and put my head on his shoulder. We sat there together in the destruction of my bed. The pleasant burn of hot salami lingered on my tongue, and my heart sat heavily. "Don't be sorry. We're good. And, for what it's worth, I agree. We'd be a terrible match. Even if you are amazing in bed."

"From *you*, that's pretty great to hear," he said, and there was a bit of grief tinged with pride in the words. I felt good about the pride, and the sadness wasn't my fault. He put an arm around me and held me close. For a moment I let myself take some of that affection, knowing it was the last I'd claim. "It was a nice dream, for a little while. And…you've taught me a lot. Not just sex."

I laughed at his earnestness, squeezing him with one arm in a way I hoped was playful. I couldn't go deep with Arthur. It wouldn't be fair. "It's okay, mate. You don't need to soften the blow. I'm okay. You're okay. You don't want me to hit you up, I won't. I respect that." I sat up and looked at him all flushed and soft and vulnerable. "Go home, Arthur," I said, gently. "I'll still be here to keep you on your toes."

He nodded and let out a long breath. "I should."

I gave him time to find his clothes and finish the pizza, then walked him to the door. His touch on my cheek lingered.

"I wish I was the kind of person who could screw without needing more. I thought I was."

I pressed a kiss to his palm, then stepped back and let him go. "Listen to yourself, Arthur. You've got a good heart. And listen to people you respect. Not the ones with the power. The ones doing things you admire."

"I'm here, aren't I?" He asked me, and shame crawled, sticky and hot, in my veins. He meant it. He really did look up to me. And not just when I was on top.

"I am not a shining example," I said dryly. "Go on. Think about it. Sleep well. Don't regret what wasn't meant to be. There's a lovely person out there for you."

Something flickered over his face. "Person?"

I shrugged, smiled, eased back a bit further. He wasn't quite out the door yet. "Bye." I blew him a kiss and swung the door closed, forcing him to step back.

My fingers lingered on the doorknob, though. The sound of his steps fading made me sad in a way I hadn't expected. Hells, was it wrong to regret not clicking with him? With my head full of those bittersweet wonderings and my belly full of pizza, falling asleep was easy.

My phone rang in the night and long habit kicked in, along with an unhealthy dose of adrenaline. "Yeah."

"Aurora, it's Bethany."

I kicked the covers off. *Vampires. Taig.* "Yeah. Awake. Go."

"Contract on the way. Probably won't be signed in time." And her voice was like ice.

I was already dragging out my Retrievals bag. "Vampires?"

"Yes."

"Wizard?"

A short pause. "Yes. I won't ask how you know."

"Intuition," I told her, grimly. "Give me an address and a time."

I caught a lift with the cops from East to Central and rode in the back of the van with them out of Melbourne, along the freeway and then up winding streets. Richardson was in the first van, already en route, and because of where I'd started from, I was riding with Taig and Greene. Greene was living up to his name. Apparently travelling sideways didn't work for him.

I'd looked over the blueprint, heard the plan. Two-pronged attack. Master bedroom and back door with vans blocking the drive. Then we just had to raid.

It sounded like chaos to me, but apparently the family had been tipped off twice already, and they didn't want to wait until we could contain it.

Something about that nagged at me as the van moved around corners, and I adjusted the wooden knuckle dusters for the umpteenth time on my hands. They didn't fit perfectly over the gloves. I sent Dad a text and told him I needed a new set. And a knife. "Heard from the team on Amor?" I asked Taig, because I couldn't *not* ask.

He didn't look at me. "Chat later."

Ice ran through my veins. I hadn't been notified when Vix died. Would they leave me out of the loop on this, too? I'd spoken to Bethany just a few hours ago. She told me she knew nothing, then. Could it have changed?

I let out a long breath, felt the roll and slide of the coffee in my belly.

The worst part was that I could picture it in detail. I knew how one misstep, one assumption, one moment of bad luck, could bring it all down.

The guy beside me shifted on the seat and cleared his throat. Feet were shuffled. The van's engine whined as we went up a steep hill, and I closed my eyes but found no solace in the dark.

I didn't need to ask if they were kitted out for lycans this time. I'd already seen. Two guns, not one, on most of them. Shields, a few charms, a few vials of Homecoming Fires and similar, low risk magicks. Nothing that would make much of a difference, really, but sometimes it was the little things that got you over the line.

And sometimes it was the little things that got in your way.

We rumbled to a halt. The door was opened quietly, but, really, if there were lycans around we were already made.

I remembered Beo's eyes going black and depthless. The utter absence of anything that made my belly clutch just to remember it.

Bones, shattering. Afternoon sun.

I fell in behind a local guy who was waiting as we jogged, and I felt for the folks hauling all the weapons. Mine were compact, my highly effective Lupetec armor light.

Maybe that was why most of them were breathing pretty hard when we reached the point we were meeting Richardson's team. She waved me over and I trotted up, spotting a wizard beside her. "Rearguard," she told me, softly, and pointed to me.

The wizard was wearing jeans and a beanie. He looked about my age and had a hard set to his mouth. *Out to prove himself.* And his staff looked like something out of a fantasy novel, complete with glowing crystal gem.

They were fucked.

"You sure?" I asked her, against my better judgement.

She nodded once, hard. I shrugged and jogged back to Taig's group. "New guy?" Greene asked me, still somehow pale and clammy from the drive.

"Temporary wizard," I murmured. And maybe I should've argued with the decision to put him in the lead. He was a liability.

But I didn't *want* to go first.

We hydrated. They caught their breath and I tried not to notice Taig was doing just fine despite his soft belly that was exaggerated by the vest he was wearing, despite the weight of the rifle over his shoulder and the pistols at his hips. Dad bods could be deceptive.

The sun was up but the mist was thick as we split and approached. I breathed in air so cold it burned. Leaves and sticks crackled under feet around me and tension thrummed in my limbs. We moved as a group.

Something was wrong. I could *feel* it.

I eased my headgear down over my face as the back door came into view. The sun was piss-weak but simultaneously warm as an afternoon in summer.

Through the mist I could make out vague swirls where Richardson's team were going in low and hard. We had an easier path, which made sense. They'd had a longer breather after that billygoat track.

Quiet, calm, and still.

I stopped, anxiety clawing at my chest. My internal alarms were wailing and my feet had become cement. There was just no way I could go through with this. So I straightened, turned, and caught Taig's eye.

I could say no. Pull them all out.

I drew in a deep breath. Someone brushed against my shoulder then shot me a quick, searching look before they kept moving. And a scream started to bubble deep inside me.

I swallowed it and shook my head. *Focus. Breathe. One foot. The other.* I stretched my legs. Ate up the distance. *Just jumpy.* The words echoed in my head. *Just jumpy.* We went through the garden beds, then across the lawn. Somewhere far away a car started up. It was just background noise though, nothing alarming.

We were at the back door and nothing was wrong. But I couldn't breathe.

I hadn't had this sick feeling before the lycans had hit. It wasn't like I was an Oracle.

Just jumpy.

There was ice in my veins.

In front of me the same woman who'd taken out the door to Vincetto's place so deftly was swinging the big black key they used to break locks. I hadn't been asked to cast a Silence Ward and alarm skittered through me. But maybe there was a reason. If Richardson hit the house first, then—

But it was wrong.

Working on instinct, I cast my Impenetrable. The spell snapped into place neatly, ill-planned but well executed.

It carved through the building, smashing brick and wood. Cops went down around me, hitting the dirt and lifting their weapons, but they were safe in my ward.

And then came the fire.

CHAPTER 28

THE FORCE OF THE EXPLOSION THREW THE WOMAN SWINGING THE BLACK ram at the door aside, even from her place inside my ward.

"Trap!" someone was roaring.

But I *knew*. I knew those shouts. I knew those screams. I heard them in my sleep. We all sounded exactly like that. We were all just scared animals…

Breaking bones. Afternoon sun.

There was no time for thought. Shoving past a faceless cop, I barely heard him fall as I dove through my ward with a crackle of power into the inferno.

The scorching heat, the suffocating smoke, became my world. Still there was movement around me, even in the airless firestorm.

I kept low and ran into someone—a few *someones*. They were screaming as I grabbed hold of anything I could. Wailing. Running. Chaos. Guns, firing. Crashing, rushing, noise. Glass exploded nearby as I hauled them through the maelstrom.

"Grab everyone!" I tried to shout, but the words were lost in the roar of the orange, white, red, and *hungry* beast that had surrounded us. And they couldn't get inside my ward without me. The thought of that, of people potentially dying, trying to get entry to my sanctuary, sent another shot of adrenaline coursing through my bloodstream.

I dragged people I'd found back with me into the ward and threw them in. Burning. Burning. Keeping myself low was easy. My feet, my body, knew these moves.

I went hard.

Muscles were tight and flooded with adrenaline. The heat was crushing. The ground beneath me was soft, and studded with glass and brick. The house was going up. The bush. The road. Everything, alight.

Trap.

Not vampires.

I grabbed a few people. Three or four. They let me pull and drag them. We couldn't see through the billowing smoke or past the painfully bright flame. Couldn't. Breathe. The weight of them was immense but simultaneously nothing at all. My legs burned and I could feel that fire *in my bones.* Someone fell, their helmet blackened, the logo peeling off like an aged sticker on a kid's notebook. I reached down and grabbed them. One of their joints popped and their scream of agony was just part of the soundtrack of failure. I pulled them over the grass, into the circle of green inside my ward. It was far enough. They'd be safe.

Again.

More.

How many more?

My head was spinning. *Go low. Go hard. Get more.* I stumbled and got up. My eyes were streaming. There was a body at my feet, glass in their eye, a big, deadly sliver. The image burned into my brain like it was a freeze frame. I stepped over them. I didn't have time to mourn. *Where are the survivors?*

The heat was an immense wave. It consumed air and hope alike.

I found someone trying to protect another in a heap that I almost mistook for a pile of dead. I reefed the top person up. They looked up at me, tears running from their eyes. I helped haul their comrade up and staggered under their weight. I had to carry them and my shoulders screamed in fury. There was a rush of warm blood. Not mine.

Pumping. Spurting. In time with his heart. The afternoon sunlight. Low growls.

"This way!" I tried to shout, but there was no air and my legs weren't strong. I staggered again, managed to fall forward. The grass was green. *I'm inside my ward. Have to. Hold. The. Ward.*

My head was spinning. I couldn't. Breathe.

Ice in my veins. Sun on my face. Smoke in my eyes.

The crackle of power from my spell was like a lover's kiss. I was grabbed and shoved onto the ground, into the dirt. The person was dragged off my shoulder.

Words surrounded me, hemming me in. I got up but felt my leg go out. Someone caught me amidst the roaring, crackling chaos.

Beo's paw on my hand.

I tried to pull away toward the edge of the ward. There were more. So many more.

But I was yanked back, hard, by a hand on my arm. Someone was shouting, but the noise was burned up in the crackle and roar. An object struck the barrier and I barely heard it. Again, I was pushed down roughly. They yanked and shoved at me but I could barely make them out. Were they swimming? Was my head? They were pulling at my boots. I could feel it. I didn't kick but my body screamed to fight.

I looked up at the huge dome of my spell. The smoke and fire raged around. Parts of the house were burning against it. Beside me, a flattened fuchsia and damp mulch looked horrifically normal. This time when I rolled to a sitting position, I wasn't shoved down. I could see Taig in front of me.

His mouth was a grim line and his helmet was off, showing where sweat dripped down his face. There was no soot though, not on him. And something about that eased the terror in my heart to let my lungs expand. Rapidly I inhaled, exhaled, as I watched his lips form words. The world lurched.

My boots had been ripped off. Before me the sight of my woolen, mismatched socks seemed almost hilarious. I'd been close—one was navy, one was black. Did I get points for trying?

Because I'd tried.

I flopped back against the ground as the adrenaline drained out of me. They weren't screaming, now. It was just the roar of flames.

Amor.

CHAPTER 29

They lost fifteen people and the wizard. I couldn't help but second-guess my decisions. Had I jinxed him?

I'd grabbed Richardson. The woman I'd carried was the worst off, but everyone I'd hauled into my ward had burns, shrapnel injuries, smoke inhalation.

And the sirens rang in my head long after I staggered home, into my shower, into my bed.

Somehow I got to Dierdre's, where she took over, humming to the music struggling out of her phone's speakers and I did my best to match her joy rather than dampen it.

Vampires.

Angels.

Fuckery abounding.

I sat still while she spritzed my hair with some sort of magickally-enhanced hair mist and coiled another few curls up onto my head. "You've got such *amazing* hair," she said, not for the first time. It was a fruitless battle, really, trying to tame my hair. But she'd been *so* keen to try.

"I'm attached to it," I agreed, blandly, my voice rough from the smoke. But I made her laugh. Then she scowled as one of the chunks of hair slipped a bit. "Hmm." It wasn't singed, at least. I'd had my head-gear on. I'd been protected.

Not like the others.

She put the spray bottle down and marched out of the bathroom, leaving me looking at my reflection. With makeup done, and pretty sharp, too, I looked good, but my mismatched eyes were piss-holes in the snow. I couldn't bring myself to care.

When she came back it was with a little bottle with a dropper in it and a mutinous expression. I kept my mouth closed as she drew the dropper, murmured some words, narrowed her eyes at my hair and started working on the more independent strands.

Not scrolling on my phone was hard, but I didn't *really* need a client seeing the mess that my socials were. I felt a text arrive and, wondering if it was Lilith, dug out said device and glanced at it.

Taig.

"I won't look," she said, with a smile in her voice that told me she'd already looked.

Shit. "I'm waiting on news about my old Retrievals team," I told her, not lying. We hadn't exactly had time to chat. But I stalled until she shifted her focus to quickly glance at it.

He was hoping to catch me tonight. Hadn't forgotten he was my guide.

I sighed and put it down. "Bad news?" Deirdre asked, as a singer warbled about reclaiming her power from the shitty phone speakers.

"No news."

"Is that...bad?" she asked, frowning. "People say no news is good news."

"It's bad in this situation." And it wasn't mine to carry. There was nothing I could do. Well, nothing I hadn't done, anyway.

Maybe I could've done more.

I shoved that away. "But, we're here, safe, and have a fruit platter, so."

"Sweet of him to keep you updated."

I grunted, not fooled by her phony nonchalance. She just smiled a secret smile and ruthlessly gathered another few dozen curls, draping them artistically.

Time dripped past. I hummed along when I could, smiled when I was smiled at. And when she was done—having actually succeeded, at least for now—I joined in her bad dance moves with equally bad ones of my own as we went into the kitchen and ate from the fruit platter I'd bought pre-prepared because I was bone tired.

Where the fuck is Lilith?

Surely I wasn't the only one joining the dots. Taig was clever. He'd see the links. It's not like they were subtle.

It was the *exact same spell* that she'd almost taken us out with at the warehouse.

Except Beo hadn't been there.

Except I'd been able to hold my ward.

My heart hurt. "There's just something about kiwi fruit," she was saying, with a sigh.

"Especially sliced," I agreed, resisting the urge to look at the time again.

"Agreed. Are you sure I can't get you a tonic for your eyes, or..."

She'd already put drops in them. They felt better, but I wasn't going in for magickal healing. Who knew if I'd lose my thrice cursed job if I didn't show? And I was going to show.

Grimly, I bit into a slice of apple that was absolutely not fresh and yet somehow had avoided browning. Maybe it was plastic? Probably.

When a knock on the door came, I sprang up and beat her to it. Lilith, bag in hand. The sweetest sight in the world.

Her brow furrowed as she looked me over. "Heard you got into some shit today."

"Yeah." I shut it behind her. "Did you have any luck tracking whoever gave Arthur's address to the vamps?"

"Some." And then Dierdre was there and Lilith's smile was huge. "Oh, your hair looks *amazing*. And so does Rory's. I can smell the rose hip. Your tonic?"

We primped and preened, blended and contrasted, then went separate ways to get our clothes on. Once again we joined forces in the bathroom, where Dierdre was doing Lilith's hair, the good music on her bad speakers once again. *Nails on a chalkboard*, my Oma would've said.

When there was another knock on the door, I leapt off my perch on the side of the bath. "I've got it," I told them, hastily. "You two keep polishing."

I didn't miss the quick, loaded look Dierdre shot Lilith but didn't bother to roll my eyes, just went out, the sound of my heels on the wooden floor making me wonder if I should remove them. I didn't want to chew up the wood.

Taig stood behind a big bunch of flowers. Surprise flickered over his face and I got a quick once over, but resisted doing the same to him. "Not the witch I was expecting."

"Uh huh." I stepped back, checked out the flowers, a big, cheerful cottage style arrangement. I ignored the hurt that swelled in my chest. There was no reason for it, after all. "I'm her Caretaker. You break her heart, I'll eat yours."

His brows rose. "Does she know you're speaking for her?"

"She's busily dancing to pop hits and doing hair." I grabbed my coffee. "You okay?"

"Yeah." He set the bouquet down. "You should be in hospital. Or bed, at least. Heard you didn't let them take you in."

I shrugged it off and hid behind my mug as I checked the time. I could probably skip out early. Maybe.

"It's an encouragement gift," he said, quietly. "Felt right."

"Sure." I took a gulp of coffee. It travelled like a lump down my throat. I didn't want him anyway. "I'll go get her."

Lilith chose that moment to appear, her hair halfway braided and held tightly in one hand, wand in the other. "Not an assassin, then." She frowned at the flowers, cocked a brow at me. Silently I shook my head, warning her not to ask questions, and drank some more coffee. "Nice suit, O'Malley. That tie would look better on Roars." And with that, she left.

Fucking deserter.

He was smiling a bit as he wandered over and leaned on the bench beside me. "She's right," he admitted. "Don't know how it'll sit without a collar, but it *is* a black-tie affair."

I knew damned well she was right. It'd look great between my mostly bare breasts. And, fuck it. "Well, hand it over."

I half expected him to laugh it off, to make some excuse. But he reached up to his throat and eased the knot. He'd shaved. His hair was still damp and he didn't smell of sandalwood, but some other stuff that I didn't like half as much. "You're pissed."

"Yeah."

He eased it out from under his collar, offered it to me. "Because I brought someone who's sad flowers?"

I shot him an irritated look. "A gorgeous, lonely, very *single* sad someone."

He cocked his head a little, his expression almost calculating. "I didn't know a gorgeous, tough, honorable and fierce someone would be here, or I'd have tried to figure out what to bring her. Not flowers. You aren't a flowers woman."

My mouth went dry. I held the tie, warm from his body. "Are they alive, Taig?" I asked, feeling sick.

He shrugged. "I don't know. Second team went dark about ten minutes after they arrived."

I paced away, feeling sick. "And no one is sending up alarms."

"Oh, I didn't say that."

"Today's fire was—"

"Amor."

I paused, glanced back at him. "And?"

"And wheels take time to turn," he said, quietly. "But I'm glad we had you. Again. But you don't get paid to run into infernos to save people."

Rage rolled through me. "You want me to let them *die?*" And I felt my arm move as I hurled the tie at his face.

He caught it neatly, not even dropping my gaze. "I've got my priorities," he said, calmly. "I like you alive. I know that's easy for me to say." He shrugged. "Nothing I could've done."

"It doesn't make it sit better," I said, before my brain could kick in.

"No," he agreed, quietly. "No, it doesn't." And there was real empathy in his eyes, a kindness that extinguished the fire in my blood before it could really take hold and left me feeling charred. "Come here," he said, loosening the knot a bit more in his hands. "I'll try not to upset your hair. That must've taken serious time."

"I'll be picking pins out for weeks," I muttered, lowering my head so he could ease it on.

"Looks great. Doesn't sound worth it, but, hey, what do I know?" I felt the weight of the fabric, the warmth of him, the softness of the fabric, on my skin. I straightened up, making sure my jacket wasn't showing more than I planned. "You'll need to tighten it up."

I looked down at the thing and lifted the knot. The classic oval mirror Dierdre had in the hallway showed me in all my severe glory—with a wonky tie.

The effect would have been hilarious if it'd been the end of the evening. I pinched the two sides like I'd seen others do, tried to shuffle the knot up. It bunched up.

"You need to—" he cut off and pressed a hand to his jaw, then folded the other arm over his chest like he was trying hard not to talk or laugh or something. "Sorry. Go on. I won't mansplain."

"It's not mansplaining if you actually know a thing I don't." I looked at myself in the mirror. Drunken femme fatale? Not tousled enough for post-quickie. I sighed, put my hands on my hips. "I don't want the tie anymore."

"Sure? I can help." And his eyes dipped down to the knot between my breasts. "I didn't even know you could mess them up that badly."

I was way beyond caring. "Just," I waved a hand tiredly. "Take it or fix it. I don't care. But I'm not going like this."

"No," he agreed, a smile tucked into the corner of his mouth. He came around behind me. My heels put me comfortably taller than him, but he studied the knot in the mirror without appearing concerned by that. "Are you okay to go tonight?" he asked, the humor fading. "I can put in some paperwork. Rock some boats."

"Aren't you supposed to be super neutral?" I asked, because I was a bitch.

"Yeah, no one believed it anyway." He met my eyes. "I'm not good at pretending not to notice important things."

My heart squeezed. I ripped my eyes away but couldn't make my feet move.

"Lilith or Dierdre can fix the tie," he said, that low, sexy rumble going straight to my core. "Or find a video. We've got time."

Alarm bells rang in my head and told me to run. But I couldn't run with lead feet.

My arm, however, wasn't weighed down. My fingers lingered on the borrowed warmth in the fabric. I held it up, offering it to him.

His arms went around me. "Like this," he murmured, but I wasn't watching what his hands did. There was something wonderfully solid about his chest being pressed lightly against my shoulder blades. The warmth of his breath against my ear made ripples of awareness wash through me. He'd stopped me going back out. He'd probably saved us all, because if I'd gone down, my ward would've, too. He would've died.

But I didn't think that was all he meant when he spoke about priorities.

His fingers brushed against the skin of my throat as he settled the knot and tightened it. The ice inside of me was melting—or had melted. I didn't know. But I knew what the simmering, humming awareness meant. He smelled wrong but he wasn't. I settled back, just a little, and felt him shift to accommodate me. "Here?" he asked me, the word low. "Or," a few movements did something different to the tie. His arms were strong and warm but his hands didn't touch my skin. In a last-ditch effort to focus I looked in the mirror. But all I could see were those hands, so close to my breasts. "Here?"

"Yes."

He paused for a moment, the pace of his breathing changing. My blood hummed. "Here?"

"No."

He shuffled it a little and there was a featherlight touch, some accidental pressure, against my breast. Heat stirred deep within, liquid and beautiful. "Better?"

I looked but didn't see. "It isn't straight." I could stop in a moment. A few more touches wouldn't hurt.

"It isn't," he agreed, the words quiet. "Maybe I ought to help you out with that."

"Yes," I said again, and it sounded like a sigh to me. Alarm bells rang again. I ignored them and closed my eyes as his fingers skimmed down between my breasts, deliberately, now. Heat lanced through me and I felt myself unfurling. I was suddenly, agonizingly aware of my bare skin under the jacket and how close his fingers were to my nipples. My throat was so close to his lips. My hips could just nestle into his.

His fingers scraped lightly, exploring, enjoying. They cruised down the exposed vee of my jacket, his pace leisurely. And the blood in my body swept down with them, ahead of them, in anticipation. I drew in a breath and felt the answering rush of wanting.

"It looks good," he said, and there was not a hint of laughter in his voice. "More than good. Excellent choice."

"It's still wonky," I managed, drawing in another breath.

His lips were against my neck. Not kissing. Not quite. Just lingering, full of promise. The backs of his fingers smoothing back up my chest and I felt the breath he drew in deep as his fingers unfurled. The pads of his fingers were a soft, gentle pressure as he traced the underside of my breast, exploring my exposed curves. I held my breath as pinpoints of desire demanded attention. I burned.

"Check it now," he recommended, voice rough.

"It's good." The words were intelligible. My tongue was fantastic. Oh, fuck, his would be, too. The thought made my knees weak. "My jacket, though."

He'd almost melded with me. My head swam. Part of me wanted to stay here forever, drowning in sensation, in the promise that sang in my body. I arched back into him, wanting more, and heard his breath catch. "Yeah," he agreed. "Yeah. We might need to..." his fingers slipped down the lapel slowly, over my aching breasts. But the caress was blunted by the fabric of my jacket and the need only grew.

I was a fucking puddle at his feet and I didn't even care.

The backs of his fingers brushed over my nipples, my breasts. I breathed deeply, drawing the heat in deep, and wished I could get closer. His hands cupped me through the fabric, his thumbs moving over me in slow circles. My breath was caught in my lungs but I didn't want to exhale, to move away from that tenderness. I couldn't miss a moment of it. I wanted more but I didn't want to move—didn't want to risk this sweetness coming to an end. I was all but draped over him and his lips brushed against my throat, warm and soft and hungry.

I arched my neck, hoping for more and felt the kisses become firmer. Teeth scraped, ever so lightly, and my breath caught. His fingers found my nipples and captured them gently. I felt the wash, the roll, the wonder of it and pressed my hips back to feel the hard length of him. It was just us, and it was all I wanted. His hands. His mouth. His skin. The future lay before me in fragments.

I just wanted this part. Him. Us.

My ear was caught in his lips and teased gently. My hands groped behind me, searching for something more. Something to hold onto as the sensations swelled. His hair was soft in my hands, and I held him close as I sank into the sensory delight. Every nerve, every cell, felt alive. I breathed him in deep.

"We should stop," he said, the words breathless. "Or relocate."

"Don't stop," my tongue said without needing my brain. Thank the Elders. My brain was gone. Out for a long lunch. Probably wouldn't get back in until Monday. I tightened my fingers when he went to pull back a little and was rewarded by a nip, a suck, of my earlobe. I was vulnerable and I knew it—but I also knew I was safe. Maybe even cherished. And that was a heady combination.

"I want you." That was all I knew. "All of you."

Against the damp of my ear his breath shook. "Good. Because I'm pretty stoked about all of you, too." The way he kissed my neck with finality made me want to weep. "Not here, though," he said, roughly. "I want more time."

The thought of drawing it out, wallowing in this, in the heat, the glory, the sheer wonder of it—I couldn't wrap my head around it. But I couldn't imagine ending this. "How much time?" I didn't have forever but I didn't know how much time I *did* have. I didn't care. I needed to, but I didn't. He did, though, so I had to. "Like—fifteen minutes?" I could buy us some time.

He laughed, a silent, quick expulsion of breath that made me shiver. "I'm not talking minutes."

The promise went straight to my bloodstream but alarm bells sounded, somewhere far off in the back of my brain. *Maybe later tonight we could—*

But when I managed to focus my eyes and meet his in the mirror, ice ran through my veins.

He wasn't talking about minutes.

There wasn't just heat in his eyes. Oh, it was there. He was in it with me. Maybe not as far, not as deep yet. But there was wonder in his gaze. There was awe and warmth.

I straightened and stepped away, almost twisting my damned ankle in my damned sexy stilts and grabbed the wall as my damned knees half gave out.

That wasn't a casual move. *I knew he wasn't a casual guy.*

And I was a fucking *puddle.*

"Go easy," he murmured, hand hovering at my elbow. "You okay?

Fuck. I pressed a hand to my mouth, felt the smolder and scream of my body. And the traitorous aching of my battered heart.

Hiding my face, I gulped in air. I didn't know what he'd see and I didn't want to figure it out. *Oh, fuck.* If something started—I wouldn't be in control, with him. I didn't—I couldn't—

"That got a bit out of hand." My words were wry and rough. "Can't say I didn't enjoy it, though."

It had been in hand—in *his* hands, anyway. And he'd known just what to do.

My body wept for more.

I shook my head wordlessly. It wouldn't be neat, with him. It wouldn't be clean. And the knowledge of that made tears rush into my eyes. There was a knot in my throat and it tasted like grief and fear. I didn't want to feel grief *or* fear. I couldn't go down this path again.

He was saying something. I don't know what. And I just couldn't let myself get drawn in.

I'd just end up at his feet again.

Boneless.

I turned and fled, seeking Lilith's strength and solidarity.

"Rory," she said as I barreled into her, jostled the bag of cosmetics in her hand. She caught me. "Are you—what's wrong?"

I fell down on the toilet, put my head between my knees, and gulped air.

Nothing was wrong.

Nothing.

I could do this.

CHAPTER 30

THE SOUND OF LAUGHTER, OF THE LIVE BAND LOSING AGAINST THE competition of the wind, of the rise and fall of polite nothings, surrounded me. I saw Arthur approaching and kind of wanted to turn the other way, to drag Lilith and Dierdre to the bonfire to dance. But half the coven was around us and a bunch of others as well. Dierdre was laughing, a champagne flute in her hand, the wind throwing her red hair around like it was too full of joy to contain.

I sighed and Lilith shifted a little closer. "Don't ask," I told her, not for the first time this evening.

"Not asking." She lifted the apple juice to her lips. Through the illusion—the woman's mask—she drank. It was an odd visual I wasn't used to yet.

But Arthur didn't come straight to us. He circulated. I was relieved to see Bernie take his arm and tow him away from Dierdre quite firmly toward a group of young witches.

My eyes skimmed the crowd slowly. I was grateful for the little pocket of quiet and the witch at my shoulder. No threats here aside from the oversized egos of some of the partiers.

All too soon Arthur extracted himself from the wolves Bernie had thrown him to and started his path again. "This is boring," Lilith said. "Next girls' night, let's stay home and play games."

"Done."

"Can't believe I did my hair for this," she muttered, shifting her weight to save her feet from her gorgeous, but doubtless agonizing, icepick heels.

"You look great." And she did.

"Yeah, well." She blew out a breath. "Why do people leave the house? I don't get it. All the best stuff is at home. And there are less people."

It was so true. Over the way, Arthur's eyes locked onto another wizard doing the rounds, a dark-skinned, young guy I'd seen spending more time with the grey-hairs and outcasts than the movers and shakers like Arthur.

Arthur didn't have his mask on and I watched, with interest, as his dimples flashed while he talked to the wizard. I nudged Lilith. "Hey. Check it."

She glanced over. "Oh, it's Shepherd."

"Who?"

"Shepherd. He's a good bloke. Keeps a low profile, but does good work. I hear he was going to go Retrievals, but his mum got sick, so he stuck close to home. His skin's the wrong color for a promotion."

"That's fucked."

"That's life, witch," she drawled and looked away, losing interest. "I'll introduce you if he comes over. I'm hoping to bump into Vince."

"Vince." The ICT guy? I'd met him, what, twice, when I had my devices hooked up to our software and networks? Before me Arthur moved in and touched Shepherd's arm. There was color in his cheeks.

"Vince," Lilith repeated. "He's got access to *everything*. I've had some permissions granted so I could access a few of his files to do genealogies. I can't imagine what I could do if I could access that every day. Old information *and* new, he's got it on all the magi families."

My head snapped around. "What?"

I couldn't see her expression through the mask but I didn't need to; I could feel that sassy brow arch in my bones. "You heard me."

I grabbed her arm. "Let's find him. I want to—"

"Yes, well, if I'd spotted him, I'd have hauled you over." She patted my hand on her arm, then gently removed it.

"Sorry." I blew out a breath. I knew better than just to grab people. I was more rattled than I wanted to admit. The sleep I'd had that afternoon hadn't gone long enough, obviously. I was just too tired. That was all. "Sorry, Lilith."

"You're good." Another sip. "Chill, Rory. You're ruining my dinner."

Since her dinner had been a fast-food burger about an hour ago, I doubted I could've done much to harm it.

"Why, if it isn't my favorite mortal."

My dad's voice made me smile and turn. He was wearing a ridiculously old-fashioned coat and tails. He thought it was cool. The top hat and antique walking stick only took it to the next level. Beside him, grinning like the birthday kid and looking like a queen, was Aspen.

"Okay," I sighed, as I reached over, folded them both in my arms. "Where the hells did you two come from?"

"I was invited," dad said, feigning injury. "And dragged this one along." He jerked his thumb at Aspen, who was already sighing over Lilith's underbust skirt thing.

Dad reached into his jacket and pulled out a velvet wrapped bundle. "Knife. Didn't have time—or measurements—for the dusters."

I took it automatically, running to keep up. "I told you today."

"*You* told me today. *Cooper* told me last week." He pressed a kiss to my cheek and the mask on my face tickled as the illusion shifted, broke and reformed. "Nice moustache."

"Thanks," I said, distracted. "How did *Coop* know I needed a new knife?"

Dad sighed and shook his head wisely. "You and your fast city life. You've left us all in the dust." Impatient, I jabbed him in the ribs with a finger and made him laugh. "He's Retrievals now."

"*What?* Little Coop? Elders!" The kid had been nineteen last I'd seen him? "He's, what, twenty?"

"Three, and *you* were *barely* twenty when you got your first contract."

Yeah, but. "Shit, dad. Wait. He's reading my reports?"

"Yeah. Word travels. He's up in Western Australia, but keeps tabs on you. He always looked up to you."

"He had to. He's a short arse." I was going to have to reach out, touch base. I looked at the velvet wrapped knife, struggling to get my head around the skinny kid Dad had taken under his wing now taking contracts, keeping the peace, and looking out for *me.*

It made me feel pretty loved, really.

"Here," Lilith said, holding out her hand. "My skirt has pockets. Unlike your manly pants over there."

"Huh. That's not how it's supposed to work," Dad mused. "Pants need pockets. Where else do we store the keys to the patriarchy?" He dipped his head a little and my attention sharpened. "I'm hearing a lot about vampires."

"I told you," I muttered, glancing around. Pretty sure I'd broken some confidentiality laws.

"What about the fae?" he asked me, the words soft beneath the rise and fall of conversation around us.

I glanced up, met his familiar eyes with the crows-feet at the corners from smiling all the time and felt a wave of love wash over me. To think there was a being that weaponized such things. "Dad, you always blame the fae."

"Is it *really* paranoia if they're out to get you, though?" he asked, mock-thoughtfully. "Seriously, Sunshine. You've got vampires. You know if you've got one, you've got the other. But I haven't heard anything about the fae."

I'd already considered that. "I know. But I've got bigger fish to fry right now, Dad, okay?" I glanced around, wishing I could grab some free champagne. A headache was gnawing low in my skull.

"I'm worried," he said, seriously, glancing around.

And, just to annoy him, I said, "Hi Worried, I'm Rory."

He nudged me lightly with his elbow. "Chip off the old block. Oma says she forgot to mention something to you the other day."

My headache cranked up a notch. "Oh?"

"Major banishment if the thing manifests," he said quietly, while simultaneously smiling and lifting a hand to wave hello to some random grey-haired wizard passing by. "Whoever it's riding will be the sacrifice. This is one that can't manifest by itself."

I thought of Amor's eyes changing, of the reek of roses. Shit, I could happily sacrifice her. "Cool."

"Not cool," he corrected. "Scary. Once it's manifested, if you just kill the host, you've got yourself a pinball situation."

That was definitely not cool, he was right. "Okay. Shit." So, if I'd been a bit slower cutting Amor's throat, I could've got myself possessed. *Great.* "I hate beings who can't manifest solo."

"I hate beings," he said, blandly. "Why, I'm suddenly thirsty. You three have young legs," he said, to the group of us, interrupting Aspen and Lilith's animated conversation about quality leather. "Maybe you can find me something to drink."

He was smiling at us but I glanced in the direction he'd been looking before the sudden change and saw, immediately, the three slight women who all-but shimmered. And my heart sank. "Faeries."

"I hate being right," he agreed, grimly. To the group, "drinks?"

He was trying to get rid of us. "I'm working, Dad."

"Cool. Work near the drinks table." And he shooed me. Actually raised his hands and made flicking motions.

The urge to grab one hand and crush his fingers was strong. I didn't, mostly because I was too busy trying to figure out where the vampires were. Because fae meant vamps, and vamps meant fae and the whole thing meant my headache was going to get no better this evening.

As soon as we weren't looking, Dad moved off in the direction of the faeries. I saw him grab a few of the old guard with a glance and a raised hand. If he needed me, I'd know about it.

Dierdre danced with Janet by the fireside, her smile huge. Guilt crawled through me. I hadn't seen her leaving. I was too caught up in my own shit. The crowd hadn't moved much. The friendship groups changed a few members as people floated, but the clots of magi and company were in similar positions.

Aspen's hand settled on my upper arm and I caught the end of a story she was telling Lilith about an escapade we'd been in a few years ago. But it was the smile, the way her eyes glittered, that hit me right in the guts.

How long had it been since I'd just been happy?

"Red head in the sparkly cream dress," I said in Aspen's ear. "Keep us close, yeah?"

"Pleasure," Aspen said. "Can you dance as well as you dress wounds, Lilith?" And Aspen took over as I felt the tension in my neck and shoulders. Over a sea of heads, I spotted Arthur again chatting and he met my eyes for just a moment.

My heart twisted and the shame of what I'd done to him was real. Lilith's hip bumped into mine and jolted me.

"You okay?" she asked, pausing in the middle of the group, music flooding in around us.

"Yeah," I said automatically, catching the edge of the warm smile Arthur sent our way before he turned back to the wizard he was talking to. Shit, I was tired. "No," I amended, suddenly. "No, I'm not."

Lilith and I stood in the eye of a storm for just a moment, a tiny second of peace. I was so not okay. What in the hells had I done? Jeopardizing a job I loved, running from a good man to the arms of someone I'd never in a million years be happy with? Running ridiculous risks and never once stopping to think? But those mistakes didn't mean I deserved to be miserable forever.

"Let's go somewhere quiet," Lilith said, studying my face. "You can talk it out."

But I didn't want to talk it out. There weren't words for all of the big, gross things. I just wanted to exist, for a moment. I just wanted to *be*.

So I took a deep breath and felt the flood of dark, sticky horror. Yeah, I'd screwed up plenty. But that didn't mean I wasn't allowed some joy.

"I just want to be here," I told her, feeling the tears in my chest and letting them sit there. "I'll be okay later. For now, I just want to be here."

Aspen's arms snaked around my waist and the tightness of her hug almost made me explode. "Dance it out!" she crowed, and laughter got all tangled up in those tears in my chest as I stayed there, in the moment, with the two of them.

It hurt. It hurt my feet, but more, it hurt my heart. And it mended it too.

I didn't see what happened with Dad and the fae. But I saw the old guard returning, and there was no more sign of faeries.

It was never that simple, but for tonight, it was enough to let someone else manage everything that went wrong. It was okay for me to step back.

By the time we fell into Taig's car, Dierdre was rubbing her cheeks from smiling and I was even more exhausted but felt strangely at peace. Nothing had gone terribly wrong just because I'd had some free champagne and danced with my sisters.

"I think my smiling muscles are jelly," Dierdre said, the words carried on a happy sigh.

I let the conversation ebb around me and watched the rooftops, the cars and the sidewalks. It was one in the morning but it was Solstice night in Melbourne. The traffic was less, sure, but far from none. Anxiety hummed along my skin and I let it, sitting with it as the lights flickered through the interior of the car.

There had been faeries at Solstice. Dad was right. Maybe it was hereditary. Either way, it was shit, but it was shit I couldn't deal with right now, if ever. And I didn't need to. I checked my phone, but he hadn't contacted me. I'd chase that up tomorrow, maybe. But if he needed me, he'd let me know. I trusted him to do that.

As the car lights blurred past, shapes shrouded in mist and mystery, I took my knife back from Lilith.

"We need to talk to Vince," I told her, quietly. It made sense to discuss the guy with the keys to the kingdom, after all.

"I need to sleep."

"Same. But tomorrow..."

She shot me a quick, worried look, but didn't argue.

We needed to do something. We couldn't sit and wait forever, minimizing risk and reducing lives lost. And while I couldn't control everything, and the situation with Amor was horrible, I could do *something*.

I saw Taig glance at me in the rearview mirror and I avoided his gaze as well as I'd avoided his advances tonight. While I remembered it, I pulled off the tie—*that fucking tie*—and tossed it on the seat between Lilith and I.

Instantly I wanted to snatch it back. My heart ached. There was no point pretending, though, that I was in any sort of place to take what he was offering, even if my hormones disagreed.

If I was Amor—or Tobias—what would I spring my trap *early* for?

I saw Dierdre, her head tipped back, a soft smile on her face as the streetlights brought it into sharp relief, then deep shadow.

Her.

I felt sick.

So, how did I make them think they had her?

Or... how did I make them think they *couldn't* if they didn't act immediately?

In the ebb and flow of the light, Deirdre closed her eyes, peaceful and happy. My stomach twisted. If word got back to them that I was going to kill her, would they believe it? Could I make it look authentic enough to draw them out early? There weren't many ways out of this. If Tobias had taken out *two* teams—well, it wasn't ending happily.

Not if we did it on their terms.

CHAPTER 31

TAIG PULLED INTO THE PARKING GARAGE BENEATH DIERDRE'S PLACE. I was quiet as the pleasantries were shared and climbed out after Lilith.

"I'll wait down here while you get your keys," I told her, breathing around the knot of yuck in my chest. "Want to talk to Taig."

With a swift, concerned look in his direction she acquiesced. I waved off a skipping Dierdre and didn't stomp on the bloom of pride in my chest. Okay, so I'd been against the whole idea, but I'd listened in the end. And it had been good.

Pretty much the story of my life. Screw up, manage to salvage something, make the most of it.

I sighed as Taig got out of the car and came to stand beside me, looking into the quiet shadows in companionable silence.

"I rushed you," he said, the words matter-of-fact.

"No." He hadn't, really. "No, I did." Because when things went wrong, I leaped before looking. And even though things were still just as wrong as they had been, I needed to be kinder to myself than that. "I need to catch my breath, Taig."

He nodded, and there was warmth in his eyes I didn't expect to see. "Makes sense. I'm glad you're doing that." He jingled his keys idly in his hand. "I can drop you home. Not making a pass, just might be easier."

But I wanted to sit with Lilith for just a few minutes more. And I didn't want to risk my brain short-circuiting again. "Thanks. No."

"No worries." He glanced in the direction Dierdre and Lilith had gone. "I can wait with you."

But being alone didn't scare me. I put a hand on his arm and felt the warmth of him through his jacket. I didn't want to curl into that warmth, though. I wouldn't be able to breathe.

"Go home, get some sleep." He'd be as tired as me, I had no doubt. "I'll see you soon."

He nodded again and straightened. "I'd love to kiss your fingers good-bye."

My fingers? Amused, I lifted a brow and gave him a bit of a smile. "Interesting."

He took my hand on his arm and lifted my fingers to his lips, brushing a kiss across my knuckles. And it felt...nice. "Thank you," he murmured, against my fingers. "For looking after you. Goodnight, Rory."

I stepped back, folding my arms over the warmth in my chest, and only lifted a hand to wave him off.

The peace of the night settled over me like a blanket and I breathed it in. That chill on the air was in my bones, and maybe it always would be. But there was a fire in my heart, too. And maybe it wouldn't level out totally. But I knew I'd be okay.

Removing my makeup in my quiet apartment was an almost meditative exercise. I curled up in bed by myself and felt my own warmth seeping into the cozy nest around me. And the longest night of the year I slept contentedly alone.

A knock on the door dragged me out of bed before nine. Expecting some half-remembered delivery, instead I stared blearily at Greene, dressed in his uniform blues.

Taig was nowhere to be seen, and neither was any other cop. "What'd I do?" I asked, shoving some hair out of my face.

He grinned. "Morning. I hear it was a late one. O'Malley sent me, because he thought you'd be interested to know there's a group of vampires holed up at the Docklands."

The last of the sleep blew out of my mind. "I am." I stepped back to let him in, but he shook his head. "Anything relevant on them?"

"Oldest is estimated to be three centuries. This is all speculation and second-hand information. They aren't currently being investigated for anything." He cleared his throat. "Don't, ah, text anything about it, though, okay? This is just a quick check of the building. Totally didn't even see you."

I gave him a thumbs up. Was this information useful? I'd decide after coffee. "Thank Taig for me." Then I paused, frowning. "Wait, is he okay?" He hadn't been called out on anything, had he? I would've been, too, surely.

"Oh, he's fine," Greene said vaguely. "He just needed a messenger, and I guess he knows I can keep my mouth shut. Got Franko double-parked waiting for me, so I'd better go."

I waved him off, puzzled. Since when did Taig send a messenger? Surely this wasn't about giving me some space. This sort of information might be useful. I could definitely use it to start asking questions. And three century old vamp heading up a nest? That was dangerous. That sort of fire-power—

My phone screamed at me before I'd even reached for the coffee. Bethany's name lit up the screen and I was groaning as I answered. "Again?" I demanded.

"Good morning to you too, Aurora," she said, the words icy. "How unfortunate for both of us that you're the only one I've got access to right now."

Bitch. I listened to the brief with one ear and took enough time to make myself a coffee, because the world could just wait two minutes before I went and rescued it.

At least this time when the lycans hit us I was ready with the

Impenetrable Ward. At least I didn't have to listen to breaking bones, except in my head.

Once the dust had settled on the chaos of the Retrievals operation, I couldn't silence the anxiety humming at the back of my brain. *Afternoon sun on my skin.* I tried to listen to Lilith's words, but my reception was terrible and my attention was worse.

Still, I was grateful that she'd managed Vince without me. Having a witch like her by my side meant I didn't need to do everything myself. Damned if I knew how to tell her how precious that was without sounding like a sappy card, though.

"—by vampires," she was saying, the words quiet and hurried on the other end of the phone. A flock of cockatoos passed overhead. Or in my head. I breathed though it, not checking to see what was reality and what was memory, trying to position myself so the cacophony wouldn't interfere with my ability to hear my friend.

I'd missed too much, though. "What?" I asked her.

"Vince. He was *taken by vampires,* Rory."

Again, I had to turn away from the gory scene as a trolly went past with what was, probably, a lycan beneath the sheet. I wondered dimly when they'd invest in lycan-sized bags. Or at least trollies the poor things didn't fall off of. It seemed such a horrific way to go.

Vince, the IT guy. Vampires. "Is he okay?"

"He will be," Lilith said, softly. "He's rattled. But, Roars—he's the one who gave them the information."

My heart ached for the guy. "Involuntarily, I assume. Is there anything I can do to help you help him?"

"I got it," Lilith said, sounding tired. "But thank you. I thought you'd want to know, though, that he can tell us exactly where they are."

. ₀.ₒ ₒₒ ₒₒ . . . ₒ ₒₒ.ₒₒ .

"I'm not saying this is poorly thought out or completely irresponsible," Lilith said, as she strode along beside me eyeing off the dying sun. "But if I did, I wouldn't be wrong."

280

"We've established it's the best option," I reminded her, glad to have her along even if she was going to bitch constantly. And it wasn't as poorly thought out as she was saying it was. A long shot, yeah, but it was a shot.

"*You* established it's the best option." She paused, her eyes narrowing as she scanned the shipping containers ahead of us. "*I* think there had to be an option C."

There was an option C. But it involved Beo, who was gone. We could manage without him.

Option A was to wait and respond. It meant waiting for more people to die at the hands of Amor, Tobias or their angel. It meant hoping they made more mistakes than we did. I wasn't a fan of that option.

"We should've told O'Malley," Lilith muttered, not for the first time.

"Taig is busy." And I needed some breathing space still. I needed not to run to him…or away from him.

"Not *that* busy." When I just ignored her, pulling my jacket a bit tighter, she sighed and waved a hand. "This way."

Option B was forcing the angel's hand and make them come to us. We couldn't win a fight on their terms, on their turf. But if we could get them to come to us, we'd be okay. And anyway, I worked well on the fly.

There was no way what we were planning on doing was legal. The time warp charms at my ears alone would get me thrown into SuperSec if I used them when I wasn't contracted. And I gave no fucks about any of that. Everything was screwed. Retrievals were basically down, and the supernatural cops weren't equipped to deal with angels.

Dierdre was a sitting duck, and she wasn't the only one. I was taking control back.

We turned a corner and Lilith lifted a finger, pointing at a shipping container stack at the end of the row that was taller and wider than the others. "Looks like the one Vince described."

Anticipation and dread hummed through me. He'd identified four vampires, but he'd also been charisma'd to the nines. How the fuck Lilith had got anything out of him, I had no idea. I guess she was pretty charismatic, too. Poor guy had been almost sick when he realized he'd basically given vampires the personal details of every single magi in the system.

Pretty smart on behalf of the vamps, though. No one suspects the ICT guy. And Lilith didn't seem to mind protecting him.

"Stay behind me," I told her, feeling sick.

"Yeah, yeah, I got it." She shot me an annoyed look. "We should've brought Janet. The whole coven."

Probably, but I was breaking a lot of laws. I wouldn't have even dragged Lilith along if I'd had a choice, so I didn't bother replying. We'd had this conversation a million different ways this afternoon.

She didn't think my plan B was a real plan. But, shit, it was the best I had, and the best *anyone* had. And if she didn't agree with that on some level, I'd probably be hog-tied on her couch eating ice-cream awkwardly.

A woman came into view, bone-white and exhausted, stumbling as she pulled on a coat. She saw us and cringed. I didn't chase when she turned and ran erratically in the other direction. My heart skipped a few beats. *Vamp food.* "Well," Lilith said, slowly, "I guess we're in the right area."

The door to the shipping container was ajar and the sun was dying. I stepped up the pace. I'd warned her about the time warp charms. She knew what to expect and what to do. It wasn't the safest plan, but neither of us were pushovers.

As soon as I activated the charms I felt the difference in Lilith's pace, the way the wind skimmed through her purple hair, the way her eyes slowly tracked to me then back to the ajar door.

She didn't speak, just lifted a hand like her actions were slow motion.

Yes, I noticed the door. I drew the wooden knife in one hand, the silver knife in the other, and rolled my shoulders.

I didn't need to kill them all. All I needed was to send a message.

What Tobias did to the messenger wasn't my problem.

And anyway, who didn't love waltzing into a vampire nest on a lazy Monday evening? *Me, that's who.*

If the oldest was three centuries, as Taig's information indicated, well, that might be okay. But if the recently transferred Hollywood ancient was here and in a bad mood, we were fucked with a capital F. And a capital 'Ucked', too.

Anxiety hummed and my bladder shrank to the size of a pea while I struggled to stay with Lilith, matching her now painfully slow pace. The charms burned my ears and I knew it wouldn't be long before that pain was going through to my skull. But I breathed through it and let the pain wash over me. I knew the risks. I knew the rewards, too. So here I was. And I'd probably have time to recover before tangling with Amor.

Lilith lifted her wand as we approached. Her mouth formed words in slow motion, the sounds strangely elongated. I breathed and waited as light flared and filled the container.

Three levels, decked out in luxury. They had all a modern vamp nest needed, according to Vince, and then some.

I hated the idea of him being here, alone in a vampire nest.

And I hated the idea of those vampires having access to our entire network.

Thank fuck Lilith figured it out. I wish I'd been there, with her, helping. My belly clutched and tightened. Alarm bells were ringing in my head and I acknowledged them. *Yes, walking into danger. Anxiety is normal.*

I shoved the door open and strode in, braced for the worst.

But the sight that met me wasn't what I'd prepared for. No vampires ready to fight. No lycans ready to defend. A television streamed an old vampire movie, something with lots of sex. On the couch in front of it, there was a vampire.

Their head was bent at an unnatural angle, a wooden stake through their mouth, and their body had shriveled and aged.

Dead.

My heart turned in my chest. Someone had beat me to the punch.

I swallowed down bile. I hadn't planned on going in and doing a full recon. I'd planned on them coming to me.

I couldn't walk away, though. That vampire had been caught totally unawares. Infighting was the only answer, and that meant there was division within their ranks.

Which meant my plan was fucked.

Maybe it was sunk cost fallacy, but I was committed now. So I ran. Up the ladder, into another lounge-style room—three vampires. *Dead.* They were fossilized around a card table, cards in their hands. A cigar burned in an ashtray, the smoke coiling slowly through the air. *Recent.* Terror pumped through me, gave me strength. *Who could have—*

Up. *Don't linger.* I hit the lights to reveal two huge beds. Three more vampires. *Dead.* Naked, shriveled and taken by surprise. But here there was sign of—something. The sheets had been pulled and half-dragged away as if someone had run. Or tried to.

I didn't wait or think or figure it out, just flew back down to Lilith. The smell of the cigar smoke hit my nose as I shot out of the container and deactivated the charms. My head was spinning. The pain of the charms was far away. "They're dead," I told her, flatly, trying to gulp air and figure out what my next steps were.

There were more vamps around, but these were the ones we *knew* had ties with Tobias. Had their allies turned on them? How many had there been? To take so many, so quickly, so completely—

Lilith's mouth fell open in shock. "You—"

"Not me," I said, impatiently. "I was never going to kill them." Okay, maybe some. I paused and shook my head. "Sorry. Stressing out, here."

"What—who—"

The woman who'd fled us. We could catch up with her. Question her. Shit, if Lilith could get something out of Vince… quickly I turned, ushering to Lilith.

Something caught my attention, some flicker in the corner of my eye. Time slowed, but I hadn't activated my charms. I grabbed Lilith, my wooden knife pressing against her coat and making my grip sit awkwardly. Spells swam in my head like the mist already rolling in off Port Phillip Bay.

The figure was tall and dark—probably handsome, too. A long trench coat moved around his calves in the sea wind.

And then he was gone.

Just *gone.*

No blurring. No nothing. Just there. Then gone.

The air rushed out of my lungs. I reached for my phone, stabbing myself with the silver knife I'd forgotten I held in the process. It didn't pierce the Lupetec leggings, but I felt the pressure of it. *Holy fucking fuckballs.* I fumbled, my heart in my throat.

"What. The. Fuck."

She'd seen it. I shoved the silver knife back in its sheath with a hand that shook. I would've cut the shit out of my hand if I'd not had my gloves on but that came under the category of 'who cares' right then. Somehow I got my phone out. My heart was hurling itself against my ribs, trying to flee.

I couldn't make my fingers work. I couldn't dial the number. Lilith was pulling me, dragging me. Gravel under my boots was treacherously uneven in the dying light. "We have to go," she was saying, horror in her voice. "We have to go *now.*"

I got the fucking phone unlocked and turned. Followed. Ran. Felt the wind. The icy cold. The damp of the air, thick with fumes from the freeway and the smell of the ocean. Running steps. *Ours?* Roaring in my ears. Every cell in my being screamed at me to flee.

My instincts knew I was prey.

<h1 style="text-align:center">CHAPTER 32</h1>

LILITH HIT THE LOCKS THE SECOND THE CAR DOOR CLOSED BEHIND ME. "What. The. *Fuck*." And she turned on me, horrified. "What the *fuck?*"

I pointed wordlessly to the road, trying to catch my breath and straighten my head. "Drive." The doors wouldn't do shit against a baby vampire.

And that wasn't a baby.

She did, accelerating abruptly. The car lurched and my heart did too, but it was just her driving, totally understandably erratic. I fumbled at my phone and found my contacts, finally. *Taig. Taig.*

It rang forever. When he answered it with a half awake, "Rory?"

I felt no relief at the sound of his voice. "Found your vampire nest," I told him, trying to put the panic aside. "*And* the ancient."

"Are you safe?" he demanded. "Where are you?"

Laughter bubbled in my chest and I crushed it. "Getting the fuck out of here. Meet us. Somewhere."

"Where are you?" he repeated, the words simultaneously deadly calm and an absolute order.

I didn't even mind. "Shipping container place, near the Westgate. You know—fuck. Address, Lilith. No—it doesn't matter. We're almost at the freeway." But, holy shitballs, that thing could *move*. I had no doubt whatsoever it could catch us in a car if it wanted to. "Somewhere quiet, Taig. So I can explain."

He was silent for a moment. "I'm about half an hour from you. Come to mine."

"My place is twenty," Lilith said, through chattering teeth. "And it's charmed. Tell him to come to *mine*."

"I heard her," he said. "Send me the address. I'll be waiting. For God's sake, Rory, be careful."

I hung up on that utterly ludicrous request. As if there was a single thing I could do against that level of power. I sat back and shut my eyes, listening to the roaring of blood in my ears.

He'd killed them.

There was no question. It fit too neatly. Explained it too well.

Who in the ever-loving fuck was he, and why is he taking out vamp nests?

And, on the back of that. Why had he let the woman go? Because if you're powerful enough to take on that many vampires without them having an opportunity to lift a finger, you were more than powerful enough to kill one vulnerable woman.

Or two witches.

"Can Vince get information on clients?" I asked Lilith, trying to remember what she'd said about his resources.

She braked abruptly for lights, her breathing still a bit quick. "Vince can get information on *everything*. If he doesn't like his job."

I resisted the urge to remind her he'd given us all up to the vamps. It wasn't his fault. Without charisma protection, we were all just putty in their hands.

"We should talk to him."

She shot me a hard look. "He's been through enough." Her hand was white knuckled on the wheel, but when we got a green she took off smoothly. "How about *you* talk to O'Malley and *I* talk to Vince."

I opened my mouth to object, then closed it. It made sense. I didn't like it, though. I didn't like being out of the loop. I'd been out of the loop today, and look where that had gotten us.

I shook that thought off. It wasn't Lilith's fault there had been a random, ridiculously powerful vampire there staking out the competition. But all I'd needed was *one vampire*. Just one. To send a message to Tobias. To make him think Dierdre was in danger, to make him come to the party. I scrubbed my hands over my face.

Exactly *how* I was going to make it work I still wasn't sure. And it didn't matter, because every single vampire was *dead*.

I drew air in deep and reached for patience. "Okay, so, I'll see Taig at yours, then? And catch you when you get back."

"Uh huh."

I tried not to look while she pulled into the left-hand lane to do a hook turn. The whole thing made me feel out of control. I couldn't deal with a fucking hook turn right now.

"It's going to be super awkward to call him, you know."

"Taig?" I asked, surprised.

"Vince."

"Oh." From my limited interactions with our ICT guy, they all seemed pretty awkward. But he was only at our coven part time, so I hadn't worried about trying to get around the bloke's painfully obvious social anxiety. "Want me to do it?"

"*No.*"

I held up my hands, surprised by her vehemence. "Hey, not going to blackmail him." Although I'd considered it, briefly.

"You're like a dog with a bone," she said, flatly. "And I don't want you…gnawing on him. I love you."

It stung, a bit, but I tried to understand. "Okay. It's fine. You're right." I hadn't been at my finest recently.

"Sorry if that was unkind. It wasn't supposed to be." She let out a long breath. "Hells, Roars. That's not what vampires are supposed to do."

She hadn't even seen the inside of the container. "No," I agreed, grimly. "No, it's not." Especially not when there was still light. Not enough light to be a true danger, sure, but enough that it should've made him cautious.

He hadn't been cautious. He had been *curious*.

My stomach was starting a rebellion and I had no time for it. I jumped out at the lights near Lilith's apartment to save her navigating the parking maze and bolted through the misting rain. Taig was near the door in the scant cover, huddled low in a windbreaker. He looked like he'd just done a double shift and the information barely touched me. "I don't have her keys," I realized, out loud.

He looked over my shoulder. "Where is she?"

"Long story." I glanced around grimly. The pizza place over the road was *terrible*, but any port in a storm.

He stopped me with an arm over my body before I could steer us in the direction of the light and noise from the greasy shop. "It's public."

"And?"

He shot me a withering look. "Come on, Rory. Vampire one-oh-one? Private property is protective."

"All right, Detective Arrogant," I muttered, falling into step beside him. Darkness had fallen and the hairs on the back of my neck were still up. "Fuck."

"I'm going to assume we're not in immediate danger," he said, the words clipped.

"Who fucking knows." He'd just *vanished*. Not a flicker. Not a shadow. Just…*gone*. My skin crawled.

His stride lengthened and keys came out. "Get in." Car lights flashed. Locks clicked.

I didn't argue, just climbed into the passenger seat and let out a long, shaky breath. "I think I'm in the wrong line of work."

"Well, you'd be a shit beekeeper, with the way you go stirring up trouble." It hurt. The guilt, the shame. I wasn't—I just couldn't, right now. I reached for the doorhandle.

"I'm sorry," he said, quickly, through his teeth. "I'm sorry, Rory." I paused, for a moment and tried to think. But I couldn't. I could only feel. One raw bundle of nerve endings, that was me. "I'm rattled and I was a shit. I hurt you and I regret it. Next time I'll let you know I just need a minute, or take a walk."

I swung my eyes on him, studied his profile.

He'd done a *shit-ton* of communication courses. Or a lot of therapy.

Something about that knowledge made me feel just a little better. "Don't be a dick."

He exhaled slowly. "I try. Sometimes I have to work harder than others. But I'll try harder." He shook his head a little. "I can just do some laps. Cars are almost private property."

"Almost doesn't count," I admitted, tiredly, feeling myself deflate. "And you know it."

"Yeah." He shrugged. "I'll drive you home. Can't be that long a story."

But I wasn't going home without talking to Lilith. "Yours is closer."

"You want to be alone with me?" he asked, bluntly.

The look I sent him was, I hoped, pure venom. "Look, mate, I've got bigger problems right now than how you'd look with my legs draped over your shoulders, okay? And so do you."

He didn't say anything. Maybe he had nothing nice to say. But he turned on the indicator and watched the traffic for a gap. I wasn't offered his phone to turn on music. The wipers, the hum of the traffic around us, were our mood music. And it wasn't a light mood.

I couldn't sleep with him. I didn't need the complication of anyone else right now. Getting my own head straight was enough.

But I needed the wonderful sexy arsehole.

"I've been doing long hours and no housework," he said, flatly, as we pulled up.

I braced myself as we left the car. His eyes were everywhere, his hand hovering somewhere in the vicinity of my shoulders as I was ushered up the stairs and down a hall. I don't know what he thought he was protecting me from when I was the one packing all the legal weaponry, and a shit-ton that wasn't, too.

When he opened the door the smell of Indian hit my nose. Shoes had been kicked in some semblance of a pile beside the door. A pile of bottles, rinsed and ready to be recycled, sat on the end of his bench. Passionfruit fizzy drink. The man must drink his weight in it. Some empty boxes were in their general vicinity, just chilling, waiting. His bin was full of takeaway containers.

"There's no moldy dishes," I said, looking around. "No piles of laundry. No bongs."

He shot me a look that seemed actually insulted. "Moldy dishes? What do you take me for?"

I shrugged, decided not to tell him some of my wilder stories. "Single guy who works dog hours." I tossed aside a jumper on an armchair and found a book, a young adult fantasy thing with a clown on the cover. I threw it onto the coffee table, too, then flopped down in the space I'd cleared.

He didn't ask if I wanted a coffee, just went into the little kitchen area. "So. Talk."

"This is between you and me."

"No promises."

I felt a twist in my gut. *Rejection?* Betrayal. It was betrayal. No wonder it hurt. "Okay." I stood. "Thanks for the ride."

"Trust goes both ways, Rory." He hadn't even looked up, was scooping up coffee. "Since when did you need to tell me when to keep my mouth shut?"

I could've told him right then and not been far wrong. Anger simmered in my veins. Why was he suddenly so pissy? "Is this about the other night?" We'd sorted that out, hadn't we?

"Last night. I don't know. Is it?"

I drew a breath to shout at him and felt it turn to stone in my lungs. I walked over, my feet heavy, and fell down on a stool. "Not from where I'm sitting."

He nodded. The smell of coffee filled the air. "Okay. Well, from where I'm sitting, you've copped some pretty big hits recently."

He leaned on the bench before me. "I get that. I'm not looking to hit you in a tender spot. I'm having a hard time keeping it together right now. If you'll recall, yesterday you ran into a magickal inferno *three times.* That cost me to watch." He shrugged a little. "No point denying it. And it was still in my brain, last night. So, I didn't make good choices tonight, and I'm sorry."

I scrubbed my hands over my face. I couldn't do this now. Another example of me not thinking things through and somehow managing to not completely ruin everything. That shame wasn't useful right now. "Okay, look, we've been polite, we're good. I don't know if I should be apologizing to you for last night. But, fuck. Vampires, Taig."

He turned and finished the coffee making ritual as he said, "I don't need an apology. Except that I might not be able to wear that tie again without getting hard."

I couldn't help the smile that tugged at my mouth at the thought of him choosing his wardrobe to avoid that particular problem. "Sorry, not sorry."

"Yeah, same." He slid a coffee over to me then went to the fridge and pulled out a bottle of the passionfruit sugar water. "Want?"

I shook my head and watched as he poured a measure of it, then drew in a deep breath, visibly bracing himself as he said, "Vampires."

"So," I began, warily. "It occurred to me that we're running in circles and people are dying."

The slight arch of his brows, the way his eyes narrowed fractionally, told me he knew exactly where I was going.

Did I deserve that annoyance? *Fuck, who knows.* I stood and followed him back to the seat I'd cleared as he sat his drink down and fell down on his saggy old couch. "I'm not *that* predictable."

"No," he agreed, dryly.

I picked up the paperback, tossed it at his face and was shocked when he caught it one-handed. The grin he shot me was as lazy as his catching hand was fast. I let it go. "Long and short of it. Angel's lackeys are working with vamps. Amor wants Dierdre. I figured I'd lure them out by sending a message, via vamps, to indicate she's in danger. My terms, my turf."

His brow furrowed. "*Why* would the ex believe a message you sent via vampires?"

"Because I'd murder them if he didn't."

His face was blank. "I see."

It wasn't a *huge* flaw in my plan. I waved it away. It sounded bad when I said it like that, but it had potential. The point wasn't the plan, it was a bunch of murder, *not* done by me.

By the time I'd finished describing what I'd seen, his eyes were cold and his mouth a hard line. "And now we can't do anything with this information, lest we get you, Lilith, and her source in trouble."

"Yeah."

"Okay." He took a pull of his drink. That shit was pure sugar. I was kind of tempted, actually. But the coffee he'd made me was pretty good. "Why would an incredibly powerful vampire kill a bunch of other vampires—at least *one* of which was likely a centurion—and not you?"

I shrugged. "Dunno. Want to visit him and ask?"

Taig set down his drink very deliberately. "No."

I shrugged again. "Okay, that's fine. Look, I can report it anonymously—"

"You can't visit him," he said, quietly. "Rory. I'm dead serious. This isn't a time when you can," he waved a hand. "Smash through some barriers. This guy is a nuke."

I raised my brows and made no attempt to hide my irritation. Heavy-handed Taig wasn't my favorite incarnation of the man. "Oh?"

"From what I hear, his paperwork was submitted while he was staying in Hollywood. He got approval. He didn't book a plane, Rory. He didn't jump a rift. He *walked.* And he got here in one night."

I tried to juggle that information so it could somehow make sense. "That's, what, a twenty-hour flight, plus the oceans he'd have to cross?"

"Greene did the math while we were shooting shit the other day." He held my eyes, grim and deadly serious. A chill went down my spine. "That's faster than the speed of sound. Significantly. And he *sustained* that."

That didn't really mean much to me. I had no idea how fast average vamps moved. Who tracked that shit? Especially when the subject matter was so prone to eating the tester. "Got it. He's badarse. That's already registered."

"Has it? Because you just invited me to speak to him. And I don't think you meant a video conference."

I shrugged and looked down at my coffee, feeling sick. "It's all I've got."

"Right now," he agreed, quietly. "But something will come up. We know where Tobias and Amor are. We'll get them."

The idea rolled around in my head, heavy and slick. "The teams are still dark, aren't they?"

He didn't look away. I respected that. But his expression softened, a little. "Yeah."

I stood and cradled my coffee close, but I couldn't feel the warmth of it. I paced in front of his big television. Anxiety hummed low in the back of my brain. I checked my phone, but there was nothing from Lilith.

"Want to talk?" he offered, gently.

"No." I took a fortifying swallow of coffee. "You don't go dark for this long. They're dead."

"You don't know that."

No, I didn't *know* that. But I knew what it looked like. What it felt like. The smell of fear, sweat, and death. The desperation. The slow, creeping retreat. The shifting extraction points. The shattered charms. The sleepless nights.

Taig was a brilliant detective, but he wouldn't understand that. He hadn't been there.

"They're calling teams from all over Australia," he said, quietly still. "And specialists. Assembling people for a major assault."

My heart twisted. That wasn't unheard of, but it wasn't done lightly. Aside from anything else, the financial cost was huge. And they couldn't plan for this push. Their intel was bad, otherwise they wouldn't have had two teams go dark.

He hadn't mentioned it, but it must've been in the works for a while. It took time to pull everyone from everywhere. *He hadn't told me.*

Another thought occurred to me, a darker one. "How many teams have they sent?"

Hesitation, now. "Four," he admitted.

I couldn't breathe around the sudden lump in my throat. Four teams. Forty magi. If even *half* of them didn't walk out…

"That's more teams than we have in the *state*."

"Yes."

I ran my hands through my hair and found another pin. Brutally, I yanked it out. Fucking pretty hair. Fucking *bullshit*. "What kind of specialists?"

He picked up his drink again and swirled it.

My heart sank. "They've contacted you."

He lifted the glass and drank it like it was scotch. "Yes."

I paced away from him. I didn't need to ask what he'd said.

He wasn't Retrievals.

He was amazing. Great. Good at his job. Quick on the uptake. Knowledgeable. But he wasn't *Retrievals*.

And he'd be torn apart.

My heart ached. *Afternoon sunlight. The cacophony of black cockatoos and splintering bones.* I could lose Nic and Taig both in one fucked up day. And I might not even be there for them, at the end. "They haven't contacted me."

"You're too close," he said, quietly. "Conflict of interest." I whirled, lifted a finger, and he held up his hands in surrender. "Isn't my call, Rory. I put in a word for you. You know I always do. And I believe the words I put in, too."

The anger flooded out of me and I fell down in the chair, defeated.

He was going to die, and I was left sitting here, worrying, wondering, and wishing for a plan D.

He let out a long sigh, scrubbing a hand over his face. "I wish they'd let you come."

I wished they hadn't asked for him. But I couldn't tell him that. I looked down at my knees, helplessness a weight on my chest. I breathed and wondered how my ribs didn't creak under that crushing pressure.

I remembered Amor on her knees, surrendering. The way they'd been about ten seconds away from being ripped to shreds.

He was too good for that end.

"You're waiting on Lilith, right? You never told me what she's up to."

I considered lying. Instead, said, "Following up with our source."

"Okay. I heard the job this morning was pretty smooth, considering." He picked up the book beside him, shifted it onto the armchair. "But you must be beat. Sit down. I'll put on some bubblegum for your brain. If you fall asleep, I'll throw a blanket over you."

I wavered. Curling up beside him, putting my head on his shoulder, sounded good. More than good.

He's going to die.

"I'm not going to take that sad look you're giving me personally," he said, around a yawn. "But I gotta say, I liked Velvela a lot more before he made you second-guess everything. Shit. I shouldn't have said that out loud."

A glimmer of humor snaked through me. I didn't know if I wanted to laugh or cry. Because it wasn't Beo I was thinking about. "Are you on an adrenaline dump, O'Malley?"

"Mm." He sank a bit lower. "I reckon. Why fight it?"

Though I was kind of tempted to see what I could nudge him to do in that weakened state, I didn't. *Witch of the Week.* "I'll let you go get some rest. Sorry to lump useless information on you." I needed to get my head on straight, get a new plan.

"No information is useless information." He blinked, then straightened. "Don't go out there. It's dark."

I glanced out the window. It was, indeed, dark, and freezing cold too. "I can see how you made detective."

"I'm too tired for snark. I'm serious, Rory. I'd put money on you any day of the week up against pretty much anything, but why borrow trouble? You get injured when we need you…"

He was right, but it didn't matter. If I stayed here, I'd end up curling up to that promise of warmth, of care and maybe even love. I'd drink that shit up and I'd be gone.

And I was just starting to find myself.

I finished the coffee and set the cup down. "Thanks, Taig," I said, as gently as I could. "I'll text you when I get home. Don't wait up."

CHAPTER 33

I SAT ON LILITH'S COUCH LATE INTO THE NIGHT READING THE GIANT FILE on one Wesley Stoke, a vampire who had last resided in Hollywood, California. I worked backwards for a few weeks. His transfer papers. The flurry of communication when he'd disappeared. The flurry when he'd reappeared, here, hours later.

Hours.

He'd made the trip, on foot, in *hours*. From America to Australia.

Prior to his transfer, he'd been a favorite of his Caretaker and their adoration came through clearly in their reports, even though I'd put money on the fact they'd been edited. You couldn't edit out everything.

Flipping through to the back I looked at the first date we had for him. Twelve years ago. The day we'd been made legal, the day that supernatural beings were granted permanent residency if they came forward.

He'd been first in line to sign up for protection. And, from what I read, had worked faultlessly within the system since the start.

He was rich as sin, and a philanthropic investor who sought to stop climate change and social inequality while also turning a profit. He had a penchant for pop culture and had kept a staff of people he'd fed from. They'd undergone all of the expected tests. The health, the psych, at his expense, and *more* regularly than was mandated. And always passed. He'd expressed his grief in a long, flowery letter when the laws changed. He continued to pay for medical expenses for people on his Approved Feeding list. Apparently he didn't *advertise* that—it wasn't a drawcard to lure the down and out. It was all done through legal channels, meticulously managed.

"You're a real gem, aren't you?" I muttered, sifting through the pages. Gushing accounts of Stoke being part of search and rescue teams in natural disasters all over the country. Of him donating large sums of money to help struggling children to access lifesaving medical interventions. Of him opening a pop culture museum and donating all funds to at-risk youth. Of him founding an indie film festival that was shifting cultural norms. Of his time on movie sets and his career as an actor. Of him participating as a volunteer fire-fighter until someone got their knickers in a knot and made it illegal.

The vamp had posed for charity calendars and done photo shoots with *kittens*.

And for some reason every single damn picture was in his file.

Lilith was asleep, and I sat there in the glow of the crystal ball shaped lamp on her side table looking at the photo of Stoke laying on the grass in the twilight, wearing sunglasses and nothing else. He had kittens sleeping all over him. The crook of his arm. His belly. His chest. In the curve of his hip.

Hats off to the photographer. They'd managed to not get his junk in the photo, somehow. Good angle.

I tossed it down on the table, frustrated. You didn't get to be however many hundreds of years old this guy *had* to be from pulling Timmy out of the well to keep the townsfolk happy. Not when those townsfolk were your snacks.

He had an angle. And fucked if I knew what it was.

I eased out from under the blanket and went back to the front of the file. Bayside address, Saint Kilda beach. He'd already submitted paperwork for…I skimmed my eyes over the list. More than a dozen people on his Approved Feeding list, with more pending.

He certainly wasn't going hungry.

I stood and debated making myself a coffee but didn't want to risk waking Lilith. I went over to her desk, rummaged for paper amongst the jumbled piles of paperwork, bills, parcels, boxes and cute stationary options that weren't being put to good use.

Her work bag slipped a little, the open flap dragging it half off the chair. I caught it before it could fall, but a bunch of paper spilled out.

Beo's face stared at me from the first printout.

My heart did a slow roll. I straightened her bag but took the paper back to the circle of light, feeling sick.

She'd pulled his file, too.

Why?

I couldn't sit but went straight to the most recent. All my notes. The police reports, the investigations. He'd come up shining, but I knew that. I'd read any report in there I hadn't written. The transfer request. Approved.

I skimmed through the names of his pack members, mourning them.

On the bottom of the list. *Dawn Velvela.*

She'd chosen a name.

The illegally migrated child that he'd—*we'd*—protected. She'd chosen her name.

My heart.

Hurt.

Unable to swallow away the lump in my throat I kept flicking through the information. He was on the coast in New South Wales, working as a jiu-jitsu coach. Incident reports came, thick and fast, then. He and the pack had tangled with local vamps, faeries, leprechauns, had actually murdered a banshee and had suspected runins with some other shifters.

I turned away from medical reports, grief burning in my chest.

I bet that shit would've been smoother if I'd been there.

And I would've gone. I would've stood beside him. I could've been a BJJ coach, too, or something. I was flexible and resourceful. I could've helped the whole pack. But his scars were deeper than I'd known.

It hurt. I was glad Lilith was keeping her finger on the pulse, but it still hurt. Not as much as I thought it would, though. And that, in itself, was bittersweet.

I tucked the files back into Lilith's bag carefully, letting my fingers linger on that for a moment. *I hope you're all okay. I hope your road is smooth and your sunsets bright.* It could've been so different. I hoped it was, for both of us, in the future. I hoped he could heal and find peace.

Letting out a long breath I turned away and refocused on the here and now. I needed to leave Lilith a note.

To lie, or not to lie?

Fuck it. If I got unalived, she'd need somewhere to start. I didn't lie. But I did ask her to trust me.

And then, with the city settling around me, I set off.

Public transport at that time of night was balls. Wait times were blown out dramatically. Some services just didn't run. But I made it, eventually, at three in the morning.

Wesley Stokes' house was over the road from a swathe of council land leading down to the ocean and a wide footpath that was being used even at this hour in the freezing cold by hardcore exercise enthusiasts or partygoers. Inside, lights burned.

Of course. Vampires didn't keep our hours.

I drew in a deep breath and didn't even bother taking hold of my wooden knife. What was the point? At the speed this guy moved, I'd be dead before I even knew I should start swinging. There was a sick, sinking feeling in my gut.

Hello, Plan D.

I lifted my fist and knocked.

Before I'd rapped a third time it was opening. And there he was, sans kittens, complete with sunglasses. The trench coat I'd seen earlier was leather. His pants were, too. And he wasn't wearing a shirt.

I wasn't complaining, but I did make note that the guy didn't feel the cold.

"Ah," he said, a smile tugging at his mouth as he looked me over.

"The witch who moves like a vampire. You found me quickly. I didn't think you would."

My breath misted as I regarded him. "I'm Rory." I didn't offer my hand. He knew I was a witch and he'd seen me in the container, if he'd noticed me using the charms. Which meant he'd been in there.

Somewhere.

My skin crawled at the thought. Had I overlooked him? Was he so fast, even with the slowing charm? I didn't linger on that thought, because there was no good answer.

"I was hoping to speak to you."

He stepped back in an offer of entry. "I do have guests, so I'm sure you won't mind keeping it brief."

"Absolutely." Shit, if I could be in and out in two minutes, I'd be ecstatic.

The house was contemporary; clean lines, glass guard rail on the polished concrete stairs; white walls broken up by framed prints of old movie posters, games and actors. I was led through an empty lounge with the heavy curtains raised over the windows to let the streetlight and moonlight in, into a big kitchen with a giant granite bench. A platter that had the corpses of cheeses and fruits sat to one side with empty bottles of wine.

Guests. Snacks. Same thing.

"Can I get you something, Rory?" he asked me, following my gaze. "White, red? I have spirits, too—my cocktails are somewhat lacking, but they're passable."

Vampires didn't need to eat, but they could. It helped them blend in, I guess. How regularly they chose to eat, and whether they enjoyed it, I had no idea. But this one obviously knew the standard human conventions. No surprise. "Do you have coffee?"

He smiled a little. "I certainly do. It was one of the reasons I wanted to come to Melbourne. You have excellent options in that regard. How do you take yours, Rory?"

I really didn't like the way he kept using my name. I should've given him a fake one, fuck it. "Black."

"Ah. A woman after my heart. I've got a lovely batch of beans I ground not long ago that are *perfect* for long black."

And he was, immediately, in front of the coffee machine. Crossing the kitchen without so much as a *flicker*, like stop motion without a bunch of frames between. My hair lifted and swirled as the machine whirled while physics caught up with his speed.

The hair on the back of my neck rose as I watched him making the coffee. I swallowed around the lump in my throat and took a seat. "And what brings you to my home in the middle of the night?" he asked, the words lazy.

He'd fed recently. I didn't know all his signs, but I knew he wouldn't be half as content if he hadn't. "I've found myself in an interesting position."

"I do like those," he murmured, not looking up.

A sliver of awareness snaked through me. The ring on my finger that defended me from charisma grew a little warm. I ignored his attempt to dazzle me magickally—and my human response to having a gorgeous being giving me attention. "I was going to attempt to cut a deal with those vampires you murdered tonight."

"Were you?" he asked, amused. "That's lovely, Rory. Very sweet." He walked over and the way he moved was pure, undiluted sex.

My mouth was a desert. I reached for the coffee gratefully. "I figured I'd probably kill most of them."

His smile widened. "Ah. You're *that* witch."

I raised my brows. "Which witch?"

"Is which?" he asked, his brows lifting. "Word gets around. Leticia died from wounds inflicted on her by you. Such a shame." There was glee in his voice, though. "And you fought off her pets, too. Quite the accomplishment. I'm honored to have you in my kitchen not trying to stake me."

Well, fuck. I was infamous in the underworld. "I'm not here to take swings at you, Mister Stoke."

He snorted. "Mister Stoke. Please. I'm Wesley, or I'm Wes, or Stoke, or I'm whatever cute name you come up with."

"I'm not big on pet names myself." I sipped the coffee. Maybe it's just that it was hot, or maybe it was his charisma, but, *shit,* it was good. I sighed and sipped again. "So, Wesley. Why are you reducing my workload?"

His grin was fast, rakish, and went straight to my bloodstream. "Why, because I understand how hard our law enforcement works. And I don't want them losing any sleep over the…darker parts of my own society."

Hooking a foot over the bottom rung of the stool, I cocked my head. "You're upholding our laws."

"Well," he shot me a self-deprecating smile, "I wouldn't, of course, ever be identified in any violent, vigilante acts if they were to happen. But if they *did* happen…to bad people. Wouldn't that be convenient for everyone?"

There hadn't been a whisper of it in his file, but I had no doubt this guy had murdered those vamps, quick and clean. I didn't want to think about the power that would've taken. I'd probably have a panic attack. "I'm not questioning the convenience, although tonight it most definitely wasn't. I'm questioning the motives."

"Oh." He laughed a little, spread his arms. "Look at this place, Rory. *Look* at it." I waited for the other shoe to drop while I sipped. "This world. The things we can *do.* I live like a king and all I need to do is look after those who offer themselves to me."

Convenience. That was his angle? "Lots of folks want more."

"Yes, well," he shrugged and reached for his coffee, mirroring me. "That's a very unfortunate side-effect of the deeply toxic society we struggle to properly divorce ourselves from. How can one possibly ever believe that one is safe?"

I turned that around in my head while I savored the full-bodied taste of the coffee, the bitter heat of it. "So, you like our rules."

"I do," he sighed, content. "But I have something others don't."

"Safety."

"That's right. I don't mind that there are kittens guarding me. Why should I? They're lovely."

Another chill went up my spine. The whole thing was a joke to him. He played by the rules because he wanted to.

Fuck, we were lucky he did.

I took a deep breath. "I'm not going to be pointing the finger at you. It wouldn't matter if I did, but I wouldn't anyway. Those vampires were dangerous to us."

"Yes, they were," he agreed, seriously.

And suddenly I realized they were dangerous to him. To the laws he enjoyed, to the reputation of his people. That could complicate his life and make it harder for him to enjoy his kingdom.

Shit.

"I've got a problem," I told him, bluntly. "There's an angel involved. The group of magi around this angel have been working with those vampires to further destabilize the city's power structures."

"Yes," he agreed, still smiling. "Oh, yes, they have." The validation was nice. And, curse it, so was his smile. "I did hear you had some personal beef with them."

Beef. I had beef? "Personal. Professional." I shrugged.

"And you want me to kill them?" he asked, his smile widening. "Is that why you're here, Aurora?"

I hadn't told him my full name. I felt utterly naked, right then, coffee cup in my hand and vampire leaning nonchalantly across the island bench in front of me. "No."

"Good." He sipped again. "They aren't my problem. Isn't this an excellent brew?"

"It is." I sighed, turning the cup between my palms. "I don't want to ask for a favor."

"But you will," he said, smiling softly.

"But I will." I looked up and saw myself reflected in his glasses. Chaotic hair, damp hoodie, one blue eye, one hazel, in a tired face. "I want word to get back to the angel that I'm going to kill her witch."

His brows rose. "And you think they'll believe that."

"Sure." I shrugged, trying to keep it neutral. "Angel of love is fueled by my witch's ex, who's obsessed with her. And, anyway, better she dies than end up possessed. Right?"

He laughed and leaned forward a little more. "Keep going. This is excellent."

"That's as far as I go. I want them to know I'll kill her."

His grin just widened. "To lure them out? Because you think the wizard won't think clearly about her safety. You want them to rush you. That's your goal, isn't it?" It wasn't a question and I wasn't going to tell him the answer anyway. "My dear, I can do *much* better than your little threat. Why, by the time *my* story gets to them—which would take about, oh, six hours, I expect, give or take time for tantrums—I could have them *positively salivating* to get to you." And the ring on my finger hummed, warming against my skin. I didn't glance at it. I had no idea what of his magicks he was trying to use on me. It wasn't going to work, though.

I said exactly nothing.

"Oh, it's beautiful. I haven't played these games in far too long. Can I have tickets to the finale?" he laughed at his own joke. "You know what? I love it. I can make it happen." And he looked at me, smiling widely. And waiting.

Oh, fuck. "What'll it cost me?"

"Oh, please, Rory. We're practically friends now. I wouldn't ever demand anything from a friend." He took a leisurely sip of his coffee, amusement still tugging at his mouth. "But, if you were to *offer...* "

I was damned if I did and damned if I didn't. I wanted to know the cost, though. My mouth somehow formed the words, "I am."

"Well." He drew in a deep breath. "You are *delicious.*"

Alarm skittered down my spine. I'd known I only had one bargaining chip when I walked in. "And I have some clout."

"Oh, yes, well, clout is always lovely, isn't it?" And there was a paternal smile on his lips like I'd just been given an award at school. I wanted to squirm but refused to give in to the urge. So, he didn't give a shit about the little power I had. *Good to know.* "I do hope you aren't worried. Some people give off...extra. Life just"—he waved a hand gracefully — "*Rolls* out of them. It's lovely to be around such people. And you're definitely one of them. Why, I haven't tasted anything like you for some centuries. There aren't many of your kind."

Centuries. Plural. Some of them. Oh, fuck. "Cool," I managed.

"Mm." He moved toward me again. "I like our chats. If you were to return." He reached out and touched my hand. His black skin was soft and cool. Horror warred with the flare of animal wanting in my veins. "Leave this off, darling," he murmured, running a finger over one of my charms. "I'd hate to break it. It's such a pretty trinket."

I glanced down at the ring in question, trying to make my brain work. It was the one that had gone warm a few times, my anti-charisma charm. I swallowed, hard.

He could break it.

Fuck, he could probably break the whole *world.*

"You've tried to use charisma on me twice since I've been here." The words were firmer than I felt.

Surprise and disappointment sat better on his face than I would've expected. "No, I haven't. I've tasted you twice. What would I possibly gain from dazzling you? I enjoy my guests' for their personality, their individuality."

He'd tasted *me. Holy fucking shitballs.* "You've tasted me," I said, out loud, disbelieving. I knew what vamps looked like when they fed. I would've *noticed,* even if he'd gone through my protection.

"Like I said, you just give off life, my dear." And he was back to his smiling self again. "Think of it like the fruit that's fallen from the tree. It does no one any good, really." But he was looking at me thought-fully. "You felt it?"

"Apparently."

He hummed. "And did you *enjoy* it?"

My mouth went dry. "We both know how humans react to vampires' feeding on them."

He pulled a face. "Such a crude phrase. I don't *feed.* I might take some fruit from the branches, here and there." He reached over and I didn't pull back, letting him stroke my cheek. He'd broadcast the move, gone in at human speed. "Never do I rip off a whole branch, Rory. Just sampling, here and there, the *ripest* parts."

I couldn't tell, then, if the roaring in my bloodstream was chemi-cally induced or sheer human desire. "So, you want to pick my fruit."

Why the fuck did that sound so boring when I said it and so sinfully delicious when *he* said it?

"I would like that," he agreed, shamelessly, still stroking me. "I think you would, too."

"And then you'll pass on my message?" I heard myself asking. Shit, maybe I could go crawling back to Beo and beg him for help. Plan C didn't look so bad.

"No," he said, still stroking my fingers. "No. I'll do that just because it sounds like fun. And because you're one of the good guys. Aren't you, Aurora?"

I felt myself swaying toward him. The ring on my hand was *hot*. Just fruit off the ground, right? I pulled back, deliberately, and took a fortifying swallow of coffee that rolled in my belly. *Elders, I don't know what I'm doing.* "Good is subjective." I set the cup down.

"Of course." He smiled at me like a parent to a kid who'd just glued some junk onto a page and called it art. "And I mean it when I say this favor is free. Why not? Your plan is hilarious, and I was already sorting out this group. The enemy of my enemy is my friend."

My skin crawled. "What will you do?"

"Oh, I'll make them believe your heavy-handed lie. Tonight." A smile tugged at one corner of his mouth as he rolled his hip away from where it was propped on the bench. The flex and shift of muscles, of light on his dark skin, hypnotized me. "Why don't you wait until you've sorted out your angel conundrum. If you want to visit me afterwards, well, I'll be here. I promise I'll do everything in my power to ensure you enjoy it thoroughly."

My belly turned over. I would, too. I knew the looks on the victims' faces. The way they begged for more. "But this favor is free."

"It is." His smile vanished. "I don't usually do illegal meetups, you know."

"Of course you don't."

"But, you're in the field. You couldn't be seen with a client in such an… intimate fashion. If you ever needed another favor."

My lungs weren't working. "No."

"So, just for you," he said, conspiratorially. "I'll keep your secrets, Aurora. You'll keep mine. You know where I am if you ever need me. Why, we'll make a fine team, won't we?"

I couldn't possibly find an answer. Not when I could barely find the exit.

CHAPTER 34

BESIDE ME, DIERDRE TOOK THE DONUT ARTHUR PASSED HER WITHOUT juggling the jars full of glowing liquid she held nestled against her ribs. "Who are we waiting for?" Arthur asked me, glancing at his watch. "Bernie," he muttered, answering his own question with irritation. "Of course."

I didn't bother looking at my watch. I'd already given Lilith and Dierdre a run-down of the situation in as much detail as I could. I'd given Arthur a summary of what he needed.

We had time, yes, but I had no idea how much time. There were worse places to wait than beside the eternal flame at the Shrine of Remembrance. The cold wasn't a problem for me in my Lupetec, though I felt for Janet in her sensible work clothes. There was decent visibility, and there weren't too many visitors on the business hours side of nine in the morning.

And, yeah, I didn't like the situation. I was worried as hells about them all. But I also knew damned well they understood the risks and they were choosing to be here. And that made my heart glad.

Arthur stopped at my side and cleared his throat. "I thought I'd mention this afterwards, but, since I've got you…" I drew deep on my patience, took a bite of donut, and turned to listen to him. "Well, I've been doing some reading."

I barely resisted groaning. He looked so *sincere*. "Oh?" I managed, somehow.

He nodded, apparently pleased at my response. "Yes. It's all fascinating, I must say. And I noticed your—" he glanced at me a bit sheepishly "—risk-taking behaviors are common with people who have disordered attachment and unprocessed trauma."

Then he stopped talking, clearly waiting for a response. *You created this monster, Rory, you deal with him.* "Yes, well, there you go," I offered, hoping it would be enough. "I'll add it to my to-do list." *After* living through whatever happened next.

"I wasn't really sure if some of what you did might've been the, ah, love potion," he went on, frowning a little. "My research indicates that's unlikely, though, and you may have maladaptive coping mechanisms."

The donut tasted like ash. "Yeah, I know."

He looked surprised. "You do?" Then he relaxed and dug into his pocket. "Excellent, then. I don't need to explain further. I also looked into therapy options. I said I would." I didn't have much choice but to take the business card he was passing over. "This woman does E.M.D.R. and some other things to help process trauma. She's local, and when I called her office yesterday, the wait list is only about three months, which is actually very short. And I'll make sure your schedule allows you to attend." I looked down at the card, torn between laughter and horror. "Unfortunately, we don't have access to quality therapies through our roles. However, I understand Retrievals is more flexible. If you indicate it's to process the trauma around killing Amor..."

My heart swelled. He was bending the rules. I tucked the card into the pocket of my pants, gratitude a big, warm ball in my guts, and pressed a kiss to his cheek. "Thank you for doing all that for me, King," I said, moved. "Can you remind me in a few days? I'll probably forget."

He gave me a knowing look. "Sure. No worries. Glad I could help."

My phone went off and I stuffed the rest of the donut Arthur had given me in my face so I had a free hand to grab it out of my pocket, feeling tired. Maybe if I'd done the work earlier, I would've seen the writing on the wall with Beo. Maybe I *could've* helped him manage his own demons, instead of just holding my own off.

I hoped he had a friend like Arthur to help him find his way forward.

I smiled at the name on my phone. *Taig.* Swiping to answer, I turned away from the gathered magi and walked a few steps toward the shrine. "Hey," I managed around donut. The ship with Beo had sailed, but there was no time like the present to get myself sorted…or at least start working on it. Elders knew I needed to.

"Wanted to make sure you weren't dead," he said, around a yawn. "Thanks. For answering. And being not dead."

Guilt gnawed at me. I'd pretty much done the exact opposite of what he wanted. I glanced over my shoulder at the gathered witches. Last time I'd tried to keep secrets from a guy, I'd done huge damage to him. But Taig was nothing like Beo, and this situation wasn't the same. I was doing the best I could by them, by me, and by him, too.

I glanced over at the group of witches. At their feet, shopping bags full of herbs and salt waited. Hot drinks and baked goods, courtesy of Arthur, were vanishing.

Shit was about to go down. And I couldn't *not* mention that to the district's favorite detective, right?

Shuffling my feet a bit, I sat with the guilt and cleared my throat, doing what I needed to do. "So, I've noticed when things happen, you're usually not far away," I said, slowly, trying to figure out how to navigate this situation.

He let out a groan. "You're about to tell me something I don't want to hear."

"Well…I could not, if you'd rather be surprised?" I offered, swirling the too-hot coffee around in its paper cup and kind of hoping he'd take that out.

A long sigh. Something creaked in the background. Door? Shoe? "Go on," he said, tiredly.

I wandered toward the flags at the other end of the forecourt. It had only been last night when he'd flat out told me not to go near Wesley.

Whoops.

"Look, it's not a big deal." It absolutely was. I expected an angel before lunch. But it was on *our* turf, and that would make all the difference. I hoped.

I heard the kettle boiling in the background. "How long do I have and where are you?" It was said with resignation. "I'm about three weeks behind my paperwork already and Samhain is coming."

Did I ever know that feeling. "Don't know how long." I put aside the urge to lie, because, fuck it, I *liked* having Taig on my team. "I'm playing the waiting game. Shrine of Remembrance."

He was quiet for a moment, his spoon chiming as he stirred his coffee. I could just about see his super neutral cop face. I wondered if he had a shirt on. I wondered if he'd be okay with someone stroking that soft, curving belly once I was sure of myself again.

I wondered if he'd figured out what I'd done.

"I can't just rock up in tactical gear, Rory," he was saying, the words low and rough and sexy. "I'm not even on duty until—"

My phone buzzed. I pulled it away, saw Bethany's name on incoming call and felt my heart squeeze. "I gotta go, Taig," I said, quickly, and with some relief that I refused to feel guilt over. "Got another call."

"Keep in contact." And then the line went dead.

"Report," Bethany told me, briskly.

I rolled my eyes toward the sky. "Hi, Beth, how are you?"

"What's your status, Gold?"

If only her words weren't quite so painfully neutral, I could've thrown them back at her. "Cold, mildly annoyed at the temperature of my coffee, and tired."

She paused for a moment. "I've got information indicating you're on Summers. Is that not accurate?"

I glanced back across the paving toward the eternal flame where Dierdre was showing Janet one of the glowing jars. "I am."

She let out a long-suffering sigh and I loved that I'd annoyed her, petty as it was. A pen clicked repetitively in the background. "I've got a contract for you. I'm trying to get some others, too, but…"

But they were all dead or hiding.

I swallowed around the sudden lump in my throat. "Yeah, I know," I said, to make it easier. "Contract is on Tobias—Dierdre Summers' ex?"

She was quiet for a moment. "There's an extra waiver on this one, Aurora."

Fuck. I hunched my shoulders and turned into the wind. "Because of the angel."

"And, with current availabilities—"

"We're understaffed and under resourced," I cut in, irritated. "Come on, Bethany. This is me. I know the dance."

Keys clicked in the background. "I have another situation I need to manage. I'm sending the contract through. It's only active if you accept the extra waiver."

I felt the phone case bite into my hand. "What's happened to my team, Bethany?"

"You don't *have* a team, Aurora," she said, stiffly. "Call me if you want to clarify anything."

The barb went home. Feeling sick, I opened up my emails, but Wesley must've been as good as his word if Amor was on the move. Was that supposed to be comforting? I wasn't sure. *Electronic signature enabled. Great.* I glanced at the second waiver. As expected, I was basically signing away my fucking life.

At least the hazard pay was half decent.

I looked across at my gathered coven. They weren't a Retrievals team and there was no denying it, but they *were* my team. I wasn't alone.

I signed the waiver. Whatever I made, I'd split between us. It was the legal ramifications I was hoping to dodge right now. I had enough of them.

Clint would have a kitten if he saw what we were prepping for. The thought made me smile.

I was just skimming the contract when I saw Bernie arrive with a big, beaming grin on her face and thermos in her hand that was absolutely fortified. She offered a bag of lollies to Cici with flourish. The phone I tucked away as everyone gathered around. We probably stood disrespectfully close to the eternal flame, huddling around its warmth and hoping our eyebrows would be safe.

"Quick summary," I said, with a wave, trying to be the energetic, chipper, in control leader they needed. "We've got an angel-possessed wizard on the way. I'm expecting he'll land sometime today. Just got a Retrievals contract for him." A scowl snapped onto Arthur's face and I shot him an annoyed look. "I didn't even clock on this morning," I reminded him, under my breath. "I'm on *leave*, Arthur."

I thought I was being quiet, but laughter rippled around the circle and his face went red. Guilt snarled inside me. He was just doing his job, even if it was in a typical annoying Arthur fashion. I wished I'd been a bit gentler on him.

"Good," he told me, with a firm nod.

While he struggled with his own embarrassment, I cleared my throat and turned back to the group. At least I could draw attention away from him. "We're going to have three groups to run a banishment spell," I said, briskly, as Bernie stomped her feet and rubbed her hands together beside me. "Salt and obsidian wards around you to protect you from at least the lower-level stuff. It'll be major."

"*Major?*" demanded Cici, her eyes huge. "We're doing a *Major* Banishment? But—the law—the sacrifice—the Abyss—"

Janet nudged her from the side. "Hush," she said, quietly, then cut her eyes back to me.

My heart swelled and ached. "This angel can't manifest. Whoever it's possessing will be the sacrifice. As for the Abyss..." I shared a quick look with Lilith, feeling vaguely unwell. I knew some of the things in that dark prison. I'd sent some there.

Which meant I'd set some free.

Limited real estate meant hard decisions. Sometimes, they were the wrong ones.

"We won't Banish if we don't have to," Lilith said, briskly. "No point if we can just take out the mouthpieces. But if they summon the angel, we don't have a choice. And we aren't going to have a repeat of the Salisbury Circle. Right?"

Silence stretched out, broken only by Bernie's mutterings about uppity Brits. I saw Dierdre huddling over her jars, her eyes huge and her beanie pulled low. Hells, I ached.

"Rory, Lilith, and I will manage any combat," Arthur said, with finality. "Dierdre's the bait, so Lilith will cast an illusion to look the part, but we want some protections around the real Dierdre. Subtle ones. Janet?"

"I can do subtle," Bernie objected, then laughed at her own joke and slapped Cici on the arm. "Hoo, did you see that boy's face?" she asked, the rough whisper carrying to my ears.

I turned away and pulled out my phone again. Inside my glove, my wand bit into my wrist, but I ignored it as I opened the email from Bethany.

I'd just started scrolling through the standard stuff to the real information when my phone rang.

Nic.

My heart almost stopped. I fumbled it in my hurry to answer, felt my charmed earring carve a path across my screen protector as I held it to my ear.

The roar of helicopter blades took me back in time. I could see the rivers, the trees, the valleys and towns, the team around me. My heart swelled and broke. Exhaustion and determination shimmered through my veins. I could all-but feel the wind on my face, the harness over my shoulders, the half-controlled panic in my gut.

I couldn't do that anymore.

But I could do this.

"Rory?" Nic shouted over the noise.

Tears burned my eyes. He wouldn't hear most of what I said. I didn't know if I'd have words, anyway. But he was okay. I could rest. Wasn't this why I'd set all this in motion?

I drew in a deep breath and all those big feelings drained away, leaving me exhausted, but lighter.

"Look, if you can hear me, witch," he was shouting, "We've got a *massive*—"

I strained, tried to make out the words, but the reception dipped, broke up. The roar of the chopper faded and I turned to watch my coven moving around, making protective circles and chatting.

Nic was up and running. I had a contract for Amor and Tobias. Coincidence?

"—hear me, Rory? Watch for her—" I held my breath, tried to angle myself so there was minimal background noise. "—brooms!" he was shouting. "Say something, Sunshine!"

"Something!" I tried to shout, but the word cracked and crumbled.

I'd done this. I'd set this in motion. I'd lifted the heat off my team—maybe off *all* the teams—and let them move.

And I was about to cop the fallout.

The now-silent phone I shoved back in my pocket as I lifted my head, bracing myself. "Expect them from the air," I called over the racket. "They're on brooms." I wished Taig was there to tell me what level of offence they were committing. I wished he was somewhere safe.

"Rory," Arthur called. "Circle or triangle for the obsidian-secured ward?"

Well, at least he was asking and not just assuming, even if he *should* know that answer.

"Circle," I told him, then went over to the group with neither Lilith nor Arthur to guide them and let myself fall into the rhythm, the back and forth of it. But my feet were heavy and my thoughts were slow. We were basically done. I just wanted it to be over.

Taig hadn't asked me how I'd got word to Tobias. Was it because he was half asleep, because he didn't want to know, or because he already knew? My heart ached at the thought. I hoped he'd understand why I'd done it.

I pulled out my phone and opened the messages, taking a quick selfie for Taig. I captioned it *still not dead.* And resisted bitching about the fact I was still wearing a top with bitemarks in it. At least Retrievals replaced gear quickly when it was needed. I looked at the photo for a moment, watching the little ticks that said it was delivered. I wanted him here, too, and that surprised me. Because I wanted him *so far* from any angel shenanigans that went down. Somewhere safe and cozy, that's where he ought to be. And, hells, that's where I wanted to be, too. But that wasn't how I rolled. And it wasn't how he did, either. We were people who got it done. But sometimes that cost us more than we could pay.

I was sitting with that knowledge when the air vanished.

Grimly, I reached for my magick. I didn't waste any time reassuring my coven who were gasping like fish as they looked around for the threat, the spell, the reason for their terror. In the middle of us the eternal flame had suffocated.

I knew the reason.

That was *my* specialty. And, curse it, I did it better.

Breathe freely and smash this ward. The counter-spell felt clean and controlled. One day I'd be both of those things, too.

I drew in air, turned my face into the wind, and felt the anxiety ripple up my arms. My phone was vibrating in my pocket and I didn't dare reach for it.

"Game on, bitches," Bernie hooted.

Clouds sat low in the sky, a typical dreary winter day. Nearby, one volunteer was walking toward the visitor center, looking warily in our direction. It was too late for those who might come to greet the dawn, too early for the school trips—and that meant there would be minimal civilians to get hurt. That was important.

"Rory, did you feel the—" Lilith gave Arthur a bit of a shove and a hard look that shut him up. I loved that witch. And the wizard was actually pretty cool, too.

The wind had changed direction at some point and there was a mist rising from the ground. It crept over the pavers and manicured lawns as the clouds rolled closer.

Arthur shifted his staff from hand to hand, watching the sky. "That's two spells," he told me, quietly. "At least."

Lilith, looking all the world like Dierdre sans glowing potion jars, was hunkered down in a salted circle that would protect against neither Jack nor shit. But it should draw them in.

"Could be two Amors," I agreed. "Or six, for all I know." But I doubted it. Who had the energy to look after six witches? I couldn't even look after one. Granted, I wasn't an angel.

As if on cue, thunder rolled forebodingly. Wind tossed the thick cloud cover over the sky like a blanket settling across a bed. Darkness unfurled over the city and there was something achingly sad about that. I wished I'd had my phone out recording that, though. Sad, yes, but also hauntingly beautiful.

Unaware, Arthur absently lit the eternal flame and cranked it up to ten. It was almost as dark as night and I didn't like the long shadows or the thickness of the mist.

"Can you disperse that?" I asked him, waving a hand at the mist.

"Not without breaking the law," he said, glancing over his shoulder at me as the fog crept toward Cici's group closest to the Shrine.

The hairs on the back of my neck prickled as thunder rolled again. We probably didn't have time to debate the lesser offense that was a weather spell compared to the risk of waiting to see what was going to come *out* of that mist, who it killed, and then responding with greater force to put it down. That conversation would require an hour and a mind-map with Arthur, blessed be his rule-loving heart.

So instead, I offered, "I'll say I did it."

He gold fished at me, opening his mouth, closing it, then eventually shot me a look somewhere between confused, relieved, and disgusted. Then he lifted his staff and wand together toward the sky and finally started casting. I followed the path of his spells rather than look at him, putting aside the guilt. If he understood the situation, he wouldn't have looked at me like that.

"I'll explain later," I told him, because we both deserved it.

If he heard he didn't have time to respond. A swarm of crows appeared above him, arrowing down through the sky, screaming their fury, and adrenaline shot through me. Arthur ducked, and I lifted my wand-loaded hand. *Through this shield you can't touch me.* The crows hit my shield, flickered and dispersed.

"Got us illusions," I called, on the off chance someone hadn't noticed that little detail. Another swarm of crows came low out of the mist from the direction of Saint Kilda Road and, impatiently, I cast the shield spell again. Again, they flickered out. "Sorry," I said to Lilith, preemptively, as I grabbed her and positioned myself strategically at her back.

I should've been scared. Or angry. *Something.*

I just felt tired. Tired, heavy, and ready to sleep for a hundred years. Maybe my name wasn't so far off-base, after all?

Fake it 'til you make it, witch. "The ritual is almost complete. You want to join her?" I shouted into the mist. A pedestrian crossing in the distance went off at me, and I resisted the urge to cringe. I just wasn't good at dramatic threats. They didn't teach us this shit in Retrievals class. All I had to go off were action movies and it worked *there.*

"Ritual?" Lilith said in a fair impersonation of Dierdre's voice. "What ritual? You told me we're making Solstice charms!"

The woman deserved an award. She knew what she was doing.

Arthur was chanting, his eyes on the clouds above us, his expression one of fierce concentration. I gathered that meant that, no, he couldn't easily fix that small problem.

"That mist is too close," Lilith said quietly. "They could be cutting throats any second."

"I can use my Blowback charm," I said, turning warily. "Once."

"Janet could burn it off. But if she's doing that…" She wasn't ready to banish. I nodded, understanding what Lilith hadn't said.

I heard more cawing as another flock of crows appeared and sighed. The whole thing was getting old. *Through this shield you can't touch me.* I threw it up haphazardly to protect Arthur's flank, not paying much attention to another round of illusions.

And real birds hit the shield. Feathers appeared in a puff and bones crunched in a way that made my stomach roll. *Real* birds? Lilith, still wearing Dierdre's face, gagged. If I'd known, I could've done *something*—

One flank was protected from my shield, and Arthur was flinching away from the horrific mess of probably innocent creatures. And where he'd stood a moment ago, lightning poured down, three strikes in rapid procession.

"Heavy, wet, thick or dry, send this air into the sky," Arthur bellowed as I collapsed my spell and lifted an arm to protect my eyes against the sudden rush of wind.

A shout of discovery had me turning in time to see a blonde, previously hidden by the mist, level her wand at Arthur as she ran toward us. I recognized the circle that was carved into the pavers at his feet without needing to hear her cast.

Impenetrable Wards were *my* jam. And, unlike some folks, *I'd* had to figure it out myself. I hadn't had an angel give me the damned recipe. Stepping in front of Lilith, I deliberately left us open from the back, hoping to draw out another Amor if one was lurking. Better to know as soon as possible.

Like, *before* an angel appeared.

Inside the Impenetrable Ward there was an explosion of fire. Time became as thick as molasses in the winter as I swung my eyes toward that neatly contained inferno. *Arthur—*

Amor hit me as I searched for an answering spell, and we skidded along the ground. The blow to my jaw I didn't even see coming had enough force to have me seeing stars. Fighting her was different. Lupetec made it different. Normal strategies didn't work against her, just like they didn't work against me. I *knew* this, but my brain still spun on it. *Punch drunk?*

Arthur.

I'd just broken him in too. Making friends with wizards took real work.

Muscle memory was about the best weapon I had, right then. I drove my knee up, my arm down, caught her in a choke and took her back. She threw me hard against the grey pavers beneath us as I caught a glimpse of Arthur in a bubble of steam.

Water. He'd watered a fireball? Poor guy. This was why anyone who messed with elements needed to spend a lot of time in the kitchen. You learn these interactions, and—

She threw me into the ground. Stars filled my vision, and I tried to roll free and get my bearings. The whole world spun around me. *From without or from within, this dome will not impact where I go.*

As I cracked the ward the steam rolled away from Arthur. He tipped his face back and sucked in air, frantically loosening his tie. And, honestly, the sight made me want to put a bow on him and pinch his cheek.

There wasn't time for that, though. I mean, I could've made time. Shit was just—dull. There was another Amor coming up from the Remembrance Garden, and I had to trust Lilith and Arthur, because the one I'd pissed off had a knife in her hand and it wasn't for a cheese platter. I just wanted a fucking *nap* and no more angel. Was that so much to ask?

I rolled away again, and the Lupetec stretched and flexed over my back and shoulders. My knives dragged on my belt. It was all the same.

It was all pointless.

The roar of helicopter blades, rushing air, warmth of afternoon sun. Fear and blood stank. Time dripping by. Days, weeks, months.

All the same.

I was empty.

Amor grabbed me and I lifted my arm, her blade sliding harmlessly against the Lupetec, then biting into me as it hit actual flesh.

Of course. Because they hadn't replaced my thrice-cursed lycan-chomped top. Not like I'd done them any favors, was it? Not like I'd kept half the fucking VicPol alive on those missions.

Maybe not half. Maybe they'd done some work. They would've been fine without me. It didn't really matter.

I caught a handful of her hair, yanked and twisted, but my heart wasn't in it. She struck out wildly with the knife and I let the blows land, just kept hold on her head.

I just had to get this done so I could go and have a nap somewhere.

So I drove my knee into her face.

The dance was hollow. Monotonous. We'd fight. We'd both get in a few licks. Eventually, surely, she knew, I'd win—after all, I had my coven behind me. And then I'd have to do it all over again.

I was too tired for this shit. Way too tired. Tired to my *soul.*

While I contemplated that, wearing a few hits, dishing a few out, I saw, in the background, lightning and birds. A cage of some sort bounced across the open area in front of us, scraping nosily against the concrete. At least it was empty, but still, who threw *cages*? *Honestly, these people have no class.* Next they'd be hurling fireballs like it was the eighties. It was all painfully boring.

Silver flashed, giving me a split-second warning. I let myself tip over backwards and ate some ground, trying to get my head in the game.

The fog hadn't touched me. But it rolled through my mind thickly, settled into my skull.

I watched, my back to the ground, limbs like lead, as she shifted her weight, up on her knees. Blood dripped from her mouth onto me, which was probably a bunch of hygiene violations. It was a super vulnerable position she'd put herself in. She really had no base, no grips, no defenses as she smiled down at me. Shit, I could've...

But moving just seemed so hard.

The wind roared. The helicopter blades struck air. Aspen's tears when reality sank in. Brandon's bones, breaking.

She knelt over me and the illusion flickered around the blood on her mouth. I watched as she raised her wand, smile turning up one corner of those disconcerting lips.

I didn't even hurt, particularly. Not physically. I just felt...empty. There was no real point in any of this, no real purpose to continuing. And, honestly, it was nice not to have a knot of shame and guilt in my belly.

The wind lifted her braid. She moved in slow motion. I wondered if Taig was on his way. Behind her, in the actual important part of this scene, Lilith sent a silver spear into another Amor. An illusion Amor. If this was a movie, the camera would've been on *that*, not this woman's fucked up mouth that I couldn't quite drag my attention away from.

Realization seared through the mist in my head and shot fire through my veins. My belly clenched as I hip-escaped.

Finally. Brain. Body. Working.

I took her down.

Fucking *angel* bullshit, stealing hope, suffocating life. How was that *fair?* Could it just turn love and hope on and off like a fucking *tap?*

Well, I had my own thrice-cursed supply and damned if I was letting anyone mess with it.

The anger was there, but far away. I couldn't hold onto it. Not like the despair, right there, surrounding me, suffocating me. I acknowledged that but refused to give in to the angelic meddling. Behind Amor, Lilith turned a snake into a balloon and popped it with a spear. My heart swelled and a little more of the mist lifted. *Purpose.* I had plenty of it.

And, yeah, I was fueled by love.

The last of the hopelessness lifted like sleep fog after my morning coffee. Amor lunged and we scrambled, searching, seeking dominance. More due to good luck than skill, I caught her in my guard. The ground rippled beneath us and I shifted, tightened my grips, rolling with it. I laughed at her and it felt *good*. Bitch was going to have to do better than that to get to Dierdre.

Another jolt of purpose shot through me. I had to hang onto what was good and real. I couldn't let the cloying mist of whatever the angel was doing smother that.

"There's nothing for you," Amor said, between her teeth. "You walk in the cold. Alone."

It really *was* cold. But I wasn't walking, and I sure as shit wasn't alone. My heart huge and full, I avoided her knife swing. That warmth, that strength, I breathed in deeply, pulled it into myself as motivation rushed back into my limbs, protecting me from whatever shitfuck spell they'd used.

She scrambled away, casting a quick, searching glance around. Arthur was redirecting lightning and holding back the mist while Lilith kept the illusions at bay and dealt with whatever was real. Respect burned in me, keeping the mist at bay. The ground exploded at Arthur's feet and I saw him arcing through the air but didn't move to intervene. I trusted my team. Someone else would go for that catch —I needed to make some runs.

I dived, hard and low. In my grip, I locked Amor down and tightened my arms. She writhed and I rode it, the beating of my heart in my ears. Crows cawed and witches cast, bystanders squawked and lightning crashed. I breathed through it and felt the burn of the wound in my arm, the cold hard ground beneath me, the slip slide flex of the witch in my grips, and the fire in my blood.

A flurry of wind made my skin crawl. *Vampire!* My brain screamed it at me. I gritted my teeth but didn't move. I couldn't do everything— but I didn't have to. When the air rushed past again I heard the clatter and hiss of metal and wood against the pavers. Her Lupetec bit into my fingers but the arch of her neck was against my forearm. Fruitlessly, she drove her head frantically into my shoulder.

Arrows.

I was being shot at.

Tucking my head, I tightened my grips further, rolling as she kicked us over and let her knife grind into my Lupetec clad leg. My heartbeat would've rivaled a hummingbird's wings but I couldn't let go.

Burning, on my cheek. *Fuck.* A minor wound. This time.

I forced my eyes to Lilith, hoping the arrow had been laced with Love and not Rapid Decay, and watched as she leveled her wand at a patch of clouds, casting a spell I couldn't hear. Blood roared in my ears.

An arrow bloomed in Lilith's chest and the noise.

The noise.

Stopped.

I let go of the woman in my arms, scrambled to my feet. Staggered. Ran.

My heart.

Stopped.

The afternoon. Sunlight.

The ground was slippery, the air thick. Lightning danced, shrieked, screamed. "What?" Lilith demanded, looking past me as I grabbed her, dragged her toward a ring. A ward. "Bitch is charmed to hide!" she snarled, purple hair flying, eyes searching. "I've tried the illusion-lifting sweeper, but—"

"You're hurt!" I shouted at her, desperately. We had healers. We could save her. Crows were swooping at Arthur. Cici was screaming something, pointing over our shoulder, her wand shaking danger-ously in her hand.

I followed her gaze and saw nothing, but kept dragging Lilith toward their protective circle. She dug her heels in. "You're hurt!" I shouted again over the racket. Why didn't she—

"What?" And she shook me off. "Help me figure out where she's—"

Her hip met mine. I staggered, fell, and took her weight. The ground exploded behind us.

I threw up a ward and hauled her to her feet. An arrow struck and it sounded like a church bell ringing. But she was unharmed.

Illusions. Oh, fuck, illusions.

Behind her I saw Arthur, his suit trashed, dodge a wild knife-swing by the Amor that should've been unfuckingconscious. *Next time,* I thought grimly, *I'll choke the bitch for longer.*

Witch—powered by obsession, meet witch powered by fury and caffeine.

"I'll tag Arthur!" I told her, collapsing the ward. "King!"

He leaped away, his shiny leather shoes slipping on the edge of the grass dangerously close to that mist. I gritted my teeth. *Homefires, answer my call. Homefires, don't let me fall.* The fire sprang up around Amor and she flinched back from the trick flames, trying to dodge them. "Homefires," I told Arthur as he stood staring for a moment while the fire leapt at her, clawing its way up her braid.

He blinked. "That's a kid's—"

"Staple," I cut in, as she dropped to the ground and rolled. *Burn, witch, burn.* Grass flew as the spell went wide and then the whole world was tilting.

My pulse kicked as air whistled around me. *Gravity sucks and I sure don't.* I spun midair. *I could be my own fucking stunt double, if only some silver screen folks were here to witness this.* I planted both feet onto the shrine list thing with the names of all the places conflict had happened, or something. I hoped they'd understand. Kicking off, I arrowed back to where Arthur was on the ground near one of the wards, bleeding and stunned. *Amor's target.* His hand clawing at his throat, his staff on the ground beside him. His eyes bulged. *Choking ward.*

Grabbing Amor, I went down in a tangle of limbs. Maximal damage, maximal disruption. As I lifted my arm the fiery reminder of my wounds lanced up the limb and sank claws into my brain. *Breathe freely and smash this ward.*

Arthur's hand dropped from his throat. He snatched up his staff and then I couldn't see anymore as lightning struck the ground beside me. I went over, dodging some of the blows from Amor, wearing others. As best I could I rolled with it and saw stars. Or lightning, above us, maybe. Redirected? It hit the ground harmlessly, taking an unnatural path sideways. Mist tangled around me, seeping into my brain.

The din of my coven all screaming out their information, their encouragement, filled my head like my headphones had just paired with my phone. I wished they hadn't.

"Help Lilith!" I shouted over the background bullshit, hoping the wind would carry the sound to Arthur.

Amor's blonde plait hit me in the face and all I could smell was roses. Her forearm on my throat would've made me laugh if it hadn't been for the knife strike I knew would come next.

Bridging, I went for her knife arm and pulled her in close, blocking the swift forehead strike she gave me with my face. Reeling, I let my body carry me on instinct as I rolled away. *Fuck, I thought* I *was pig headed.* I couldn't keep going for much longer—I needed traction.

A spell hit me a moment too late for me to deflect, and the ground fell away as I flew. I saw her wand after the fact. *Better than never.* With hard, furious hands I keep her locked to me. A possessed witch was my co-pilot.

The edges of the world were hazy, and the grass wasn't soft when we landed.

My bones rattled as I bounced, but I kept her locked in my guard, trying to use her to buffer the impact. In my peripheral, lighting streaked toward us and then angled away at the last moment. My heart was in my throat and a glowing line was seared into my vision. Around it I made out the gleam of her knife, and my guts twisted.

I threw up an arm, felt the drag of the weapon against my armor. *Harmless.* But her fingers dug into my throat, and I felt the pounding of my blood in my head like a rolling boil. Writhing, I threw my head aside and bridged, but I couldn't dislodge her.

Arthur or Lilith would be there to help me soon. Again I bridged, struck out, felt the strength of her grip on my Lupetec, her fingers too long, too strong. Inhuman.

Glowing eyes. Blood. Pounding. The world felt further away.

Charms. Charms. Thoughts and memories whistled past me like the wind.

And then her fingers suddenly eased and her weight increased. I blinked away the lightning's glow as she melted to the side, disoriented by the sudden stillness.

There was a hole in her throat.

The world stopped for one moment. Another.

Swallowing hard, I put that sight away for later, bridging again and turning away before I witnessed that inevitable slide of puppet with the strings cut. My skin crawled beneath *afternoon sunlight.*

Lightning arced. The ground shifted, swayed and undulated under my feet. I went down again and realized it actually *was* moving. It wasn't just me.

Gunfire. There's gunfire. Of course there was gunfire. *I* hadn't shot out Amor's throat. And Arthur wouldn't, even if he had a gun, unless it was legal. And either my phone was ringing or I'd accidentally dropped a vibrator in my pocket earlier.

Someone screamed. Outside of the warded segments of people to look after, that was. And my heart shuddered.

Taig.

Somehow, despite the earth's best efforts to kick me off, I got to my feet. It could just go fuck itself. I watched the rippling surface, the cracking pavers, the pretty eternal flame brazier thing go rolling away with a clang like a giant cymbal.

Shit. Maybe not such a great location?

I moved with the ground, trying to run along in the flat bit like it was a game and I had limitless lives, but as soon as I'd hit some sort of rhythm it ended and I was left standing in the middle of grass looking at a group of cops who were moving—oddly.

Taig stepped out from behind the shield, fuck-off gun over his back, ripping his helmet from his head and waving a hand rapidly at his throat.

Breathe freely and smash this ward. I cast my eyes around, fury tugging at me. That shit was getting really old. Why not just fireball me again? Retro was cool.

He gulped in a breath. "Got a problem in the air," he told me as I swept my gaze across the group. Another cop outcrop on the flag side of the area. "Can you expose her?"

My head was ringing. The circle of witches nearest to me had stopped squawking, which was a boon. But they'd also stopped helping.

Something about the way they were all smiling and chatting together made hair rise on the back of my neck.

Lilith was down. Not seriously down, just on her arse. But Dierdre had broken rank and was trying to apply first aid. Arthur was redirecting lighting into the area he suspected another Amor was lurking, obviously defending them. Taig was saying something beside me, the words loud and urgent.

Afternoon sun.

I breathed. My limbs were lead again.

Behind me, someone said, "Hey, Greene, you busy this weekend? There's a great microbrewery out Geelong way. We could go with the boys."

And it was—jarring.

I drew the cold air deep into my lungs. *Winter. Melbourne.* The air was thick with roses. And then a hand on my shoulder jarred my focus.

Taig, his light blue eyes bracketed by worry, was studying me. He hadn't shaved that morning and his stubble was mostly grey, but there were surprising glints of copper that made me look at his hair, a tawny base with generous salt in it. The wind blew and a chunk of hair flopped down onto his forehead. I followed the curve of it with my eyes. I wanted to feel the softness of his cheek above the high-tide mark of his facial hair. I wanted to rub my lips against his throat where the beard and skin met just to feel the contrast. Warmth filled my chest. I could've floated, in that instant.

His hand tightened on my shoulder.

My mouth was bone dry. Pulling my eyes away was an act of willpower, and even after I did the image of him was burned into my brain.

Desperately I wriggled my toes in my boots. Lilith was beaming like a proud mother at the nearest group of witches. They were hugging each other, smiling, sobbing. Janet was fluffing someone's scarf, tears streaming down her face.

Angel.

I breathed in deep and concentrated, hard. All I could smell was fucking *roses.*

Angel!

I drew my obsidian knife. Taig's hand tightened on my shoulder. "Rory," he was saying, the word low, urgent, and hungry. "Rory." And I wanted him to say my name like that. From the bottom of my heart, I wanted that so badly that it hurt.

There wasn't enough knife to go around.

Laughter bubbled in my chest and it was probably the hysterical type. I bit the fingers of one glove and ripped it off, shoving it into my belt. My body wanted to float away, to just glide in a sea of bliss and take him with me. Every movement was hard. Every fiber in wanted— *needed*—to relax.

No, I need to move. I needed to…get hold of myself. Yeah. *Shit, yeah. Just like always.* And something about that made me feel good. I could do this dance. I did it on the daily.

My fingers coiled around the obsidian blade. "Rory!" And it was a demand, now, stern.

That's not my Taig. I imagined one of those kid's picture books. *Not my puppy. Not my circus. Not my monkeys. Not my Taig.*

Except this *was* my circus, and I'd brought these people here. They needed me to not just nope out of this whole ridiculous situation. In my hand, the blade was cool, smooth, and shockingly solid.

And I felt the mist lift.

Urgency poured through me. My eyes skimmed the battlefield. It wasn't a battlefield, though—it was a country fair.

Taig's hand was heavy on my shoulder and he shook me, the movement short and brisk. "*Look at me,*" he said, frustration, need, in his voice. "Please, Rory."

My heart ached. Even without the angel's influence I wanted to listen to him, give him some time, but I couldn't. Amor was—and the angel—My thumb pressed against the tip of the blade. The sound of it cracking was lost beneath a wave of laughter from the cops behind us. A shard of the broken obsidian knife fell into my waiting palm.

I looked up at Taig, at those beautiful pale blue eyes, at his earnest expression. The depth of adoration on his face made all the alarms ring in my head. We weren't there. Not yet, anyway.

With one hand I grabbed his wrist and he didn't object when I reefed up his sleeve, just drew in a deep breath and moved closer. I'd been here often enough that I knew damned well he was going in for the kiss.

I ached for him. And I could see the cold white glow coming from the direction of the shrine, the length of my shadow getting shorter. Terror flooded through me. We were sitting ducks, all of us. And I'd never really been into roleplay. *Fuck this.*

His arm was warm, his hairs almost white. The underside of his forearm was a lot paler than the top, the skin soft and vulnerable. And that was where I drove the shard.

He barely flinched. "Jesus, Mary and Joseph," he muttered, pulling back, reaching for the weapon over his back. "Is everyone feeling that?"

I put aside the memory of that hollowness, of the bright, shining adoration, of the buoyant bliss. Instead, I turned to face the man walking down the shrine steps with the huge apparition behind him.

Four wings, clawed feet, and a face that was something between bird, snake, man and a jar of googly-eyes from a craft store. *That's colossally fucked up.*

The bottom fell out of my belly. "Don't shoot Tobias," I warned him. "I've got to get the coven to do a banishment spell." And that was it. That was all there was to it. It didn't matter that my knees shook.

And then the world exploded. Fire and rain, steam and wind.

In the aftermath I picked myself up like always, wiping dirt out of my eyes.

"Magi," Taig said, like that explained everything.

Knife in hand, I started toward the nearest group of witches. Someone had out their phone, and was showing Bernie a picture on the screen. "I know, but they're so *hardy.* They tolerate over *and* under watering. And the foliage is fantastic, bright and green. They do like some sun, but—"

There wasn't enough obsidian for me to stab them all.

Frustration warred with horror as I spotted Janet with a mixing bowl in her hand. A *mixing bowl.* And it was *full.* She was scowling at the rain but her expression cleared as she turned to speak to a witch who touched her elbow, her eyes soft, her smile wide.

Arthur had his arm around Lilith and was helping her up. Behind him, I could see one of my witches showing another their crocheting.

They were comparing fucking *wool.*

It was chaos. Mayhem.

And Dierdre was on the ground, hunched over her glowing jars. Her shoulders shook as she sobbed.

Forgotten.

CHAPTER 35

MY KNEES DIDN'T WANT TO HOLD ME. TOBIAS WAS GOING STRAIGHT FOR Dierdre.

He looked—average. Absolutely, overwhelmingly forgettable.

Except that horrific creature possessing him.

Except that obsession in his too-big, too-bright eyes.

I tightened my hand on the obsidian knife. I could take a shot and hope. Possibly I'd fuck it up, probably it'd fuck me up. All in all, it seemed like a bad option, really.

"Dierdre!" I shouted, over the rain and rise and fall of excited conversations.

"Two o'clock, Rory!" I heard Taig roar.

Adrenaline poured through me. I scoured the clouds and threw up the shield out of pure instinct. *Through this dome none shall leave or come unless it is with me.*

The sky rippled and shimmered. The sound of a bell striking reverberated in my bones, followed by a flash of movement as the background beside Dierdre blurred.

I had to move. But nothing made sense. Nothing was quite…*real.*

My legs worked. They were real. I desperately clung to the sensation of them stretching, pulling me onwards, toward Dierdre. The magick of my ward slid over my skin, over my soul, and I grabbed Dierdre. *As I will, so shall it be.* The ward wouldn't stop an angel for more than a split second. It'd just knock me the fuck out when it was smashed.

Her arm was small in my hand, thin. The knife I forgot I was holding bit into her and she cringed as she looked up at me—but her expression cleared.

Well, that was three of us un-angeled.

Shame only two could cast, wasn't it?

"Homefires," I told her, quietly. "It'll buy us some time."

Her legs wobbled less than mine as she stood and hefted her jars. Her jaw was tight and her shoulders hunched, but she was on her feet. And I wanted her the fuck out of there.

Running wouldn't work. There was an Amor literally in the wind right now. We had fuck all backup.

"How's your Banishing?" I asked her, taking a slow step back.

"I know how." The words trembled but they reached my ears.

I didn't withdraw the knife, just took another step back, then another. But Tobias' legs were longer and his eyes were fixed on her.

As he passed by a ward, the obsidian on the ground flared and the witches all burst out in gleeful laughter, focused entirely on one another.

You could see how people might think that sort of happiness was good. Maybe it was, sometimes. But my heart broke for them.

"You should run," she told me quietly, and the words didn't shake, now.

I snorted, ignoring the way my heart squeezed. This was it. This was as good as this situation got. So I drew up the memories of the first spell I'd ever learned. *"Walk in the shadows and blot out the light,"* I began.

I heard her swallow. *"Walk in the shadows and blot out the light."*

The mist was back, snaking around our ankles. *"Find your home in the deepest of night,"* I continued. My ankle rolled as the ground beneath me shook.

"Find your home in the—"

"Hey, arsehole!"

Clint's voice made a reflexive flare of fury spurt through me. My fingers bit, hard, into Dierdre's arm. *"Find your home in the deepest of night,"* she said, stumbling over the words.

"Smith!" I heard Taig bellow. "Stand down!"

Of fucking *course*.

"Need not your name or proof of your spite." I was jostled from behind and knocked into Dierdre.

"Get your filthy hands off her, you ugly slut," Clint snarled.

I was grabbed and pulled but kept my grip on Dierdre. *"Need not your proof of a*—no, no," Deirdre sucked in a breath, and I could *feel* the spell deflating as Clint shoved me again, a typical schoolyard bully shove in the shoulder. I wore it and stuck to Dierdre, more worried about Tobias and his immortal driver than this man of below average credentials making his demands.

"Don't worry, beautiful, this loser can't hurt you anymore," he crooned to Dierdre. His eyes were overbright as he stared at her. The guy *reeked* of roses.

As he lifted his service weapon I realized, suddenly, that today had ruined roses for me forever. If that was all it ruined, it was going to be a great day.

Deirdre's eyes widened and her mouth opened as time slowed to a crawl. Spells swam through my head like bees. Oh, I knew what was happening. But I, very deliberately, didn't cast any of them.

Because, you know what? Fuck Tobias. And fuck Clint.

A gun barked and light flashed from the muzzle. Dierdre jumped in my hand and I put myself between her and Clint grimly. Tobias fell, dead as a doornail.

Some of the conversation around us stopped for a moment, like everyone could suddenly breathe again.

"Oh, Elders!" Cici breathed, nearby. "Someone *shot* that man!"

"Banishment spell!" I shouted, relieved.

There were nine of them, in three groups of three. My coven worked together as well as any other. We knew what we were doing, and we'd be strong enough to do it. If Clint happened to get Banished, well, I wasn't going to lose any sleep over him.

"No," Deirdre was saying, horrified. "No!"

Yes, yes, yes. I walked her backwards as Clint's body arched impossibly, his eyes glowing like two spotlights on the back of a ute. He was still holding his gun, but you didn't bring firearms to a magick fight, and I gave no shits about that.

Janet spoke up first, leading her group in the Banishment spell, the mixing bowl dangling, forgotten, in her hand as they began to follow her lead.

And Amor came whistling out of the clouds, her expression grim, broom between her legs and wand in hand.

My heart stuttered. "Arthur!"

He lifted his staff and she saw it coming. I knew she did. I felt her disdain in my *soul.*

There but by the grace of a random angel go I.

Arthur was blown back, and she swung her wand toward the coven. *No.* Furiously, I locked my hand around Dierdre, went heavy, and sent my magick into my Blowback Charm.

Amor was knocked flying and Arthur ate dirt. The coven was scattered by the force of my charm. Even with me anchoring her, Deirdre fell back a few steps but I didn't let her go, sticking to her like a cheap shirt in summer.

Unaffected by physics or magick, Clint was straightening. Growing. Glowing. His gaze swinging toward us.

My mouth went dry. I had no qualms about sacrificing that specific guy. *Just, you know. Time. Spell complexity. Keeping folks alive while that goes down.*

Details.

CHAPTER 36

Clint's gun was levelled at me. The kick in my chest came the same time I registered the flash and bark. I staggered back with the force of it. *Thank fuck for Lupetec.* I was going to *hurt*. What a dick move.

"*No!*" Deirdre screamed, furiously. My heart lunged into my throat as she shoved him in the chest. "No!"

Above Clint, the angel's wings unfurled.

Her knees went out.

But Clint paused, for a moment, a tiny flicker of doubt in his eyes, the faintest frown on his face.

I was hit from behind and grabbed by hard hands. "Get her out of here," Taig was saying. "Get her out. Get out."

The urge to stab him was pretty fucking strong. I stomped on it.

I needed more firepower. I couldn't do a major banishment myself being fucking *shot* every two seconds. I glanced down at my Lupetec shirt, annoyed to find a slight pulling between my breasts. Arsehole. Who fucking *shot* people?

"Rory, we can't—"

But I could hear the chopper blades again.

My hand tightened on the obsidian knife, willing the mind-tricks

337

away. Dierdre was cowering and Clint was just standing, confused. He reached out to stroke her hair with one hand, a gun in his other. *Oh, yeah. True love.*

Fury kicked through me, and I heard the whistling in the wind. I looked up, joy and hope exploding in my chest as familiar black streaks came from the helicopter above us. They hit the ground. Boots. Lupetec. Wands. Charms. *Oh, fuck, just like always.* I'd been glad to see them so many times before, but that rush of relief never got old.

"Sunshine!" I heard Bang shout, and my heart leapt. She threw a dark green ball into the air and I cast an Impenetrable Ward around us a split second later, just like always. Her green ball hit the center of the ward and popped, spraying the contents over what we'd figured was pretty close to a kilometer in every direction.

Calmer Surroundings was the official name of that potion. Chill Juice was what Bang had always called it. And suddenly the situation felt so much more under control. Whether it was the potion, or my old team, I didn't know and didn't care.

Nic's staff hit me in the chest and I didn't even mind that agony screamed through my ribs at the shock of it. "Disperse some obsidian," he said, like I was still one of them. "Let's dance!"

I collapsed the ward as the team, down a few members, split into two groups—one for Amor, one for Clint. Bang took another pod off her belt, tossed it from one hand to the other.

She grinned hugely at me. "No worse than fossil fuel emissions, right?"

"Right," I agreed, the word light. My eyes burned with the rush of emotion I couldn't have named if I tried. I threw up another ward around the area. *Airlock.* I still knew the moves. Somehow, I hadn't expected to.

From the corner of my eye, I saw Amor's fireball redirected and thrown back at her. The wand in her hand been transformed into a bottle of water and obsidian-studded rope looped her chest. Nic stepped up, hitting the weighted end of the rope with the flat of his staff like a cricket ball. "Six!" He laughed, grinning as it tightened around her.

He used that move in totem tennis, too. Jerkoff. Hells, I wanted to hug that guy.

Bang tossed the pod at the sky, and I covered my eyes as the wind whipped and flurried. Grit burned against my skin, but it died down as quickly as it had come. I collapsed my ward and lifted my head.

Arthur was with the coven, blinking his eyes as if rousing from a slumber. Everyone was coated with a fine layer of ground obsidian and I wanted to stand and enjoy the sight of them, whole, alive and autonomous.

But I couldn't.

Clint was being driven to where the eternal flame was burning erratically from the broken gas pipe. Homefires flared strategically around him and obsidian-tipped ropes flashed as it darted around him, forcing him onwards. Whoever was in charge of that did good work. I eyeballed the young magi doing the ropework. Newcomer. I'd get myself invited along to the wind-down.

I should probably meet my replacement.

I propped my hands on my hips and realized my face *hurt*. My arm did, too.

"Miss you, bitch," Bang muttered, beside me. "Specially these last few weeks. Could've used your ward skills."

I watched as they drove the angel into position, the rise and fall of my coven casting the banishment spell, with Arthur bolstering anyone who faltered. I felt the energy, the urgency, ebbing. It was okay, now. It was under control.

"What happened?" I asked Bang, in the moment of calm.

"Trapped, then locked in your fuckin' Impenetrable." She turned her head, spat, and gave the edge of my ward some side-eye. "You can end that anytime you want, by the way. Did you know angel's commands reverberate endlessly? No? Well, let me fuckin' tell *you*."

My heart ached for them. I opened my mouth to try to find some words of comfort, some words of gratitude, and I heard the wailing that sprang forth.

It puzzled me for a split second before I realized it wasn't *my* wailing. The noise hadn't come from *my* mouth.

Dread speared through me as I spun, searching out the person responsible. Deirdre, crying in Taig's arms, reaching for Clint. "Don't kill him!" she was pleading. "Don't kill him! It isn't his fault!"

The spell was a cartoon snowball, though, gathering momentum around us, swelling and spinning.

Either Clint or the angel heard Dierdre's pleas. He stopped struggling away from the Homefires, stopped ducking the flashing obsidian dagger. It sank deep into his arm as adrenaline rippled through me.

"No!" Deirdre wailed. "No one deserves to die!"

The angel above him folded its wings like some sort of monstrous bin chicken at the end of a long day, and alarms sounded deep in the tired recesses of my brain. *Nothing's ever easy.*

"Shit," Bang muttered, on my heels as I started to move toward Dierdre. "Nic!"

Through the chaos I heard Nic shout, "Nail him! Him! The—with the scope on his rifle, the cop—*Jem!*—"

I wasn't listening, though. I knew what was happening.

The light receded and darkness swept in, cold. Clint collapsed as the angel ripped itself free of Clint's body before my team could contain it.

The spell rose and fell, undulating around us. Three sets of voices in three rounds. The power was palpable. And it was almost unstoppable, now. We needed that spell to go off. My team could buy us a bit of time, but humans couldn't go toe to toe with angels.

I'd been complacent.

The angel wanted love. Total, all-consuming devotion, obsession, whatever it was. It didn't care *who* loved or *how.* Deirdre stumbled away, sobbing.

Taig arched his back. His eyes weren't blue, now, but—

Lights like beacons.

My heart froze and broke.

CHAPTER 37

My team swarmed Taig, switching targets like the well-oiled machine they were. He was still arching at that impossible angle and Homefires was already making smoke raise from his skin. In my chest, behind my bruised ribs, agony was encapsulated. The angel, the glowing, hideous thing, unfurled from above him.

Taig.

It had.

Taig.

And the banishment spell was coming to a close.

He'd be worse than dead.

One of his hands lifted. He ripped off his helmet and threw it aside. It wasn't Taig—or not just him. Not anymore.

The crackle of the fire rose and fell in time with the chanting around us. Dierdre was sobbing.

My heart. My bones. My soul. Trembled.

Ached.

And I just stood there, feeling the swelling, spreading hopelessness. There was no answer. I *knew* there was no answer. We couldn't *not* banish an angel. The cost in lives would be horrific.

He was gone.

I couldn't draw air into my lungs or make my body work. *Taig.* I remembered the way we'd bumped into each other when I'd first started with my coven, how I'd picked him for a hard arse. And he was, but he had a good heart, too. That combination was everything. And now I was going to lose him.

His gaze swung toward me. And I barely saw the angel behind him.

There were seconds left. The spell would banish him with the angel. And there was so much I wanted to tell him, still. So much I wanted to do. We could hang out, shoot the shit. And maybe I'd be brave enough to let myself melt against him, if only I had some time to let myself heal, first.

But I didn't have that time. And soon, I wouldn't have him.

I could hear in my head my Oma's voice. *Give it what it wants, it'll chill its beans.* Was that what Dierdre had done? Given Clint what he wanted?

Horror and hope bloomed in my chest, a toxic flower. I knew. I knew what Taig wanted. My heart twisted like an overstretched elastic band. I knew. And I couldn't—

But I couldn't not.

I doubted I could fake it. But I didn't need to fake it. *Oh, fuck.* I was so far gone and I hadn't even known. He stared at me across the distance like I was his whole world.

Power was heavy in the air, and the spell rose and fell around me. That thing would take him with it.

Deirdre was pulled away by someone, and she dropped out of my sight. Everything around us fell away. It was just a cold, dark morning, some thick mist, and two people with too much tension between them for too long.

The rise and fall of the end.

He reached for me and I fit into his arms. I felt the obsidian knife in my hand vibrating. It heated, cooled, and cracked in a split second. His armored vest was peppered with obsidian dust but it didn't matter. A bit of dust wouldn't be enough to even slow a manifesting angel at full force. His not-Taig eyes stared into me, starving.

I closed my eyes, my heart in my throat. I couldn't look.

But I moved closer and felt his hands. *His.* They scooped up my hair securely, firm but gentle, sexy and sweet. And my heart screamed.

His lips were cold and gritty but I didn't care. I poured myself into the kiss, let myself be a pathetic fucking puddle. I gave him everything I had and more. His hands were on me, grabbing, holding, as he never had. *Not Taig.* There was a coldness to his skin, an order in his hands.

YES.

The word shook my bones, the utter truth of it.

I let myself melt into him, begging him, silently, with my kiss, with my heart, to come back. He took, though. He just took and drank, and it was all I could do to keep pouring those feeling in, to keep him with me. To feed the beast that wanted to control us all. Tears burned and he feasted.

So, I let him.

His lips were hard against mine but it didn't matter. I surrendered. The hurt fell away, and the fear.

The spell burned. My tears seared, carving a path down my cheeks. I could *feel* where they displaced the flimsy barrier of that obsidian dust. But it was irrelevant, now.

My spell swam through me, offering itself. From the depths of my soul, the marrow of my bones, the beating of my heart, I drew on every fiber of magick I had, gathered it all up and infused those words. And I cast.

Through this dome none shall leave or come, unless it is with me.

Every word. So clear. So powerful. So huge.

With me. My choice.

I fisted my hands in his vest as he devoured me, barely even feeling him, now. The banishment spell rose, trembling on the cusp of completion.

And, gently, I pushed Taig through my ward. Him, but not the angel.

He *screamed.*

And the angel roared in fury, the noise reverberating in my bones and swamping me with agony.

But they were separate sounds. *Love conquers all, fucker.*

The banishment spell closed.

My spell shattered and I fell, agony in every cell of my body. The world went grey and the angel was over me. Four wings. Talons. Eyes, everywhere. So bright, so pure, it hurt.

And Taig on the other side of my ward, somehow, as the world spun, cracked, and collapsed.

EPILOGUE

DIERDRE GATHERED UP THE JAR THAT'D BEEN FULL OF UNBREAKING Potion before I'd been dragged into the Garden Courtyard by my team and given the good stuff. She slipped quietly out, her eyes puffy but her steps confident as she went.

I looked at Nic, still lingering with me, Brandon's best friend, my sometimes-lover, my team leader.

My old team leader.

They had to go, of course. They'd been dark for so long. They needed to eat, sleep, decompress and exist. But they'd stood by me in the aftermath, and that meant the world to me.

"Still have no idea," Nic said, grimly. "That shouldn't have happened."

I'd heard it about a dozen times. My head hurt. My heart hurt more. I didn't care why the ward had broken but still held. It made no sense; I couldn't cast a multilayered ward because there was no such thing. Maybe at some point I'd figure out what had happened. How the angel had shattered the first layer of protection—which should've been the only one—but still, somehow, been contained. Even if I *could* do that sort of spell, why hadn't I been possessed? Why had the major banishment spell worked even without a sacrifice?

I didn't care, right then.

Lilith was totally fine. She'd been showing some of my team her illusions and transmutations while Davo patched her up with his wicked battlefield medic magick. Arthur was already helping contact folks to get the shrine repaired.

Clint was, unfortunately, alive. And, of course, he'd made a pass at Dierdre.

What a shame that she'd fumbled one of her potions. Just a minor potion, of course—one to settle upset bowels in small doses. Or trigger uncontrollable vomiting in large doses. And it wasn't Dierdre's fault he'd breathed in a large dose. We'd all seen it. He'd just sat there in the vapors, inhaling them. Himself. Without any assistance. Fully conscious. Weird choice, but it wasn't like I'd *made* him.

"Hey," Nic said, quietly, nudging my foot. "You still got it, Sunshine. I saw you, today."

The invitation inferred in the words was one I'd been waiting for. I looked at his face, the hollows from lack of sleep, the grey hairs in his beard.

"It's tempting," I admitted, quietly. "But not because of the work." And it didn't matter how tempting it was. I couldn't do that anymore. It wasn't good for me.

He snorted, slapping the flat of his cricket-bat shaped staff on his leg. "Fuck the work. Started planning my exit strategy. You're the first Australian Retrievals to leave a full-time team not in a body bag, you know?"

"I know." Through the sprawling jungle of the garden courtyard, I saw my favorite detective approaching. He wasn't wearing his tactical gear and he looked like he'd just done a bunch of the paperwork I was currently avoiding.

Nic turned, a bit of a smile tugging at his mouth as he saw Taig. He gave me a friendly shove with his staff. "Want me to read it real quick?" he offered, wiggling his brows. "Friendly neighborhood Oracle here, at your service. Discount price."

The afternoon sun filtered through, soft and safe. Me and my aching head rested back against the exotic tree. Nic could've told me some possible futures, warned me of some possible pitfalls.

"I got it," I told him, knocking his staff off my shoulder. I kind of wanted to figure it out on my own. "Go on. Fuck off. Think of me after Samhain."

He snorted and pressed a kiss to my head. "You always were smarter than we gave you credit for. Blessed be, bitch," he said, a smile in his voice. "Say hi to your dad and Oma for me." And his steps were almost silent as he walked along the half-overgrown path.

I breathed deep and didn't try to make sense of any of it. I didn't need to, now. That would come later. I heard Taig settle beside me. "Most folks have cleared out now," he said, sounding tired.

It was done. They'd banished the angel. The last of the Amors were gone. Paperwork would be coming, but wasn't it always?

"How's the head?"

"Shit."

He made a noise of agreement. "I hear you're a fully-fledged Caretaker again. Looks like there *was* an angel involved after all. Who knew?"

I rolled my eyes, which meant I had to open them. He was half-flopped against another trunk of the same tree I'd claimed. "Ten bucks Clint'll try to say it's a demon when he finishes ralphing all over the place."

Against the tree Taig rolled his head, almost lazily, in my direction. Grit had gathered in the laugh lines around his mouth and the furrows of his brow. My heart ached pleasantly at the sight. "There are two kinds of arsehole in this world," he said, wisely. "And Clint is both of them."

"Yeah." My fingers itched to reach out and touch the deep lines carved into his skin and smooth away all those extra years he didn't need to carry.

He almost hadn't carried them.

"So." Clearing my throat, I tried to sit up and searched for something to say and some way to say it. The anxiety was there, under the surface, humming. Normal, really. But we were okay. "How much do you remember?"

He straightened with a sigh, eyeing me off. "I definitely remember you kissing me then ripping the angel out of me. If that's what you're asking."

I fought the urge to shuffle my feet. "Yeah. Kind of awkward way to have a first kiss."

A smile tugged at his mouth. "Don't know that I'd count it as our first, myself." Before I could figure out what that meant, he said, voice rough and low, "I hope you're not into threesomes. Because after that, I am going to really struggle."

Shock and relief ran through me in equal amounts. "Huh. That's your biggest concern?"

"Aside from the fact you literally attempted to sacrifice yourself for all of us?" he closed his eyes. "You've got a hero complex, and I don't know I like it."

I sat on the bench beside him, boneless, and stared into the garden.

He knew what had gone down. All of it. *Fuck.* There went my last hope of just pretending like the whole thing was just standard Retrievals protocol.

I didn't have a single drop of courage left. "I need to sort myself out, Taig."

He reached up and rubbed one palm over his cheek. The rasp of stubble against calluses made a funny scratchy noise, and what did it say about me that I just wanted to nestle my face against that same spot like a cat?

With a bit of a frown, he considered me. "That can't possibly be why you kissed me like you were pouring your soul into me. Pretty sure the angel would've known if that was fake."

"Pretty sure it would've," I agreed, feeling small and vulnerable. "It wasn't. Fake."

"Okay. Well. If the problem is your quality versus mine, since you seem prone to beating yourself up about stuff," he closed his eyes again, kicked out his legs and settled back on his hands. "You're not as shit hot as you think. Couldn't even take an angel solo, even with all the laws you broke. We must be made to be together."

Before I could respond a couple wandered through the gardens. How the fuck the public were still allowed in the area I had no idea, but there it was.

"I should go," I said, hyperaware that I could barely string two thoughts together.

"Sure. I just wanted to see you." And he straightened, looking at me apologetically. "Sorry. I know you had a pretty major spell broken. And." He waved a hand at my arm.

I looked down at the bandage. "Pain block." Shit didn't work on my head, but Dierdre's potions did. And they tasted better than Arthur's, too. I'd gotten off lightly.

I didn't know what came next. I had no promises for him. I sure wasn't ready to hear any, either. The silence grew and stretched. I tried to just...exist, here, with him.

It wasn't so bad. Uncomfortable, disconcerting, but not so bad.

"Any ideas what's going on with the faeries?" he asked me.

"No." I shifted a little. I'd forgotten about the faeries. "Let's cross that bridge later."

"Okay." He tipped his head back again and shut his eyes. "I'm totally consenting to any form of affection. So you know. Feel free but not obligated."

I blinked at him. "I'm sorry?"

"Well, if you wanted to plant an angel-free kiss on me. That'd be great. Probably healing. Pretty sure I read research about that. Yeah." He let out a long breath. "I think I'm crashing, Rory."

I was lost. The man still made me melt when I felt about as sexy as an old work boot.

I let myself lean my weight on him, and rested my head on his shoulder. He smelled like stress, gunpowder, and sandalwood. "Hey. At least I can now give you a killer nickname," I said, the idea popping into my head unbidden.

He turned his face into my hair. I wanted to stay there, right there, in the dappled shade of the winter afternoon. "What?"

"Angel," I offered, wiggling my brows.

He shuddered, pulled back. "Ugh. No. Too soon."

The man had almost had his soul banished. Today. A few hours ago. I wanted to go with him when he pulled away, to press myself against his back. The desire made me feel like a steaming pile of shit. "Yeah, sorry. My brain is fried. It wasn't funny. I shouldn't have teased." And, because I was human, I put that guilt aside and focused on what was important.

We'd banished a terrifying fucking angel, and no one I gave a damn about had died. And, even with all my screw-ups, I'd helped get us here. I didn't need to forgive myself for putting my foot in my mouth.

He glanced back at me, a bit of a smile tugging at his mouth. "I'll, ah." He shook his head and moving slowly, touching his forehead to mine. "I like it when you tease me, usually. Just beware ties. Especially black ones that you want adjusted. Tease me with one of those, my heart may very well just explode."

The memory made me sad. I wished I'd grabbed him and held on. "We should've skipped that boring party." But we were here.

"We should've done a lot of things," he said, the words slow and sad. "Hindsight is twenty-twenty. We've got now, though."

"We've got now," I agreed, feeling disoriented at how he was echoing my own tired thoughts.

Slowly I lifted my hand, giving in to the urge to run the back of my fingers against his jaw, his cheek. My heart bumped and rolled in my chest. The softness of his skin, the roughness of his beard, felt wonderful. He smelled wrong, but that was okay. He'd be okay.

"Now is terrifying," I admitted, quietly, cupping his face in my hands.

"Yeah." He turned his lips into my palm. "But, the thing is, it wouldn't be terrifying if it wasn't important." I searched his face, wishing I had something to give him right now, wishing I had the courage to take what he offered. "I'll be here," he said, quietly. "When you're ready to be terrified alongside me. It'll be easier together."

Warmth rushed through me. He was absolutely right. This was

important. This was real. And we could do it, together—at our pace, without losing ourselves.

Honest reviews help readers find books they love. If you've got time, please consider sharing your thoughts on your favorite sites.

For free bonus scenes during Rory's Retrievals days, or access to updates, please sign up **at ElisseHay.com**.

ACKNOWLEDGMENTS

After so long living under my rock, finding the bookish community has been a huge perspective shift for me and I'm awed by the welcome I've received and consistently amazed by how inclusive the community is.

A huge thank-you to Maddison from MaddyReads and Faye from Devoured_Pages. You both helped me hold the imposter syndrome at bay and gave me valuable feedback I hope I've done justice to.

Mez, she slept with Arthur. I'm sorry, or you're welcome. Also, I miss your face.

For my little humans, thank you for being awesome.

And Wayne, for helping me hold this space for our people, and our hopes and dreams, too.

www.ingramcontent.com/pod-product-compliance
Lightning Source LLC
Chambersburg PA
CBHW011126190726
48289CB00012B/2928